THE PAINTED LADIES

Frances Paige was born in Glasgow between the Wars, but has lived in the North of England for many years. Domestic life absorbed much of her time until her forties, when she took up first painting, and then writing, with great success. She is the author of more than twenty-five novels, including, most recently, the popular *Sholtie* series.

Acclaim for *The Glasgow Girls*:

'Written with the sure touch of meticulous research, with wholly believable characters, it is an amazing insight into middle-class Glasgow between the Wars. Frances Paige is an exciting, vibrant writer'

ELIZABETH ELGIN,
author of *I'll Bring You Buttercups*.

'Beautifully and sensitively penned, and the pain and poignancy felt by her characters struck chords deep in my own heart. This is one book I'll treasure and read again and now that I have discovered her, I'll want to read more'

CHRISTINE MARION FRASER,
author of the *Rhanna* novels.

FRANCES PAIGE

The Painted Ladies

Lines from 'The Way You Look Tonight'
© T. B. Harms Company, USA
Warner Chappel Music Ltd, London W1Y 3FA
Reproduced by kind permission of
International Music Publications Ltd

This edition published by Grafton Books, 1999

Grafton Books is an Imprint of
HarperCollins*Publishers*
77–85 Fulham Palace Road,
Hammersmith, London W6 8JB

First published as a Paperback Original 1995

1 3 5 7 9 8 6 4 2

ISBN 0-26-167354-8

Set in Postscript Linotron Palatino by
Rowland Phototypesetting Ltd
Bury St Edmunds, Suffolk

Printed in Great Britain by
Caledonian International Book Manufacturing Ltd, Glasgow

For Mary, Norrie and James

Foreword

The first novel of this series, *The Glasgow Girls*, set in the thirties, follows the lives of the three daughters of Angus Mackintosh, an established architect, and his wife, Rose, who live in the West End of Glasgow.

The three girls, Nancy and the twins, Jean and Anna, are students at the Glasgow School of Art, where they mirror in a lesser way the group of talented women painters who attended the same school in the late nineteenth century, and whose influence runs throughout the book.

Nancy, the youngest sister, conventional like her mother, marries James Pettigrew, a widower and architect, but the twins rebel against the restrictions of their background and pursue more unusual paths.

Jean, beautiful and exotic-looking, falls passionately in love with Frederick Kleiber, a tutor at the Art School, who has fled from Vienna with his wife and family. The affair ends in tragedy when he drowns in a quiet summer loch, leaving Jean pregnant with his child.

Anna falls equally passionately in love with a fellow student, Ritchie Laidlaw, already a talented painter, but with a working-class background which doesn't please her mother. Anna refuses to be influenced by her and subsequently marries him.

Ritchie wins a scholarship and goes to London, where in his easy-going way he becomes involved with Christine Bouvier who has a background of mental instability. When she traps him into a compromising situation, she then accuses him in a letter to Anna, who disappointed and jealous, throws him over. The final straw, when Christine Bouvier slashes a valuable painting of Ritchie's in the gallery where she works, makes him decide to clear out to Spain and fight in the Civil War.

Jean, meantime, when her pregnancy is made known, goes to live in Kirkcudbright with an elderly great-aunt, Jessie Craig. In her youth in Glasgow, as a pupil at the Art School, Jessie had known some of the younger Glasgow Girls, and when they established a summer school at Kircudbright she had followed them there.

She sees Jean through her confinement, but the baby is dead at birth.

The doctor who attends her, John Whitbread, has fallen in love with her, and eventually, after much heart-searching, she agrees to marry him and try and put Frederick Kleiber's death behind her. Her great-aunt has died of a stroke, having bequeathed her house to Jean, and she and John elect to make their home there.

Anna and Ritchie have become reconciled by the time he returns from Spain, and *The Painted Ladies* moves into the fifties, with the three girls raising their families. Nancy and James have one son, Gordon, Jean and John a son and daughter, Roderick and Sarah; and Ritchie and Anna also a son and daughter, Hamish and Vanessa, known in the family as Mish and Van.

One

July 1956

What makes me despair, Anna thought, is the emergence of a pattern in Van, this daughter of Ritchie's and mine. This morning had confirmed it. She flicked through the pages of the newspaper over the breakfast muddle the children had left in their usual dash for school, not finding much to capture her attention.

Those old fogeys in the House of Lords still for capital punishment. Marilyn Monroe with Arthur Miller. Odd coupling, that. But wasn't she beautiful, that something, that vulnerability . . . Elvis had it. She would trade three Bill Haleys with his 'Rock Around the Clock' for one of Elvis. Suez, Suez, Suez . . . Eden was another vulnerable one. Would crack under the strain . . .

She poured a cup of coffee, her third, now tepid and bitter . . . perhaps it was the penalty of being a mother, this unease about Van. But not about her brother, Mish. Vanessa and Hamish, their school names. She screwed up her face and put down the cup. Ritchie would have made the coffee before he went up to his studio. He liked to get an early start when he had a project on. The one he was working on came from one of the New Towns in Scotland.

He had said when he'd come back down south from visiting the site, 'All they want is expensive wallpaper. No, I take that back, one of them did say, "Something like that bloke Picasso, if you can manage it."' He had squeezed her waist, laughing. 'Nae bother, eh?'

'Give them a copy of *Guernica*,' she had said. The time he'd spent fighting in Spain in 1938 had been a rich seam for him.

He thought her anxiety about Van was excessive. She was all right, he had said in bed last night. 'Thirteen in a girl is a difficult age, a hovering kind of age.' And she had 'good bone structure'. Anna had laughed, as if that was all that mattered. 'Don't you remember that trouble with the cats? She'd be about nine . . .'

At first she'd thought what a kind, sympathetic little girl Van was when she began to bring home those mangy, rheumy-eyed cats, reminding her of that rabbit they had seen in the woods with its face half-eaten by myxomatosis. No, that was going too far . . .

'We could have a cat of our own, Van,' she had said, being reasonable, 'a nice tortoiseshell, or an orange marmalade one like Orlando.' She had pointed out that cats picked up from those back streets near the school were infested with fleas, or even carried disease. Van had her characteristic stance even then, head down so that their eyes wouldn't meet, nodding dumbly when Anna said patiently, 'You promise, don't you, not to bring any more stray cats home?'

Those *encounters*, she thought now, I never have them with Mish. She turned the pages of the newspaper, seeing only the children's faces as they had

2

been in the car mirror this morning, Mish alert, composed, neat in his school blazer (he was captain of the school), Van with those triangular blocks of black frizz on either side of her face, the same wiry hair as her Aunt Jean's, the great eyes unfocused, striped tie bunching her blouse collar too tightly round her neck. Once when she had been examining one of Ritchie's paintings she had been astonished to see Van's face embedded in the design, reduced to black and white triangles, a recurrent Mondrian-like motif.

She had reached the Arts page in her restless flicking. Yet another critic's opinion of *Lolita*. 'Nabokov hates Freud, loves butterflies.' His book had disturbed her. The girl was too close to Van's age for comfort.

Ritchie had a glass case of butterflies upstairs which he had bought in a junk shop. When Van was born he had said of her eyes, showing off his erudition, 'Adonis blue, *Vanessa cardui*, the Painted Lady.'

They were the same colour as Jean's. 'Vanessa's nice,' she had said. It had conjured up for her an image of the decorative woman she might become, duskily beautiful, given to wearing brilliant dashing colours – again like her twin sister in Scotland.

In any case they had wished to steer clear of the usual Scottish names like Jessie, Mary, Annie. Hamish had been embarrassed early on by being asked why he didn't wear a kilt, and he had suggested the abbreviation. In due course Van followed his lead. 'Vanessa's like someone in the Pony Club.'

That day, four years ago, Ritchie had come clattering downstairs when she had shouted for him. 'Gee whiz!' he'd said when he found her in Van's

3

bedroom staring at the cat stretched across the sheets like an empty fur bag, four kittens nuzzling and mewling at its side.

'It's her slyness!' Her voice had been trembling because of the shock. 'She said she would stop bringing stray cats home. She *promised*. She went to school without telling me about this.'

He was muttering to himself. 'Look at it. Terrible. Beautiful. Birth-blind. Impossible to paint. Bathos. Easier than pathos. Those huge heads, fumbling . . .'

'Don't go on about them, for God's sake!' She had been suddenly infuriated. 'What are we going to *do*? They can't stay here.'

'No . . .' He looked at her without seeing her. Painter's eyes. Compositional eyes. Then, clicking back: 'You don't expect me to drown them in a bucket? Come on, Anna!'

'No, of course not! It isn't the kittens. It's the thought of Van watching the birth and then going off without telling me. She's only nine!'

'Don't prejudge.' He had lifted one of the kittens and run his hand gently over it. 'Boneless.' He put it back with its mother. The she-cat made a slight, weary acknowledgement with her head. 'You're prone to do that with Van. It's midday now. It could have happened after she went to school.'

He had been right, of course. She tackled Van when she picked her up in the car. Ritchie had put the cat and the still-damp kittens in a box and taken them to the RSPCA, then come back and gone straight upstairs to his studio. She knew better than to expect anything else.

'You hid that cat in your bedroom, although you promised –'

'It was its face, Mummy. It followed me from

4

school and I lifted it. Mrs Porter didn't notice it in the car.'

'Did you know it had kittens in your bed?'

'Oh, that was what it was! Poor thing. Having its babies! It kept moving during the night. And sometimes it made little moans.' She smiled timorously at Anna as if everything was all right now. She steeled herself.

'It was naughty, Van. You brought it home and smuggled it upstairs. That was secretive. You should have asked me . . .'

'Mrs Porter was in. You were having tea with her in the kitchen.'

Damn Mrs Porter, Anna thought. Years of living in her parents' home in strictly conventional and salubrious Clevedon Crescent had not prepared her for the English suburban habit of women who just 'dropped in'. Any spare time she had was spent in her barn in the garden where she designed and made clock faces and photograph frames in metal. Rose, her widowed mother, had always set an example with her organized life-style.

'Yes, that's right, Mum.' Mish came to his sister's defence. 'Piggy Porter's Mum was nattering away per usual.'

Her defences went. Some instinct, perhaps the anxious look on Van's face – a child of nine shouldn't look like that – made her say, 'We'll forget it.' When she got home she gave her some little chore to do, a symbol of expiation. 'But remember, Van, no more stray cats. Cats will tell other cats that this is a good howff.' She tried to get her to smile. 'That knock-kneed tom you brought home last week looked up from its saucer and gave me a very knowing wink.'

Mish had chuckled, Van had snorted and rushed into her arms. This was her daughter, Anna thought, stroking her long back, whom she loved, this white-faced girl with her black frizz subdued in bunches on either side of her face, those suffering eyes, reminding her of Jean's when Frederick Kleiber, her married lover, had drowned . . .

And now, four years later, when the Cat Phase was forgotten, they were into the Odd Girl Phase. Not Elvis Presley. That would have been too ordinary. Not scrap books of film stars or the Royal Family, not boring hockey – Van thirteen, still undeveloped, not pretty but with the promising bone structure and fine eyes, so different from her brother who could talk intelligently about Abstract Impressionism with his father and was going in September to the Glasgow School of Art and boarding with Granny Rose at Clevedon Crescent.

Ritchie was unperturbed about the girls Van brought home. 'They look as if they could do with a good square meal.' He was as proud of Mish as he was modest about his own work, although his murals were now widely exhibited abroad. Glasgow still coloured his work. The silver streak in many of his paintings Anna identified as the Clyde, although there was a period when they had lived in Clerken-well when she had thought it might be the hidden Fleet River which had captured his imagination.

Their move to the Thames Valley had been prompted by Ritchie's need to be handy for London, and the old house they had bought had satisfied that, as well as Anna's longing for a garden for the chil-dren. The second floor was converted into a studio and there was an old barn in the paddock where Anna hammered away at her metal work to her heart's content. The outlying part of the town where the house was situated, once a village, had run to seed, but as Ritchie said, you couldn't have everything.

He loved the space at Greengarth. He loved Anna. He was happy. 'You're right for me,' he told her. 'Sometimes you make me want to spit blood when you criticize my work but you're right there too. And when we make love. Remember those sparklers we used to buy in Glasgow at Hallowe'en? That's you. Sparks fly when you're lit up . . .'

The sound of Vivaldi floated down from his floor. Sparky music. It was a shame to spoil his paradise, but they were a couple, he had to share, not lock himself away and play Vivaldi. She got up and went quickly out of the room.

The second-floor stairs were narrower and steeper today. Perhaps at forty-three the rot began to set in, although she was not conscious of age. Each year, she supposed, would make the stairs steeper until they both became old and moved to a bungalow or a house in Spain, Ritchie's dream.

He was up the ladder working. He wore a large butcher's apron tied round his middle. He hadn't heard her come in or was too engrossed.

'Ritchie,' she said, crossing the room and looking up at him, 'could you stop? I have to speak to you.' He nodded and went on painting for a minute or two like a runner who must continue after he has reached the post, then put his brush in the large pot of turpentine fixed to the ladder and came down quickly. He grinned at her.

'So he nipped down the ladder and had her,' he said.

'What are you talking about?' He could be infuriating at times. He recited as he wiped his hands on a rag:

> 'As Titian was mixing rose madder,
> His model was nude on a ladder,
> Her position to Titian suggested coition,
> So he nipped up the ladder and had her.'

He leered at her comically.

'You're crazy. Ritchie, my purse is missing. I'm sure that girl Winnie Good took it.'

'Oh, no.' He sobered. 'She wouldn't, would she? Have you looked in the car? She appreciated being here while her mother was in hospital. When I took her home last night she was singing your praises . . .'

'I had a fiver in it and some change. I've looked in the car, but I'm methodical, you know me. I didn't like her. She was shifty-eyed and she made Van giggle but I could never hear what she said, just that whisper, whisper, whisper in her ear, and Van's eyes on me while she listened . . .'

'You're prejudiced. And we don't want her to be class-conscious.' The concept of class-consciousness had only dawned on Ritchie since he came to live in the Thames Valley.

'I know we don't, but it's the lack of variety! Just girls from those dirty houses in Vale Street or the tinkers from the caravans at the canal. They make me feel so guilty the way they gawp at everything. They're not . . . house-trained. There was the girl whose father and mother had split up and she had that screaming fit. I told you. You were in New York. Her nose bleeding and the rest of it. I had to deal with it on my own as usual.'

8

'What did you do, as a matter of interest?' His eyes were with her now.

'Got up and slapped her face. Oh, hard-hearted Anna!' She was suddenly bursting with rage at his academic interest. Never there when he was wanted. Swanning about all over the world, or sacrosanct when he was at home. Vivaldi! 'You take nothing to do with the upbringing of the children! You go off to exotic places, or if you're at home you mustn't be disturbed. Well, that Susan Something-or-other was bloody well disturbed and I had to cope with it. Lay on the floor and pounded it with her heels. Then there was Jenny – you remember Jenny, the one with the twitch and the wry neck. Or was that the time you had your show in London and stayed up for a week?'

'You're coming on a bit strong, darling.' In his Glasgow days he had never been able to say 'Darling'.

'Yes, I'm sorry. I sounded awful to myself. But now this Winnie Good. It's too much. What's in a name? You might well ask. Winnie Bad would suit her better. Yesterday evening when I went upstairs for something I found her coming out of our bedroom. She said she had got mixed up. Well, she's been with us for a week and we don't live in a palace. Nothing seemed touched. My bag was in its usual place inside the wardrobe on the shelf when I went to get it this morning.'

'So?'

'The wardrobe door was unlocked. I always lock it because it swings open of its own accord sometimes. I know she took the purse, Ritchie, I just know. I found I hadn't got it when I stopped off on the way back to get some onions.'

'How much did you say?'

'A fiver. You know that purse Mother gave me with the section for notes? It's super, all in one, and a nice wide opening so that you can see the change. A woman must have designed it.'

'And you really looked round the bedroom?'

'Yes, on my hands and knees, under the bed, everywhere. I'm sure she took it. That creeping around upstairs, that sliding glance, like a stealthy animal . . .'

'Or one that's been whipped. The father's a drunk. We can't accuse her.'

'I know that. They probably needed the money. I gave her a pound note when you took her home last night. She did quite well out of us.'

'I saw the mother, a poor, frightened-looking soul. They probably filleted her in hospital.'

'Bleed away. Like Van. Maybe she put her daughter up to it.'

'Anna, that's unfair. Those stories the girl told us about her father were heart-breaking.'

'Okay, okay, I'm horrible, but I'll miss that purse more than the money. I treasured it. But don't you see? It's not Winnie Good I'm worried about, nor the money. It's Van. It's the pattern I'm worried about. Those mangy cats, and never wanting to join in and now those girls. I'm sorry for them, dead sorry, but everything has to have a flaw in it to interest her. What is she looking for?' He had been pulling the paint-spattered apron over his head; now he threw it on the ground and took her in his arms.

'She doesn't know. She's searching, trying to understand, to help in her own way. Poor you.' He put his cheek against hers. 'I know you're worried. And poor Winnie Good who was bad. Poor all unfortunates. Let's call it our donation to the RSPCA and the NSPCC.'

'She gave me a look of pure hatred yesterday when I said you would take her home that evening. "Well, if *you* want me to go, Mrs Laidlaw." Making me feel bad.'

'She liked it here. Can you blame her? She got proper food. I don't get drunk and beat her up . . .'

'I'm not Oxfam,' Anna said, almost weeping because she wasn't happy with herself. She took a deep breath, tried to speak steadily. 'Anyhow, that isn't the point. It's Van who's the problem with her constant wish to crucify herself.'

'Don't make a great thing of it. In a few years she'll have a boyfriend and her crusades will stop. It's a credit to her that she has such a tender heart. Let's go and have a pub lunch. My painting is buggered up for the morning. That's one thing about living here, pubs you can take women into. Not like Glasgow, all sawdust and spittoons.'

'Only where *you* lived. They're quite jazzy now in the centre of the town. I'm sorry about your painting.'

'Don't be. It's part of the whole thing to be taken off it at an exciting stage. I'll go back to the attack later on.'

'You're a wee gem.' She spoke jokily in the Scottish idiom, but suddenly there was a flurry of tears and she released herself to mop her eyes and blow her nose. 'It's worrying.'

'I know. And you should be concentrating on your work.'

'I'm getting a few commissions now that I've advertised.'

'You're good. Great sense of form.'

'Coming from you, that's praise. Don't forget we

11

were called "our own Glasgow Girls" at the Art School. Jean and I were bowled over at being linked with that illustrious lot. It's funny, Mish has never been any trouble and yet he's the one who should be, given his artistic inclination. But he's more like a budding accountant.'

'So you get double rations with Van.'

'Maybe if I called her Vanessa it might help. It's crazy, mutilating good names.'

'Life's too short for long ones.' He took her in his arms again. 'But never too short for some things. Should we skip lunch?'

'Listen to the canny Scot.' She laughed at him. 'No, I want to see people.'

Two

Anna planned to be casual when she talked to Van, to treat the matter without intensity. She insisted on Ritchie being there too, although she knew he would rather make good the money to her and consider the matter closed.

She spent the day in her studio in the garden, and as always the hammering got rid of her tension. Discipline came from within, she remembered her old tutor saying, and there was nothing quite as absorbing as designing a motif and then transferring it to a piece of metal. Jean had been the one for colour, and was now part of a select band of women painters who had never moved out of Scotland as Ritchie had done, to wider fields.

Men were free to roam, of course. How vehement she and Jean had been in the cause of Women's Rights when they were at the school, and now both seemed to put their children and husbands first.

Mish was out with friends, Van was in the sitting room. 'Don't go storming in like the Gestapo,' Ritchie had said to her in the kitchen where he had been helping her to clear up. She thought his remark unfair. She preceded him when they went in, taking her time.

Van was stretched out on the sofa. 'Oh, Mum!' she

said when Anna turned off the television. She had been watching a nature programme.

'Sorry, but we want to talk to you. It's about Winnie Good.'

The girl sat up. She had a wary look. 'Why did you rush her away? I thought she was staying until the weekend. You said so.'

'She stole my purse. It was in my bag in the wardrobe. She was snooping round upstairs.' It sounded childish, and strictly speaking, she had no proof. She looked at Van. Her face was pale, startlingly so between the wedges of black hair.

'She wouldn't do that. I know her. I'm sure she wouldn't do that although they're poor. Her mother's just back from hospital. It was terribly serious, the operation . . .'

'I know. I'm not concerned about the money. It was the purse. Granny Rose gave it to me. Your friend probably needed the money in it, but she could have asked . . .' The misery on Van's face made her want to go over and hug her, break this barrier between them.

'She was afraid of you.' The words stung. Ritchie knew that. He waded in.

'Anyhow, what's money?' He waved his arms. 'It grows on trees. The leaves are five-pound notes. We all know that in this house. We have a money tree in the garden, like a ginkgo tree with bright yellow leaves of gold leaf.' Van didn't laugh. Nor smile. Her face was closed against him.

'We want to understand,' Anna said. It was only she who wanted to understand, who was pursuing the topic, who was obsessed. 'You have nice friends at school whose parents we know, who ask you to their houses.' She had a fleeting memory of her own

14

girlhood in Glasgow, of the house in Clevedon Crescent, of the mothers with their pearls and twinsets
who had afternoon tea in town with *her* mother to
organize select parties 'for the young'. Don't forget,
she told herself, that you and Jean scorned them at
the time. It was only Nancy who fell into Mother's
pattern . . . 'And yet you prefer those village girls or
the gypsies. You know we aren't snobbish.' She met
the girl's eyes and they were cold and scornful. 'It's
just . . . it's just that the kind of girl you bring home
is . . . is . . .'

'Is what?' She wanted her to damn herself.

'Not . . . not *likeable*.' It wasn't right at all. She
sounded like a class-conscious nitpicker. 'From the
first time you brought Winnie Good I mistrusted her.
She was . . . like that spaniel we had to get rid of,
it was sly, always stealing, grovelling, wetting the
floor.'

'You said it had to be put down because it had
kidney trouble.'

'It had. As well. The Vet said it would be
kinder . . .' She gave up. 'What is it that you
like about those girls?' And the cats . . . no, that
couldn't be said. 'I know they're all in difficult circumstances. I would willingly help them, give them
money . . .'

'Oh, that's easy. Anyone can give them money.
You give Mrs Tompkins money to work for us but
you don't ask her into the *drawing* room.' Sometimes
she did say that because Rose, her mother, always
said 'drawing room', thought 'lounge' was estate
agents' parlance only. 'They want to be accepted into
a decent place, don't you see, sit at a properly set
table, eat decent food . . .'

'Maybe we should start a boarding house,' Ritchie

said, 'for girls. And cats.' Where angels fear to tread. Anna gave him a look.

Van's eyes on her father were black, full, her voice trembled. 'I thought you of all people would have understood, Dad. With your painting. You told me once that you mixed your paints with your blood,' her face was grave-white, 'and I understood. I feel it too,' she put her hand on her chest, 'here.' Her face was screwed up now. 'I feel this awful pain for . . . desolate creatures. Anything that's living and desolate. I can't get to sleep for it sometimes. It's worse than an ache . . . it's like a wound inside, bleeding . . .'

There was silence in the room. If she would weep, Anna thought, only weep, then I could comfort her, but it was past that, strange territory which only Van knew. It was embarrassing almost, because of the seeming exaggeration, and yet, looking at the white face you knew she meant it, that she was telling the truth.

Anna didn't dare to look at Ritchie. She straightened in her chair, swallowed painfully. Her throat had thickened. 'We're trying to understand you, Van. We know there are thousands, millions of sad people, deprived people, homeless people in the world. They're there. But there are the other kind too. It's necessary to see both sides, and you're young. This is the time you should be having fun with people like yourself, playing tennis, swimming . . .'

'I'm not a joiner. We've been through all that.' Anna was a joiner, right from her Brownie years. She had always walked away with all the badges, was covered with them, Jean had taunted her. Societies were always looking for people like her, organized, not afraid to take on responsibility, the Art Society, the PTA. 'I only feel lonelier in societies.'

Ritchie spoke. 'You'll soon have to decide what you are going to do when you leave school, at least where your interests lie. Mish knows already.'

'He'll never be a real painter like you. He's too . . . competent.'

She saw the fleeting look of pleased surprise on Ritchie's face. 'I think you're cut out for social work with your interest in people. You could take a Social Science degree. You would be equipped to help people then. Does that appeal to you?'

'It might.' She didn't look interested. 'It's so . . . businesslike somehow, and anyhow that's not for ages yet. This winter I thought I could do something for the real down-and-outs, the ones you label as *gypsies*,' she shot a look at Anna, 'but they're only poor people who've given up the struggle.' Her eyes burned with intensity. Anna felt as if she were being scourged.

'But you *have* been doing that more or less, don't you see?' Ritchie said. 'For those girls like Winnie Good, under-privileged girls. They aren't exactly down-and-outs, but they needed help.'

'You can see that, Dad, but Mum doesn't like them in the house.' Her glance at Anna was cold. 'Now she thinks they steal money. But I wouldn't bring the down-and-outs here. I was reading in the paper how at night they go to St Christopher's in Baldock Road and get soup. I could help there.'

'Look, Van.' Ritchie got up from his chair and went and sat beside her on the sofa. He put an arm round her shoulders and pulled her comfortably against him. *He* didn't feel a barrier. 'You might as well face up to it, life's sad, bloody sad. Not only in council

17

houses and caravans. Not only because of money. You say you read the papers. Do you read the national ones, not just the weekly rag with the local news? What about the killing that goes on all over the world? Kenya, Algeria, riots in Alabama. Do you know anything about black civil rights? About Rosa Parks, the black woman who sat in the whites-only part of the bus as a protest? Be aware, but you have to get on with your life, your education, be constructively selfish as I am with my painting, as I was in the war when I was an official artist.'

'You fought in Spain.' Got you there, Anna thought.

'Yes, I did. That was a crusade, and then it turned out to be more complicated than I thought. But I was much older than you. All you can hope for is to feel fairly comfortable and that means accepting sadness – that's what growing up means. Then you can make up your mind. Am I getting through to you?'

'Yes, but there are the down-and-outs here, the ones who hang around the Market Square whom the teddy boys laugh at. I can't *not* see them, *not* see their haunted eyes . . .'

She has to be a saviour, Anna thought. It's the stigmata she's after.

'Daddy's right,' she said. 'You can't go around wiping everyone's tears. There's your own life to be planned – university, possibly marriage and children. Of course you have to help where you can . . .' She saw a single tear roll down Van's cheek, the dejected downward bend of her head. They weren't getting through to her. She spoke briskly: 'Anyhow, that's enough talking. I'm going back to the barn. I'll give you a hammer if you like. It helps. What are you doing, Ritchie?' He pointed to the ceiling. He went to his studio like a lover. She smiled at Van but there was no response.

In bed that night Anna admitted she had failed.

'She makes you feel small, though,' Ritchie said.

'Yes. Worldly. Where does one draw the line?'

'I sympathize with her. Feeling like an alien. I used to feel like that in your mother's *drawing* room. And you know how annoyed you got with me because I wouldn't go to the PTA meetings.'

'Not any more.'

'I let you down, you being the President or whatever. But I didn't fit in. I've no complaints about the school so I wasn't crowding round the teachers, not huddling with men talking about stocks and shares or football or golf. Besides they think I'm odd because I don't go to work every morning on the eight five up to town, nor work in a local factory. Nor make jokes about my typist's legs. They think I've inherited money, not that I paint because I must, for a living. If you don't hunt with the pack you're an alien.'

'Perhaps, then, she gets it from you? But Mish's talent doesn't segregate him.'

'No,' he admitted. 'Van's right. He's competent.'

I wonder, Anna thought, if it's an easy talent like Mother's or Nancy's, facile, not restless and struggling like Ritchie's. And he was good at sports.

'Maybe this house was a mistake after all. We stick out like a sore thumb, just as it does. It's an anachronism. We'd go unnoticed in London.'

'Don't bring that up again. All I want is for Van to have a normal life.'

'What's "normal", for God's sake?' He came close to her because he was going to make love to her. He fondled her breasts. His hands moved down over her

19

body, hands rough from being scrubbed with turpentine. 'At least Scotland will be a hiatus when we go up with Mish, a breaking of the pattern.'

They had arranged to go to Glasgow in September for Mish's enrolling at the Art School, install him with her mother and also visit Nancy, her younger sister, at Hyndland. Afterwards they would spend a few days with John and Jean and their family, Sarah and Roderick, in Kirkcudbright.

'Yes?' He spoke softly, lovingly, fitted his body to hers, closely, closely.

'Perhaps when Van falls in love she will be obsessed by that as I was. Remember?'

'Aren't you still?' His mouth was on hers, forcing her lips open with his tongue. 'This is the first step to breaking and entering,' he said. He was a creative lover in his conversation as well.

'Do you remember Van was quite impressed by Gordon? Nancy saw it, and said Gordon would write to her when he went to Glenalmond. She bosses him around. He's more her son than James's. Come to think of it, some weeks ago there was a letter with a Perthshire stamp on it addressed to her. But she's so fiercely secretive . . . Mmmh . . .' she moaned. This was the thing that blotted out all worries. She responded to him with a kind of desperation, trying to convince herself that this was the most important thing in their lives.

But she knew it wasn't. The grave-white face of their daughter kept coming between them, stood in the way of her passion.

I can't understand her, Van thought, secure in her room with its view over the paddock to the canal beyond. She could see the caravans, dirty-white, huddled together on its scrubby bank, specks of paper lying in the grass. She's so conventional, although when she tells us about her young days at the Art School in Glasgow it's all about how she and Aunt Jean were *un*conventional.

Granny Rose, of course, has very strict ideas about the 'right' people and the 'right' clothes – wearing your best on Sundays and not stubbing the toes of your shoes and how to set a table and how to behave 'in company' and so on, and yet I don't object to that. It's part of her. So why don't I accept Mum's outlook as being part of her?

Dad understands how guilty I feel in comparison with those girls at school who come from poor homes and caravans, especially with Winnie Good when she hints at not being good enough to be invited to our house. 'I'm not posh enough for your kind,' she said. Last winter she wore ankle socks and her legs were blue with cold.

Maybe he understands because his father and mother are quite poor, though I know he's very good to them, taking presents and things. But it's a clean kind of poorness, not like the Goods'.

Everything is so puzzling when you're growing up in the fifties. Could it be because of the last war? When Dad and Mum were young they seemed to be so carefree – at least according to the way they talk. They didn't seem to have any worries. Dad says to remember that it is what you *are* that counts, but it's easy for him. He's so likeable, and good-looking. Mum's friends go nuts about him. She gets mad at that. Her face is a scream, trying not to show it.

She got up and went to a drawer, took out the tin cash box which Granny Rose had given her when she was six. She had loved it because it had a lock and key, and had used it ever since. That was one good thing about this family: no one ever pried, even Mish, who was the absolute end with his airs and graces about being grown-up.

She unlocked the box, lifted its shiny black lid striped gold and red, and took out a letter from a neat pile, spread it out on her knees and bent over it, muttering the words like an incantation.

3 April 1956. Trinity College, Glenalmond.

Dear Vanessa, I got your letter a month or so ago but honestly I've been so busy studying for my extra Highers, and running my House, not to mention practising for the Swimming Trophy and the Fencing Cup and goodness knows what else . . . yours truly is considered quite a star in the sports department!

Did I actually ask you to write to me? You shouldn't take me so seriously. Mother stands over me while I write my Christmas cards, and perhaps I put something on the one I sent you. Don't worry. I'm glad if I did.

Now to see if Uncle Gordon can give you any advice. I don't think you should lose any sleep thinking of poverty and that kind of thing. Mother says most of that lot have nobody to blame but themselves. They won't work, and see where that gets them! This is generally before she gives me my usual lecture about getting my head down. It's always mothers who go on like this. Fathers usually keep out of it, at least mine does.

My mother's right, of course, about the competition being keen in Glasgow. Of course, being at a school like this is a help. It gives you that extra polish, and that's what counts. Take my advice, Vanessa, stop thinking about those girls you tell me about and concentrate on yourself. I always thought you'd turn out to be quite pretty if you took more care. I know girls who could give you a tip or two, even if they're not quite . . .

Some of the boys here slip out when they're supposed to be swotting, or if they're doing a run, and see the shop-girls. There's one called Lily, a real bobby-dazzler, bouffant hairstyle, high heels, painted nails, but, of course I'm only going by what they tell me, ha-ha!

I'm very flattered when you say I'm the only boy you've ever admired. You make me blush the way you describe my manly beauties. I've always had a soft spot for you, Vanessa, but, please, don't be disappointed if I don't write again. But the next time you come up to Bonnie Scotland . . . well, there's no saying . . .

Life is very complicated at the moment. And if I behave myself I've been promised a skiing holiday by the parents.

Don't do anything I wouldn't do.

Your loving cousin, Gordon.

She folded the letter and stowed it away in the cash box. He didn't understand, of course, how important it was to her to try and help the poor deprived souls in the world. It was something you couldn't explain, this pain in her heart.

But he was sweet. And so good-looking, that golden quiff . . . 'Daredevil Dan'. 'I always thought you'd turn out to be quite pretty . . .' *He* could fill her thoughts to the exclusion of everyone else, he could heal her pain, hold her gently in his arms . . .

She locked the box with the key she kept on a ribbon round her neck.

Three

Ritchie had bought her a car, her first, in which they were going to Scotland, but at the last moment he was delayed by negotiations for a commission. The arrangements had to be made in London, and afterwards he had to go to Barcelona.

They decided that Anna would drive up with the children on the day they had arranged as Rose 'would have a fit' at any alterations to the programme (the expression echoed down the years). Ritchie would follow on the night train from London and spend a few days in Glasgow to see the galleries and introduce Mish to the Art School, then go back to make the flight to Barcelona. Anna would go on to Kirkcudbright with Mish and Van.

She didn't mind driving although it was a long way from the Thames Valley to Glasgow. Not many women in Scotland were allowed to drive by their husbands; the three sisters were the exception. 'We're avant-garde,' Jean had said, 'because we were at the Art School.' Mish assured Anna he would be able to share the driving with her next year.

They needed a car for the amount of luggage they were taking. Mish had a 'flitting' of all his possessions – Ritchie told him he would have to learn Scottish expressions – and there were presents for their cousins in Glasgow and Kirkcudbright. Rose's came from Harrods. Nothing else would have been good enough, and even then it was invariably compared with what they might have got in Daly's, her favourite Sauchiehall Street store.

Then there were presents for Walter and Lizzie, Ritchie's parents, and there would be a substantial envelope slipped to Walter, who had a mild passion for gambling. 'Poor old bugger,' Ritchie said, 'life hasn't been much fun for him. On the dole for twenty years and his wife washing tenement stairs and closes for those who could afford it.' That had been stopped when Ritchie was earning enough to give them an allowance. Anna liked to give her mother-in-law a smart coat and dress. She still had a neat figure at seventy.

The journey up through England had been easy, with two stops, one at Birmingham, the other at Preston. Now they were crossing the border at Gretna Green. 'Welcome to Scotland', the notice said.

In the car mirror Anna saw Mish miming the Highland fling with arm movements. 'Look at that fool,' she said to Van beside her, and laughing. 'From now on we call you Hamish since we've gone through the Tartan Curtain.'

'They think we speak awfully funny,' Van said.

'Just wait till we get to Glasgow and you'll hear *me*. You should hear Granny playing bridge with her cronies. Jean and I used to be in fits. "It's your *tern*, Grace."' She gave a passable imitation of her mother's accent. 'And they hum little tunes like this.' She hummed the melody of 'Tea for Two'. 'She's so coy! "No keekin', gerls," she'll say, holding her cards against her chest.'

Van snorted at her side, 'Oh, Mum!'

' "No looking", that means. Oh, we were carefully brought up, not like the freedom you kids have. Jean and I were the despair of Mother because we didn't like the Jaeger ensembles she chose for us. Especially Jean. She loved making dresses out of old bits and pieces. We had a settle in the hall where materials bought at sales were kept, and Bessie's mending basket was a rich treasure trove.' She laughed, remembering. 'Once she dressed up Tumshie, Bessie's cat, and sent it into the drawing room in the middle of one of Mother's bridge do's.'

Mish chimed in: 'And Bessie said, "Yon yin needs skelpin'." I've been practising Bessie's way of speaking since I'll be staying there. But since we're talking, how about Gordon's voice? It's the absolute end!'

'No, it isn't!' Van was incensed. 'He's just polite.'

'Like a smarmy shopwalker. He's a comic turn.'

'It's the Glenalmond brogue,' Anna said. She changed the subject. 'Oh, I'm looking forward to seeing Jean afterwards.'

'I shouldn't think it's easy for her,' Mish said in his precise adult fashion, 'I mean, because of Roderick.'

'Still, he's loving. That's better than being easy.' Van's voice sounded sad. Her head was turned towards the window.

Anna drove on in the silence, beginning to recognize landmarks now, the signpost for Moffat, all those stops with Father when they drove to see Aunt Jessie at Kirkcudbright, who had left her house to Jean when she died. She and Jean in their kilted skirts on those outings . . . 'Sit up straight, *gerls*, and don't wriggle about. It spoils your pleats.' Gargantuan lunches, afternoon teas, Father always amenable as he shepherded his brood of four females, not saying much, never looking entirely happy, the look of a Highlander far from home.

She remembered him saying to Mother as they drove through the soft hills of Galloway: 'Those aren't *proper* hills, Rose. If the girls could have seen Carn Ben with the sun on it.' Rose hadn't liked Ross, 'too wild and barren.' She was city-bred with a pathological fear of untamed countryside. Country noises, and worse, country silences, disturbed her. Behind a practical exterior she had numerous fears.

The Thames Valley, she said when she visited them, was her kind of place, with 'nice' trees and little teashops in the pretty towns. Ritchie regarded Renton as too well bred. It was simply a convenient resting place for his wife and family, with space to move around and convenient to London.

They had passed through Lesmahagow and were on the flat land, becoming aware that the outskirts of Glasgow were not far off. You could almost feel its pulse beat, she thought, that great sprawling city which was her home and where her roots were. At that moment she knew what belonging meant, felt a mixture of pride and shame which every Glaswegian feels for the city's reputation for violence, but scorn at the Englishman's inability to understand the Scots, their tenderness and passion, their aggression, their intolerable smugness and compensation for that smugness in their feeling for art, a dramatic, infuriating, lovable city.

'Can you smell it yet, Glasgow?' she said to the children.

'It's like a city behind a veil,' Van said.

'That's the smoke pall.' Mish.

'Your father claims he got most of his inspiration from wandering about the city streets absorbing images and remembering the past, the famous Glasgow murders, Madeleine Smith sinning in the grand way in Blythswood Square, poor little Dr Pritchard of Charing Cross hanging by a rope, the last person to be executed – he haunted the Necropolis, you know . . .'

'Dr Pritchard?' Van said.

'No, Daddy. He became obsessed by John Knox for a time.'

'He's certainly not a disciple of John Knox,' Mish laughed.

'Definitely not. And he loved Kelvingrove Park with lovely Park Terrace sailing like a cruise liner above it, and the Botanic Gardens near our house. Granny Laidlaw once said to me that she thought Kibble Palace there – the conservatories – were a dream of delight. He loved the sweep of the Georgian terraces and the contrast with the squalor of the Gorbals, and all the streets running like arteries to the river where Sam Bough painted. And most of all, the Glasgow voices. He says that's why he feels so much at home in Barcelona. It's like another Glasgow, a port. I'll have to drive down to Central Station tomorrow to pick him up off the *Royal Scot*.' She said it casually, but felt apprehensive. Could she park beside the taxis in Gordon Street, or drive right in?

It would be like going back in time to stand at that barrier, she thought. And to see his lifted, welcoming face, full of love.

'Mother!' They were in the drawing room at Clevedon Crescent, a room which with its balanced proportions and plaster cornices certainly deserved the title. She went towards her. This would be the only time they would kiss. Daily comings and goings had always

29

gone unmarked. Funerals, though, Father's funeral, Mother walking between Jean and Anna in becoming black, Nancy walking behind. Mother didn't approve of women being at funerals (only Catholics permitted that), but she had no living relations, and Father's only brother, Calum, was in far-off Australia and hadn't thought it worthwhile to come.

'You look as smart as ever, Mother.' But she seemed faded, although still rose-like in her soft pink blouse and matching cardigan and pearls, although her cheeks were rouged more noticeably than last year. Her lipstick was a mistake. Too vibrant. But always decorative, a painted lady. She remembered Nabokov's butterflies.

'You look well, Anna,' Rose said, standing back, 'but thinner. It suits you. You can't wear clothes if you're fat. And here's wee Vanessa! Now *you* could do with more colour in your cheeks, dear. Maybe you're growing too quickly . . . and Hamish! My goodness! We'll have to get you both against the door when we go to Nancy's.' This was an annual ritual, the measuring of the children back to back. And Mother's annual joke, which would now be out-of-date since Gordon was no longer at school in Glasgow: 'Gordon's *got* it, but then he goes to the High School!'

'I drove up, Mother. My new car . . .' Lift of chin, no sprowsing allowed.

'Now sit down and Bessie will bring you a cup of tea before you get settled in properly. Just wait till you see the grand room she's prepared for you, Hamish, up above.' The drawing room was on the first floor. Mother thought that a *sine qua non*. 'You'll be able to see the whole of Glasgow from the windows, back and front. And a fine desk for you to sit at and do your drawing and suchlike. Your grandfather was always busy with *his* drawings.' She touched her eye with her handkerchief, a *de rigueur* gesture at the mention of her husband. 'Angus's desk. We got the removal men to lift it and take up the carpet in your room as well. Just rugs, which I think you should roll up if you're painting. There's a bathroom next door. Your mother and her sisters loved being up there, didn't you, Anna?'

'Yes, it was great!' How easy to slip into the Glasgow idiom.

There was a bump at the door and Anna jumped up and opened it. How often she had done that in the past. 'There's Bessie dunting . . .' Bessie had never mastered the art of putting down the tray on the landing table to knock first. She came in with the laden tray.

If she had diminished over the years, hair streaked with grey, a rounded back, the quality of her teas hadn't – scones, strawberry jam in the crystal dish, sandwiches, ham or gentleman's relish, Father's favourite . . . those summer holidays at Kilcreggan when he had stepped off the boat at the pier, the three girls standing there to greet him, being proud of this good-looking father of theirs with the briefcase and bowler hat, a city gentleman.

'Well, Bessie,' Anna said, when she had put down the tray, 'here we are to plague you again. You're going to have a lodger this time, Mish . . . Hamish.'

'Aye.' She gave him a sideways glance. 'Well, there's to be no morning trays for you, young man. They stairs are getting a bit much for me noo, even up to the *drawing* room.' She glowered at Rose, and then went back to Mish. 'You'll come doon for your breakfast like ony decent person.'

31

'I'll do that, Bessie,' he said politely. He came forward and held out his hand. Bessie looked at it first before she wiped her own hand on her apron and presented it to him – she didn't go in for any fancy nonsense like hand-shaking, her look suggested.

'I'm sure you and me will get on fine, Hamish.'

'I'll try and not be any trouble. And just ask me if there's anything you want carried up.'

She looked astonished and pleased. 'Well, you can't say fairer than that.' She turned her attention to Van. 'And this is the wee lass? No' so wee noo. I dare say you'll be the next one for a lodger, if I'm still here,' she added darkly.

'Have you still got Tumshie?' Van asked.

'Aye, but gey ancient noo. No following at my heels like the last one, much to your Granny's disgust . . .'

'Pour the tea, Bessie, please,' Rose commanded, 'or it won't be worth drinking with your chattering on. Anna must be dying for a cup.'

'Could I go into the kitchen and see him?' Van asked.

'Aye, you can, but he'll no' take to you. Bad-tempered. There'll never be one like the old Tumshie, God rest her soul.'

'After tea, Vanessa.' Rose was firm and a little tetchy. 'One thing at a time. But the same rule still applies. No coming into the drawing room with any Tumshie.'

'She wouldn't come in if you went down on your bended knees and begged her, Missus.' Bessie was busy pouring tea and handing it around.

'Mrs *Mackintosh*, Bessie,' Rose said. 'Will you pass the scones, Hamish, please? You'll have to get used to helping Granny when you're here.'

Anna smiled to herself. Mish would. He was eternally amenable. And he'd be tactful with Bessie. She would point out to him when she got him to herself that the relationship between the two women, mistress and maid, was strong and unbreakable, founded as it was on an equal measure of love and recognition of the established hierarchy.

Four

Hearty shaking of hands, Ritchie by her side – she had successfully gathered him up at Central Station this morning – kisses between Nancy and Anna (not bestowed on Rose because she and Nancy saw each other most days), a kiss for Van from Uncle James, now lean but not so defined, Anna thought, as he had been at thirty-five when he had married a twenty-two-year-old Nancy. She had taken the spark out of him.

'Sherry, Mother?' James asked Rose when she was seated. 'Sherry for the ladies, isn't it? And, Gordon, will you pour out a soft drink for Vanessa and Hamish? Now that Gordon is in his last year at Glenalmond, he's allowed a wee tot of whisky.'

'Very kind of you, Father,' Gordon said gaily, as if to humour him. He was a fine-looking young man, dressed in a Mackintosh kilt and blue tweed sports jacket, stockings with red tabs. He had manly polished knees. Anna saw Mish looking covertly at them.

'Now you'll see why we don't call you Hamish in England,' she would say to him later. 'They would have expected you to dress in a kilt and sporran.' 'Fancy dress,' she could imagine Ritchie saying.

He was accepting his whisky from James with a surprised grin.

'You said a *wee* tot, James!' He looked at the same time bemused, but his eyes were lively. She knew him of old. He wouldn't miss a thing.

Nancy, in a flowered and frilled dress, with her blonde hair carefully waved, was plumper than she had been. All that rich food she got on their luxury cruises . . .

'When's your next cruise, Nancy?' she asked. She knew from experience that there would be very little information sought from them. You got the impression when you visited in Glasgow that you had dropped from another planet with no past, present or future, just an instant in their busy lives, details of which they were prepared to retail to you until you were glassy-eyed with boredom. How you grew away! And yet how you understood it so well, their capacity to make drama out of everyday incidents.

'Will it be the Caribbean?' She might as well start the ball rolling since it would roll in any case, details of sitting at the captain's table, the lectures on flower arranging, the woman who tried to outdo everybody by changing four times each day, Gordon's prowess at deck quoits, in the swimming pool, on the dance floor, and so on and so on.

'Oh, we're not going this year,' she said, shaking her blonde head sorrowfully. 'James's mother's pretty frail, not to put too fine a point on it she has . . .' she mouthed the dread word '. . . just a matter of time.'

'Oh, I'm sorry.' She remembered Nancy's mother-in-law at her wedding, a little round-bodied widow like Queen Victoria, dressed in a two-piece and flowered toque. 'I doubt if we'll even get to Lamlash.'

'Couldn't you take her there with you?'

'No. She couldn't make the journey. Besides, she only likes Pitlochry. They know her at the Hydro. She always went there with James's father. Gordon's very good. He's agreed to go with us to Lamlash after he comes back from OTC camp, if we go.' Gordon overheard her, looked up, smiling.

'But you've promised me a skiing trip to Austria when I'm at the uni.'

'Did you ever know me not keep my promise?' Nancy smiled coyly back.

Anna looked at him, handsome, ruddy-faced and kneed, hair in a golden quiff, a young Adonis. Her glance went to Van and saw that she was transfixed, her eyes glued on him. Her soft drink in her hand was untouched, her mouth was a little open. Oh God, she thought, I should have tumbled to it. That letter with the Perthshire postmark which Mish teased her about, and how she flared up at him and rushed out of the room . . . Her glance shifted to Nancy, perched coquettishly on the arm of her husband's chair, her arm round his shoulder. Their glances met, and Nancy bent forward, speaking softly, presumably, so that their mother wouldn't hear. 'Grace Binnie died, you know.'

'Mother's friend?' The memories that name brought up. The skeleton at every feast in the Mackintosh household, sad or glad. The Greek chorus. Grace Binnie, always the spectator, never interfering, seeing everything. She would make a good watchdog for St Peter, 'sitting on the right hand of God, the Father Almighty, from whence He shall come . . .' The Creed, which she had learned in English churches, where she had felt that she was halfway to Rome on a visit to His Holiness. 'Grace Binnie!' she

36

whispered. 'I thought she would go on for ever.'

'So did I. Everybody thought it would be Stewart Binnie who would go first. He was older for one thing. It just goes to show. You never know . . . Did I tell you that Gordon has decided to take his degree in architecture and follow his father into the firm? Then you and I can go on an eternal luxury cruise, can't we, dear?' she said to James who had been listening, putting her cheek against his.

'Yes, Nancy,' he said, looking too drained for any luxury cruise, unless indeed it *was* eternal.

'A lovely funeral, wasn't it, James? Grace Binnie's. Wylie and Lochhead did the arrangements. Beautiful. Nothing fancy, but all in perfect taste. It pays in the end.'

'They're famed for that, Wylie and Lochhead. It would be a great comfort to Mr Binnie.' If Ritchie were listening to Nancy, he'd have a fit. How could a tasteful funeral make any difference? She became terrified when she thought of losing Ritchie. She had always been afraid of death, its finality. As a small girl she had worried about losing her father, felt she would die too, and yet, when it came, it was bearable.

Was there indeed some satisfaction to be gained from 'the turnout', as they called it. 'A good turnout.' She hadn't thought of that aspect at the time; now she remembered her mother saying hours after Father's death, 'Of course, we'll have Wylie and Lochhead,' as if that were a solace.

And she had been gratified that the whole of the City Chambers had 'turned out', a tribute, she said, to the finest man who had ever lived.

She and Ritchie hadn't decided whether they wanted to be buried or cremated, were toying with

the idea of a suicide pact when they were sixty-five
and the juices had dried up. She hadn't asked him
whether he meant his painting juices or the other
ones.

Nancy jumped off the arm of James's chair lightly,
or as lightly as she could. She would be girlish at
eighty, or perhaps it would go when James went. She
had always been his 'little girl'. 'Before we go in for
dinner we've got to have our annual measuring.
Come on, boys! I think Gordon's going to be the win-
ner again although he's not at the *High* School now.'
She smiled at her mother. 'He's excelled himself on
the rugby field.'

Mish and Gordon crossed to the door and stood
obediently back to back, neither protesting. They had
been inured years ago to this ceremony. It was easily
seen that they were both the same height, even without the ruler which Nancy produced.

'Do you measure horizontally or perpendicularly,
Nancy?' Ritchie said.

'It's height, of course. It's always been height! I
know you of old, Ritchie Laidlaw. You're pulling my
leg.' She made eyes at him.

'Finished with us, Mother?' Gordon said, laughing
at Mish. 'What we have to suffer with parents!'

Anna studied her nephew, his undeniable good
looks and humour, his breadth accented by the tweed
jacket with its epaulettes, his handsomeness marred
slightly by his mouth, what Bessie would have called
a 'petted mouth' when the girls were young. 'Away
ye go oot o' ma road. I don't want any petted mooths
in *ma* kitchen,' when they had run to her with a complaint.

He was smiling at Van. 'Would you like me to take
you for a game of tennis at our club, Vanessa, before

you go to Kirkcudbright? You too, Hamish. We've a great crowd.'

Van sat back in her chair as if she had been struck. 'I'm . . . not very keen . . .' She looked anguished.

'Listen to her, Aunt Anna!' He smiled in her direction. He was charming in his boyishness, his sureness of his charm. 'I bet she's another Mo Connolly. You're all brilliant players down there.' 'Down there' was the composite Glaswegian expression for anyone who lived in England, implying that it was a huge amorphous *nothing*, a piece of nameless ectoplasm. 'What about it, Hamish?'

'I don't mind.' Mish was always equable, as if to make up for Van. 'But I don't think you'll get my sister to go. She's against all that.'

'All what?'

'Tennis clubs. The kind of people in them, ordinary people.'

'Ordinary!' Gordon was horrified. 'But they're anything but that!'

'Well, you know what I mean. Like us. But *she* likes odd people, misfits.'

Van muttered something, head lowered.

James surprisingly intervened. 'Everyone has to learn to mix, Vanessa. I was shy myself when I was young. You have to learn to swim with the tide, isn't that so, Ritchie?'

Ritchie looked up from his whisky, jerked momentarily out of his 'non-uttering policy'. When he was younger he had offended Nancy once or twice with what she called his 'Red' views. Now he claimed he got his best thinking done about paintings while they were all chattering on. 'Well, neither of our two are keen on sports to tell you the truth, James. Maybe it's something to do with me being a painter and the

39

kind of people who come about, and Anna with her metal work. Our friends are not exactly . . . tennis players,' he finished lamely.

'Ah well, I can see that,' James said and sat back in his chair, mission accomplished.

'I'd quite like to go,' Van said in a small voice. She had raised her head, her eyes luminous, large, fixed on Gordon, like a scared rabbit meeting a stoat. Anna's heart bled for her. 'But I don't have tennis stuff, and there's Kirkcudbright. When were we going, Mum?'

'There's no hurry. We could soon get you some tennis clothes at Rowans.'

'Oh, don't bother, Aunt,' Gordon said. 'I don't want you *buying* stuff. It was only a suggestion. And if Vanessa doesn't play much she might feel at a disadvantage.'

Nancy, the arbiter, stepped in. 'Of course she'll go, Gordon. Lumley's is best now, Anna, more up-to-date. And if Vanessa doesn't play much, all the more reason for her going to a decent club and seeing how it's –'

A trim maid appeared at the door, putting poor old Bessie in the shade. 'Dinner's ready, Madam,' she said with a little bob.

'Thank you, Eileen.' Anna noticed the Highland lilt in the girl's voice. 'Can I help you, Mother?' Nancy went towards Rose who was gathering her beaded evening bag and her chiffon scarf together.

'I'm not an old woman yet, Nancy,' she said petulantly. She must have noticed the contrast too, but Anna doubted if Eileen would have the staying power of Bessie.

'Coming, Vanessa?' Gordon, all charm, held out his hands to her. Anna saw the immediate blush

40

which swept over Van's face as he pulled her to her feet. She looked across at Ritchie. Yes, he had noticed too. Those bright, beautiful painter's eyes met hers, one eyebrow raised. Those compelling eyes. They had compelled her for years, would go on doing so for ever.

The following afternoon Anna and Ritchie sat in an old-fashioned tearoom they had found in Byres Road, above a baker's shop. In the morning they had driven out to the north-east of the city with the children to see Ritchie's parents.

'We crowd them into a morning,' Anna said. 'Your mother's not daft. She knows we always give more time to *our* family.'

'Mine couldn't put us up. She knows that too. When I'm earning really big money I'm going to set them up in a decent house. Her dream is for a garden.' Anna thought of the gaunt little woman whom she loved, who loved her son and therefore her, whom her mother didn't see eye to eye with because Lizzie Laidlaw had politely turned down her invitation to have tea with her in Fullers and then go shopping together in Buchanan Street. Father had been the go-between, he had made the effort. She remembered him putting up the Laidlaws in the Selkirk Arms when she and Ritchie were married in Kirkcudbright.

'If we get a really big house to match your really big money, I wouldn't mind having them. We could share the garden.'

'We'd have to live near a betting shop as well,' Ritchie laughed. 'Don't worry. I'll never forget them. They did too much for me without understanding the first thing about art.'

'I'll miss you,' she said now.

He was leaving by the night train for London, she was driving to Kirkcudbright the following morning with Van.

Mish was staying on in Glasgow to be 'shown the ropes' by Gordon. 'The boys have really hit it off,' Nancy had enthused. 'And he can come to us any time, Anna, if he gets too much of Mother . . .' Mish would be all right.

'Quel relief!' Anna said now, smiling across the table at Ritchie. They always felt inhibited at Clevedon Crescent in spite of its size, and somehow felt that their lovemaking had to be conducted silently when they were in the habit of 'talking themselves through it'.

'Curbed passion doesn't suit you.' He could read her thoughts. 'I wonder how poor old Van's getting on at the select tennis club.'

'For ordinary people.' She laughed. 'Don't say a word. She's all moony-eyed, and she wouldn't stop brushing her hair to try and get the frizz out. "Black girls have it straightened," she said to me, looking pathetic, poor love. She's *in* love. I shouldn't like her tied up to the golden boy, but it might wean her away from the misfits . . .'

'Isn't she a bit young for all that?' Ritchie asked. 'Boys. She's not fourteen yet. I'd rather have the cats.' His eyes were on the waitresses in a black and white huddle in the corner of the room. 'I thought these pleated cap things went out with Feydeau. Strange place this, Edwardian. I like the ambience. Do you see the height of the ceiling? And the cornices? And there's a cashier sitting in a box at the door, for God's sake! I remember my grandmother telling me that at Anderson's Royal Polytechnic – it became Lewis's –

they had that system of wooden cash holders, like pepper pots, which went whizzing around on overhead wires to the cashier. I would have *killed* to see that. I had dreams about it, thought I could get into a giant one and go whizzing about the emporium – that's what they call it, an emporium . . .'

'Antediluvian. We were discussing Van.' You always had to stop Ritchie when he got on one of his surrealistic tracks.

'You wouldn't want her to get hitched up to her *cousin*, for Christ's sake?'

'So what? I bet you're thinking if they did they would have loony children. That's real lower-class thinking. No, I wouldn't as a matter of fact, she's far too young to think about anyone, but going to the tennis club lets her see that it might be fun to be normal – at least what is called normal. Anything's better than Winnie Good. Did you see Gordon looking horrified when Mish used "ordinary" in its proper sense?'

'Yes, that's his upbringing. "Ordinary" to him means the crowds in Partick on a Saturday night, swarming round the chip shops, packing out the corner pubs, the men coming stottin' out and buying a bunch of flowers for the wife . . .'

'Miles away from skiing in Austria with "your own crowd". Lord preserve us! Are we being over-critical? But I couldn't stand it here for long, could you? It seems so parochial.'

'That's only one bit. In any case, I think the younger generation may break away. There are signs already.'

'Nancy's the dominant influence with Gordon. So hidebound . . .' A doubt about herself crossed her mind. 'She showed me her shoes last night. Rows of them in her bedroom. All with peerie heels, bought in Russell & Bromley's.'

'She wears high heels because she has fat ankles.'

'Is that it? I never noticed.' She had, and had come to the same conclusion. 'And she said wasn't it nice that Gordon had "hit it off" with Van and been *nice* to her, then she gave me some advice on where to buy clothes for her, make her more "with it".'

'But you took her advice, didn't you?' His look made her feel shabby.

'Van wanted it. A complete tennis outfit, a bandeau for her hair, all in Lumley's, and if there was any nonsense to use Nancy's name . . .' She thought of that expedition this morning with a tense Van, but one who was subtly different, as if driven, possessed. 'I want something really up-to-date, Mum. Don't try to push me into what *you* would like.'

She had been hurt because she had thought she was completely innocent of that besetting sin of mothers. Van had two types of outfits, school uniform and jeans with an assortment of jerseys. Sometimes she wore Mish's which had become too small for him. In summer she wore shirts and shorts. She was unadorned, in every sense.

She looked out through the great windows on to the busy street. 'The sun's shining. How would you like to walk along to the tennis club? It's not far from here.'

'Won't it look like spying?'

'Don't be silly. Nancy says the parents often go. There are facilities for them in the Club rooms.'

'All right. I haven't been that way yet.'

'You always walk miles,' she said to him as they waited for the bill.

44

'Glasgow's rich in memories for me. And hilly. I never noticed that when I was young, really young.'

'You were young enough last night.' She gave him a lascivious look. 'Maybe it's like Rome. The city of seven hills.'

'There must be even more here. Think of the steep climb from Bothwell Street to Sauchiehall Street, the ascent from St Vincent Place all the way to Greek Thomson's church. I would love to see the contour of the land without the buildings.'

'The Cathedral at the top of High Street . . .'

'I might try to make a map of it, stripped of everything, to see how it looks. I might just do it in my head . . .'

'Thank you, sir,' the waitress said, at their side now, holding out the bill.

'Thank you. Do you know the age of this place by the way? I thought that possibly you'd been here for quite a time.'

Her leathery face broke in an amused cackle. 'Is that you casting nasturtiums? Thinking I was put in with the bricks?' Ritchie laughed with her. You could talk in clichés for ever in Glasgow without having an original thought in your head.

They walked in the sunny afternoon to the corner of Byres Road then turned left into Great Western Road, going towards Anniesland Cross. He put his arm round her waist and she felt young and happy. This was her childhood, her girlhood. Life had been pleasant and she had not known at the time how circumscribed it was. Had Ritchie been an architect like her father or James, she would never have known it could be anything else.

She remembered how dubious she had been about Ritchie when she had met him at the Art School, knowing that he wouldn't fit in, but determined to have him all the same. Her father had been her supporter, had won Mother over. Excellence in any field impressed Angus Mackintosh. Besides, Ritchie Laidlaw was a likeable lad with a presence.

'Are you happy, Ritchie?' she said.

'Yes. And fortunate. This trip to Barcelona is quite something. Being asked, I mean. I don't deserve my luck.'

They were walking past Bellhaven Terrace, and he stopped in the middle of its imposing frontage and kissed her. Two elderly ladies dressed in the usual West End summer uniform, flowered two-piece, pearls and straw hat, had to go round them. Anna heard one of them say, 'Did you ever see the like? In broad daylight!'

'You should see us when it's dark,' Ritchie muttered.

It was Anna's old tennis club, tucked down one of the salubrious drives off Great Western Road. It hadn't changed. The handsome stuccoed building, white-washed, red-roofed, the green lawns of the bowling club on one side with its smart elderly ladies and gentlemen playing. The women's legs looked thin because of their clumsy white plimsolls.

They sat on a bench not directly in front of the tennis courts where they could see and not be seen. The September sun shone blandly down on them, the beds of dahlias blazed circumspectly within their lobelia and alyssum borders, and the white figures darting about on the red blaes had a *déjà vu* quality. She might have been one of them. Nothing had changed in thirty years.

'There's Mish in that singles court,' Ritchie said. 'He plays like how he is, capable, neat, composed.'

'Do you think he'll make a painter?'

'He'll use his talent. I don't think he'll be like me. It's the market place for him. He's got what I lack, a business sense.'

'There's Van. Playing against Gordon and a girl. Golden-haired. But doesn't Van look pretty?'

'Like a young colt. All legs.'

'That's because of the short skirt. Accordion pleated, her choice, and frilly knickers, if you please. The shirt's Aertex. Do you like the wide bandeau?'

'Nothing keeps that hair in place. She's like a Rossetti woman except their hair is red usually.'

'There's a certain resemblance, but they never looked vulnerable the way Van does. I fear for her . . . now they're chatting across the net. Gordon looks like every young girl's dream, doesn't he?'

Even from this distance the girl playing with Gordon was striking. The golden hair was held in place by a white spotted red scarf which was knotted behind one ear. Her face and legs were a golden bronze against the short white dress she was wearing. The skirt flicked flirtily as she ran forward after serving.

Anna watched how she and Gordon played strongly together. Once, when they ran up to the net together, she saw his hand on her shoulder. They looked . . . suited.

She turned her eyes to Van, feeling that apprehension again. She ran awkwardly, she was unco-ordinated, surely more so than she had been; now Anna saw that her knees were too bony for such a short skirt, a skirt which did not flick sensually but seemed to slap lumpily against her thighs. She fluffed balls, she put her hand to her mouth in dismay, her partner, a dark-haired boy, turned away

47

from her with apologetic gestures to the other two.

'I wonder if she's short-sighted,' Ritchie said. 'She missed that one although it was played right to her racket.'

'I don't know. I'll find out.' The sun on her head was no longer a benison.

'Your serve, Wendy!' she heard Gordon call out. It would be 'Wendy' Anna thought. The girl took her place behind the serving line, one foot forward, raised her right arm slowly, her body one long fluid line from hip to wrist, the racket poised above her head. Her other arm came up with the ball, there was a moment's pause and then it went hurtling swiftly and surely over the net to land in the far corner of the court.

Van was caught off guard by its velocity. She started towards it a second too late, on the wrong foot, hurtled herself after it, somehow stumbled, and the next second she was sitting awkwardly on the court like a stuffed doll, her legs outspread, her racket spinning away from her to land at her partner's feet.

Anna saw the swift derisory look exchanged between him and the other two before he lifted it and ran towards her. She got up quickly, shaking off his arm held out to help her. Gordon and Wendy, coming up to the net and standing there, looked like spectators at the edge of a bear pit. Their set faces showed they were controlling their laughter.

'Are you all right, Vanessa?' Wendy's Kelvinside vowels rang falsely. 'Poor you! You must have felt such a fool!'

'You didn't hurt yourself, did you, Vanessa?' The cousinly, equally false tones of Gordon.

They couldn't hear if Van even replied. They could see her fiercely shaking her head, adjusting her bandeau, which was over one eye, and walking back to her position. Her nonchalant wave was pitiful, her smile like a grimace.

'Oh God, I can't stand this,' Anna said, half-rising from the bench.

'Don't move just now.' Ritchie pushed her back. 'She'll be even madder if she sees us. She's not hurt. Only her pride.'

'Or her soul.'

They played again, the other three with half their previous energy and expertise, as if the game was already over.

Anna saw the two couples shaking hands, watched as they gathered up their racket cases and cardigans. Van bunched the expensive cashmere she had bought for her under her arm, Wendy put hers round her shoulders, the empty arms swinging. She was laughing at something Gordon said, her backwards-thrown head making the golden hair swing, as her skirt had done, flick, flick . . .

'Come on,' Anna said. 'I don't want them to see us.' She couldn't bear the pitiful sight of their daughter trailing behind the other three like an outcast as she tried to put the racket in its case, dropped her cardigan, picked it up again. The image of Van's dejected figure stayed with her as they walked back to Clevedon Crescent.

Five

Anna was sitting at the breakfast table when Van came in with her grandmother, the latter rose-fresh, rose-scented, in crisp pink linen with a diamond pin on her lapel. In contrast Van was listless, pale, hair sticking out unbecomingly behind her ears. The dark tinge under her eyes showed that she hadn't slept.

'Good morning, Anna,' Rose said, taking her place where Father had once sat. 'Vanessa and I met coming down. Of course I've been awake for hours. Bessie brings me my morning cup and then I read the paper before I have my bath.'

'You look as fresh as a daisy.' Or a rose. 'What would you like for breakfast, Van?'

'Nothing, thanks.' She was sullen.

It hadn't escaped Mother. 'I was just saying to Vanessa that she needs smartening up. Girls like to have pretty clothes. I'm going to take her to Daly's to buy a party dress for a little present. You and Jean and Nancy always had such pretty party dresses.'

'That's kind, Mother, but she hasn't any need . . .' Distance blurs, she thought. Nancy had worn hers obediently, but she and Jean had invariably wriggled out of wearing Mother's choice. Jean liked to make her own; Anna herself had always preferred smartness to prettiness. She remembered a dress she had worn when Frederick Kleiber had come to the house with his wife, slinky black and fringed from bust to hem. 'No flouncy dresses, please,' she had told Ritchie when he had said yesterday he would like to bring her back something Spanish, 'but an embroidered shawl would be very acceptable.'

'Not even some toast, Van?'

'No, thanks.' She raised her head. The great dark eyes looked as if they were falling out of her head. 'Mum's right, Gran. I don't go to parties, and besides we're probably going to Kirkcudbright quite soon . . .'

Bessie came into the room unceremoniously, as she always did. 'Here's the boys,' she announced, 'your yin, Anna, and Nancy's. This place gets more and more like Charing Cross every day. Ma carpet . . .'

Gordon and Mish had followed her in, laughing, obviously on the best of terms. 'Sorry, Gran,' Gordon said. 'I wanted to catch the visitors before they went out, so Hamish suggested I come back with him.'

'Sit down, boys.' Rose indicated seats. 'I have to strain my neck nowadays looking up at you both. Have you had breakfast?'

'Oh, hours ago!' he said. 'We've been swimming this morning at the Arlington Baths. Hello, Vanessa!'

'Hello,' she mumbled, playing with her knife.

'It's really Vanessa I came to see. There's a hop on at the tennis club tonight before we all go back to school, or in my case the uni, and we . . . I wondered if you'd like to come. Hamish is game. He's got his eye on someone.'

'I've got my eye on the grub,' Mish said, smiling. Nancy's behind this, Anna thought, and she's already rung Mother, hence the offer of the party dress. They're forever organizing . . .

'That's very kind of you, Gordon,' she said to prompt Van. 'Well, what do you think?' The girl raised her head and looked at him.

'I'm going off to Kirkcudbright with Mum. Sorry.' She looked at Anna. 'Whenever you like.' Anna shrugged, smiled, and shut up.

Gordon was at his most charming. 'Don't *think* of yesterday. It happens to everybody sooner or later. Wendy says she once fell in a tournament.'

'I wasn't thinking of that . . .' She toyed with her knife, her eyes downcast.

'She should come, shouldn't she, Aunt? Mother thinks it would do her good, at her age. She'll send us all there and back in a taxi.'

Van was melting. Her eyes were on him, eating him up, his slicked golden quiff, his strong throat, his smile. 'But I haven't anything to . . .' He'll think we go around in woad 'down there' Anna thought.

'We were just on the point of going out to buy a party dress,' Rose said. 'How opportune! You can't possibly refuse, Vanessa. A little bird must have told us there was a "hop"' – she used the word gingerly – 'in the offing.' The little bird being Nancy, that plump little wren who perched on James's chair.

Van's lack of sophistication showed. She was cornered, had no guile. 'What do you think, Mum? We were going to Aunt Jean's . . .'

'A day won't make much difference. I can phone.' She made an effort to be motherly. 'I think Granny's being very kind, and Gordon too. Even if you don't know anyone there, Mish will be in the same boat.'

'Gordon says I might meet one or two chaps who're going to the Art School,' he said.

'Will there be a lot of people?' Van appealed to Gordon.

'Oh, it's not a big affair. About sixty, I should think. I'll take care of you.' His manly chest swelled. 'Great band too. The City Warblers. They play at the uni.'

'Do you ever think of *anything* but enjoying yourself?' Her eyes engulfed him. Did I ever look at Ritchie like that, Anna marvelled. 'All those poor people begging in Argyle Street . . .'

'There's nothing I can do about it.' His chin lifted. 'My job is to work hard and become an architect like Father.' Rose gazed at him fondly. Van's eyes were fastened on him like a leech. 'But who said you couldn't enjoy yourself as well, eh, Gran? What about a waltz?' He held out his arms.

'Away with you! He's a caution, isn't he?' Rose said to the others, shaking her head in admiration. 'Gordon always cheers me up.'

Anna smiled, looking at Van. Her eyes were luminous. She was laughing. 'Daddy sings like you. Mish is too prim.'

'There's only room for one clown in the family,' her brother said. 'Dad's always clowning. You should see him chasing mother about the house. Sometimes he throws her over his shoulder when –'

'Oh, Mish, really!'

Rose frowned slightly at this revelation. 'So that's settled,' she said. 'Vanessa and I will go out this morning. You'll probably meet girls from your mother's old school, dear. You have to be as smart as them.'

Anna tried to redress some of the balance. 'But there's no need for your mother to send a taxi, Gordon. I'll bring them over.'

Van came into the drawing room that evening with an attempt at nonchalance. She had been with her grandmother all day while Anna and Mish were at the Art School to show him her old haunts. Gordon had been going to spend the day at Helensburgh with friends, but he would be back in plenty of time for the dance. He hadn't asked Mish to accompany him.

'Do you like him?' she asked Mish.

'He's all right. But he's run by his mother.'

'And you aren't?'

'Nobody runs me. No, you and Dad are sensible. I didn't realize it till I came here. The families live in each other's pockets!'

'Well, that's smart,' she now said to Van. She thought it was awful. Her hair had been 'done' by Rose's hairdresser – 'You can't go wrong with Antoine' – who had completely changed her appearance. He had attempted to tame the frizz by dragging it back from her face and torturing it into little curls on the nape of her neck. Her eyes had an oriental lift as if the skin on either side of them was too taut.

'I would have preferred pink or blue,' Rose said, 'but I learned my lesson from them.' She sometimes spoke as if 'them', Nancy, Anna and Jean, had lived a separate existence from her in their childhood.

The red dress with the tiny waist and cap sleeves was hardly longer than the accordion-pleated tennis skirt, but Van was wearing pale stockings which smoothed out the boniness of her knees. She had red shoes with grosgrain bows on the front. She wasn't at home with herself. It showed in the stretched, closed mouth – it was scarcely a smile – and her frightened eyes.

'You look lovely, Vanessa,' Rose said. 'I wasn't sure about the red at first, but you're just like your mother. Smart.'

'She'll have to run if she meets a bull,' Mish said, trim in his school blazer, grey flannels and smooth hair.

'Isn't that just like a brother?' Rose said. 'Well, off you go and not keep Nancy waiting. She likes everybody to be on time.'

Nancy was at the oriel window of her drawing room as Anna drew up. That does seem a little anxious, she thought, considering we're on time. And Nancy's smile seemed rather forced as she opened the door.

'We're not late, are we, Nancy?' she said, as they were led into the room.

'Well, this is a smart young couple and no mistake.' James got up out of his seat to greet them. 'Glasgow hasn't changed, eh, Anna? These women . . . a whirl of activity all the time. But I can't blame Nancy for being a little annoyed –'

'It's that boy!' Nancy broke in. 'Now we're *all* waiting. Really, you do your best –'

'Where is he?' Anna said, looking from one to the other.

'He went sailing!' James said. 'I've just heard half an hour ago. Nobody tells me anything in this house.'

Nancy looked embarrassed. 'He *assured* me he'd be back in loads of time. He left with Wendy. Her parents, the Armours, have a summer house near Shandon, a beautiful place. It was just to see their new yacht and they were going to get the five o'clock train back. They're very nice, really, Anna. You'd like them. Mr Armour is very high up in banking circles, away above the ordinary manager . . . they say he'll be the next one to have his face on the banknotes . . .' Her glance raked Van distractedly. 'You look very nice, Vanessa. Your hair's different . . .'

'I didn't know Wendy was going to the hop too.'

'Well, it's a crowd, you see. If you're in the right *crowd*, you're home and dry.'

'Would you like a glass of sherry, Anna?' James said. 'And Vanessa and Hamish? Some lemonade?'

'No, thank you.' Anna looked away from Van's face. She couldn't bear it. 'Shall I just leave Mish and Van here?' And to hell with Hamish and Vanessa.

'Now, don't you rush away,' James said. 'Have a sherry. The train's probably late.'

'They're really very nice people, the Armours.' Nancy had taken up her usual perch on James's chair, like a bird returning to its branch. 'Thanks, dear.' He had given her a sherry also. 'I can do with this. That big house at Shandon, and their flat in Bellhaven Terrace is really beautiful. It's to be handy for schooling. Mrs Armour gives lovely bridge parties, and she's a great worker for charity, isn't she, James?'

'So you tell me. Don't you think you should telephone Mrs Armour? Something might have happened.'

'Oh, do you think I should?' She got up immediately and tripped away on her high-heeled court shoes. Little piggy feet, Anna thought, as she watched the round bottom disappearing through the door. 'They're very nice people . . .' the words came floating back.

Van was sitting beside Anna on the sofa. She turned towards her, but she was staring straight ahead. A flash of irritation went through Anna. She really must learn to hide her feelings. 'A little bit of social hypocrisy,' she would say to her later, 'oils the wheels.'

'It's a lovely room this, isn't it, Van?' She let her eyes travel round the swathed pelmets, the eye-

hurting pictures of Scottish hills and rushing rivers –
no deer on rocky crags, thank God – no wonder
Ritchie went into a fugue when he was here. She
winced away from the huge gilt mirror above the pink
marble fireplace and contemplated the small tables
placed strategically and littered with photographs of
the family on their luxury pleasure cruises smiling
out from their silver frames.

'As long as nothing has happened,' James said. He
didn't look unduly perturbed. He must be used to
his son.

Nancy was back in the room, her face flushed, but
she was determinedly smiling. 'Mrs Armour said they
went sailing and they got becalmed. She saw the
yacht from their window with binoculars. She's
awfully apologetic. Anyhow they're back now and
just leaving. She offered to drive them, but I said it
would be just as quick on the train. Wendy has to go
back to Bellhaven Terrace to dress, but they're quite
used to taxis, the Armours, for everything . . .'

'You told me he said he was just going to *see* the
yacht,' James said.

'Yes, I know, but I suppose it was tempting. You've
been young once too, James.' She spoke to Mish and
Van. 'You won't have long to wait. I'll get Eileen to
make up some sandwiches.'

'I'll go back with Mother,' Van said.

'Oh, you mustn't be upset at Gordon!' Nancy was
soothing. 'He'll be *full* of apologies. He has a way
with girls . . .' She shook her head smilingly at the
thought of her son's charm.

'I'm not going to the dance,' Van said, looking
down at her hands.

Nancy sighed, then spoke severely. 'We went to a
lot of trouble to get those tickets for you, Vanessa.

57

And there's the dress my mother bought. You'll meet a lot of very nice people. Gordon will be here in no time. It's a very fast service from Helensburgh.'

'I'm not going,' Van repeated. 'I'll go back with Mother.'

'I know you're upset, but –'

Anna got up. 'She's not at all upset, Nancy. But she's a stranger, and she would be without a partner, wouldn't she? Gordon's with Wendy. She doesn't at all mind missing the dance. She gets plenty at home. Are you staying, Mish?'

'I don't mind.' Mish, the mediator. He gave her a family look. She understood. Better to keep on comparatively good terms.

The journey between the two houses was mercifully short. Anna, unable to think of anything valuable to say, kept quiet. She busied herself watching the Glasgow night-time traffic, everyone intent on going out for the evening, a 'tare'. It's liveliness came through to her. Ritchie said New York was the same.

Bessie opened the door. 'That was quick,' she said. Van rushed past her without speaking and made for the stairs. They heard the bedroom door shut. 'Whit's up wi' her?' Bessie never stood on ceremony with any of them. 'Has she lost her scone?'

'Something like that.' She hadn't time for Bessie's witticisms. Her mind was busy on what she would say to her mother. It's all so trivial, she thought, but it wasn't, not to Van. She would never have consented to stay on after that contretemps at the tennis club, never given in to being dressed up like a Christmas tree, if she hadn't thought Gordon would be her partner at the 'hop'. But he'd hopped away. He was

58

her first love, her first experience of meeting someone who could take her away from people like Winnie Good. She went into the drawing room, smiling.

'Here I am! Isn't it a shame? Gordon was delayed at Helensburgh where he was sailing, but Vanessa was glad of the excuse to come back here. Hamish stayed on.'

'Why did Vanessa come home?' There were no flies on Mother. 'Is the dance off?'

'No.' Anna made the appropriate face. 'Womanly troubles, Mother.' Rose made the same face back.

'Oh, well. I can sympathize there. Some people get off scot free in that department, but she must take after me. The *pain* each month. Even a hot-water bottle and a wee tot of whisky from my mother didn't do much good. But, what a shame! Nancy will tell me all the details.'

Anna went to her room early with the excuse that she had to pack. The thought of Jean was welcome. How close they were, how close they had always been. It would be good to see her.

When she had finished she knocked gently on Van's door. There was no reply. She pushed it open and saw she was sitting up in bed stiffly, a book in her hand. The red dress was crumpled on a chair, the pale stockings trailed limply over it.

'I'm not crying,' she said, looking up. Her eyes were scrubbed red, their beauty gone.

Anna lifted the dress, shook it, got a hanger from the wardrobe. 'Why should you cry over a rude boy?'

'That's what I thought.' Her voice shook. 'But he said . . . in his letter . . .' She bit her lip. 'It's my own fault. I should have known . . . I'm not his style. Nor his friends'. I know where I'm happiest. Now.'

'Oh, darling.' Anna sat down on the bed and put

her arms round her. 'There's plenty of time. All we want is for you to be happy.'

Her voice was strained, as if it hurt her to talk. 'I *know* how to be happy, Mum. I was so stupid, thinking . . . I've *told* you. Everybody's got their own way. I'm sorriest for Gran dressing me up. That dress cost pounds! I'll never wear it but I'll tell her I will. I'll write a nice letter when we get to Kirkcudbright. One thing, Aunt Jean and Uncle John don't organize . . .'

'No, they're too busy with their own problems.'

She freed herself from Anna's arms. 'This is really a good book,' she said, lifting it.

Anna took the hint.

Six

'I love this road after we go through Dalbeattie,' Anna said. 'This is the first time I've driven on it myself. Shall we be adventurous and take the long way round?' She sang lustily, '"Oh, you'll tak' the high road and I'll tak' the low road, an' I'll be in Scotland afore ye . . ."'

'Scotland always goes to your head.' Van wasn't going to be easily amused.

'Robert the Bruce country. Did you know? He defeated the English at Glen Trool near here. Don't they teach you any Scottish history at Renton Grammar?'

'They've hardly *heard* of Scotland, some of them.'

'"Scots wha hae wi' Wallace bled, Scots wham Bruce has aften led . . ."' Anna intoned.

Van tittered. 'You always act like a fool when you're going to see Aunt Jean.'

Anna acknowledged the justice of the remark. 'If you had a twin you'd feel the same. She understands me through and through, from the beginning, not as you see me, a warder with keys.'

'Oh, Mum!' She laughed out loud. 'But I like her too. I like them all.'

'Maybe Sarah will interest you in horses this time.'

'Not a chance. You're either horsey or you're not

and they know it. They nudge me with their great long faces and they're horrid when they smile. She has that friend of hers at the posh farm, Bunty Logan. They talk about nothing else.'

'If it keeps them happy . . . Anyhow, I expect you'd rather go to Aunt Jean's than to Aunt Nancy's, even if they don't have a fatal attraction like Gordon.'

'If you really want to know,' Van's voice was low and fierce, 'I'd rather have Roderick than Gordon.'

'Well, that's saying something.' She shut up and kept her eye on the road. Mutehill now, and running along the lovely coast road with St Mary's Isle anchored over there in the blue water. Anyone could be seduced by the idea of happiness here. Jean certainly had, helped by that loving husband of hers. If there was any railing against fate it was on her own side, not Jean's.

Somebody up there must have it in for Jean, either a sadist or a seeker after vengeance, someone who was going to make her pay and pay for that one silly mistake, if it could be called a mistake, of loving too well but not wisely.

But what a charmer that man had been! You could hear the soft swooning sighs that rose from the girls at the Art School when he came into the classroom. 'Good morning, young ladies!' The break in his voice, its Viennese intonation, the slow, charming smile which must have been the first stage in the fatal attraction he had exercised on Jean.

Those hidden meetings she had with him! The room Anna shared with Jean had vibrated with her sexuality when she came in from seeing him. Of course, Mother had fondly hoped it was Robin Naismith who was the source of her happiness, that eminently suitable young man who lived in

Kilmacolm – where else? – who had been at Glenalmond School – of course – whose father was a rich industrialist who was training his son to take his place – naturally . . .

A tiny warning bell rang in her head. Was it something of the same ilk she was hoping for for Van – not the modern equivalent of Robin Naismith, but at least a young man who would be acceptable in any company, who spoke more or less the Queen's English, had limbs and eyes in good working order and a stable psyche?

Jean had tossed those ideas aside without looking back, had chosen to love an Austrian ten years her senior, presentable without a doubt, but a married man with three children, who had impregnated her in a wood in the little seaside village of Kilcreggan and then had the misfortune to drown the same day.

'Kirkcudbright,' Van said. 'It's pretty, isn't it, Scottish, all of a piece. At least we'll get some sense here.'

Anna laughed. All is not lost, she thought.

The Whitbreads' house was interesting. It was in fact Jean's own house, which had been left to her by Great-aunt Jessie, who had cared for her during that ill-fated pregnancy, and in whose house the baby had been born and died.

John Whitbread, Jean's husband, the local general practitioner, had his own house, but they had made the decision to use it for surgeries. He had installed his old housekeeper, Mrs Beith, as caretaker, and moved in with Jean after their marriage.

The situation of the house in old High Street, with its joco Georgian frontage, hid the delight of the old cottage behind it and its long garden running down to a stone wall which bounded the river and the harbour. There was a studio for Jean converted from an old outhouse. Anna drew up the car at the porticoed and painted front doorway.

John Whitbread was standing behind Jean, who had thrown open the door before Anna had had time to ring. 'Anna!' she cried. 'I was worried sick about you!' She flung her arms about her. 'I thought you had driven over a cliff!'

'Show me a cliff first. Gosh, you look good!' She could never get over her twin's dark beauty, not quite so voluptuous as it had once been, but still striking. 'Let me have a look at John. You're hiding him.' He pushed forward, smiling, and embraced her warmly.

'Thank God you and Jean aren't alike.' He kissed her on the cheek. 'Variety is the spice of life.' What a steady rock of a man he was, Anna thought, enjoying being in his arms.

'We're the same but different.' She stood aside, remembering Van. 'And here's Vanessa, as Nancy called her. "Spoiling a good name . . ." Mish was seduced by the opulence at the Pettigrews' and the promise of Glasgow delights by Gordon.'

Van was kissed and welcomed. 'We have very rude children,' John said. 'Neither of them is here.'

'It doesn't matter.' Van was prim.

'Well, come in, come in! We've given the neighbours enough to be going on with.'

Anna looked round when they were in the sitting room. 'So different from dear Clevedon Crescent.' She laughed. 'Do you remember, Jean, how Mother insisted on us all standing on the Persian rug ready to welcome guests, the tweaking and the twitching, the "Keep your shoulders back, girls"? Oh, this room's nice. So welcoming, and familiar . . .' Her mind flashed back to the day when Jean had gone

64

into labour here, at the same time as Aunt Jessie had had a stroke, and Nellie, the midwife, bustling in to take charge had asked for a cup of tea. 'My only tipple . . .'

'Yes, and Nancy always hogged the mantelpiece mirror to see that her pageboy was turned under all round . . . Sit down,' Jean said. 'What a smart suit! Chanel come to stay. Oh, it's lovely to see you. I'm complete now. Sit down, Van. I'm sorry Sarah isn't here to welcome you.'

'Where are they, Aunt Jean?'

'Need you ask? Sarah's at Logans' farm, for "afternoon tack", as she calls it, but she'll be back soon.'

'Is Roderick with her?' Anna asked.

'No, he's down at the harbour. He likes to see the boats come in. I don't stop him. It's only during the holidays, and he doesn't have many friends. The school draws children from a wide area.' Her face was calm. 'I'm going to bring in tea right away. John has to dash off to his evening surgery.'

'Okay. Need any help?'

'No, it's all done. I thought we might walk down after and bring Roderick home.'

'Great! I'd like to stretch my legs.' She turned to her thin, sandy-haired brother-in-law, the mainstay of Jean's life. The hair was sparser than last year and growing further back, but his brow looked noble as a result, she thought. 'Busy as usual, John?'

'Oh, yes. All the time. Especially in summer because of visitors. The population's growing. I'm thinking of taking on an assistant soon.'

'That's a good idea. After all,' they always teased each other, 'you aren't getting any younger.'

'I'm at the dangerous age now. I'm looking for my last fling. Interested?'

'Well, Ritchie is away a lot . . .' She looked at Van to see how she was taking this. She was smiling benignly on them, as if on two children. Generation swapping, she thought. It probably occurs oftener the older you get. 'But Jean would kill me.' Jean had come into the room with a laden tray. 'John and I are thinking of running away together, Jean. Just thought we'd let you know.'

'Well, as long as *your* heart-throb is around, why should I care?' She looked at Van as she set down the tray. 'Have *you* any boyfriends, Van?'

She shook her head, her face closed. 'I'm not interested.'

Jean and Anna exchanged glances. 'What's up?' Jean's look said. Later on, when the children were in bed, John would go to his study as he always did and let them have a good chin-wag. As she sipped her tea, there was a sense of completeness in Anna's heart which even Ritchie could never give her.

You couldn't mistake him even from this distance, Anna thought, but as they came nearer she saw the change in Roderick since last year. He had grown coarser in his features, broader and bulkier in his frame, his gestures seemed more flamboyant than she remembered. Last year there had still been a trace of the child in him which made his appearance endearing in spite of his affliction – 'Wee Chinky', Sarah called him – but that had gone now.

His skull seemed more bullet-shaped, his hair scantier so that the pink scalp showed through, his features were more flattened, his eyes smaller and more slanted, and there was a semblance of a squint as he turned his head. His tongue lolled as he jumped around the fishermen. One made a friendly lunge towards him, and he jumped back in pretended fright, then bent double, laughing. As he straightened he turned his head and saw his mother, Anna and Van. He waved delightedly, beamed in recognition and ran towards them.

'Aunty!' He threw himself into Anna's arms. She thought she detected a stale smell of urine off him.

'Hello, Roderick!' She disengaged herself. 'Are you having a good time?'

'Oh yes, grand.' And then in comical grown-up parody, 'Well, well, long time no see! And my lovely cousin as well!' He embraced Van, nearly knocking her over. She took it well.

'Don't be so boisterous,' Jean said, smiling, and to the nearest fisherman, 'I hope he isn't being a nuisance, Robert. Just send him away if he is.'

'I'm not a nuisance, Mummy.' His voice rose indignantly. 'It's good fun here. I help with the nets and things,' and as if he was repeating a lesson, 'How are you keeping, Vanessa? Is everything hunky-dory in the south?' He giggled, seemingly at himself.

'Everything's fine.' Van smiled. 'How are you liking school?'

'That,' he said portentously, 'is a different kettle of fish. Robert told me that one, although he doesn't see how you could get fish into a kettle.'

'Down the spout,' she said, face straight.

He looked at her, mouth open, tongue lolling, brow furrowed.

'That's what Robert said. No, Vanessa, the big ones would never go. I told Robert that.' Anna saw the man called Robert looking towards them, as if embarrassed.

'Well, maybe you could take the lid off and drop

them in one by one?' He looked at her, then smacked his brow with an exaggerated gesture.

'Now, why didn't I think of that?'

'Say good night to the men,' Jean said. 'We'll have to get back now.'

He suddenly sulked, his head lowered, his bottom lip protruding. 'I want to stay!'

'You know you can't, Roderick.' She was patient. 'They'll be going out in their boats and we have to get back for supper. I've got something nice, something you really like. Guess what it is?' He raised his head.

'My favourite? Toad-in-the-hole?'

'Right first time. And chips.'

'Oh, yummy-yum!' He rubbed his stomach. Anna saw the men watching, grinning, as they busied themselves with their nets. What did they think of him? They would be good-natured, the doctor's boy, but he would overhear their adult conversation, pick up adult ideas and words . . . That's rubbish, she told herself. If he's happy, why should it matter?

'Well, good night one and all,' Roderick called to them. 'Thank you for having me.' He went towards them, hand outstretched. The men laughed and turned away.

'You'll see them tomorrow again. Come along.' When he came back Jean put an arm round him. Anna saw how he snuggled against her.

'I can go back again tomorrow, Mummy? I'm not a nuisance.'

'Yes, you can go back.' She turned and called to the men, 'Thanks for . . .' She stopped as if she realized she was repeating him. 'Have a good catch.'

They went up the Mote Brae together, Van and Roderick ahead of them. She had held out her hand to him and he had gone willingly. Anna saw how attentively he listened to what Van was saying. Jean met her look.

'What do you think?' She kept her voice low.

'Cheerful and outgoing. He could be a lot worse. How does he do at school?'

'Not brilliant. His attention span is short. And he's mischievous.' Her face brightened. 'But he's musical. That's good.' She raised her voice. 'After supper, Roderick, you could sing some of your songs to Van.'

He did a little dance, turning circles, clowning. 'I know some lovely songs, and I can play them too, can't I, Mummy? I can play them on the piano.'

'Yes, you can.' She said to Anna, 'He picks out the tune and accompanies himself. We have a music teacher who comes in and gives him lessons.'

'Miss Ross, Miss Ross!' He jumped up and down. 'Looks like a horse, looks like a horse!' He went into paroxysms of laughter.

Sarah was there when they got back. They found her in the kitchen with Janet, who had been with them since Roderick's birth, a cheerful girl, a farmer's daughter. Sarah, unlike her brother, seemed more sober than last year. Her sandy-coloured hair, like her father's, was in two thick plaits, her brow was freckled, her brown eyes small, but her whole appearance was redeemed by her charming wide-mouthed smile. She was open-natured, perhaps unimaginative, Anna thought, only like John in appearance; in temperament not like either of her parents. She would give no trouble. It was written over her straight, compact figure, her competent movements, her willingness to please.

The toad-in-the-hole was a great success, though Jean apologized for its ordinariness.

Roderick's performance at the piano afterwards was even more of a success. The trouble came when he was told it was bedtime. He sulked, his slanted eyes narrowed to slits, became malignant. It was John who took him in hand then.

'Sing that nice song about pigeons you learned at school, and then you can go to bed like them. Van and Sarah will go upstairs with you – but only if you're good.'

The sulking disappeared. He lifted his head, his chin, took up a pose in front of them, his feet together. 'A song with actions,' he said, and gave an elaborate bow. Everyone kept their faces straight. Anna looked at Jean. She seemed exhausted, her eyes had dark circles under them. Roderick must tire her out. Mother thought he should be put in a home. She would never do it. Now her eyes were on him, encouraging, prompting him with the occasional word. She was full of love.

'"My pigeon house I open wide . . ."' he sang, flinging his arms out.

'Mind that vase!' John said. Roderick went into fits of laughter.

'Shut up, John,' Jean said.

'Shut up, John!' Roderick repeated. He straightened his face, stood to attention and began his song again . . . '"And set the pigeons free . . ."' His hands waved from the wrist and he did a little dance about the room. Van and Sarah giggled.

'"They fly over hill . . . and then over dale . . . and light on the tallest tree . . ."' He came to a standstill, his face serious, and dramatically pointed to the corner of the ceiling. He put his finger to his lips, then sang softly: '"But when they return from their long, long fli . . . ght . . . They shut their eyes . . . and say good . . . night . . ." '

Now his hands were clasped together under his chin, his round head resting sideways on them. ' "Coo . . . ooo . . . cooo . . . ooo . . . Cooo . . . oo. Coo . . . oo." '

'They're asleep now,' John said, his face expressionless with suppressed laughter.

'You've nearly put *me* to sleep,' Anna yawned affectedly behind her hand. 'That was a lovely song, Roderick.'

Sarah got up. 'Come on, then. You can sing it again when you're in bed.'

'Would you like that, Van?' he said.

'Yes, please.'

'I want to give my Aunt Anna a big kiss.'

'Well, go ahead but make it snappy,' Jean said.

Anna submitted herself to the slobbering kiss, turning her head slightly to avoid it landing on her mouth. She hoped Jean hadn't noticed.

John got up too when the three children had gone. 'I'm off too to my study. Have a good talk, you two. I know you're dying to get rid of me.' And then, 'Do you see any improvement, Anna?' He was a father, not a doctor.

'Yes, a great improvement.' She met his steady gaze. 'He's grown a lot, and he has a great sense of humour.' She made herself say it. 'He's . . . lovable.'

'Don't forget his musical genius.' Jean's voice was sarcastic. They had never been able to pretend with each other.

Seven

'Tomorrow we go to the Logans' for tea,' Jean said. 'Christine Logan says she's tired of hearing about this wonderful sister of mine. She wants to see you in the flesh.'

'Don't tell me you sprowse about me when I'm not here?' Anna said, smiling.

'Well, I can't do it to your face.' Jean looked fondly at her. 'Our way is to be chirpy with each other. I suppose it's the usual Scottish shyness of displayed emotion.'

'Well, I don't know about that. I'm far from shy with Ritchie, and I don't suppose you are with John.'

'Ah, that's different. Are you still in love with Ritchie?'

'Passionately. And jealous as hell into the bargain. How about you with John?'

'The jealousy was the other way round. I think he felt inadequate at the beginning because of Frederick.'

'And how does he compare?'

'This is worse than the dentist. Different, but I don't think anyone could ever take the place of your first love; it's more obsession than love, in a way. I didn't really know Frederick, nor respect him in the way I respect John, nor like him for that matter, fundamentally. And I admire John, his temperament, his

72

innate kindliness and common sense, I'm proud of his standing in the town.'

'And he's a great help with Roderick?'

'Well, he's his too, but I couldn't have managed even the *concept* of a mongol child without him.'

'Or he without you?'

'He's a doctor. It wasn't the first Down's syndrome he had seen, but this one was his. He loved him. Sarah loved him. She said he had a "cute little Chinky face". I couldn't *stand* it. I never told you this. I was too ashamed. I thought, another failure . . . Janet and Sarah looked after him at the beginning, and a nurse. We had to have a nurse because he had chronic bronchitis and needed regular treatment. John did it, clearing his tubes every day, nursing him. "He's our child," he said, and do you know what I said?'

'No.'

'"He spoils everything." That's what I said. "Just when life was perfect for us he spoils everything." And do you know what he said?'

'I'm not a mind-reader.'

'That it wasn't Roderick who was spoiling everything, it was me.'

'That was a fact.'

'He gave me books to read. The term "Down's syndrome" was first used by a man called Langdon-Down in 1866. Well, it's one way of getting immortality. There is only one mongol in six hundred births, and the likelihood increases the older the mother is. John says I was a bit young at thirty-two, but that it was just our luck.'

'He's sure about the diagnosis?'

'From the first day almost. Well, weren't you? I saw your face that first time you came. But all the signs are there. He has bronchitis. He has a congenital heart defect. John doubts if he will reach his teens, so let's not have any weeping or wailing or gnashing of teeth, he says, let's give him a good time while he's here. That's what he said. That did it for me.'

'You sound like a couple of angels. Where are your wings?'

'Oh, you have to work at that. We wept together, we felt heart sorry for ourselves. John only allowed himself one day for the taking down of his hair – what's left of it. I took longer. The thing that made me really ashamed was Janet and Sarah's attitude. There were no reservations with them. Janet cuddled him and loved him the way she would have done with a lamb at her parents' farm, and Sarah came running home from school to see her wee brother. Even her pony – it wasn't Satan then – took a back seat. Janet pushed him out in his pram without turning a hair, although everybody stopped to look at him, the doctor's child – "My, my, *they*'ll no' have their sorrows to seek" – and then the presents started coming, knitted bootees and mitts – he could do with these, he's always cold – matinée jackets, woolly toys. I think Kirkcudbright went through more wool in a fortnight than they'd done for a "twel'-month back", that's how they speak here.'

'There but for the grace of God go I . . . it's the equivalent of a rabbit's foot.'

'Maybe we've done Kirkcudbright a favour!' Jean laughed. 'Even although it means keeping them in the Dark Ages. But I realize when I'm lucky, with John. He's taught me so much. "We'll have no old-fashioned ideas in our enlightened household," he says. We're lucky with our men, Anna.'

'I wonder if Ritchie is as well-balanced as that.'

Jean, looking at her sister, saw a shadow cross her face.

'Of course he is. Don't you trust him with all his to-ing and fro-ing?'

'Of course I do. What rubbish!'

'You always say "What rubbish!" when I touch a sore spot. You'll have to get used to it, the way I had to with Roderick. Any man as attractive as Ritchie will always have women after him.'

'It must be his artistic temperament,' Anna laughed, not very convincingly.

'Van has some of his charm.'

'Van? She's not interested in charm, nor in being attractive to men. She fell by the wayside, very briefly, when she saw her gorgeous cousin in Glasgow, but he spurned her. That was a bitter blow but it only made her more convinced than ever that her mission in life is to save the world.'

'What do you mean?'

'Ritchie says she's a bleeding heart. Anyone who is ill-served by Nature, or circumstances, Van is there to champion them.'

'Roderick's in for a high old time, then.'

'Oh yes, she would take care of him permanently, given half a chance. Do you remember how she pushed the pram so proudly each time we came, when other girls of her age might . . .'

'. . . have been ashamed? Say what you like. I had to force *myself* to take him shopping at first. It was only when I saw the kindness of other people that I was ashamed.'

'My God, Jean, you take your problems on the chin!'

'Practice makes perfect. That's why I wanted to live here instead of in John's house. It's dear to me. It all happened here, Great-aunt Jessie's illness, birth of my baby, and its death.'

'Forget the death. John was there, loving you. And don't forget I nearly ruined your wedding reception in this very room by going into labour.' They both laughed.

'Your face, like a turkey cock's!'

'I was trying to hold it in, it being Mish, as it happened.'

'And being dragged out of the room by Ritchie and John with your feet sticking up in the air.'

'Laugh away! One thing, your John knew my private parts intimately before he knew yours! I never saw anyone get out of their morning jacket so quickly!'

'Can you verify your first remark?' They laughed at each other, tears in their eyes.

I'll never know this feeling of rightness with anyone else, Jean thought. She knows me, through and through. She knew me before I was born, lay in Mother's womb beside me.

They set off the next afternoon to pay their visit to the Logans' farm, a low, spreading stone house, quite grand in its lovely gardens, with the working part tucked out of sight. The husbands would not be there. It was to be a wives' and children's affair. Sarah went joyfully because she would be seeing her best friend, Bunty Logan, and her horse, Satan, which was kept beside Bunty's in their paddock; Van reluctantly, Roderick, equably. Unlike most boys of his age he took great pleasure in being dressed in his best grey flannel suit and striped tie.

'Roderick's going to see his girlfriend,' Sarah said in the car. 'Aren't you, Roderick?'

'Going to see my girlfriend,' he agreed, nodding.

'Bunty?' Van queried.

'No, Alice, her young sister. He's crazy about her.'

'I'm crazy about her,' Roderick nodded again, pleased.

'Don't tease him,' Jean said, who was driving them in John's car. He had left it for them as it was bigger than Anna's, and had walked to his afternoon surgery.

'I didn't know they had two daughters?' Anna was sitting beside Jean.

'Yes, Bunty and Alice. She's a little pet, about the same age as Roderick. Like Alice in Wonderland. And there's a boy, Graham, who's at Agricultural College.'

Christine Logan was not the usual bustling farmer's wife. She was the owner of the property, and Tim Logan had married into money. She was thin, with thick blonde hair, like a horse's mane, Anna thought. She wore a cream silk shirt and a smart tweed skirt, and her tan leather belt had an embossed silver buckle.

'Well, what do you think, Christine?' Jean said as she introduced Anna.

'A strong resemblance.' She stood back to view Anna. 'It's inner, mostly, but there's the way you both hold your heads . . .'

'Would you like to see my teeth?' Anna said, laughing.

'Are you objecting to my keen eye?' She laughed too. 'Yes, I can see you're from the same stable. You have the same sense of humour.'

Country life wasn't all bucolic, Anna found, listening to Christine Logan. Her mind was as well-furnished as her sitting room, her tea-table with its delicate china and silver tea service. The children were to have their tea in the kitchen attended by Mrs MacLellan, her housekeeper. 'We don't want them careering about our feet all the time,' she said. And to Anna, 'Do you hunt with the Vale of Aylesbury?'

'To tell you the truth I've scarcely heard of them. Terrible, isn't it? Our interests are entirely different. My husband's a painter.'

'Yes, Jean told me. You're an arty lot, you Glaswegians. You must have a look at our collection after tea. Late nineteenth century from the Glasgow School. There's a Graham Gilbert and a Sam Bough, what else, a Guthrie, and a Muirhead Bone.'

'Some people have all the luck.'

'It's thanks to my father. Oh, and one of Joseph Crawhall's. Father thought most of the English stuff wishy-washy. Jean says your husband is a coming man.'

'Coming and going.' She smiled at Jean. 'He does mostly murals now. Municipal stuff, he calls it.'

'I bet he gets all the praise. Jean didn't forget to tell me about your work. I'm interested in the clock faces you do. Tim has a birthday soon. He sends his apologies to you, by the way. He's gone to a show today.'

'I'll be the middleman,' Jean said. 'You can tell me what you want and I'll pass it on to Anna.'

'Stop promoting me! But let me know, Mrs Logan . . .'

'Christine. It's only in Kirkcudbright they take five years to drop your title, if that, and I come from the Borders.'

'I'll be in Barcelona a fair amount. We intend to buy a house there. Ritchie seems to spend half his time there now.'

'That's what I'd like! A clock face with some kind of Spanish influence, Gaudí-esque, perhaps. I remember his flats.'

Anna laughed. 'And here I was thinking you'd want chickens or a cow or two.'

'Do I look like that?' She didn't. 'No, I like Spain. I don't know Barcelona as well as Valencia. I used to go there with father to see his friend's horses. He was a breeder.' Anna was impressed.

After they had looked at the pictures, they went into the big kitchen to see the children. They were seated round the table being tended by a *real* bustling plump farmer's wife this time. 'Are they behaving themselves, Mrs MacLellan?' Christine asked. Anna thought how easily one trained children if you laid down rules, or had someone like Mrs MacLellan to supervise them.

'Yes, Mrs Logan. They've been like little angels.' She didn't look too sure.

Alice Logan was a lovely child, answering Jean's description, a Tenniel Alice in Wonderland with her mother's thick blonde hair kept off her forehead by a velvet bandeau. She had wide open blue eyes, pink cheeks. Her checked gingham dress with a bow at the back was in character. Anna wondered if it was the girl's wish to be dressed like that. It didn't seem to be her mother's taste. Bunty, on the other hand, was like Sarah, sensible, good-looking, fair hair in plaits. You could see already the handsome woman she would become.

'Are the girls looking after you, Roderick?' Christine asked.

'I like Alice.' He simpered and hung his head.

'Well, Alice likes you.' Anna saw the quick look of denial the child shot at her mother.

79

Roderick giggled. 'I've been telling Alice a funny story,' he said.

'Have you? What about?' Anna saw Mrs MacLellan's flustered look. She turned away and busied herself at the sink.

'It wasn't funny,' Sarah said.

'It is so, Sarah! It is so, funny! It's about two dogs.'

'Well, tell us and see if we laugh.' Christine Logan was brisk. She chairs meetings, Anna thought. She doesn't let anyone waste her time.

Roderick giggled again and squirmed on his seat.

'Get a move on, Roderick,' Jean said. 'We'll soon have to go home.'

'You won't like it, Mummy,' Sarah said. A whiff of apprehension came from the girl. Anna looked at Jean and saw she had caught it too.

'We have to go home, Roderick. Never mind the story.'

'Want to tell the story!' He made a dismissive movement with his shoulders. 'Want to! It's funny! The dog was leaning on the back of the other dog with its paws,' he was gabbling the words, 'and it was pushing the other one. The fishermen laughed and one of them said they'd soon be up the Mote Brae but Robert got a pail of water and . . .' He buried his face in his hands, his shoulders shaking.

'All right,' Jean said, 'you've told it. It's time we went, Christine.' Her face was impassive. Anna looked at the two older girls. Their heads were lowered, their eyes were on their plates, but Alice's eyes were wide with a mixture of curiosity and disbelief.

'He's making it up, isn't he, Mummy? Anyhow it's not funny. Just a cruel dog.'

'Yes,' Christine Logan said. 'Don't go without your

raspberries, Jean. The girls picked them for you this morning.'

Mrs MacLellan bustled away and came back with a basket covered with greaseproof paper. Her face was red. 'You'll get a fine pot or two of jam out of those, Mrs Whitbread.' She smoothed the paper which was stained pink. 'Mind your skirt.' Her head was down, as if she was distressed. Anna could imagine her saying to Mr MacLellan, if he existed, 'I didn't know where to look . . .' She hoped Jean wasn't in for a hard time as Roderick became older.

When they were driving home she put a hand briefly on Jean's on the wheel. 'Don't give it another thought,' she said.

'Och aye.' She was silent for the rest of the way home.

John and Jean were in the kitchen washing up after supper. It was Janet's night off.

'Well,' John said, 'did you both empty your souls?' Anna and Van had left the day before.

'Partly. We don't have to *say* everything. But I've thought for some time there's a little resentment brewing up in her about Ritchie's frequent absences. He's single-minded about his work, but then he always has been. Perhaps if you're as good as he is you have to be. Now there's talk about a place in Barcelona because he works there a lot, but she's worried about that too. She has to stay put more or less because of Van's schooling, and she feels he doesn't take a fair share in bringing up the children.'

'You can see both sides. And, of course, no man other than Ritchie has ever meant anything to her.'

'That's Anna. Then there's Van. She seems to be a thorn in her flesh.'

81

'Not fitting into Anna's design, perhaps. She has a great capacity for love, that girl. Did you see her with Roderick?'

'Yes. Poor Sarah was disappointed she didn't show more interest in her beloved Satan.'

'She was totally indifferent to Satan's devilish attractions.' They laughed together. A more docile creature had never lived. 'How did she react to Roderick's *faux pas*?' She had told him earlier about the episode in the Logans' kitchen.

'She copied Sarah, head down, because she thought it was what she should do. At least that's how it looked.'

'She's deep.' He polished a plate in his usual meticulous way. 'Of course he's a fairly elusive sort of chap, Ritchie . . .'

'Maddeningly attractive to women. And Anna knows it. And worries about it. I don't think he takes her worries about Van seriously. He accepts, loves. Anna on the other hand has always cared a great deal about presentation. She would spend hours in front of a mirror in the old days. It's not vanity, it's a wish for perfection. Not a hair out of place. She's always had great style and she wants her daughter to be the same. They don't see eye to eye.'

'She's a designer, Anna, with people, and in her work.'

'That's astute, and acute,' she said admiringly.

'Well, while I'm basking in your praise, let's go up and see if the wee lad's asleep.' He kissed her as they turned from the sink, drawing her to him. 'I want comfort too. Talking about Ritchie makes me wonder . . .'

'What?'

'I'm only a stay-at-home, stuck-in-the-mud GP.

Sometimes I think I must be too dull for you, you exotic creature.'

'That's just the way I dress. Anti-Kirkcudbright. I've always been gypsy-like.' She said in a low voice, 'If I could somehow convey to you the *regard* I feel for you, as distinct from love, sixteen years of steadiness in my life after the early turmoil.'

He drew apart to look at her. 'My dearest wife. And I've got rid of the jealousy I used to feel for Frederick Kleiber, his romantic charm, foreign charm, everything so different from this homegrown Scotsman . . .'

'Don't ever feel jealous. That rapture, yes, I have to call things by their proper names – you taught me that – went with youth. Let's go upstairs.'

'To bed?'

'Not yet, silly.' She kissed him on the mouth. 'Later.'

Roderick was sitting up in bed beating a drum. Sarah, in a dressing-gown, her hair loose, looked round when she saw them. 'I can't get this little Chinky to stop the row. I'm trying to read.'

'We'll quieten him. Off you go, Sarah,' John said. 'I know you've been held up by our visitors. By the way,' he stopped her at the door, 'what did you think of Van this time?'

'She's weird.' She pushed her unplaited hair back from her face.

'Weird? How weird?'

'She said Satan didn't need any of her love. He got plenty from me. Fancy not falling for that beautiful horse!'

'She preferred Roderick,' Jean said. 'Stop that noise!' She turned to him. 'Did *you* like Van?'

'Van, Van, the funny wee man,' he recited loudly.

'Combed his hair with the leg of a chair . . .' He banged his drum in time, giggling.

'She taught him daft things to say.' Sarah looked disgusted. 'Honestly, Mummy. And would you hush him, please?'

'Off you go. I'll keep him quiet. Night-night, darling.' She held up her face. She encouraged goodnight kissing since it had been absent at Clevedon Crescent. Rose didn't approve of 'sloppiness'.

She stood with John, looking down at their son. There were those moments of detachment when they examined him, looking, perhaps for some kind of sign. His eyebrows were so fair that they were nonexistent in the low brow. His nose was lost in the fat folds of his cheeks, his small eyes were red-lidded, as red as the nostrils of his snub nose. John leaned forward and wiped it with his own handkerchief. 'This damned catarrh, clogging up your lungs . . .'

'Dam catarrh, dam catarrh . . .' Roderick sang.

'*Van*,' Jean said, 'your cousin with the long black hair, did you like her?'

He giggled and stuck a finger in each ear. 'I told her a funny story. And little Alice. About two dogs . . .'

'Yes, you did.' She looked at John. He shook his head. The boy had thrown himself down, giggling, kicking his legs, his head lolling from side to side.

'This dog –' he began.

'Stop it!' She put a hand under him where he lay. The sheet was wet. I can't, she thought momentarily, I can't take any more of it. I'll be glad . . . Oh God . . . She looked at John. 'You go to bed. I'm going to change Roderick and make him nice. Say good night to Daddy.'

John bent down. 'Good night, son.' The boy clung to his neck in an exaggerated fashion. Did he weep for his condition too, she wondered. His face when John released his arms gently was tear-stained. If anyone should weep it should be this poor damaged child.

'Sing song for Roddy,' he said when John had gone. He sometimes reverted to baby talk when he was tired.

'I'm going to make you nice first. Take off your pyjamas. That's right. You're a big boy. Put them on the floor.' She stripped the wet sheet off the rubber one underneath it, went to a drawer and brought out a fresh sheet from the supply which was kept there. She would wash the soiled linen and clothing tonight. Janet had to be spared. She lifted a talcum bottle from the chest of drawers and shook its contents liberally over Roderick's body, making him squirm with pleasure before she helped him into fresh pyjamas. 'Now you smell nice,' she said.

'Smell nice. Mmmh!' He sniffed ecstatically and lay down. 'Sing song for Roddy now.' There was love in the eyes which looked up at her.

She sang softly the first words which came to her, stroking the bullet-like head, watched the eyelashes which were darkened and wet with tears slowly fall on the round flushed cheeks. '"The way you look tonight . . ."' She had a low, husky voice, her Marlene Dietrich voice, John called it. Seductive . . . Robin Naismith, tall, smooth, with his Glenalmond tie and his big house in Kilmacolm. Anna, Ritchie, she and Robin at the University Union Saturday night hop, slow-foxtrotting, covering the floor in long, slow steps, 'The way you look tonight . . .' 'You're a good dancer, Miss Mackintosh, may I call you Jean?' Holding her closely, circumspectly, as befitted Kilmacolm, while her hot blood and her whole body yearned for

Frederick. She would never tell John that she hadn't known with him that ecstasy of loving she had known with Frederick, never would . . . and Robin Naismith had been almost invisible . . .

Roderick's outstretched hand was in hers as she sang. She turned it over and looked at the palm, the one transverse line where there should be two, a sure sign, or one of them. Her heart had grown too big for her body, swollen with the pain which never really went.

The boy gave a wriggle of impatience, as he lay. 'Sing song!'

'You cannot say . . .' she sang her own words to the same melody. '. . . I don't see life . . . with all its heartaches, trouble and strife . . .' She looked down. He'd fallen asleep, suddenly, as he often did. She kissed the top of the Aryan-like head.

Eight

1957

Nancy always used their house as convenient stops for her shopping trips to London. Rose occasionally came with her, James only once. He seemed unhappy transported from his Glasgow stamping ground of office, Automobile Club lunches and golf club. Ritchie said Nancy had sucked him dry. She didn't mind coming alone. She liked a good 'chin-wag' with Anna, which meant that her chin wagged while Anna's remained static.

'I don't know how Jean copes with that boy. I made myself go last year, although it took a lot out of me, because James said I must. I took Gordon with me for support, although maybe that was unkind, I mean, the comparison! I told her she couldn't sacrifice her life to a child who couldn't repay her, but she says he helps her painting by giving her love. Well!' Her beringed fingers spread out, her shoulders lifted in complete non-comprehension.

'What did Gordon think of him?' Van was sitting with them, Ritchie was upstairs painting. He always pleaded an urgent deadline when Nancy came to visit.

'Well, you know Gordon, he's the soul of politeness. He's been brought up that way. The best of schools.' She took a poor view of Renton Grammar. 'You found that, Vanessa, didn't you?' Van rewarded her with a blank stare. 'It's a pity you two didn't hit it off, just as cousins, of course, but Wendy – well, it's difficult to compete with *Wendy*. I think there's something brewing there, but first things first, I tell him. Get your degree and then we'll see how things go.'

'Did he play with him?' Van said with her intense look.

'Play with him?' Nancy looked bewildered. 'Oh, you mean Roderick! Well, if you mean getting down on the floor with him, he's no longer a child, Vanessa. He's a young man. But he took him an expensive jigsaw of Edinburgh Castle which I may say the little rascal scattered all over the house as soon as he got it. I even found pieces in my bed!'

'He's funny!'

'Well, I wouldn't call it *funny*. Gordon reprimanded him but it didn't do any good. But he took Sarah out to dinner at the Selkirk Arms one evening. Jean lets her slop about the house in those jodhpurs, and she's always at that farm even although it's different from the ordinary kind with cows and things. I bought her some perfume, a flowery one. "A girl of her age has to smell sweet as well as look sweet," I said as a joke . . .'

Anna realized that Van had slipped out of the room. Perhaps Nancy, without knowing it, had rung the death knell on her infatuation for Gordon.

Nine

❧

1958

It seemed to Anna in the bleak winter months of the following year that Ritchie was in Barcelona more than ever. She knew he was making an important niche for himself, there had been a remark in one of the national newspapers that Ritchie Laidlaw, the talented Scottish painter was becoming internationally known. He had accepted now that because of Van she couldn't accompany him, and rarely mentioned it.

She said to him one evening when he was packing to go off early the following morning, 'Some people have all the fun.'

He looked up at her, curls flopping over his brow, shirt showing gaps of flesh where it had escaped from his belt. 'Do I detect a note of self-pity there?'

'I wouldn't call it that.' She was lying on top of the bed, arms folded behind her head. Usually that posture was an invitation. 'Resentment, maybe.' She felt an obscure sense of shame that she was deliberately trying to pick a quarrel. 'Now that Mish has gone, Van doesn't even try to be companionable. She's in her room most of the time doing her homework, and sometimes she trails home very late from school. Probably with Winnie Good. And she isn't interested in shopping expeditions with me, or my work.'

'Your competence frightens her.'

'Competence? I'm bereft of ideas these days.' What a whiner, she thought. No wonder he escapes to Barcelona . . .

'It's the winter, darling.' He had gone back to his packing, sporting a long-suffering face. 'You've always been affected by it. You should become like a little dormouse, just snooze at the fire till the sun shines again.'

'It's not much fun snoozing alone.' The whinge was back and she changed it to lightness. 'As long as you aren't having it off with some Spanish beauty. You always say your juices rise when you're painting.' To her surprise he didn't reply. She waited. His voice, when it came, was not light.

'I miss you, naturally.' Another pause. 'But don't let your resentment spill on to Van. She's sensitive. She wants your love but she won't ask for it. We all need . . . at least an expression of love.'

Her heart quivered as if it had been struck. There was a corresponding tremor behind her knees. It was what was behind his words . . . She got up abruptly. 'I'm going to make the supper.'

He caught at her hand as she passed him. 'Oh come on, Anna! We're sticking pins in each other.'

She shook off the hand fiercely, and got to the door before she turned. 'I'm sorry I disappoint you so badly.' She slammed it behind her.

There's something wrong, she thought, as she assembled vegetables and meat, pots and pans – she was competent even in her misery – 'We all need at least an expression of love,' he had said. There was never any difficulty about that between us. What has happened? She tried to stifle the fear.

In bed that night he took her in his arms and said, 'I'm sorry, Anna.' His touch had the magic it always held for her and she trembled but didn't speak. Words were a barrier.

But in the morning, sitting at the table after Van and Ritchie had left in the same taxi – she was being dropped off at school – she found that the fear was still there. Was it only his painting which fulfilled him in Barcelona, made him happy without her? She sat staring into space, then went to her studio and banged away at some metal for a time, trying to make a tactile shape out of the fear.

In July Ritchie was at home when Jean and the children came to stay. John was attending a gynaecological course in London. She found Roderick, while engaging in so many ways, unusually exhausting. He was mischievous, and sometimes sly, and this she found irritating. He hid things in the house, he broke off the heads of flowers in the garden, he left taps running. The cat hid from him because he roared at it. He broke a valued little Giacometti-like sculpture of Ritchie's, and she was more upset than he.

Ritchie was like Van. He took the boy's condition for granted. He played with him, rolled on the floor with him like a puppy. When she analysed her feelings they were two-fold: sorrow that her beloved sister had been 'allotted' such a child, and an odd kind of jealousy that she was coping so well.

And painting so well. There was a flourishing artistic colony in Kirkcudbright, founded by the original Glasgow Girls, plenty of summer visitors from further afield. Jean had sold five paintings out of the seven she had done during the winter. Anna herself had made the clock face for Christine Logan, but although she had been pleased with the result, nothing further had happened.

She was finding that her kind of work was not popular where she lived. Had it been wrought iron, or wire sculpture, like Ritchie's little statue, it would have been sought after, but metal work with Art-Nouveau designs, based on the work done by the Glasgow Girls, was considered rather passé. Jean suggested her renting a shop in Marlow where there were always American visitors, but she couldn't find the energy to arrange it.

Mish, on the other hand, was doing well at the Art School. He had decided he would like to be an art historian or work in a gallery. He would never be a painter like his father, he told him, but he would be selling Ritchie Laidlaw's work in his own gallery. He had been home for a fortnight, and had now gone off to New York on a summer course with several other students.

Van worked doggedly enough at school, but she had few friends. The other girls at fifteen were keen on clothes, boys, and sports. She was uninterested in all of them. Her hair was still untamed, and she had been found to be myopic when Anna took her to an optician and now wore glasses.

She was in the seventh heaven while Jean was there, not because of Sarah, but because she could take charge of Roderick. He was soon shambling after her wherever she went. 'You don't get cross with me like Aunty,' Anna heard him say.

Because there was seldom opportunity with so many of the family around, she and Jean had little time for their usual chin-wags. But Jean did say before she left: 'You've changed, Anna. You look as if you had a worm inside you. Has it got green eyes?'

She was furious with her. 'Trust you with your acid comments! No one seems to notice around here, but I've been feeling low for a long time. No energy. A feeling of . . . worthlessness.'

'My God!' Jean said, looking at her. 'I never thought to hear the good-at-everything Anna say anything like that.' Her voice became tender. 'You do look peaky, but I thought you had been too busy to apply the old *maquillage*.' She laughed. 'Do you remember Mother called it that because she once bought a jar of French face cream? You're run down. It's nothing to do with the old charmer upstairs, is it?'

'No . . . except that he's away a lot . . .' She wouldn't put the fear into words. 'No. It's this . . . feeling.'

'Go and see your doctor and ask him for some pep-up pills. Or better still, board Van out somewhere and go back with Ritchie to Spain.'

'She's on holiday next week.'

'Couldn't be better. Take her with you.' She hugged her. 'I know you. You're keeping something back. I'm there when you need me.'

Later on that evening, Anna said to Ritchie: 'I wonder when you go to Barcelona next week if Van and I could come with you?'

'Great idea!' But *he* hadn't suggested it.

'She's on holiday then and I feel in need of a break.'

'I was thinking the same thing, but would Van like it?'

'I'm sure she would. She's only been to the south

coast and to Kirkcudbright. It would be an experience for her.'

'Well, that's something for us all to look forward to. I'll have to go upstairs again for a few hours. Something I have to finish . . .'

'Okay.' She felt better.

Van looked embarrassed when she told her. 'It would be a wonderful opportunity for you. Dad would take you around the galleries, there's a fine collection of Picassos, we could take trips together, and you could swim and sunbathe. Aunt Jean was telling me off for not having gone more, but I didn't want to leave you . . .' She made the overture, smiling.

'I could have stayed with a friend, Mum, any time, or been alone. And you miss Dad. It's in your face. You kind of . . . wither when he's not around. The thing is,' she stumbled over the words, 'I should have told you earlier, but we were busy with Aunt Jean here . . . we did a project at school where we went to Low Wood Orphanage, on the London Road, remember?'

'Yes, I think I do.'

'I really loved it, and the matron said she could always do with extra help during the summer holidays when some of the staff were away . . . so I volunteered. For a week, or a fortnight . . .'

'When?'

'The beginning of August. The time you're talking about.' The fearful look was back in her eyes again. They hadn't been like that when Jean was here, as if they had shared that intense brilliant blue.

'You might have discussed it with me first.' Those eyes . . . but she had to admit it, Van staying behind gave her an opportunity of being alone with Ritchie, to tell him that she honestly did feel below par and she missed him and now they had time to be together, to love. 'Okay,' she said, 'I'll go and see the matron, and if it seems all right, you can go.'

'Oh thanks, Mum!' She threw herself into Anna's arms and they hugged awkwardly. Unexpected tears came into Anna's eyes.

'We'll be good friends,' she said. 'I know I'm a bit short these days, but,' she tried to joke, 'young girls go through phases which are difficult for Mums.' And greatly daring: 'I've sometimes wondered if that rude cousin of yours, Gordon, had something to do with it.'

It was a mistake. Van seemed to freeze in her arms, withdrew herself and went out of the room without speaking.

She liked the matron, Mrs Sanderson, and the orphanage seemed to be well run. It was set in pleasant gardens. There could be nothing wrong with Van going there.

'We would love to have Vanessa if you could spare her,' Mrs Sanderson said. 'I'll take good care of her. You know you're blessed with such a daughter, Mrs Laidlaw, she has a rare gift of communication with those less fortunate than herself, and so much love to give. She must be a joy to have at home.'

'Yes, she's . . .' They were having a cup of tea together, and without intending to, she found herself confiding in this woman she had never met before. 'She has a tendency, all the same, to feel more at home with the disadvantaged. I know it shows what a fine girl she is, but sometimes I wish she were more . . . normal.'

'Normal! She's unique! You should realize that. Normal girls are ten a penny, but to come across one who is so full of the milk of human kindness, so noble, is unusual nowadays. Take my advice, you go off to Barcelona with your husband for a holiday. I should think you need it. Are you always so pale?'

'I must admit I haven't been feeling up to the mark lately. Maybe that's what makes me . . . over-critical.' She said with a tentative smile, 'Maybe it's my age.'

'You look just a girl. But you're right. There's a hiatus. Husbands appear, I say *appear*, to become less involved. They may well be approaching the peak of their career, and don't feel the pain of seeing the children you've reared leaving the nest. I know. My husband was like that, and one day he had a heart attack and died.'

'That must have been terrible for you.' The thought of a similar loss in her own case was like a dagger going through her.

'Terrible, but bearable eventually. I determined I wasn't going to be a drag on my daughter – she had just married – and so I took this job. I was a nurse. Work's the answer. I won't say I'm as happy as when I was married to Jim, but at least it's given my life some meaning.'

Anna came away feeling that she would have to take herself in hand. She would look for a shop in Marlow to rent, she would find an agent in London when she came back from Barcelona, and she would see the doctor before she went.

'I've decided to go and see the doctor,' she informed Ritchie that evening.

'What's wrong?' He looked anxious.

'Periods,' she said, 'or lack of them,' and smiled to see his look of embarrassment. She had once told him that any mention of womanly complaints made him

96

blush, and he had said it was his working-class background showing through.

'Poor soul.'

'I want to feel good when we're in Barcelona. We'll be alone.' She told him about Van.

'A second honeymoon, eh? Well, you mooch along and see good old Doctor Brown. "And what can you cure?"' he said, chanting from an old Penny Geggie.

'"I can cure the itch, the skitch, the scurvy and the . . ."' It was like old times.

But it wasn't good old Doctor Brown, but a younger and snappier version, Dr Gerald Masters.

'He retired a few months ago,' he told Anna. 'Now he goes to painting classes. Your husband had better watch out.' He smiled at her. 'I believe he works abroad quite a lot?'

'Yes, Barcelona.'

'Does that give you a chance to go too?'

'Not always, but I'm planning to go next week. There have been . . . family problems. My daughter is still at school.'

'Is that a problem?'

'No, no, I meant she was too young to be left alone . . .'

'So, are *you* having a problem, Mrs Laidlaw?'

'In a way. I've felt below par and my periods are irregular. I wondered if,' she laughed, 'I was having an early menopause, and if so – what about hormone replacement therapy?' She said the last words in a rush.

'My word, you are advanced! It's early stages yet. Where did you hear about HRT?'

'My brother-in-law is a GP. He's been on a course in London and he was telling us about it.'

'And did he tell you about the dangers?'

'Cancer? Yes, he did. No, I wasn't really thinking about it. It's just, those symptoms I'm having . . .'

'Suppose you tell me about them?' He leaned back in his chair. Dr Brown's eyes hadn't been so keen. Nor his hearing. Had this one heard the tremor in her voice?

'And there's this general feeling of gloom, dis-appointment in myself. I'm . . . letting myself down.'

'You're . . . forty-five?' He consulted his notes. 'It's early for the menopause, but I can arrange for a gynaecological checkup, if you like. Do you feel low in the morning?'

'Like death. Especially if Ritchie, my husband, is in Barcelona . . .' She laughed to show that it was a joke, but it wasn't. His eyes were on her.

'Tell you what,' he said at last, 'you go off with your husband as you've planned and I'll give you some anti-depressant pills to take. When you get back we'll have you checked. And forget HRT meantime.'

'I wasn't really thinking . . .'

'Is there anything else?'

I suffer from jealousy concerning my husband, always have. I can't believe that anyone so attractive to me won't be the same to anyone else. I have this fear . . . 'No,' she said. 'Except that I can't work. That's upsetting.'

'To have a talent is a great solace. I can see that. Well, if there's nothing else, you get off and have that holiday in the sun. Learn to relax. Scots people tend to be too analytical about themselves. I know. My wife is Scottish.'

On the way home she stopped at a boutique she had often admired and bought a backless sundress and a straw sombrero. As a morale booster. And she

would begin making up her face again. It helped a
little, but didn't kill her regret that she hadn't told
the new young doctor about her fear. That she was
losing Ritchie.

Ten

Anna determined to make her trip to Barcelona a 'distancing', the leaving behind of any worries. She would try hard to adopt a positive outlook, to make herself an enjoyable companion. Such striving, she thought, had never been necessary before.

Barcelona surprised her. 'Now I see what the attraction is,' she told Ritchie, after two days of wandering about finding peepholes into the past, a hidden cloister, a delicate wrought-iron gate, a small square half-hidden by plane trees. Those were the real delights, but there were also the set pieces, the Barri Gòtic, the *plaças*, the *casas* by Gaudí – she wasn't ready to express her opinion of his cathedral yet.

It had the same atmosphere and vitality as Glasgow, the feeling of being a seaport, a mixture of races which was reflected in the lively air of the people as they went about the streets.

They had booked a room in a spacious but shabby hotel near the Liceu Theatre on the main *Rambla*. 'How could you have stayed here so often?' she said. 'The decor is so depressing, those shitty colours!'

He laughed at her. 'It's recovering from the war. I suppose I get all the colour I want in my work. This was only a staging post for me, a place to keep my clothes. And it's so impersonal. I can come and go without anyone keeping tabs on me.'

While he was busy with Manuel Folguera, the head of the architect firm who employed him (he was also Director of Art for Public Buildings), she was happy to stroll about the squares and streets, to browse amongst the stalls on either side of the *Rambla* with their flowers and books and curios. She saw Ritchie's Honduran finches, which appeared as yellow flecks in so many of his paintings, darting madly about their tiny cages, and she spent hours in the Boqueria market wishing she was running a house. She had never seen food which was quite as colourful nor sold with quite the same enthusiasm.

The weather was hot. Guided by the statue of Columbus she explored the port, and standing in the bow of one of the *golondrinas* which made trips round the harbour, she felt like a pirate with her scarf knotted around her head to keep her hair in place. It was a buccaneering city, she decided, it had élan, or whatever the Spanish equivalent was; she could well understand the appeal it must have for Ritchie who could stay in a drab hotel because he was surrounded by so much beauty and colour.

She saw him differently. He was relaxed and yet excited, taut, yet distracted. At times she wanted to clap her hands in front of him and say, 'Here I am!' He said he and Manuel were absorbed in a new project for a municipal building near the Gaudí cathedral. 'So is Maria.'

'Who is Maria?' She had the feeling that the name had slipped out inadvertently.

'One of the team. Manuel's right-hand man. Haven't I mentioned her before?'

'No.' She looked at him. 'Is she new?'

'No, no.' He looked irritable, caught out. Caught out? 'She's been there all the time. She's full of ideas.'

'What age is she?'

'Thirty. I think, thirty.'

'Married?'

'Separated.'

'Family?' She felt she was filling in a form.

'Yes, a daughter. What is this, an inquisition? Yes, I know she has. A little beauty. She wears the whitest dresses I've ever seen and has the blackest hair.' He looked at her. 'It's difficult getting divorced if you're a Catholic. Juan Roig, her husband, worked in the firm. It's been traumatic for her. She wants to keep the daughter but his family don't agree. They're very influential in Barcelona. I feel sorry for her.'

'Don't let your feelings run away with you.'

'You know me. I'm a sucker for hard-luck stories. Don't worry. It wasn't important enough even to mention, and you had your own worries.'

From being happy and relaxed, sure of herself and her future, she plunged back into the edgy apprehension she had known at home. Something was squeezing her gut, like a warning, as if she were once again standing on the edge of a black hole of misery and indecision. And then it was gone as suddenly as it had come. It was surely too dramatic to feel like that, too neurotic because he had mentioned a woman of thirty called Maria who had a daughter and was separated from her husband. Ritchie had always been a good listener.

'Don't you think it's time you let me meet those wonderful people?' she said. She widened her eyes to try to look limpid, and unsuspicious.

'Would you like that?' He was schoolboyish, trying

to please. 'I'll ask both of them to have dinner with us tomorrow evening.'

'Hasn't Manuel a wife?'

'No, nor likely to have. They can't all be macho.' Well, that's interesting at least, she told herself, trying to make light of the darkness which was creeping back again.

Maria was small, fair, childlike, the antithesis of what Anna had imagined. Her aubergine-coloured silk suit looked like the ones Anna had seen in the smart boutiques around the cathedral, cut with too much spareness for Anna who was tall and liked clothes which were casual and gave her room to move. Only the green and aubergine scarf she wore was voluminous. Her fair hair slid over it as she turned her head towards Anna. The small hand seemed boneless.

'I hear you have a daughter, Señora . . . ?'

'Roig, but please call me Maria. You are Anna. Ricardo calls you Ann*a*,' she emphasized the last vowel.

Anna glanced at Ritchie who looked sheepish. Ricardo? She wouldn't let him off with that.

Maria's skin was pale olive, her eyes brown. Her teeth seemed exceptionally white as she smiled. 'My daughter has a name like yours, but spelled differently, Ricardo says. A-N-A.'

'And this is Manuel Folguera,' Ritchie said as if to deflect this analysis of spelling of names.

'I've heard a lot about you.' She shook hands. He had a plump face and double chin. He smiled, the chin tucked down as if he were amused, as if he and Maria were on show, and expected to give a good performance.

'I hope it was good. We are trying to give a good

impression, aren't we, Maria?' She smiled at him as if she too were playing the game.

'But we are as we are.' She spread her hands charmingly like one of Velasquez' *Meniñas*, Anna thought, or even Picasso's, which were more apposite since Maria could not possibly be as childlike as she looked. The waiter was suddenly there and Maria turned, breaking into a flood of Spanish. He smiled down at her, talking as volubly as she did and smiling, even laughing.

'Maria makes every man fall in love with her,' Manuel said to Anna, 'except me. Give it up, Maria,' he said. 'We know Jaime loves you. Actually, Anna, it's very dull. They're only discussing the menu.'

'I am so sorry.' Maria looked like a child who had been reprimanded, but not very seriously. 'Ricardo gave me permission to organize. Jaime is telling me how good the swordfish is tonight. He must be one of the few waiters in the Passeig de Gràcia who doesn't speak English.'

'Shall we have the fish, then?' Ritchie said. 'Leave it to Jaime. Unless you'd like something different, Anna?'

'Their paella is fine,' Manuel said.

'No, I'll go along with everyone else. I like fish which is really fish, not an oblong of some white substance dipped in batter and breadcrumbs.'

'Batter?' Maria looked as if she genuinely wanted to know.

'Flour and milk. It gives the fish an overcoat, like armour, when it is fried.'

Maria smiled and shook her head, wonderingly, like a child, looking at Ritchie. 'You did not tell me about the batter.'

He shrugged. 'Does it matter?'

'Does it matter,' Anna repeated, 'if he doesn't tell about the batter?' making a poem out of it, but no one laughed. She wondered what else he had been keeping quiet about.

'Ritchie has been quite good at speaking Spanish, you know,' Manuel said.

'He's kept that dark too.' She decided to be provocative. 'But then I don't know what he gets up to in Barcelona.'

'Ah, he works.' Manuel put up his hand to his hair which was drawn back in a ponytail by a piece of black ribbon. 'Have no doubt about that. Until late at night in our office or in the old warehouse where he keeps his moquettes.'

A small fat Spaniard like a pouter pigeon seemed to have alighted by their table. He tweaked at napkins, rearranged dishes with a deft touch. There was another flood of Spanish in which Manuel joined this time. The man looked in Anna's direction and bowed, a smile sliding under his moustache. He spread his fat hands in a gesture of welcome. He spoke quite good English.

'It is a great pleasure to meet the wife of Señor Laidlaw. I hear you have no Catalan, madam. Please learn Catalan, not Spanish.' And turning to Ritchie, 'But she is charming, Señor Laidlaw! An English lady. So correct, so formal. So elegant.'

'Thanks, Felip,' Ritchie said, smiling at Anna.

'I come to say that we will design a special sauce for her, not for Señora Roig this time.'

'Thank you,' Anna said. She felt like an unattractive dowager. She tried to smile.

'We have business lunches here, of course.' Manuel spoke too quickly. He waved his hand in dismissal.

'Off you go, Felip. No, pour the wine first, if you would. Señora Laidlaw is tired of you.'

'No, I'm fascinated.' Anna shook her head, smiling, at the same time giving Ritchie a sideways look. He was playing with his fork.

While they ate she answered Manuel's questions about Renton and its convenience to London. 'It suits Ritchie because his agent's there.'

'We think highly of him *here*. We would willingly win him over. Barcelona has a great future ahead of it after its troubled years. A few enlightened people like myself are helping it along that way. We want architecture and painting of our time so that in the future people will know what we thought *now*. We have plenty of examples of what it was like in the past. Art of the present day, no dead copies, that is the way forward.'

She nodded. 'Ritchie would agree with you.' She took a morsel of the fish on her fork. 'This is delicious.'

'Everything in Barcelona is delicious. And exciting. I know Ritchie is toying with the idea of buying a house or a flat here. Do come. You'd love it. And you could learn the language in no time.'

'We've talked about it. I think I'd like it.' The wine was making her feel happy again. She didn't mind that Ritchie and Maria talking together. They had to, since Manuel was engaging all her attention.

'If I were you I'd persuade him. But there are certain commitments at home, he says, children, their education . . .'

'And me. Another commitment.'

He laughed. 'A charming one. Education is good here too, and the life is more relaxed than in London. We are Mediterraneans, don't forget. It is so grey and

106

cold and formal in London, with so many unhappy-looking people. I remember travelling in your Metro.' He assumed a frozen impression, sat up straight, knees together. She laughed. 'No,' he said, 'even with Franco. Ignore that.'

'We call the underground the Tube.'

'It is. A dark tube. Everybody ignoring everybody else. Is it the lack of sun, do you think? Do come! Try it for a time at least. There is so much work we could give him. He is at his peak. Easel paintings are for old men when they have to tie the brush to their wrists or paint with water – I ask you, water!'

'I have responsibilities,' she said. The dread was back again, the edge . . .

'What are those responsibilities?' An Englishman would never ask a direct question like that. A Scotsman might.

'My daughter's at a difficult age. My son's all right. But she would think it was a ruse to make her give up . . . what she wants to do.'

'Ach, children!' He took a sip of wine, shaking his head. 'Wine, good wine, conversation at the end of the day of creative work. These are the things that matter. Children make too many demands. Why do parents let them rule their lives? Even Maria. I have no children, but I have something more lasting, my buildings, my interiors, my fountains, my sculptures. And no backchat from them. That is a delicious phrase I have learned from Ritchie. They remain in their places, they give pleasure instead of demanding sacrifices. That is how I see it. But these commitments you speak of, they are your husband's as well?'

'Not to the same extent. He's an artist, single-minded. You should know all about artists, Manuel – their selfishness, their conviction that they are

107

different from ordinary people.' God's gift to mankind . . .

She turned away from him, looking at Ritchie. He was telling Maria something, expounding. So often men were telling instead of listening. She interrupted. 'You live in Barcelona with your little daughter, Maria?'

Her eyes were almost as beautiful as Van's. And full of comprehension: You deliberately interrupted, because you were jealous. 'Yes, with my little daughter.'

'Here is Jaime,' Manuel said, 'bearing another piece of the Mediterranean on a plate.'

Yes, she said the morning after, which was Sunday. She had liked Maria and Manuel very much. She even managed some enthusiasm. She felt she had Jean at her elbow saying, 'Don't spoil it by being bitchy. We've outgrown that . . .' Ritchie had fallen asleep immediately they were in their room in the hotel, and she had felt very bitchy about that. But he had apologized and been very loving in the morning, saying he had been pissed, and they had been caught in the act by a chambermaid who brought them their breakfast on a tray. They had frozen under the bedclothes, he inside her, trying not to move.

They went to see the *sardana* danced in the Cathedral Square. Manuel had told her of it. 'It is symbolic of Catalonia,' he said, 'deceptively simple but complicated underneath. Pure ballet. It tells our story.'

At first there were only a few dancers on their own with their hands behind their backs as they performed the steps, as if practising, then they joined hands and made circles as more people came out from

Mass. Soon the whole square contained its circles of dancers. The dancers didn't speak. There was no fooling around, no awkwardness, it was a statement which deserved proper respect, a proper approach.

'Could you imagine the same thing in the Market Square in Renton?' she said. 'Or for that matter in front of St Paul's? We're far too self-conscious as a race.' She laughed. 'Maybe not so much nowadays. That new dancing – Cliff Richard's.'

'Slow, slow, quick-quick, slow at the university on Saturday nights. But we weren't performers.'

'You are. You perform in your paintings. You're a show-off.'

'Manuel says every life is a performance. Did you like him?'

'Very much. I get along with him.' She hesitated. 'Maria I'm not so sure about.'

'Why?' She thought he was studiedly casual.

'She looks too sweet and little girlish for thirty. Wasn't that the age you said she was?' Now the dance was in full swing, the bands rising in a crescendo, hands clasped with hands, arms uplifted, small, neat, back-tracking steps, then slowing down smoothly, slowly, until once again the high notes of the flute quickened their steps again. It was like life, she thought, it had a surge, then a retrenchment, then an inevitable surge forward. People were solemn, as if they knew it was like life.

'She really is like that, temperamentally speaking, all the way through. Sweet. But she has a brain like crystal.'

'You can see through crystal.'

'But it's rock-hard. Manuel says we need her sweetness because he and I are too harsh. Well, I am, he's in between.'

109

Did *he* need her sweetness? Was it missing from their marriage? 'She designs the most wonderful fountains, Grimms' fairy-tale fountains, like stalactites.'

'Aren't they silent when they dance?' she said, turning away from Maria and her fountains. 'Each circle is like a political statement. Proud. They pride themselves on their pride.'

'It's in their bearing. But do you remember when I was fighting here I said they were cruel as well? Cruel and kind.'

'I wouldn't say Maria was proud. She's feminine. And she makes eyes at women as well as men. She made soulful eyes at me. I don't believe there is all that sweetness behind them.'

'Are we talking about Maria or the *sardana*?'

'Both. Manuel explained it to me. The steps are composed of rhythms. If he hadn't told me that, I might have joined in, but I wouldn't dare, here.'

'It's serious stuff.'

'He asked me if I would like to live in Barcelona.' She turned to him and saw his eyebrows rise. He looked wary.

'He's been asking me for ages.'

'Did you go off the idea?'

'I thought it was maybe the wrong time to talk about it with you. There was Van.'

'It could be a holiday house to begin with.'

'And you hadn't been up to the mark.'

'I'll be better now I've seen the doctor.' She watched a man's bobbing head, counting the steps between the bobbing. She waited, then said, 'At least we could consider a flat in Barcelona, and I could join you for some of the time.'

'I honestly never thought you'd consider that. Or

agree to it. You like me at home as much as possible. And I *have* to be here, worse luck, although it's very attractive . . .'

'You're not trying to put me off?'

'Good God, no!' He looked irritable.

'Then we could try it.' She took a deep breath. She'd had enough of being neurotic about her health, and being suspicious of Ritchie, when chiefly she was worried about Van. 'It might do us both good. I could get new ideas for my metal work, or perhaps sell some. I like their tiles. I might study their designs.'

The band made a wailing, ascending sound, like someone running up a ladder and finding a pot of gold at the top; the wailing disappeared into the clashing sound of cymbals. Was that the stage her life was reaching, if she could take what it was offering, something momentous, something she was being rushed towards, the sweep of inevitability?

She looked at her watch. 'I think we should go now. Manuel said one o'clock. How far is it?'

'Yes, we'd better. Not too far. Arenys de Mar. It's a mile from the coast. Sunday's like Blackpool there, or Saltcoats at the fair. But he can see the sea. Wait till you see his place.'

When they were driving along the coastal road she said, 'Do you really make a lot of money with Manuel's firm?'

'I could make more. They want me to become a partner. He says I have an English sense of form. I corrected him. Said it was Scottish and hadn't he heard of Mackintosh, my hero?'

'I'm surprised you haven't talked more of all this at home. It's as if I've just discovered you're leading another life, a double life.' She looked at his profile, but it was giving nothing away.

'Everybody lives double lives, or treble lives, or more, boxes within boxes, even husbands and wives. I can't tell you about every one of them, or expect that you want to come in. You've always been a great judge of my work, but only when it's in front of you. But you haven't seen what I'm doing here . . .' He swung his head as if he was shaking off the subject. 'Great road, this. I like the feeling I get in Barcelona. Its . . . courtesy. It welcomes you.'

'Okay, it welcomes you. So does Glasgow. I don't shut you out of my boxes, do I?'

'Don't go on about boxes. Or make a row out of it.' His hands came down on the wheel with a bang of exasperation. 'We'll arrive with sour faces. You can always tell if couples have been rowing in their car on the way by how they whip them off and smile too brightly. You should know me by this time. I don't externalize very easily. You should know that too. I use my painting for that, and possibly I dropped the idea of a place here because it wasn't the right time. But I'm making a lot of money. Van and Mish might like it as well.'

Her anger faded away. A *family* flat. 'We have a flat in Barcelona,' or 'We have a house on the Costa Brava, not the busy bit . . .' She liked the thought of Nancy's face if she said that.

'It would be fun. A complete change. But we could keep on the house as well?'

'Oh, yes. London is just as important to me. I have to have my base there.' And so had she. There was still the idea of a shop at Marlow although that now seemed unimportant compared with the opportunities there might be for her in Barcelona.

'I must say being here has given me some new ideas.'

'That's the feeling I get too, a culture I understand. You need a fillip. Maria could help you there. She knows people interested in furniture, general bric-à-brac, tiles and so on. Wrought iron. Grilles. A barrier, but something you can see through. An invitation.'

'You don't want to be in Barcelona to be near Maria?' She made her voice light.

'Good God, no!' Was he too vehement?

'She's very sweet. You said it.'

'I prefer you, sourpuss.' He put his hand on her knee. 'Nice puss.' The hand slipped between her thighs. She groaned, feigning passion and they laughed together.

Manuel's house was halfway up a mountain, white-stuccoed, one-storeyed, with cool, splendid rooms, not definitely Spanish, but definitely modernistic. The furniture in the huge salon was steel and the floor was of marble. He would never know the wall-to-wall bliss of running barefoot on wintry mornings to get the post. He had no pictures, but the pottery and sculpture in strategic niches probably cost more than Ritchie's murals.

He led them through the room to a large tiled patio surrounding a kidney-shaped pool. Maria was there, another couple, and a little girl of about eight who was sitting at the edge with her feet dangling in the water. She must be her daughter. She had seal-black hair which covered her face as she bent forward.

'Sundays are pool-side days,' he said. There were oleanders in tubs, palms, and bougainvillaea growing up the wall of the house, tables with green and white umbrellas over them.

He introduced them to the couple, Señor and

Señora Rusignol. He was a museum director, Manuel told them, she a sculptress. If I lived here, Anna thought, this would be our milieu, those the type of friends we would have. Renton, in spite of a scattering of earnest artistic types, was surprisingly provincial. Anna, who was used to the lively culture of Glasgow, had been surprised at the number of coffee mornings to which she had been invited, the fêtes, pronounced 'fates', which proliferated in summer, the pointless conversation about families.

Their friends, or acquaintances, were the usual backbone of a small community, the doctors, the teachers, the solicitors, but at least there was no strain involved in the company they kept, comfortable, like old shoes. Here, she thought, I should have to be constantly on my intellectual toes.

'It's a lovely pool,' she said to Manuel as they were given chairs and drinks. 'It makes me dying to have a swim.' She had been forewarned by Ritchie and had bought a new swimsuit yesterday, a creation half-white and half-black, cut very skimpily round her buttocks. She had it on underneath her dress which buttoned down the front.

'Do. It will freshen you before lunch.'

She said to Señora Rusignol, smiling, 'My husband and I are over-dressed. We aren't used in England to being able to slip into a pool like this.'

'I understand.' She smiled back. 'We spent a week in London and it rained every day. I bought an umbrella as a memento. Now I am like the Victorian lady in the Ciutadella Park. Do you know her?'

'I'm afraid not. Do *you* go often to London, Maria?' she said. She must find out about the Victorian lady later. Maria Roig looked ravishing in a white swimsuit. Her hair was pinned up on top of her head but ringlets had escaped or been allowed to escape on her neck, and on either cheek.

'Sometimes I go. Ricardo tells me what I must see in the private galleries.' Had they met without Ritchie mentioning it to her? She mustn't be suspicious, she told herself, and spoil the day.

'Next time you must come and visit us. Our house is only forty miles from the city. I could show you the English countryside, which, incidentally, I don't think is a patch on the Scottish one.'

'Ah yes, you are Scottish. I like that better. Come and say, "Hello" to another Ana, darling,' she called. The little girl got up and came over to them obediently. When Anna said 'Hello', she gave a slight bow, smiling shyly.

She was a beautiful child without a doubt. She had the same olive skin as her mother, but her hair was the colour one would have expected, richly black and lustrous. Her thin body had grace, her legs were well-shaped, although slender. One imagined that she and her mother had never known an awkward phase, and in Ana's case would never know it.

'You must come and see *my* little girl,' Anna said, 'although she's not very little now. She's nearly sixteen.'

'You have a name for her?'

'Vanessa. It is the name of a butterfly.'

'That is pretty, to be called after a butterfly. Vanessa,' she repeated the name.

'It is also called the painted lady.'

'The painted lady,' the little girl repeated.

'You speak very good English.'

'I have an English nanny who is called Isobel. She teaches me. And Mama. She likes to speak English for Ricardo.'

Anna got up. 'I'm going into the pool. Are you coming?'

For Ricardo. Movement was essential to get rid of that one, otherwise it would fester. Maria had overheard her.

'I come too. Consuelo won't. She likes only to sunbathe, or is it that you can't swim, Consuelo?' She laughed like a child, teasing.

'You are naughty,' Señora Rusignol said. 'Everyone knows how naughty Maria is.' She looked around, smiling, eyes shaded from the sun by a large hat as she lay back in her chair.

'Naughty but nice,' her husband said. Anna smiled at him. She had no idea of the expression in his eyes behind his densely black glasses. He had a stringy body which contrasted with his wife's plumpness. She seemed about to topple out of her swimsuit. Anna thought with pleasure of her own trim figure.

She felt even better in the water. It was a natural element for her. She and Jean had always swum wherever they were, and had gone twice a week to the Western Baths as girls in Glasgow. She took a delight in the fact that Maria only took little dips in the water, keeping her head well above the surface, while she swam strongly up and down the pool, sometimes under water.

Another world, another element. This was what she had always liked about swimming. She curved her back and swam level with the blue-green tiles, thinking how different they must be from the murky depths of the loch when Jean had dived and dived again looking for poor Frederick Kleiber.

Did she ever have nightmares about it now? Surely not, but the episode had changed her. Her girlhood had disappeared in the space of one afternoon. Noth-

116

ing would ever bring it back. But now she had John to comfort her and hold her close, a healthy daughter – and Roderick . . . She felt ashamed at the puniness of her own worries as she surfaced at the other end of the pool, shaking her short hair out of her face and looking towards the men sitting chatting together.

'Come on, lazybones!' she called to Ritchie. He, unlike her, had no love of water. His ablutions were strictly necessary ones. He preferred to stand under a shower than to wallow in a bath.

'Don't be so superior!' The others laughed. Perhaps she had been showing off a little. Maria was standing waist-high with her daughter, hands clasped as they bobbed up and down. The ringlets which lay at the nape of her neck were still dry. She joined in the laughter.

Manuel called, 'You swim like a fish, Anna. Now you will have seafood to eat as well. Lunch is ready. Come and have some sangria to get the taste of chlorine out of your mouth.'

Señor Rusignol turned his black gaze on her. His mouth was stretched in what might be an admiring smile. She felt good.

'Right!' She clambered out, aware that her suit clung to her body and that the men's eyes were still on her. Yes, she had been showing off. She said, taking up a towel from a chair and draping it round her, 'I'm going to eat you out of house and home, Manuel.' He bent forward to Ritchie.

'That is a common expression?'

'Yes, only common people use it.' Ritchie's glance was teasing. It was an old joke between them. Rose had always thought he was common, coming as he did from an unfashionable part of Glasgow and having a father who was permanently on the dole. She

117

made a face at him, loving him because he was hers, bound to her in so many ways.

'I shall write it in my little black book,' Manuel was saying. 'Maria, Ana!' He stood up, 'Come and eat!'

Eleven

Van greeted them happily when they collected her from the Low Wood Orphanage. The spectacles she now wore didn't impede the beauty of her eyes. They were lively, deeply blue. Her hair was tied back becomingly with a ribbon.

Mrs Sanderson seemed equally happy. 'I'd be pleased to have Vanessa any holiday time,' she said. 'She was a great help to us. And the children loved her.'

They had an enjoyable meal together, telling Van about Barcelona, she regaling them with stories of the inmates at Low Wood. There were letters from Mish to read. He was enchanted with New York, he had been taken round the Museum of Modern Art, the Guggenheim and the Frick, he had discovered Greenwich Village and he had met some super people, artists, musicians, all kinds. 'I guess my eyes are being opened,' he wrote, which didn't sound like Mish at all. And: 'I'd like more than I can say to work here, it grabs me, the newness of it, the wealth of opportunity.'

'It'll do him a lot of good,' Ritchie said, and smiling at Van and Anna, 'Well, it's nice to know everyone is happy. Don't you think Mum looks great, Van?' Van smiled too, but in a distracted way.

'We talked about taking a flat or a house in Barcelona,' Anna said. 'I think you and Mish would like it. I mean when you're on holiday from school.'

'That's what I wanted to say to you.' Anna looked at Van. It had been too good. There was the familiar apprehension, a swift dip of her spirits. 'I want to leave the Grammar.'

'Leave!' She hadn't meant to raise her voice. 'But you're going to be working towards your A levels! You can't *leave*.'

'I don't mean leave completely. It's just that the Grammar School's too academic for me and I want to learn useful things, like shorthand and typewriting.'

'But they're only skills.' She looked at Ritchie, wanting to say, 'Why don't you say something?' but he was playing his usual waiting and watching game. 'You can't give up your all-round schooling for something like that.'

'Why do you want to do it?' Ritchie's quiet voice warned Anna. She was flying off the handle again.

'You'll be cross if I tell you.' It was Anna she looked at.

'Try me.' She willed herself to be calm.

'There was another girl working for Mrs Sanderson. Adelaide. She's at the Tech. She says it's really good. I don't want to go on to university. I want to work for some kind of charity. I read an article the other day and it said that anyone interested in that should get some office skills together, get themselves trained for administrative work . . . I can do A levels there too. I thought that might suit you, Mummy,' her look made Anna feel ashamed, 'better than just working at anything in an orphanage like Low Wood.'

Anna's heart was being squeezed. Why did this

girl of theirs make her feel so mean-spirited, and at the same time, frustrated? Why wouldn't she just be ordinary – no, normal? Look at Sarah. Look at Gordon. Of course, they couldn't be compared with Van for her sensitivity, her loving kindness – that was what Mrs Sanderson had called it – but it was the type of person she always seemed to be attracted to which was disturbing, and now there was a new one, Adelaide . . . an odd name and someone she had never even heard of.

Van was speaking. 'I'm not good at begging, Mum,' her eyes were wide, full of a kind of purity, 'but a properly run charity which I could organize . . . that would suit you, wouldn't it? You see, it's those awful pictures on television. I lie awake at nights thinking about them. Maybe I can go out there when I'm older, say, over eighteen, help in the field – that's what they call it.'

'Van,' she said, 'I understand. But you can't go round wiping everyone's tears like Albert Schweitzer. You'd never be done. If you work hard and get a degree in Social Science, for instance, you could do something really constructive. You'd enjoy university, the way Mish is enjoying Art School and all the opportunities it offers. You might even meet someone . . .'

'Like Gordon?' Her voice was icy. There was a silence which Ritchie interrupted.

'I've been listening, weighing it up.' He looked at Anna. 'Why not agree to Van going to the Tech, if that's what she wants? We both see your point of view, Anna, but she's put forward a good case.' His look was disarming, and loving. Her defences crumbled because she hated herself.

'Maybe I was too hasty.' She turned to Van. 'And

121

stupid. I keep trying to fit you into my pattern. Blame Granny Rose. She brought me up all wrong.' She subdued the tremble in her voice by laughing.

'I like Granny Rose.' Because she didn't vacillate? Her face broke into her enchanting smile as she spoke. Her eyes were full and moist. 'Oh, thank you both. I'll work hard at the Tech. I promise.' She got up from the table. 'I'll walk round to Adelaide's house and tell her. She says she'll give me some of her last year's books and that will save you money.'

When they heard the door shut, Ritchie held out his arms. 'The problems of bringing up daughters! Come here, pussy.'

'Pussy! What a nerve!' Nevertheless she got up, went round the table and sat on his knee. 'I never get it right with her. I'm the one who always complains. Never you. So you're the one with stars in your eyes, and I'm the one who objects.'

'She's found something she wants to do which she feels she's suited for, and she wants to get what she thinks is a proper training.'

'But she's academic, clever . . . university material.'

'A university frightens her. And she's stubborn. Come on, Anna. Let's just go along with her meantime and see how it works out. She wants to help *now*.'

'So I stay put. She'll still be at home.' She leaned against him, full of mixed-up feelings, resentment against Van and Ritchie, but mostly against herself, knowing she was too rigid, too intense.

'We'll fix up that place in Barcelona, and make arrangements for you to get there as often as possible. There will be ways. I hate to see you giving yourself such a bad time, Anna. Give her a loose rein. It'll work out, you'll see.'

There was a tight band across her forehead. 'I'm ashamed of being like this. It isn't me,' she said. 'My insight is always hindsight. Maybe if I can come to Barcelona oftener I'll change, become the fun-loving film-starish kind of creature you like.'

'I only like you.' He sounded weary. 'Get that into your stubborn head. You're over-sensitive. I know why you find it difficult with Van. I've come to terms with the reason myself.'

'Why?'

'Because she makes me feel humble. Guilty.'

'Guilty?' She considered that, burying her face in his neck so that he wouldn't see her tears. Where had the dashing, positive, young Anna gone to? Was it maternity which had changed her, and was she too painstaking, too involved? Perhaps if she became absorbed in her own work, regarded visits to Barcelona as an impetus? She sighed. His arms closed round her.

'Shall we nip upstairs?' he said. It was an old joke, the solution, he thought, to all their problems.

'All the same,' she said, her voice trembling, 'you shouldn't have made me capitulate like that. You should have supported me.'

'It wouldn't have done any good. You have to accept the girl as she is. Don't try to do a Svengali on her. She's full of loving kindness. That's the main thing, isn't it?'

'I suppose so.'

'It's not my way to pick holes, Anna. Love must be given wholeheartedly. Van knows that, is secure in that.' Was he wiser than she? Was it wrong to try and guide your children's opinions, knowing they

123

would thank you later? Or would they? *You're always so sure.* Ritchie was holding her very closely, solving the problem in his own way. With love. She responded as she always did, and to hide her emotion, she closed her eyes and pretended to swoon in ecstasy. 'Take me. I'm an instrument for your desires.'

To her surprise his eyes looking down on her were full of sadness. 'If you knew how imperfect I am . . .' He rocked her in his arms.

Twelve

Van seemed happy at the Technical College, and to have quite got over her infatuation for her cousin. She was cheerful, worked assiduously at home copying out interminable hieroglyphics from her Pitman textbook and practising on the portable typewriter which Ritchie had bought her.

She talked a lot about Adelaide, her friend. 'She's really nice, Mum.'

'Where does she live?' She tried to look relaxed.

'In Canal Street. They haven't been here long. They're Londoners. It's difficult getting a cheap enough place in London. Her father left them. Her mother has to clean houses to keep them.' The familiar stab in the heart. After all, she thought, Ritchie's mother had 'taken in closes', as he once told her, washed and pipeclayed them for the residents of superior tenement property at half a crown a time. She had a faithful husband, but he was still on the dole. The precepts inculculated in her by Rose about women who charred for a living were taking a few hard knocks.

'Ask her to come back with you tomorrow for tea. Daddy and I would like to meet her.' The die was cast. She, at least, was trying. Perhaps Gerald Masters' pills were having a good effect.

'Would you, Mummy?' Her face lit up, her eyes shone. She was beautiful. Her skin was so fine that you could see the blue veins on her temples. There was a russet gleam in her black hair. Ritchie had said when she told him that she had done the right thing.

Adelaide was as black as pitch with a white, fleshy-mouthed grin and bright, inquisitive brown eyes. A red wave seemed to submerge Anna's vision and blind her for a second before she came to her senses. She heard herself saying, 'Hello, Adelaide! I'm glad you could come.' The girl's eyes had a wary intelligence. She knows I'm shocked, she thought. She wanted to reassure the girl, to say, 'I don't mind you being black. That's your affair.' (What a stupid remark that would have been.) Her resentment was directed towards Van. She had known Adelaide's blackness would surprise her, but hadn't had the courage to tell her before the girl came. It's the slyness . . . or was it fear of her? 'How do you like living in Renton, Adelaide?' she asked.

'Oh, it isn't ba-ad.' She had a sing-song voice. 'The young ones liked Brixton better, but Eb says it's nearer the country here.'

'Is Eb your brother?'

'Yes.'

'What age is he?'

'Nineteen. Zach and Sam are eleven and thirteen. Eb doesn't work.' On the dole, Anna thought, resigned.

'What do you intend to do when you've finished college, Adelaide?'

'Well, Mrs Sa-anderson wants me to go back to Low Wood but me and my mum, we're London sparrows. She would like Van too; Van was real good with the kids, and of course she's cleverer than me.

126

Maybe she takes after you, Mrs Laidlaw.' The smile was ingratiating. 'You making ornaments and such like.'

'In a way,' she said.

She told Ritchie of the girl's visit in the evening. They were having a late supper because he hadn't wanted to be disturbed all day. Adelaide had gone home and Van was working in her room. 'What next? You'd think Van was trying to *get* at me.'

'Because the girl's black? For God's sake, Anna. We aren't racist.'

'No, I'm being silly. It's just . . . they're never . . . ordinary. Always misfits.'

'I'm going upstairs again.' He wasn't listening. 'I've something in my head. I might work through the night.' She went out to her studio in the garden and knocked the hell out of a piece of metal, finding when she had finished that she had made some kind of plaque with an ethnic figure on it, full, protruding lips, corkscrew hair . . .

Because of her guilt she told Van to bring Adelaide home with her any time. Sometimes they worked in Van's room, and she could hear the giggling that went on downstairs. *She* couldn't make Van giggle like that. Were they giggling about her?

Occasionally Van went home with Adelaide to the little house facing the canal. Anna had driven past the terrace out of curiosity. It was a shabby place, a coloured ghetto judging by the children who played in the street. Of course it was a disgrace that people of few resources were housed in a low-lying piece of land at the dirtiest part of the canal where the Renton factories were grouped.

She noticed, perhaps because she was always so careful of her own appearance, that Van became steadily more careless of hers. 'She's beginning to go around looking like a tramp,' she said to Ritchie.

'You know why?'

'No?'

'She's embarrassed to be well-dressed beside Adelaide's obvious poverty.'

'Does that mean wearing stockings with runs in them?'

'You give her a dress allowance?'

'You know I do. We agreed on it when she went to college.'

'Maybe she's giving her friend some of it, or the brothers when she goes to their house. Adelaide has three, hasn't she?'

'Yes. With biblical names. You're right, of course. I didn't tell you, but I discovered she had given Adelaide that beautiful navy-blue coat I bought for her at the beginning of winter. With the bright red scarf to go with it. She looked good in it, like a university student.'

'Which you would like her to be.'

'Yes, I would!' She found herself shouting. 'What the hell's wrong with that?'

'I'm going upstairs,' he said. 'Don't let's get into this again. There's no future in it.'

'Oh, sure! Brush it aside. It was only an expensive coat. It doesn't concern you. It never does.' The door banged behind him. 'Damn, damn, damn,' she said.

She realized that she was unable in her present state of mind to look rationally at this problem about Van. If she had been, she would see there wasn't any problem, except with herself. She remembered a film star she had admired years ago saying in his drawling Yankee voice, 'Don't make waves.'

She went into the kitchen and busied herself

128

preparing food, a mindless task which suited her mood. Real work was the answer. At her 'ornaments', as Adelaide had called them. Jean had found her salvation in her painting. What Anna needed was a fillip. Perhaps at Barcelona. Ritchie would find a flat and they would go there for Christmas, a new experience.

She wiped away a tear with the tea-towel and went up to the bathroom where she made up her face meticulously, taking the usual pleasure in the process. She had looked forward to sharing ideas about hairstyles and cosmetics with a daughter, laughing together. She and Jean had done that, experimenting with creams and rouges, with eye makeup. 'Our armour,' Jean had said. 'Two painted ladies.' Any resemblance Van had to that description lay only in her name.

She looked at the finished result, the soft shading on her cheeks and eyelids, the styled hair. Anyone who took such trouble with her appearance would never allow herself to have a nervous breakdown. The thought was comforting. She stopped in the act of putting a tiny camel-haired eyelash brush back in its box.

It was like a sunrise, the realization, flooding her mind. It was what lay *behind*. Presentation had become too important to her. Perhaps that was why Jean was painting so well – she was digging, probing for the meaning, the truth, with colour. *She* was only concerned with the surface. She should be able to do it with design. She went up to the attics.

Ritchie was busy on his latest mural. She thought it had inescapable Spanish undertones in its rich, almost raucous colour.

'I see Flamenco frills there,' she said, standing

squarely in front of it, 'and perhaps a bit of Gaudí distortion. It's over the top. You'll have to watch. They like you in Barcelona for being Ritchie Laidlaw, I hope, not a ragbag of Catalonian tricks.'

He smiled down at her from his perch on the ladder. 'I like you when you criticize. I was beginning to miss it.'

'Do you mind?'

'No, it's the thing you do best. I'm sorry I was bloody to you downstairs about Van. It's just that you want to set everything to rights. You're too obsessional.'

'Even about your painting?'

'There it's valuable. I depend on your criticism. I fight against it, but the resultant aggression is just what I need. More than that, it's necessary. In Barcelona they flatter me. I like it, of course, but I'm not a pussy cat to be stroked.'

'Let *me* stroke you,' she said. 'Van is in her room. I'm full of love.'

'God, you're always direct!' He came down the ladder and stood in front of her, smiling, being Ritchie as she loved him, had always loved him. He took off his apron with slow, seductive movements, like a strip-tease artist. He threw it with an exaggerated gesture of his arm on a nearby stool.

'Where would you like to have me?' she said. Her heart was thumping pleasurably.

'Did you ever know a painter who hadn't a couch?' He took her in his arms and waltzed her towards it.

Thirteen

During the Christmas holidays they all went to the new flat which Ritchie had found on the coast road to Sitges. It had a balcony facing the sea and a wrought-iron staircase running down to the garden. They did as Anna had planned, went to the cathedral, a new experience as they weren't Catholic, and ate out often in the little restaurants around the Plaça Reial.

Mish loved Spain for its colour. He soon exhausted the coastline with Sitges and its two Grecos, and embarked on a systematic trail through all the galleries of Barcelona, sometimes with Anna, sometimes with Ritchie. He took copious notes in his business-like fashion, and was soon an authority on their layout. He and Ritchie had long conversations on their contents which became so eclectic that Anna could only sit and listen.

But she was getting her own inspiration from the general architecture and feeling of the place. She was an executrix rather than a thinker like Ritchie. She had to have a hammer in her hand, unlike Ritchie who pondered over painting like music before he lifted his brush. She was looking forward with enthusiasm to getting back home to start work in her own studio.

The flat would be shut up for a month or two during the worst of the winter. Ritchie had a body of work to finish at home, and Manuel always took a winter holiday in the Caribbean or the Far East to 'compare cultures and recharge his batteries' – Ritchie quoted him. 'Spanish art is beguiling, but you have to be careful you don't get swamped with it.'

Van didn't go often with them to Barcelona. She preferred to wander about Sitges, to walk by the sea, to explore the narrow streets. She sometimes gave the impression of not being altogether with them. Anna refrained from being critical. This was a family holiday and she and Ritchie felt they should try and make it something the children should remember.

Anna and Ritchie were invited by Maria Roig to her flat in Barcelona, a large spare apartment in the Barri Gòtic at the top of an old building with wonderful views of the spire of the Cathedral of Santa Eulàlia. Her daughter was in Switzerland, she said. Van was disappointed. Anna, still being circumspect, did not say she would have found nothing to pity in the beautiful little Ana.

Maria seemed restrained, but then it had been easy to be relaxed round Manuel Folguera's pool, the last place Anna had seen her. There was a framed photograph of a gathering at it on a small table. Anna studied it surreptitiously, and found what she was looking for – Ritchie, bare torsoed, not beside Maria, but looking towards her, smiling.

'Josep Rusignol took that one.' Maria had seen her. 'Manuel had a birthday party. Summer is a happy time.'

'So is Christmas. Do you miss your daughter?'

'Yes.' Her eyelashes swept her cheek, and then the

candid, childlike gaze. 'I am a little jealous, you see.'

'Why is that?' Of course she was enchanting, that fair hair against the exquisite black dress, worn short, with high-heeled shoes. Only someone of her size could wear such heels.

'She is with Juan, my ex-husband. He is mad for skiing. He charms her with the ambience and the furry white hats and fur-lined jackets he buys for her and so on, the way to a little girl's heart. At this stage I do not know whether she will become a sports girl who is only happy when whizzing down the slopes, or whether she will follow my interests. It is a tug of war.'

'Children's careers always present problems,' Anna agreed. 'I haven't any doubts about my son. He has already mapped out his future. Van is another matter.'

'Is she unhappy? Has she left a boyfriend in England?'

'Oh no, she isn't interested in boys. She was once, but he wasn't interested in her.'

'That could be an embittering experience. I had the same situation with Juan. You have to find a substitute.' Her eyes were limpid, but was there a hidden gleam of satisfaction in them? Anna had seen the same look in Adelaide's eyes when they rested on her. All Ritchie was interested in was the purple tones of her skin. 'I've no colour sense,' she had told him. 'It's her specious humility I don't like.'

'My brothers are in rags,' she had said to Anna more than once with a pitiful look. 'They'd be grateful for any of your son's cast-offs.' But when Anna had made up a large bundle for her, her thanks had been lukewarm: 'It's always old stuff like this they have to wear . . .'

133

'We have arranged to meet our two at the Dolphin Fountain,' she said to Maria. 'Perhaps you'll excuse us.'

'Yes, mustn't keep them waiting,' Ritchie said, over-heartily. Was he like a dog brought to heel?

'She's beautiful,' Anna said as they walked through the narrow streets towards the fountain.

'Yes.' He nodded, his eyes on a shop window. 'They sell great scarves. I could buy you one . . .'

'Are you a regular customer then?'

'No, I just use my eyes.' He sounded exasperated. 'For God's sake, I *need* to stroll around. I can't work all the time. And I have to meet the people who employ me, find out what they're thinking.' He quickened his step. 'Come on, the kids will be waiting.'

It was her fault again, her sharp tongue. If she could only tell him about this feeling of gloom which suddenly swamped her, of the world darkening round her at times. Dr Masters had explained to her when she went for a supply of pills that it was due to hormonal changes in her body, but Ritchie would have felt awkward and embarrassed . . .

When they caught sight of Mish and Van standing at the fountain she slipped her hand through Ritchie's arm and smiled, shyly for her.

'You look like a couple of lovebirds,' Mish said when they met up.

'And you look terribly young, Mum,' Van wanted to be in on this, 'much too young to have us.' She was wearing tinted glasses and she looked Spanish-smart in her short white skirt and T-shirt. 'Honestly, Mum!'

'Will you listen to the flattery, Ritchie!' She was having a job subduing her face.

The rest of the holiday went well. Ritchie said there would be plenty of opportunities like this. 'Would you rather live here altogether?' she asked him, and he replied, 'Of course not, you're my wife.' But that hadn't been at question.

It was only when she was clearing up the flat that her suspicions were aroused again. She opened a book on El Greco in the little room he had appropriated as his office, and saw the inscription inside it. 'To Ricardo from Maria. Remember.' The word seemed to indent itself on her heart immediately. She could have touched the spot.

She didn't mention her find even when Ritchie absented himself on the last evening and came back in time for a late, late dinner. He smelled, not of perfume, but of perfumed soap, and his hair was slightly damp as if he'd had a shower. Jealousy ripped through her at the sight and smell of him, but she maintained a stubborn determination not to spoil the family holiday.

She discussed with Mish their visit to Glasgow – he was halfway through his last year at the Art School – and she wanted to thank her mother in person for her kindness in having him for so long.

'She's not a bad old biddy, Bessie,' Mish said. 'Nor is Granny Rose, if you go by the rules.' She joined in the laughter. She discussed her plans, to see Nancy briefly, then whip up in the train to see Jean. She wouldn't drive because of the weather. She thought they gave the impression of a very happy family.

When Ritchie said in bed that they had better get to sleep right away as they had a long journey tomorrow and turned from her, she lay sleepless beside him, her misery too deep for tears.

* * *

135

It was in a way like returning to the womb to be once more in her childhood home. The elegant curve of the crescent pleased her eye, the lofty rooms, the upstairs drawing room, the mansards behind their parapet, the ornate lamps on the stone wall outside. The quiet permanence of it gave her a sense of peace and continuity, as if the Georgians had permeated it with their leisured way of life.

And Rose had a kind of permanence too, smart, immaculate – did she take her own attention to detail from her, Anna wondered – the only difference being that she now affected rose-coloured chiffon scarves tucked in at her neckline, because, she said, her neck had reminded her of the Christmas turkey's.

Bessie was the same except that if one looked closely there appeared to be a gradual atrophy taking over: her hair was sparse and grey, her skin sallow with perpendicular lines creasing her mouth, and her movements were stiffer. Rose had bought her a spanking new trolley when she had noticed trays were a problem, and although Bessie referred to the chariot as 'new-fangled rubbish', she used it all the same. The only thing which hadn't atrophied was her tongue.

'I owe her something after all those years,' Rose said to Anna, 'and of course there's a nice little nest egg for her if I should predecease her.'

'All those years,' Anna said, 'first with grandmother and then you. Such faithfulness. And the two of you living on here alone since Daddy died. Don't you ever go and sit with her in the kitchen, Mother, maybe make her a cup of tea?'

Rose's chin lifted with her eyebrows. 'It's well seen you've never had servants, Anna. No, no, Bessie knows her place and I know mine.'

You're both a dying breed, Anna thought.

'And of course there's a special bequest to Hamish. The two of us will miss him. A man in the house and so pleasant and helpful. "Good morning, Grandmother. How are you today?" Not sullen. Children nowadays are that sullen. They don't make the effort.' Anna agreed, thinking of Van. 'Between you and me, Anna, I'd rather have Hamish than Gordon Pettigrew. Spoiled by Nancy, and now he's being spoiled by the Armours. Of course they know he's a catch for their Wendy, and parents are that relieved if it's someone suitable and not someone without any background.' She had once said the same about Ritchie. 'It's a daft sort of name though, Wendy. No name for a grown woman.'

'It's from *Peter Pan*, Mother.'

'I know where it's from but that's no excuse. No, give you your due, Anna, you and Ritchie have made a good job of Hamish.'

'He's brought himself up. It's –' She stopped herself.

'Vanessa? Not so easy? I can see it in her face. Angus was like that, quiet but implacable, a real Highlander. They have dark thoughts.' Anna remembered that quiet reliable man who'd been her father. Only a wife really knew the real one.

'But you had a happy marriage?'

'Because I put him first. I know you don't do the same with Ritchie.'

'How do you know that?'

'You're always wanting something that isn't there. Trying to make him over. Jean has learned acceptance quicker than you. But then there was that time . . . and the illness . . .'

'You mean Frederick Kleiber being drowned and then his baby being born dead?'

137

'Yes, that's you too. Always wanting to spell everything out. Won't let it be. Sometimes it does harm to name things. They don't die then.'

'So I'm a failure.' This was to be a visit to show her appreciation. She'd better watch it.

'Don't give me that kind of talk. If you are, it's only to yourself. You always want everything perfect.'

'How do you know that?'

'How could you bring anyone up and not know what they're like?' She arranged her chiffon scarf. 'I had such a job getting the right shade for this.' She patted it. 'That sweetie pink they have in Daly's! I told them it was something subtle I was after. Of course, not everyone has been to the Art School.' She preened herself.

'It sets off your complexion, Rose,' she said, and giggled. Her mother was silenced momentarily by the effrontery of having her first name used.

'Aye, I try to live up to my name.'

Jean gave her the welcome she got from no one else, her own flesh and blood, part of her. No need to explain herself, to exemplify, to clarify. Jean could feel what she was *trying* to say.

'John looks well, but thinner,' she commented.

'He's been dieting because Alastair Campbell has found out that he has a heart murmur.'

'That's the young for you,' John said. 'Insisted on examining me one morning after surgery.'

'Alastair is his new assistant,' Jean told Anna. 'Good thing we got him. I would be glad if John would slacken off a bit now.'

'Take his advice, John.' And to Jean, 'Where are the children?' They were having a glass of sherry before dinner.

'Sarah's gone to the Logans to bed down Satan, and Roderick followed her. This is a new ploy of his. I don't know what fascinates him there. It's not Satan. He hates horses. Luckily she doesn't go as often now.' She looked at John, smiling, 'She has Alastairitis. Of course she's far too young, seventeen.'

'I wasn't much older when I met Ritchie.'

'No, that's true, and Alastair would be eminently suitable from Mother's point of view, twenty-four, a Highlander from Inverary of impeccable background . . .' She laughed. 'There's even a house waiting for them. Mrs Beith looks after Alastair in the old surgery house, but I know she's anxious to retire.'

'I never thought you would become a scheming mama,' Anna laughed at her.

'That's what maternity does to you. Neither did I.'

Sarah looked the same, but with a tenderness about her expression which hadn't been there before. She would make a grand doctor's wife.

'Aunty!' Roderick pretended surprise, amazement, with his exaggerated gestures, although he must have been told she was coming. At thirteen he was bigger, coarser, more boisterous. 'Well, you could have knocked me over with a feather!' He enveloped her in a bear hug. She felt his wet mouth on her cheek. 'You came by the iron horse this time, I hear.' He nodded like an old man. 'And how did you find them all in Glasgow?'

'Very well, Roderick.' She tried to keep her face straight. 'They all send their love.'

'Grandmother must be getting on now,' he said, looking at John for approval, and then in a burst of enthusiasm, 'I saw Alice today! She was going to a party and she let me see her party frock. My eyes were out on stalks, I can tell you!'

'Oh, Roderick!' Jean said. They were all laughing, 'Where do you pick up those expressions?'

'That's nothing!' He looked pleased. 'You should hear the fishermen.' He covered his eyes with his hands. 'But I've not to tell. "Don't let the doctor hear," they say.'

'All right. Well, go and wash your hands. We're going to have supper now.'

'They make me laugh all the same, Mummy. Old Jock said . . .'

'Go and wash your hands, please!' John's face was stern.

'Right away, Daddy.' He went shambling out of the room.

'We can't keep him away from them,' Jean said to Anna. 'Do you see any difference in him?'

'He's still got his sense of humour.' She laughed. 'And he's growing. He's a strong healthy lad.'

'He can lift me off the floor. He knows he can make us laugh and he plays on it.'

'How is he doing at school?'

'Academically not at all, but he's the drummer in the school band, and he still plays the piano a little. And he sings. He has a strong sense of rhythm. They've talked about training him to be a joiner, but he's too clumsy with his hands. He might improve.'

Mother was right, Anna thought. Jean has learned acceptance.

They talked endlessly while Anna was there, walking in the clear frosty air along the road towards Gatehouse of Fleet, or along old High Street and into the town to shop. 'I love this place,' Jean said. 'I wouldn't like to be anywhere else.'

'For two Glasgow girls we've got about, and now

we have a flat in Spain. Ritchie uses it more than me, but I'll try and go oftener.'

'Do you like it?'

'Yes. I'd like to be with Ritchie. They're very keen on his work. He began a love affair with Barcelona when he was in the International Brigade. It's still got a hold on him. I could work there too, its strangeness . . . You seem inspired here, Jean. I love that one you did of Wigtown Bay. The sky's a masterpiece.'

'Oh, I'm not in the same class as Ritchie. It's a pity you couldn't go with him. I've got my painting *and* John.'

'I can't leave Van on her own. She insisted on giving up the Grammar School and now she's at the Technical College. I'm not so happy about that. She wants to be a charity worker.'

'Well, that's all right. You have an inherent dislike of do-gooders. I've noticed it.'

'No, I haven't.'

'Yes, you have. You're dismissive.'

She gave in. 'Maybe it's because Mother always sent me to the door at Clevedon Crescent when she thought it was a canvasser or something.'

'Do you remember Jesus?'

They laughed together. 'Yes, I remember. "Tell your mother Jesus is calling her," he said, and I said to her, "It's Jesus, Mum."' They laughed again.

'And Bessie knew what was going on and she said, "In the name o' Goad and me wi' ma steps no' washed!" She was being funny.' They were laughing helplessly now.

'And Mother said, "Jesus doesn't knock on doors. He's got plenty of churches."'

They drove to see the origin of Jean's picture and walked by the shore of the bay. The thin afternoon sun was pleasant on their faces. Winter never seemed to be so severe in this part of Scotland. Anna thought of the Glasgow she had left, its 'mucky' streets, as Bessie called them, with the drizzling rain, sometimes the fog, the sooty buildings, remembered the cold stretches of corridors when she had been at the Art School.

But always there had been the thrilling anticipation of meeting Ritchie when they changed classes. Did sober Sarah feel the same for the new young doctor? Of course she must. It was the perquisite of youth, but in her own case it had never died. That was the damnable part of it . . .

'I bet you miss Ritchie when he's in Barcelona.' The thought reader at her side.

'Yes, madly. I'm as jealous as hell. I want to be there with him in case . . . But there's Van. She has this friend, Adelaide, black as coal with an indigent family, and knowing her she would have them all staying in our house if I turned my back.'

'You don't like this girl?'

'No, I don't. Of course you'll think it's because she's black, but it isn't that. She's "sleekit". Remember that word? She makes the bullets for Van to fire.'

'You give yourself a lot of trouble over Van,' Jean said.

'Yes, I know, and when it's not her it's Ritchie. You know me.' She couldn't keep it back. 'Jean, I'm worried. I think I have a rival in Barcelona.'

'Have you met her?'

'Yes, married but separated, and with a girl of eight or nine. She's small and fair and not like me. She's . . . beguiling.' She met Jean's eyes and tried to withdraw the fear from hers by breathing in deeply.

'Don't jump the gun. Creative people are given hell

142

by their imaginations unless they're spilling it onto canvas or into print, or in your case, knocking hell out of a piece of metal. Are you getting on with your work?'

'Yes, well . . .' She was annoyed at the question.

'Get on with it, then. Ritchie doesn't see women as potential rivals to you. He genuinely likes them.'

'I know. It can be quite impersonal. But this one is different. She's a woman in child's clothing, experienced, creative, fair-haired, and the antithesis of me.'

'Ritchie likes your type. Straightforward. That mixture is too complicated for him. You've grown up together. You fit, fundamentally. Don't worry.'

'But I do. She's compact and neat, and that dreadful word, petite. Suddenly my feet are too large and my elbows stick out.'

'Oh, Anna!' She put her arm round her as they walked. 'We used to think life was a doddle when we were students in Glasgow, didn't we?'

'And the daft thing was we thought when we got married we'd be in clover. Do you remember that time after the baby, and you and I were living in your house as snug as two bugs in a rug?'

'Yes.'

'And I'd quarrelled with Ritchie about that other girl in London, the nutter, Christine Bouvier?' She paused. 'God, how strange! Now it's Maria Roig! I'm beginning to see a pattern . . . And you were undecided about John because you couldn't get Frederick out of your mind?'

'He's still there. I've only accommodated to him not being here.'

'But you're happy with John?'

'Happier than I deserve.'

'We could all say that. Well, despite the sadness,

143

and the memories, there we were, and I remember thinking how nice and cosy it was and would be if you and I just went on quietly together in Kirkcudbright with our painting and metal thumping and forgot about men altogether.'

'It wouldn't have worked.'

'How do you know?'

'Because I know us. We're passionate. We aren't half-lifers. And I'm glad I knew real passion, that elation, that subjugation, that tremulous joy! A complete giving, and sharing. No, it wouldn't have worked.'

'You're probably right.' Her arm crossed Jean's to encircle her sister's waist. They were silent as they walked in the gloaming. The mist hung over the water as if over the future.

Fourteen

1961

The sixties brought changes at home and abroad. The young President Kennedy's influence was felt in Britain, with its high endeavours even in outer space, and Mish got his dream and was successful in being taken on at a large gallery in Madison Avenue, New York. The company owned a block of apartments in Upper East Side, and rented him one there at a reduced rent. Soon he was sharing it with his newly acquired girlfriend, Karin Gottleib.

'You'll like her,' he wrote to Anna. 'I know you and Dad won't mind that we're living *à deux*.' She showed the letter to Ritchie. 'Our son is a cool cat now,' she said, trying not to sound shocked.

'Who would have thought how times change?' Ritchie said, half-admiring. 'Our Mish getting all the benefits at an age when I was going about with my tongue hanging out in frustration. When I think of it, it makes me want to spit blood.'

'Never mind,' he was reading the morning paper, 'we made up for it afterwards.' Last year he would have grabbed her to prove his point, she thought, as she spread marmalade on her toast.

'And he admires Hockney, he says,' came from behind the newspaper. 'Yes, he's certainly different.'

'I think Karin whatever is lucky to get him. He's mature, charming, self-possessed, knowledge-able . . .'

'You might be describing me.' She had to laugh.

Van's friend, Adelaide Carradine, had gone back to London. Her mother had gone off with a new man, taking the two younger boys, and Adelaide and her brother Eb had rented a flat in Clerkenwell. Van said the family had never settled outside London. They were true Londoners.

Anna couldn't see it as anything but a blessing, even although Van didn't seem to take up with the other girls at college. She was still awkward at eigh-teen, painfully shy and ill at ease in company, her only redeeming feature it seemed being her eyes, large, liquid, deeply blue behind her spectacles. Anna had suggested contact lenses but Van had shaken her head. The look in the girl's eyes made her feel ashamed, as if she was seeing through her and despising her. It's only for her own good, she thought, but it didn't help.

Her hair was still untameable, a black frizz which stood out like a Hottentot's round her thin face, but all efforts to get her to have it styled were met by 'those eyes', as she thought to herself. She confided in Ritchie.

'She resents you trying to make her over,' he said. 'She thinks it implies a rejection of her and all that she thinks important. Stop nagging.'

What she seemed to think important was the voluntary job she had taken on at the college, that of shepherding the boys and girls who came from a nearby spastics home to be tutored in simple office skills a few times a week. She spoke of them often. She began to go to the home some evenings to tutor the slower ones in English. She was effortlessly clever, but Anna thought she neglected her own homework to give them her spare time.

But to Anna's immense pleasure she also acquired a boyfriend, William Armstrong, who seemingly had also volunteered for this task. Van began to speak of him shyly at home: 'William says . . .' 'This time,' Anna said to Ritchie, 'it's he who seems to be showing interest. Shall we ask this William to a meal?'

'Why not? But don't make it too formal, *à la* Rose. You frighten the horses with all that palaver.' She probably deserved the dig. She had been brought up to sit round a properly set table with immaculate linen – she had not gone in for the vogue of table mats – and her silver appointments were always impeccable. It was a Glasgow West End formality which had always been observed at Clevedon Crescent, and she had brought it with her. Jean had gone ethnic, as Anna privately called it, wickerwork and a hand-woven type of rusticity which was all right in a country town like Kirkcudbright. Perhaps it showed a rigidity in her personality that *she* was unable to relax her standards.

William came for supper – she was careful not to call it 'dinner', as they had always said at Clevedon Crescent.

He was a smooth-haired, navy-blue-suited, rather mundane young man who seemed slightly in awe of them, but whether it was her or Ritchie she couldn't be sure. Ritchie was his usual casual self, chatting amicably during the meal, but excusing himself when it was over and going back upstairs to his studio leaving her to carry on herself.

William took it well. 'I suppose when you're as famous as Mr Laidlaw you have to work very hard,'

147

he said. 'I can just see him at his easel.' He looked wistful, as if he would like to have been invited to witness this spectacle.

'He'll be lying on his old couch, that's all,' Van said dismissively. Their spectacles winked at each other. His mouth narrowed under his narrow nose and he looked discomfited.

'It may *look* relaxed,' Anna said in Ritchie's defence, 'but he has to put a great deal of thought into his murals before he starts. There are a lot of problems to solve.'

'So he thinks better lying down?' William took her point. 'Wish we could do that at the college, eh, Vanessa? Can you see us all on couches, listening to old Paterson in the French class maundering on about the French Revolution?' He laughed more than the joke was worth. Had Van really fallen for this young man with his carnivorous nose and brilliantined hair, or was she only flattered by his attentions? Or was it to fill the blank in her life left by Adelaide Carradine?

'Of course you're such a clever family.' He was ingratiating. 'Me Dad says I'm lucky to know some-one like Vanessa. And you have a studio too, in the garden?' He was laying it on a bit thick, Anna thought, looking at his rapt impression.

'It's just a kind of tool shop,' she said to be wicked.

'But you're an artist in your own right, aren't you?' He looked anxious.

'Just a bit sort of arty-crafty,' she said gaily. She caught Van's look. 'You're baiting him,' it said.

'And Vanessa!' He registered amazement. 'She's always being praised for her charity work. I know it sets the other girls' backs up, but I say leave them to making up their faces and chasing boys, Vanessa.

What you're doing is worthwhile. Honestly, Mrs Laidlaw, her name is never off the noticeboard, running this thing and that.'

'Really?' Anna said. It was the first she had heard of it.

He spoke to Van. 'It used to be you and that black girl. You're better off without her. I never liked her. She's not your kind. Black tinkers, me Dad says.' Now Anna noticed he had a whining Cockney-tinged voice. He looked at her for confirmation.

'Everybody's my kind,' Van said quietly, 'black, red, yellow, white.' William nodded warily. He had the air of someone who was trying to say the right thing. 'All the same, me Dad always says we would have been better off without them, taking up all our jobs.'

'Won't it soon be your A levels?' Anna changed the subject. He took the bait eagerly.

'Yes, I'm aiming for two Cs at least. That's why I'm doing this community work with Vanessa with that lot they bus to the college. It helps your prospects. I've got my name down with the Westminster Bank.'

'Oh, I see.' No, she didn't like him.

'I've persuaded Vanessa to put her name down too. She didn't want to, but I've told her it's all very well being charitable but you've got to look after number one in this world.'

Anna looked at her, amazed. 'But I thought you were thinking of a paid job in some of the Social Services,' she said, 'because of your experience at Low Wood –'

William interrupted. 'It's all right for a *hobby*,' he looked earnestly at Anna through his black-rimmed spectacles, an embryonic bank manager, she thought, 'but not as a career. All those cripples. The bank's

149

different, businesslike, and you get lots of perks, help with your mortgage, for instance, when you're buying a house. We've discussed that, haven't we, Vanessa?' She muttered something, looking uncomfortable.

'It's difficult to get a paid job, Mum, you see.' Her eyes had that deep look, almost beseeching. 'I've been into it. And if you do it's only a pittance. The bank's a sinecure . . . William says.' It wasn't Van talking.

Anna relayed the conversation later to Ritchie. 'I can't believe in this new Van,' she said. 'The one who was going to be the saviour of mankind has disappeared.'

'I can.'

'Can you? Do you think it's because –' she broke off because the telephone was ringing. Before she could get to her feet he was out of the room and in the hall.

He was away for a long time. She sat where she was, not giving into the desire to get up and go closer to the door which he had closed behind him, but nevertheless trying to hear. She couldn't. He must be speaking very softly. She told herself it would be Manuel Folguera. He seemed to ring a lot these days. When she had commented on this to Ritchie he had said there were always things to discuss at the start of a commission, and he would probably have to go back soon. She felt out of touch. Somehow it seemed as if Van and Ritchie were living a large part of their lives away from her.

He was spending more and more time in Barcelona, she less and less. No work had materialized there for her in spite of her hopes, but she was getting a fair amount at home. She had sold a few clock faces in

London and she was beginning to get known in Scotland. Christine Logan had recommended her to some of her friends. She must have liked what Anna had done for her.

And Molly Masters, the young Scots wife of Gerald Masters, Anna's doctor, had written an article about her in the local paper where she worked as a part-time journalist. She had headed it, 'Wife of internationally known painter will soon be putting him in the shade'.

Ritchie came back. 'Was it Manuel?' she asked him, watching his face.

'Yes.' He brushed it aside. 'Where were we?'

She kept her eyes on him. 'You said you could understand Van.'

'Well, I think I can.' He was at ease with himself now. 'William admires her. He's pursuing her, maybe for his own ends, but at least it's a change from the boy wonder back in Glasgow who was pushed into it by Nancy. She's flattered. He's doing his best to talk her into his way of thinking, and she has this wish to fit into the norm, possibly to please you.'

'Oh Lord, Ritchie,' she said, discomfited, 'do you think that's it?'

'Partly. Van's deep, and at her age girls have conflicting emotions. And perhaps she was ostracized at the college because of her friendship with Adelaide. This William chap has thrown her a rope which she's grasped.'

The last thing she wanted was for Van to give up her principles because of her. 'But he's so self-righteous!' The words burst from her. 'And all that talk about the bank and the perks! He's trying to sell her the idea of a cosy nest for two thanks to the Westminster Bank. That's not Van at all!'

'You're never satisfied, are you?'

She looked at him, surprised at the change in his tone. And, as well, he looked different. Shifty. He was forty-nine, a dangerous age, they said, perhaps a desperate age for a man. Soon he would be fifty. That was supposed to be traumatic, the time when if they had any plans to make a change, they'd better do it now or it would be too late . . .

And he was so charming, her Ritchie, if he still was hers. His hair remained rich in its Botticelli curls which were only subdued for a day or so after cutting, his smile had become more consciously charming as if he had been told often that it was. He was at the peak of his powers as a painter, as a man. This last year would be a significant one for him. You couldn't be a Casanova after fifty, could you, or was it once a lady-killer always a lady-killer?

'Is that what you think of me?' She tried to be calm.

'In a way. It shows in your work, of course, the skill, the attention to detail. Not for you the big bold strokes which sometimes hit the jackpot sometimes not. But it makes you nitpicking as well. Leave the situation as it is. William has superseded Gordon for the time being, healed the hurt he left. He was a bumptious lad at best. You know you always thought that.'

'I suppose I did. And yet, I am critical. I suppose designing makes you that way. Nitpicking, you said. But,' she would stop analysing, 'there's a mystery there . . .'

'A mystery like me?' He joked, smiling his consciously charming smile.

'Like you. You're a mystery with your frequent jaunts to Barcelona.' She smiled too, joking, then shrugged. 'Oh, I don't know why I'm cribbing. If they get married and live in their low-mortgage house I think we should sell up here altogether and find a bigger place in Barcelona. With a pool. I fancy myself in a pool. Yes, that's what we'll do. A pool like Manuel Folguera's.' But it was Maria Roig she was thinking of, her fair hair pinned up, the tendrils on her cheeks . . .

'I shouldn't count your chickens before they're hatched.' The words stunned her, and were immediately followed by a swift, sickening stab of jealousy, like a knife in her heart. It *had* been Maria Roig on the telephone. It was because of her he went so often to Barcelona, not because of his work. She was part of his work. How convenient. Now that she came to think of it, there was always an aura about him when he came back, like that Christmas-time in Barcelona when he had come home with his hair damp-looking as if from a quick shower. But it would have ample time to dry coming home to England . . .

'Do you mean,' she steadied her voice, 'that you don't want me to go with you?'

He pulled her to him, his smile true now. 'You're a touchy old thing. I just meant, as you very well know, that with *Van* you can't count your chickens. You've said so often enough yourself.'

'Oh,' she said, and held up her face to be kissed. He did. But he didn't suggest nipping upstairs and having her.

Fifteen

1962

In July of that year Gordon James Pettigrew, RIBA, was to be married in Glasgow Cathedral to Wendy Grace Armour of Bellhaven Terrace, Great Western Road and The Moorings, Helensburgh. As Ritchie said, the imperious wording of the wedding invitation brooked no refusal. Van was to be one of the bridesmaids and Mish was coming home to be an usher.

Ritchie was looking tired and strained. He had spent a large part of the previous year in Barcelona, and Anna had accompanied him infrequently. He said to her when they were preparing to go to Glasgow, 'I want you to promise to come back with me this time to Barcelona. It's important.'

'Why this time?' she asked. 'There isn't much point in being there while you spend all day in that echoing warehouse in a back street.' Or with Maria – but that she didn't say, because by leaving it unsaid, it might not be true. It was better to get on with her own work at home since nothing had materialized for her in Barcelona. In her darker moments she wondered if Maria could be blamed for that.

'I told you before,' Ritchie said, 'it's important to me.' He was pale, his mouth grim. 'You've no excuse.

Van will be in Cornwall with the Armstrongs.' These were Ron and Agnes, William's parents, who loved walking, and set off with knapsacks on their backs and plastic macs rolled up on top of that. William and Van were to join them.

'I'll see.' And looking at his tired face: 'Aren't you finding it all too much for you, this constant travelling? It might have been better if you had settled for work in London.'

'It's shown there. You know that. And New York. But the source is Barcelona, and the influence, and I'm being financed from there.'

And Maria is there . . .

'But to dash back when Mish is coming home . . . He'll want to talk to you about your work.'

'I'll see him in Glasgow.'

'But he has a few days more. He'll want to be home. Home's with us, *here*.'

'He's the last person to be sentimental about home. He's a worker like me. He knows I have always put it first. And there are deadlines. He'll know all about that, working in a gallery.'

'I'll think about it. I know it's not important but I have deadlines too.' And, in case he thought she was envious of his success, she lightened the conversation. 'We shan't have any worries about Van and William being thrown together too much. Ron and Agnes will tire them out on those tremendous hikes they go in for. When I think what we were like!'

She imagined his face became tender. 'At the Art School?' And sad, as if their love was over.

'And when we were married and living in Clerkenwell.' But there, there had been Christine Bouvier, although it seemed nothing compared with her

155

anxiety about Maria Roig. 'I wonder what happened to us?'

'We grew older.' He felt her sadness, surely. 'Maybe we could recapture it, Anna. Children separate you rather than bring you together. Come to Barcelona with me, *please*.' He never pleaded as a rule. 'Will you? When the wedding's over?'

'But you'll spend a day or so at home with Mish?'

'Oh, sure, sure . . .' He took her in his arms. 'I need to know . . .' He kissed her roughly, bruising her lip. A fine sight she would be at the wedding.

The day before they were due to leave for Scotland a letter came for Ritchie with a Barcelona stamp on it. She left it on his desk and he did not comment on it. Neither did she.

She clung to her common sense. Don't let your imagination run away with you. Maria is involved in his work. She could be writing (for she was sure the letter had come from her) to discuss some point in the latest mural. Or issuing an ultimatum? And was that why it was important that *she* should accompany Ritchie next time? Her head ached, as well as her heart.

She thought of telephoning Jean, but decided to wait until the wedding. Jean was having her own troubles. The special school where Roderick went had finally told them that he had no aptitude for joinery, or indeed any skills, and they had come to the end of the road with him. John was trying to get him some kind of job. One grateful patient who had a garage had offered to take Roderick on at the pumps.

'He'd probably drench the customers with petrol,' Jean wrote. 'But he's a big boy now, and I don't want him running about the town and getting into mischief.'

They stayed with Rose so that she could accompany them to the wedding. Rose had surprised Nancy by saying that Bessie must be invited too. As she said to Anna, 'She's been with us since I was a girl in my mother's home here, and we don't know how long she'll last. I regret now I didn't invite her to any of the others.'

'Better late than never, Mother,' she said. 'I'm as bad. We used to be pretty high-handed with her, us girls.'

'You probably copied it from me. I've had time to think of things recently, and wonder if we kept her from marrying. There's not the same division nowadays between maids and mistresses. You pointed that out to me.' And without pausing: 'What's wrong with Ritchie? He's not himself.'

'He's overworking.' And mostly from habit said lightly, 'It's the price of fame.'

'I've always thought architects were safer, never mind the fame.'

Anna said to him in bed that night, 'Mother thinks you don't look well.'

'Does she? I told you. I'm worried . . .' he seemed to hesitate, 'about my work.'

'I saw you had a letter, from Spain.' She waited for what seemed a long time, until it was too long to say anything more, then turned from him, sick with apprehension.

They took the children to dinner that night in the Malmaison when they had collected Mish at Renfrew Airport. He looked well and happy, and declared he hadn't any jet lag.

Van greeted him affectionately. 'We miss you at home,' she said.

'But you have William now. I expect he's buzzing around all the time.'

'No, just Wednesdays and Saturdays. He's studying for exams.'

'He's a dedicated young man,' Anna said. 'Earnest.'

'You can say that again.' Ritchie agreed with her.

It struck Anna that there was a singular lack of enthusiasm in the Laidlaw family about William, as if they knew somehow that he would fade away eventually.

Ritchie looked more relaxed as he led them into the restaurant. 'I wouldn't have come here when I was your age, Mish, even if I'd had the cash. I thought it was only for toffs. It has quite an atmosphere, eh?'

'I guess so,' Mish agreed politely, but Van was worried when they had been shown their table and were discussing the menu.

'You could feed a poor family for a week on the price of the dinner here.'

'I hope your social conscience isn't going to prevent you from eating,' Ritchie said.

'I'll try not to.' She didn't seem convinced.

'I dine out a lot with clients in New York,' Mish said, 'but I don't let it worry me.'

'New York has always intrigued me.' Anna smiled at Mish, this assured son of theirs. 'Is it as full of vitality as they say? And what about that wonderful Frank Lloyd Wright gallery?'

'The Guggenheim? It's fabulous. Why don't you come back with me, Mum? I could show you the sights. You'd love it.'

'I have to be back in Barcelona by the end of the week, Mish,' Ritchie warned. 'Mother will be coming with me.'

'Oh, tough luck.' He looked at Anna. 'Still, your work comes first.'

'I haven't *said* I'll go.'

Mish looked uncomfortable. 'You buying me into the gallery has given me a lot of clout, Dad.' He changed the subject.

'Good. Money talks in New York.'

'I'm in the dark here.' Anna addressed Ritchie. 'You didn't tell me.' She was annoyed.

'He wanted you to think Mish became a partner on his merit,' Van said. 'I'll have chicken Kiev after all. And a salade Niçoise. There's a Waldorf one, Mish.'

'You seem to know more about it than I do.' Anna spoke loftily because she was annoyed. 'Thank you for putting me in the picture. Seemingly I'm the last one to know what goes on in our family.'

'She's peeved.' What had got into Van? 'Honestly, Mish, she wants everything to be perfect. I thought she would have been pleased about William. Now she makes jokes about his parents because they go hiking in shorts.' Anna winced. It was true she had sung 'Keep Right on to the End of the Road', when Van had shown her some holiday snaps.

'It was a good impersonation of Harry Lauder,' she said now, prepared to treat the matter lightly since it was a family party, but suddenly her anger boiled over. 'Who is this person you're criticizing anyhow? Out on a limb, questionable motives . . .'

'Don't mind Van, Mum.' Mish, the peacemaker.

'Who's minding?' But she did. And Ritchie hadn't come to her defence. She lifted the menu. 'I'm going to have lobster. Why come to the Malmaison if you don't have lobster thermidor?'

She put on her funny hat after that, making them laugh with her thick Glasgow accent when she asked for 'Black coffee with lick*oors*', but she was deeply hurt, and all the time the thought of the letter with the Spanish postmark was like a burning spot of resentment inside her.

'You were back to your old form, Anna,' Ritchie said to her later in their bedroom.

'That was my "Laugh Clown Laugh" act.'

'I'm sorry, I should have told you about Mish.' She looked at him, waiting. 'I suppose Van was right, in a way. I want you to feel really proud of our children, as I do, and I thought you might object to me giving Mish a leg up. It was stupid of me.'

'Don't apologize.' She turned away. 'I'm getting used to being pushed out in the cold.'

They both undressed, miserably, silently, and as silently, made sudden love when they were in bed. The trees in the crescent made a swishing noise, and long ago she would have been glad of it to cover their own, but there was no talking themselves through it this time, just a swift efficient climax. There had never been any doubt about Ritchie's virility, nor his ability to fire her with his touch.

She wanted to say, 'I love you, Ritchie, always will. I understand about Mish, but why is Maria Roig writing to you? And why is it so important that I go back with you this time when it didn't matter before?' She wanted him to *beg* her, but he didn't. Here in this large front bedroom she had an ominous feeling, one of dread. This man lying beside her pretending to sleep, as she was, she knew was wrestling with himself, trying to come to some kind of decision. If it was dependent on her agreeing to go back with him, she didn't want to be party to that.

She waited, feeling the very air in the room weighing on her, heavy with foreboding. If he would gather her to him again, not with lust this time but with tenderness, even with tears . . .

She slept at last when the large windows contained the greyness of an early dawn.

The wedding seemed to be a replica of Nancy's own, twenty-five years ago in Wellington Church. She had been a fairy-tale bride; Wendy Armour coming down the aisle on her father's arm was majestic, a young Amazon, her gold hair gleaming behind the veil, the wedding dress shimmering with gold thread, behind her the shining train like the *Night Scot* sliding into Central Station. Anna hadn't thought she was so buxom. She would make a splendid matron.

Gordon was a younger James, well set-up, a tailor's dream in dove grey, his gleaming cravat, his gleaming smile. You could scarcely believe in them, she thought, they were so perfect, so unreal. So surreal, not suited for the trials and tribulations of ordinary married life.

What would Gordon be like in bed, she wondered. Would they go at each other like young animals as she and Ritchie had done, or would he have to woo his Wendy? James was the kind of father who would admonish his son 'to be gentle the first time with her'.

Anna looked at Van walking behind the train, one of four bridesmaids in her apricot-coloured dress with its bouffant skirt and matching bouffant hair. She had persuaded her to leave off her spectacles, and she was peering ahead like an owl.

'What's she frightened of?' Ritchie whispered.

'She can't see very well, I think.'

'Who on earth got her to leave her glasses off? She's as blind as a bat.'

'Me.' He turned and looked at her coldly.

Jean and John had brought Roderick to the wedding, dressed in a neat blue suit and grey tie. They both looked calm and smiling, with Roderick trotting amicably beside them, mouth partly open as usual, his bullet head revolving as he waved to anyone who looked his way.

Rose was critical. 'I'm surprised at John agreeing to bring that boy. I always thought he was the sensible one.'

'He's their son, Mother. Now, don't go around making apologies for him to any of the guests. That's the last thing Jean would want.'

'Well, she should have left him at home then.' Roderick chose this moment to come bouncing up beside them.

'Hello, Granny Rose! I saw you in church, not looking.' He gave her a smacking kiss which Rose endured, setting her hat to rights afterwards.

'Now, remember, Roderick,' she said, 'be a little gentleman for today. It's a wedding you're at, not a rugby match.'

'A rugby . . . ? Oh, that's a good one, a wedding you're at, not a rugby match!' He bent double with laughter. 'Isn't it, Aunty? A wedding you're –'

'All right, Roderick,' she said, 'we got it the first time.'

'I've never been to a wedding before.' He was suddenly serious. 'Why does everyone dress up for a wedding? Dad paid a lot of money for my suit in Dumfries. His own tailor. The man said I had a good body for my age. Maybe *I* should get married.'

'They dress up,' Rose chose to ignore this last remark, 'because they're here to celebrate

Gordon and Wendy being joined together in holy matrimony.'

'Holy matrimony?' His little eyes screwed up.

'Being married,' Anna said.

'But who joined them, Aunt Anna?'

'The minister, of course.'

'Did he? But it doesn't show.'

'What doesn't show?' Rose was losing patience.

'The join.' She tut-tutted, rolling her eyes at Anna, who kept a straight face.

'He joins them with words, Roderick,' she said.

His face brightened. 'With words? Oh, I get it! When he said, "To have and to hold"? Was that when?'

'Right. Clever boy.'

'Mmmh.' He nodded, looking wise, his head swivelled towards Gordon and Wendy who were standing together receiving the guests' congratulations. 'Look at them!' Gordon's arm was round Wendy's waist. 'He's holding her already. The minister will be pleased, won't he?'

'He'll be delighted,' Anna said. And the join doesn't show . . . She and Jean would have a laugh together later. She looked again at the happy pair, Gordon's arm securely round Wendy's ample waist. *She* won't fly very far, she thought, unlike her namesake.

Jean had joined them, exotic in a yellow dress and large-brimmed black hat. Dangling jet earrings gleamed against her creamy skin. She outshone everyone as usual. 'Is he a nuisance, Mother?' She put an arm round Roderick's shoulders, fondly.

'You're doing it too,' he said, giggling, 'like the happy couple. The minister told them to have and to hold.'

163

Rose sighed. 'You would have had more peace of mind, Jean, if you had come with John on your own.'

Jean raised her chin. Her eyes had darkened. 'Roderick had an invitation, Mother.'

'I had my own invitation, Granny Rose,' Roderick said, not at all discomfited.

Nancy always comes up trumps, Anna thought, remembering how she had offered to take in Jean with Frederick's baby when it should arrive.

'There's old Bessie!' Roderick ambled off, the perfect wedding guest, prepared to circulate. Bessie was sitting listening to an elderly lady who might be an indigent relative of the Armours, judging by her dusty black dress. No doubt Mother had personally selected her for Bessie.

'I must have a word with Mrs Armour . . .' Rose looked vague and drifted away.

'You look thinner, Anna,' Jean said.

'Not like the blushing bride. Quite an armful.'

'I see her opening fêtes.'

'Going to Brodick in August.'

'Becoming a governor of our old school.'

'And head of the RSPCA.' Anna looked across the room. 'Roderick's having a grand time.' He was standing beside Gordon, gazing up at him admiringly. Gordon was totally ignoring him.

'I had to bring him, Anna. He's our son, not to be hidden away.'

'You were quite right. But you and John always do the right thing.'

'He's my mentor. But you have no cause for complaints, have you?'

'That's what I thought . . .'

'Here we go again. You're making bricks without

straw as usual. Look, if Mish is staying on in Glasgow, why not come back with us?'

'No, thanks all the same. We're going straight home. Ritchie goes back to Barcelona at the end of the week.'

'Go with him.'

'I don't know . . . things have come up.'

'I couldn't sleep last night. Tossed about. I thought, Anna's worried. Are you?'

'Yes. I have been for a long time.'

'What's keeping you from going back with him?'

'Fear . . . that my fears will be confirmed.'

'You die a thousand deaths. You've always known he's attractive to women. You should be used to it by this time.'

'If it were women in plural I *wouldn't* worry.'

'Jealousy's always been the very devil with you. Why don't you come clean? Ask him if –'

'Hello, girls!' It was James, still handsome, lean, grey-haired, a thinner and older Gordon, but with the same height. He was followed by a waiter with a tray loaded with glasses of champagne. 'Just in time to top you up.'

'Thanks, James,' Anna said, thinking it might be a good idea to get roaring drunk. 'Great champagne!' Well, he could afford to be generous when the bill was being picked up by Wendy's father.

'They make a lovely couple,' Jean said. 'They *are* a lovely couple.'

'Well-matched.'

'A credit to you, James.'

'A day to remember, James.' They mustn't joke with James. He had little sense of humour.

'And to Nancy,' he said.

'Yes, if you don't give her the credit she'll claim it.'

'We're all products of Nancy.' He smiled at them happily. 'Well, must circulate.'

'Nancy's orders,' Jean said, laughing.

'The secret is to give in.' He laughed with them. 'It makes for a happy life.'

'I expect you're off on another cruise to recuperate after this?'

'Yes, how did you guess? The Aegean this time.'

'That's one we forgot for Wendy,' Jean said when they were alone. 'Sitting at the captain's table on a luxury cruise.'

'On his *right* hand. Nancy will soon sell them that idea. She's a picture, though, isn't she?' She had caught sight of her sister coming towards them, flushed in fuchsia pink.

'Wasn't it absolutely beautiful?' She twinkled towards them on her high heels. 'I could have cried in church but I might have spoiled my makeup.'

'We're all painted ladies nowadays,' Anna said. She had noticed the perfect rose of Nancy's cheeks, the blue eyeshadow, the mascara. 'Gilding the lily.'

'We take it from Rose. She had to live up to her name. I sometimes wondered if she wore her makeup in bed with Father?'

'I shouldn't be surprised. But she's pretty marvellous. I've never seen her with a hair out of place.'

'Nor an emotion,' Jean said. 'Difficult to live with, though. God, I set the cat amongst the pigeons once, didn't I?'

'Well, you're being paid back with that boy too.'

'Do you mean Roderick, Nancy?'

'Yes. Oh, I shouldn't have said that. I know what a sorrow it is to you.'

'Only if I choose to make it so. He was overjoyed with your special invitation to him. You're good.'

'Well, he's family.' Her pert little face softened. 'Isn't it lovely the three of us together like this? The Glasgow Girls. Wasn't it some old tutor at the Art School who said that?'

'It was Frederick Kleiber, Nancy.' Anna looked at her. 'Trust you to be the soul of tact.'

'Oh well, that's the good thing about families. You can insult each other one minute and the next you're the best of friends just because you're family. But we mustn't look back. This is one of the happiest days of my life.' She sighed dramatically. 'I know *I've* been lucky. Now I must move round the room. I've promised myself that everyone will go away feeling that they haven't been ignored.' She smiled at them from under her navy straw halo. 'You look smashing, twins. You're different from the run-of-the-mill. I could never achieve that look, even although I buy everything in Daly's.'

'Maybe that's why,' Anna said. 'You're a Daly Dipper.'

'Or a Daly Dish,' Jean said.

'Oh, you two!' She looked at them. 'So different and so alike. As if you *thought* together.'

'We've only got one brain between us.' Anna was straight-faced.

'You were always cheeky.' Nancy cast an admiring glance at Anna. 'You look really elegant. Pencil-slim. And that husband of yours! The bridesmaids are swooning over him! I really must go, girls. Chin-chin.' She tripped away.

'Are you waiting for the family dinner?' Anna asked Jean.

'No, I think it would be too exciting for Roderick. He gets carried away. Contrary to what Nancy thinks, I don't want him to make a fool of himself at the

167

table.' Her eyes grew dark suddenly, and then she was smiling. 'Give me a ring when you want to talk.'

'I will. It's just . . . I don't know what's going to happen.'

'It may never. You get off to Barcelona with that Don Juan of yours.'

They hugged each other briefly. Anna recognized Jean's smell, dusky, exotic, sweet. She always spent a lot on perfume, like a Frenchwoman.

'Come and stay when you can,' Jean said.

She nodded, not speaking, then turned away. There was an immediate sense of loss as she walked across the room.

Sixteen

❧

On the way home they called in to see Ritchie's parents. He genuinely regretted he didn't see more of them. He was particularly fond of his father, probably a love mixed with pity. Walter Laidlaw was one of the victims of modern society. He had never had the drive necessary to succeed, and now that he was in his sixties he was content to sit by the fire or do the shopping and odd chores for his wife while she was out at work.

She still helped out in the corner shop although she had given up washing closes which she had done while Ritchie was at the Art School, to augment their income. Secretly Anna had been horrified. She associated that occupation with the bedraggled women wearing aprons made of sackcloth whom she saw when in the poorer Glasgow streets. At Clevedon Crescent they always had a woman to 'do the rough', as Rose put it, apart from Bessie.

Anna suspected her mother-in-law continued to work because of the variety it brought to her life. Ritchie was generous to them, paying their rent and giving them frequent gifts of money, and Anna invited them to Renton each year for a holiday. She had suggested that they come to Barcelona sometime,

169

but Walter had smiled in a frightened way and said that was not in their line.

'Your mother married the wrong man,' she once said to Ritchie.

'No.' He had shaken his head. 'For every Jock there's a Jenny. He needs her, and Mother needs to be needed. She's come to terms with what might have been in her own life long ago. It's enough for her to see me successful.'

True to type, Van loved her grandfather for his very weaknesses. She liked to watch him working on his models, and on this visit she was sitting beside him at the table in the front room while he fiddled delicately with pliers on his latest model ship which was to be inserted in a bottle. The moment when it was in place and he pulled the threads which raised the masts and sails had always been a source of delight to her.

'Isn't Grandad clever?' she said now.

'Aye, it's a skill.' Lizzie Laidlaw never took the opportunity to denigrate her husband. 'You'll stay for tea, Anna?'

'Just a cup, thanks. We'll stop on the way home and have supper somewhere.' She got up. 'I'll come and help you.' Ritchie and Mish were discussing New York.

'You always wanted me to stay for my tea when Ritchie and I were courting,' she said in the kitchen. And, looking at the loaded table: 'My goodness, what a spread! You put the City Bakeries to shame.' She laughed. 'I hadn't the nerve to tell you we didn't have high tea at home. We had dinner at night.'

'I knew. I respected your tact. You were even ashamed about your maid, Bessie. I've met her. She's a fine woman.'

'I blush now to think of it. Inverted snobbery.'

'You were always a sensitive girl, still are.' She looked at her while she filled the kettle at the kitchen tap. 'Are you losing weight to be in the fashion or is there something bothering you?'

Anna laughed. 'Someone once said I made a good clotheshorse. Perhaps I'm trying to live up to that.'

'You and Ritchie are happy?' She was sharp.

'As happy as most married couples are, I suppose.'

'True enough. But you have to give and take, not try to make them over. Once I accepted that Walter was never going to set the Clyde on fire it was fine. Oh, I know you don't see much in him, not like Vanessa, but he's got a sweetness in his character that I fell in love with. You're a one-man woman, like me, I think. And I've never had any bother in *that* quarter.' She set the kettle on the stove, lit the burner with a lighter tied to a string at the side, 'Have you?' She looked directly at Anna.

'You have an attractive son, Mum.' She looked away.

'I know that. And I know that bit of arrogance in him as well. He's always been sure of himself, Ritchie. I think his father was amazed at him courting you. He wouldn't have had the nerve.'

'Ah, but Ritchie always gave me the idea that *I* was the lucky one.' She laughed.

'He's special, very special, but inclined to see everything from his own point of view.'

'That's Ritchie.' She would never have talked to her own mother like this – she knew instinctively there would be no help there – but at this moment she would have liked to say to Ritchie's mother, 'I'm so unhappy. I'm afraid I'm losing him . . .' But she couldn't do that. Lizzie Laidlaw's happiness was wrapped up in her son's.

'Do you see much difference in Van and Mish?' she asked.

'Vanessa has changed. A girl who is loved by someone should show something in her eyes. You did in yours. But it isn't there. What is her man like?'

'Like someone who works in a bank. I don't believe in it. I think she's going out with him in an effort to conform.'

Lizzie Laidlaw's eyes rested on her speculatively for a second. 'Anyhow, she's a grand lass. I like to see her with Walter.'

'She loves her Grandad. She had a friend called Adelaide. She misses her. She went back to London. I think she was grateful when William singled her out.'

'Maybe she's trying to please *you*.'

Ritchie had said that. Was it *she* who was immature, who was still carrying about some of Rose's prejudices? But she had only wanted the best for Van. Wasn't that what every mother said, what Rose had thought when she saw *her* in love with a penniless working-class student? *You* defied your mother, she thought.

'What do you think of Mish?' She changed the subject.

'Oh, you'll never have to worry about him. He's like me, like Ritchie, single-minded and a worker, but without his contrariness.' Anna laughed.

'You have us all taped.'

'Except for Walter, you are the four people I most care about in the world. All I want is to know you're happy.' She had been busy all the time she was talking, going from cupboard to the stove, filling the teapot, then placing it on the table covered by its knitted woollen tea-cosy. She stood back, a trim small figure in her print shirtwaister, 'Well, that's it. Will you tell them we're ready? And ask Ritchie and Hamish to bring their own chairs. We haven't enough here.'

They weren't back in Renton until well after midnight. It had been a long and tedious journey, and latterly they had given up talking. Van and Mish had chatted desultorily in the back. It gave Anna a chance to think. Ritchie was evidently doing the same. When she stole a glance at him, his profile was stern.

Who was he thinking of? Was it Maria Roig? Had the letter said he must make up his mind finally between the two of them? And had he decided that if Anna didn't go back with him he would make that the arbiter? Was he tired of her, and was he finding Maria more relaxing, less short-tempered? He should have remembered that she hadn't been well for the past year or two, as if she had reached a difficult time in her life. 'It's her time,' women would say of each other in Glasgow, as an excuse. When she was working at her bench she seemed to hammer any anxiety out of her system, but in the empty house, with Van out most evenings and Ritchie away so much, her spirits sank. She was fatigued without having an explanation for it.

He had said of his mother that she needed to be needed. Wasn't it the same with her? But shouldn't she be, at forty-nine, a completely independent person? Tonight, she decided, however late it was when they got home, she would have a talk with him and ask him to be frank.

Van and Mish disappeared quite quickly to their rooms. Mish was delighted to be home again, and she could hear them laughing as they went upstairs together. Van had always adored her brother. Her voice floated down: 'Wait till you see your room. Mother's done it over.'

'Aren't you going too?' Ritchie asked. 'You must be tired.'

'No, I'm wide awake. Could you please sit down? I want to talk to you.' Her heart had started to beat rapidly.

'You've had nine hours.' He sat down obediently. His face was white and strained.

'The children were there. Ritchie, you must tell me truthfully. Are you seeing a lot of Maria Roig?'

She saw him take a breath, perhaps of relief. 'A fair amount. I work with her.'

'I'm jealous.' She steadied her voice. 'Ridiculous, isn't it? I don't mean ridiculous *now*. I've always been jealous. I should be able to take it. There was Christine Bouvier, but I felt sorry for her. And others who admired you. I've known. But this is different. I'm uneasy. You make me uneasy because I feel *your* uneasiness. What I want to know,' this damned voice of hers, shaking when she wanted it to be steady, 'is, am I right to feel that, or is it my jealousy? I think of you as mine . . .'

He jumped up as if he couldn't bear this, talking as he walked. 'That's just the trouble. You *are* jealous, bloody jealous. That's why I didn't want to upset you. But you suspect me, you don't give me enough room,' he wheeled round, 'just as you've always done with Van.'

'Leave Van out of it!' she suddenly shouted, then lowered her voice. They might hear . . . 'I've probably made some mistakes with Van, but I could have done with some help. Rose's influence may have been too strong in me, but leave that. Tell me, is this to do with Maria Roig?' He stopped walking at the window and stared into the dark garden. She saw the back of his dark curly head which she had so often cradled on her breast, *her* head. 'You don't even have to answer. I can feel it. Jean and I are intuitive. Why is this woman interfering in our marriage?'

'She isn't consciously.'

'Why does she write to you? And why is it so important that I come back with you this time? Is there an ultimatum? That you have to choose? Her or me?' He didn't reply. 'Will you look at me, for God's sake!'

He turned towards her. He looked like a small boy, he looked like a man who hadn't caught up with his age. He hesitated, then came and sat down opposite her. The curls were thick and damp on his brow. He must be sweating.

'I love you, Anna, deep down you're my girl, always will be. We go back too far. But . . . the girl I knew seems to have disappeared . . .'

'It's you who does the disappearing!' To Maria Roig.

'That tongue of yours. You're so critical, so edgy, so irritable. Maria says –'

'What does Maria say?' She kept her voice level.

'She suggested that if you came back with me it would give us more time together, to talk. She promised to keep out of the way.'

Her heart would burst, break through her ribs . . . 'How generous of Maria! How incredibly bloody generous!' She put her hands up on either side of her face. She wasn't hearing this . . .

'And,' he was determined to go on, 'we might find each other again.'

'Well, well! And so you were taking her advice, giving me my last chance, so to speak?'

'It seemed sensible. She'd been through it too, her husband –'

'Oh yes, I remember. Poor thing . . .'

'Cut it out. She knows how worried I've been about you. I've grown to respect her opinion. I'm fond of her.'

'Fond!' Now her heart *had* broken through her ribs. She got up because of the pain. 'Fond! I'm *fond* of that picture over there of yours! Not your best, if you don't mind my saying – that's one good thing about me, I'm critical – but "fond" hardly seems to be the word to describe your feelings, does it, when you seem to confide in her about us so much?' The sight of his anguished face made her walk about the room in case she would cradle his head against her. She stopped, as he had, at the window. Nothing had changed outside. Inside was different. She turned and faced him, felt the cold glass on her back.

'You've changed, you know, Ritchie, since you went to Barcelona. Does that mean Maria is more important to you than I am?'

'That's not it. It all happened because I was missing you –'

'Don't give me that clap-trap. You're nearly fifty. Why couldn't you wait until you got home? It's not *that* important, is it? Sex?'

He looked at her, seemed to breathe deeply. 'I'll give it to you straight. You've become moody and difficult to live with. You had opportunities to come to Barcelona with me which you didn't take. I know work didn't materialize for you there as you'd hoped, but we could have been together.'

'But my work is here, don't you see? And Van.'

'Okay. I give you that. But don't resent mine being *there*.'

'It's not the work I resent.'

'But don't you see, the other thing, Maria, is because you've changed? The Anna I knew has disappeared. We used to have such fun together.'

'So instead of trying to understand, you have fun with Maria Roig instead? I admit I've changed, but it's a chicken and egg situation. It's something to do with my age, my emotional equilibrium, if you like. Maybe I haven't been mature enough. I blame my background for that – Rose – but I should have been able to deal with that if you had been more sympathetic.' His detachment from her situation made the anger spurt suddenly through her veins. 'Have you slept with her?'

'Yes.'

There was no shock. Yet. The anger clouded everything, was in her eyes, choking her throat. 'How convenient. So you sleep with her every time you go to Barcelona?'

'No, no, no!' Now he shouted. 'Only since you lost your interest in coming with me. I made excuses at first. You weren't well. I even went to your doctor but he assured me there was nothing to worry about. "Perhaps a bit intense," he said. "The empty nest syndrome."'

'Poor wee birdie, toll, loll, loll . . . Remember that? What will these clever men think of next? When will you learn that it's not the end of the road for us, especially for someone like me with a little talent – nothing like yours, of course. It would have been all right if I'd come to Barcelona, cooked and waited on you, left Van . . . You know you're admired in London, the galleries would fall over themselves to get you, so why Barcelona? Or do I know the answer to that?' I'm burning my bridges she thought, but she had to go on. 'And since Van has been mentioned, I've a feeling that if you'd been more in evidence, a male figure whom she adores, she wouldn't have given William Armstrong a second look, she would have found someone more interesting, more original . . .'

'This is it, don't you see?' He ran his fingers through his curls, making them stand from his head in an aureole. 'You look like an angel like that,' she wanted to say. 'It's always what *you* want. If you'd stopped to think you know that Barcelona has had an appeal for me ever since I fought there. *That* was my real war. The place grabbed me even then in all its misery, it was like Glasgow, alive, vibrant, but with the added attraction of strangeness. I *liked* the Spaniards, they were my brothers – remember, I've never had any – I liked their outlook, I had a strong rapport with them. In those mountains and caves, there was this brotherliness . . . Van too must get mad at your attitude to her. You don't give her space. You don't approve of her friends because they wouldn't come up to Mrs Rose's expectations. Now that she's swung to the opposite extreme you don't like that either. It's got to be *your* choice, *your* way. You're not at peace with yourself. That's the trouble.'

Her heart died within her because she knew it was true. But he hadn't tried to understand. He had all the selfishness of the artist. Gerald Masters, instead of talking that empty guff to him about the 'empty nest syndrome' should have explained to him about hormonal changes in women, should have advised him to be more patient, more understanding.

I need space, she suddenly thought. I need to get

away from this situation, and that doesn't mean following him to Barcelona in case I lose him. 'I've made up my mind,' she said. 'I'm going back to New York with Mish.'

He took her hands, coming across the room to her in a few swift steps. She felt herself trembling, bit her lip. It was the old Ritchie, the beautiful painter's eyes were on her, pleading. 'You're not serious.'

'I am.'

'You mean you don't care?'

'Don't care about what?'

'Whether I go or not, even though you know I wanted you to come with me, make a fresh start?'

'What's wrong with here for a fresh start?'

'My work is *there*. I have commitments. There are deadlines for some of the murals. And we live on what we earn.'

She took her hands away because they were still trembling in his. 'I will *not* have you dangling a sword over my head. Look, Ritchie, all I want to know is, if I don't go back with you, are you leaving me for Maria Roig?'

He didn't answer. He looked away. He knows in his heart that this is a contrived situation, she thought. He has a commitment to Maria Roig as well as his murals. It's *her* ultimatum. She said, no longer trembling, 'I used to think that if you told me you had been with another woman I'd die. Well, I haven't, and I won't. Are you going back to her?'

'I'm going back to my work. It's the most important thing in my life, except you. It's important to Maria. She's involved in my work, part of it.'

She felt relief, strangely enough. The anguish would come later. She smiled at him. 'Your mother told me today that you'd always been a bit arrogant.'

His glance was that of a small boy, caught out. 'She's astute. Well, I hope you can live with your decision. I can't. Not at the moment. You've chosen Maria, not me, in spite of what you say. You and I, we had one of the best marriages going. I love you . . . like anything. I thought you needed that, needed me.' He came towards her. 'No, don't touch me. That's fatal. It's not so bad, now that it's happened. It was the suspicion, my self-confidence going, the canker eating into me.'

'Hey, Anna, what's happening? This isn't us.' The tears were running down his face.

'And don't weep for us.' She was a figure of stone. 'You should have done that earlier. Do you remember when we were young we used to weep together? But that was from joy . . . I'm going to bed. You can sleep in the spare room. Keep your libido for Maria Roig.'

'What a bugger's muddle!' He looked comical, his hair awry, the tears. 'I don't even know how all this happened. You look miles better than Maria does, your bones are better for one thing.' That made her laugh. The famous painter . . .

'Well, I hope you enjoy your choice.' She wasn't weeping. She went slowly upstairs, holding herself together.

She examined her face in the bedroom mirror, the china-thin skin, the black straight hair which cost a lot to be shaped each month, the scarlet mouth – rather old-fashioned perhaps, a *femme fatale* who'd had plenty of men look twice at her, taken in by her looks. How lofty she had been, secure in this great passion between Ritchie and herself. She snorted as she put cream on her hands. It was better than weeping.

He preferred Maria Roig, the child woman, small

180

but perfectly formed, no doubt (but not having such good bones), with a charming voice because she didn't speak English very well, brown eyes, especially charming because of the contrast between her obvious seductive femininity and her childlike appearance. She would be honey-sweet, not waspish like herself, who was always trying to improve people, to make them over to her own pattern. No wonder Ritchie always said she was a good critic of his work. And wasn't it strange how everything became crystal clear when you were dropping with tiredness?

She would tell Mish in the morning that she was going back with him. She would be mature, accepting that she and Ritchie had come to an impasse in their lives, and tell both children that Ritchie had to be in Barcelona for some time. There was no point in burdening them with their parents' problems. The decision made her feel calmer, and then sad, very sad. Her heart felt as if it was being squeezed by a hard, strong fist. She loved him so much. There had never been anyone else.

Seventeen

'Yes, I'm expecting her,' Anna said to the American voice over the intercom. She was in Mish's apartment in Manhattan and trying to accustom herself to her new surroundings, the vastness of the room which appeared to float somewhere in the sky – 'air-dwellers,' Mish had said when she commented on the height – the vastness of the bathroom, the luxuriousness of the sofas, two of them, no less, the dizziness she had experienced when she first stood on the balcony.

And the foyer had impressed her when she had arrived, tired after the plane trip with Mish, the uniformed commissionaires, the expanse of gold carpet, the comings and goings at the desk. A young man with four dogs on a lead had stood aside politely when she passed. 'A dog walker,' Mish said. She had to work that one out for herself – a child minder was one thing . . .

Now she stood in the middle of the apartment (not flat), in East Sixty-third Street and smoothed her hair on either side of her face, turning the points on her cheek between finger and thumb, a habitual gesture. Karin didn't want to 'just barge in', he'd said. 'She'll be earlier than me. She thought it would be nicer if she rang the first time.'

'Very considerate.' She had been impressed. 'But since I know she's living here . . .'

'Yes, but she was sharing with friends in New Jersey when we met, and she's quite willing to go there while you're here.' Such delicate susceptibilities.

Since Ritchie had gone off to Spain she had found to be light and brittle prevented her from weeping. Van and Mish hadn't appeared to be too perturbed. If they knew something was wrong they had kept quiet. They were used to overhearing rows. When she had suddenly wept in the plane, Mish had put his hand over hers and said, 'He couldn't stay away from you for long, Mum,' and then, 'Would you like a drink?'

The door bell rang firmly but not imperiously. She ran to it, willing herself to be cool, calm and collected. The girl who stood on the doormat was all of this.

'Hi!' she said. 'I'm Karin.'

'I'm Anna.' They shook hands. 'Come in.' She followed Anna into the apartment as if she were here on a visit.

'Well,' she said, turning to her, laughing, spreading her hands, 'what do you think?'

'Very pretty.' Anna laughed too. It was going to be easy. 'But then Mish's taste is always good. Would you like coffee, or a drink? I don't know where . . .' And then laughing again with relief, 'Oh, I'm forgetting, you live here.'

'I could stay with the girls.'

'I wouldn't dream of it. I'm probably not here for long.'

'Well, I'll get the drinks. What would you like?'

'A gin and tonic, please.'

'*Okay*,' she said it in an American way, '*Okay*.' She

183

dispensed the drinks expertly at some kind of bureau, and brought the gin and tonic to Anna. She had poured orange juice for herself.

She was pretty without a doubt, jet-black hair, a deeper blackness than her own, brown lively eyes, a nose of character. Of course she was Jewish. What was it that told you, apart from the nose? The look of intelligence in the eyes, an awareness, of being capable, and at the back of it all a kind of emanation of extra wisdom which sat easily and naturally on her and which other people had to acquire so painfully?

'Did you have a good trip?' Karin asked.

'Fine. It's the first time I've flown the Atlantic.'

'But you travel a lot. Mish tells me you have a place in Barcelona, Spain?' The upward inflection.

'Yes, my husband is there just now. I'm not going meantime.' She hesitated. The girl's eyes were on her as if she were waiting.

'That's fair enough,' she said after the pause. 'You have your own work. Mish showed me some photographs of your clock faces. They're really cute.'

'I'm hoping I'll pick up some new ideas here, once I get about the streets and museums, get the feel of the place. I hoped to do that in Barcelona but . . . it didn't work out that way.'

'I see.' Again the almost imperceptible pause. 'I've tremendous admiration for you gifted people.'

Anna shrugged. 'What do you do, Karin?' It was so easy to talk to her, not like Van, who parted with each word as if it were a precious jewel.

'I'm a psychologist, attached to a hospital. Very mundane. I interview people all day, try to help them.' That explained the pauses. 'One of the New Jersey girls where I shared is into art and took me along to a party at Mish's gallery. That's how we met.

184

I recognized him immediately as being eminently sane.' She smiled.

'He's always been like that. Mish just said you worked in a hospital. I thought you might be a nurse.'

'No, I'm not *that* clever. But I'm patient. People can live with a front all their lives, but sometimes to get them to part with it is more cruel than kind. My father's a psychiatrist. That side of medicine attracts a lot of Jews. Maybe they understand suffering.' I could do with a psychiatrist, Anna thought, even this girl, just to let it all come out, how she missed Ritchie, how she reproached herself, and then reproached him . . .

'I think Mish is very lucky, finding you.'

'So everyone's happy, except my mum.' She laughed.

'Why?' She prevented herself from bristling.

'She doesn't want me to marry a goy. I tell her that's not the name of the game nowadays, but she would still like a nice Jewish boy for her daughter who'd gone through his bar mitzvah,' she smiled wickedly, 'and been circumcised.'

Anna smiled too, seeing Mish naked for a moment. The last time had been when he was a child in his bath.

'Something happens to women when they give birth. They lose their sense of proportion. Mish has never given me any problems, but I can't see eye to eye with my daughter at all.'

'Maybe you care for her too much. Or she demands something you can't give. That's o*kay*. I know it's that with my mom. ''My little daughter!'' ' She waved her hands, reminding Anna of Jewish women she'd seen, possibly in films. 'It's not necessary to see eye to eye, Mrs Laidlaw . . .'

'Anna.'

'I'll try it. Anna. It's a pretty name. You get on with your own life and let her get on with hers. People with a talent don't know how lucky they are . . .' There was the sound of a key in the lock, the door shutting. Mish came in.

'Hi, pussy cat,' Karin said. Anna rolled an inward eye.

He came over and kissed Karin, briefly, but lovingly enough, then turned to Anna. 'Hi, you! Busy day?' The loving look was still there. Not for her.

'Give your mother a kiss, honey,' Karin said. 'She'll feel left out.'

'We're not a kissing family.' Anna smiled. 'Only weddings and funerals. Or long partings.'

'That's you being Scottish. We think the Scots are really cute here. I'm dying to get myself a real kilt. Is there a Gottleib kilt?'

'I'll find out.' Anna laughed.

'Does your husband wear one?'

Mish was laughing with them. 'They've lived in England since they were married, Karin, so thank God he doesn't. And I escaped being dressed in a skirt.'

'But you'd look dandy in one! You have lovely knees!'

'I'm going to pour myself a drink.' It's his wee Scots bit, Anna thought. He's embarrassed.

He took them out for dinner to what he called 'a neighbourhood restaurant'. It was off Madison Avenue and Anna admired the politeness of the girl who served them. Who said the Americans were brash? Afterwards they walked along the East River Embankment as far as Mayor Gracie's house to let her see that you could do that at ten o'clock at night and still feel quite safe.

'And you're as safe as houses in Central Park during the day,' Karin said. 'You don't look like a victim.' She had a way of restoring one's morale. Anna was no longer the rejected wife of an eminent painter; she was an artist in her own right visiting her son in Upper East Side, who lived with a bright lovely girl who was a psychologist.

Perforce she spent a lot of time on her own. She sat on the balcony of the apartment and thought a lot, and drew designs for clock faces, influenced by occasional visits to the Guggenheim and the Metropolitan Museum. The various ethnic displays in the latter enchanted her. She sat for hours in front of them, wondering why modern painters thought they were modern when their work was as old as time.

Her ideas came from walking about the streets of New York and catching glimpses of people's faces, of being aware of speeding traffic, hearing the constant noise of overhead jets, and police sirens. She sat in the Rockefeller Plaza and Paley Park, a little space between two blocks of buildings where a waterfall ran down the gable of one of the blocks and gave an illusion of coolness. She browsed in the book shops and got ideas from reading the many art books scattered about Mish's apartment.

She went to the Whitney Museum and fell in love with Edward Hopper's paintings, his defamiliarization of familiar motifs, real and not real. The intensity was something you sometimes experienced as if one's vision had been heightened, one's perception. His nude figures were in recognizable poses, but the quality of Hopper's vision made them a step removed from reality.

She bought posters to take home, *Night Windows* because it reminded her of the windows of the apartment across the street where she watched the man and the woman and made up stories about them, and one special poster called *Lighthouse Hill* because one look at it, she knew, would remind her of the America beyond New York City, a land of immensity, light and shadow. She thought Van would like them.

She did a conducted tour of Harlem and had an impression of black faces and white smiles, of a rich-voiced choir in the church which they visited, of jazz played at street corners, and a sail round Manhattan which was like being in another street with as much traffic as on land, and a lone sailing boat reminded her of the fishermen at Kirkcudbright Harbour where Roderick had liked to go. 'How are you, Jean?' she said, over the thousand of miles between them. 'We've both come a long way . . .'

And in between this activity she became obsessed by the couple in the apartment opposite when she sat on the balcony. It was like a microcosm of life enacted at their window. Somehow they seemed to gravitate there as if it were centre stage and the director had marked it with chalk. She was sure they didn't see her because of the angle of the apartment blocks, and each day at around four o'clock she would take her cup of tea to the table and chairs on the balcony and watch.

Sometimes they embraced. Sometimes they talked. The woman gesticulated a lot and the man was humble. Once he took her by the shoulders to turn her towards him and she shrugged him off. He was small, balding, she was taller, very blonde. Once Anna saw her naked, stretching herself. It seemed a deliberate act. An arm came out, a bare, hairy arm and dragged her away from the window.

She began to invent a story around them, a little man with a big bank account who was despised by his wife (or his mistress). His posture was humble. He seemed to beg for favours. The woman never looked loving. She *permitted* him only. Perhaps he would end up by murdering her, the worm turning. How different from Ritchie and herself, like magnets from the time they met at eighteen, unable to keep their hands off each other. Jealousy flared through her like a knife.

He had been so gentle, Ritchie, in his love, so tender, once the boisterous part was over. Violence was never part of his nature. Was that why he had found it so difficult to tell her about Maria, his dislike of giving hurt? He had his father's sweetness of temperament. Van saw that in Walter Laidlaw. She saw in Ritchie his mother's drive, and what she called his 'wee bit of arrogance'.

Once she saw the man hand the blonde woman a gift, something small in a box which she opened with, it seemed, blood-tipped fingers. She held it to the light, some piece of jewellery, because it momentarily flashed in Anna's eyes. She put her arms round his neck, her head bending and resting on his shoulder because she was so much taller, and his hand went slowly between their bodies . . . Anna got up and went into the apartment, disgusted at the vicarious thrill which shot through *her* body.

That night she lay awake in the bedroom next to Mish and Karin, and when she heard the muffled sounds of lovemaking, she lay, straining her ears, in a miasma of loving, putting herself in the girl's place. She sat up in bed and lay against the pillows. Too

189

much, too much, she thought, horrified. She had to get back.

In the morning she said to the two of them as they darted about the kitchen, snatching orange juice and coffee – neither of them ate – 'How quickly this fortnight has passed! But I've got to get back home. Van's holiday with the Armstrongs will be up and I must start work in the studio. I've got so many ideas.'

'Yes, we understand,' Karin said and, passing her on the way to the sink, put an arm round her shoulders. 'You're a great mom. Mish is lucky.'

'I'd like to take you both out tonight. You choose.'

'Oh, there's no need.'

'I'd really like to.'

'Isn't she darling, Mish? Well, there's a German place we sometimes go to which satisfies my ethnic longings . . .'

'You don't have to, Mum,' Mish said.

'It's a very small recompense for all your kindness. Both of you.'

'That's Glasgow West End politeness, Karin.' And, smiling at Anna: 'You two have clicked.'

'I think we have.' She was pleased she had passed some kind of test.

'She's a real sweet momma,' Karin said, swallowing her orange juice. 'God, is that the time? Are you going downtown, pussy cat?'

'As far as the Rockefeller.'

'Okay. See you, Anna.'

She went out to buy presents for them after she had dressed and tidied up. She wouldn't sit on the balcony any more. She would get on with her own life.

Karin as usual was in before Mish. He tended to linger with clients, whereas her department closed at five o'clock. 'We'd work on,' she had said, 'but we're ruled by the cleaners. Have you ever seen one of them on the rampage? I'd rather deal with an angry cab driver.'

'I'll have a shower and get dolled up,' she now said, 'and then we'll have a drink.'

She looked striking in her short black dress when she reappeared, her earrings sparkling, her black hair brushed back to show them.

'Snap,' Anna said. She was also wearing black. She accepted her gin and tonic which Karin handed to her.

'You have a figure like a model.' She looked admiringly at Anna. 'I'm short and tubby and I don't have your long legs. I know I'll get to look like Mom when I'm older. Hausfrau. She always wears black too.'

'Well, she probably feels right in it, the little black dress.' Anna tried to visualize Karin's mother.

'She's in permanent mourning for a different reason.' The girl's smile died.

'Why is that?'

'Both her parents were taken to Dachau when she was at one of the universities here and she never saw them again. My father lost two brothers in the same way. He and my mother escaped because they were out of the country.'

'How terrible!'

She nodded. 'They vowed to leave everything behind them and start afresh here, but she brought the past with her. Father's different.'

'Has he met Mish?'

'Not yet. He won't meet him until Mom does too.'

'If she doesn't, what will you do?'

'I don't know. I'm like Papa. I live in the present.'

'I envy you your temperament. What age are you?'

'Twenty-four. More than a year older than Mish.'

'So getting married doesn't worry you?'

'No.' She shook her head. 'Not unless we decide to have children. Mish isn't that way inclined at the moment. He's wrapped up in his work. Single-minded.'

'Like his father.'

'I wish he had come with you. I'd like to meet him. Some of Mish's friends talk about him in awe. You're lucky to be living with someone like that.'

'I'm not, as a matter of fact.' It came out naturally. 'Didn't Mish tell you?'

'No.' She didn't say the usual 'I'm sorry.' 'Mish wouldn't.'

'He's gone to live with another woman.' She had rehearsed this so many times that it was like speaking a part, had told herself she mustn't weep.

Well, well!' Karin's surprise was genuine. 'I suppose . . . I hear he's very handsome. But you're a knockout yourself.'

'Not enough. In the old days when we were at the Glasgow Art School other students envied me. My mother was the only one who wasn't bowled over. She didn't approve of impecunious art students courting her daughter. Especially if they were working class. She's a snob about class.'

'Well, that's not as bad as being an intellectual one. They're a pain in the neck. But she came round?'

'Yes. I suppose his charm worked on her too. Besides, she couldn't have parted us. We were crazy about each other. There was no living together in our time. He used to say he was bursting out of his skin . . .' in spite of all her rehearsing, her voice trembled '. . . to have me.'

'Why didn't you?'

'You don't know Glasgow West End morality in the thirties. Nice girls didn't. Jean and I thought we were emancipated, but not *that* . . . until she fell in love and kicked over the traces. It's an old story.'

'But it happens, all the time. She's put it behind her now?'

'Yes, she married her doctor. She's made a success of that. She has two children, but one of them is a mongol, the boy.'

Karin was cool. She must listen to worse every day. 'Did that floor her?'

'No. She coped. It's a good marriage.'

'She sounds like a tough cookie.'

'She's exotic and beautiful. We're very close to each other. I feel her with me just now . . . when I'm talking about her. My worries are nothing compared with hers. Ritchie is *alive*; the love of her life died. She accepts Roderick the way I seem unable to accept Van as she is. I told you about her. Now that she's over her odd phase of bringing home odd people, I can't accept her boyfriend, who is . . . ordinary.'

'Because you think the earlier Van was the true one?'

'You're smart, Karin. Yes. In retrospect, worse luck. This boy isn't good enough for her, mediocre where she's . . . unique. Ritchie says nothing is ever right for me. Do you think I'm like that? You've experience of people.'

'I'm getting it all the time. You've given me the clue, in a way, by telling me about your sister. You're close. You have a fundamental need to share everything. Did you suffer *with* her?'

'Oh God, yes. It was almost as if it was happening to me.'

'So now you have it. Your *suffering*. You want it,

in a way, so that you'll be the same as your sister? Twins, through and through. I never cease to be amazed at what goes on behind people's faces.' She shook her head, looking at Anna. 'So few people are what they seem. I'm no exception. I tend to carry my nationhood on my back. But you're so *elegant*, Anna. What's the other woman like?'

'Fair and childlike, but sophisticated, as only Spanish women can be.'

'You sound the same except for the hair.'

'In what way?'

'You seem like a child to me sometimes, but then Jews are born old. Try not to be so capable, running other people's lives for them. Be selfish. You deserve it . . . well, here he is at last.' Mish had just come in. 'I'm telling your mother she's really elegant. I hadn't got to the bit about being jealous . . .'

'I'm telling her,' Anna said, 'about your father having gone off with another woman.' He breathed deeply, shaking his head.

'You have to see them together, Karin, then you'd *know* it's only temporary. They're made for each other.' He turned to Anna. 'And we need him, Mum, Van and me. Need him around, need him to joke with. We're *family*. Honestly, he'll never exist without you.'

'Do you think so?' They were so good for her, this young pair who thought they had it all worked out.

'I know so.' The oracle at twenty-three. He came and sat down beside her. Karin got up and poured him a drink, gave it to him, at the same time bending down to kiss him.

'That's from your momma and me for being you. I'm going to the ladies' boudoir.'

'She's really nice,' Anna said when Karin had gone.

'Mish, you and Van will have to go and see your father if he stays away for a long time. It's called "having access".'

'Don't talk like that. Of course we'll see him. We love him. Van and I have talked about it. We heard you going at each other that night and we were really upset. "Not *this* family," we said to each other. "We're *special*." It won't last, Mum, this break. You're essential to each other.'

'If it does I'll die.' The gin was affecting her. She suddenly wept after being so cool. She wept unrestrainedly. Mish put his arm round her.

'We feel badly about it too. We were saying . . . maybe you haven't made allowances for each other in your marriage. He's become famous, but it's praise from you he wants. He's not so sure of himself as he looks. In spite of his stuff selling like hot cakes. Do you know, we had a small oil of his turn up in the gallery the other day, *The Rambla*, and it went in half an hour.'

'Did it? How much?' Her tears stopped for a moment.

'In pounds, two thousand five hundred.'

'The lucky devil!'

He laughed. 'Mum, he's famous! Sometimes fame can be bad for people, Karin says, if they can't share it with the one who really matters to them. They become . . . aggressive. They tend not to think of other people.'

'But I'm not other people. I'm his wife.'

Karin reappeared, her lipstick glossy, her face had a warm sheen. She took a quick look. 'You for the boudoir, Anna?'

'Yes.' She got up quickly, her face averted.

When she came back, newly made up, they were

sitting close together. Karin's eyes were tender.

'Gee whiz! Estée Lauder should have you in her firm. You'll be fighting men off, Anna. Just wait till we walk into that restaurant.'

She laughed. You don't understand, little Jewish girl with all your wisdom. I only want Ritchie. 'Lead on,' she said.

Eighteen

❧

She told herself going home in the plane that she would stop worrying and get on with her work. Mish and Karin had been good for her. And if she didn't get the same feeling with Van and William, the main thing was that Van seemed happy enough with him. Ritchie was another matter, and the empty, rejected feeling was there all the time. 'He'll never exist without you,' Mish had said. She must hold on to that meantime and get on with her own life.

Van was in when she got home. She had the table set the way she knew Anna liked it and fresh flowers in the small crystal basket which she always used. They embraced. Anna was surprised to feel tears coming into her eyes.

'Well, this is nice,' she said. 'It's lovely to be home again.'

'Do you feel all right, Mum?' Her eyes were compassionate.

'More or less. I'm coming to terms . . . with things. Karin and Mish were very kind. I feel much more cheerful, ready to get on with my work. I got a lot of ideas in New York for designs, more so than in Barcelona.' And, since she knew they were both thinking of Ritchie, 'I don't want you and Mish to feel cut off from your father because of me.' Her voice

197

broke in spite of her efforts to control it. 'I can't believe . . . this has happened.' She tried to smile.

'Oh, Mum!' She came towards her.

'Don't sympathize too much or I'll cry like a wean.' She dashed the tears from her eyes.

'He won't manage without you, honestly.'

'Mish said that too. But he's trying . . .'

'You're all too close, you and Dad and Aunt Jean.' She looked at her with Jean's eyes.

'I always thought so. But there's you and Mish. I'm really lucky.' She drew a deep breath. 'I'm dying for a cup of tea.' She looked at the table. 'And a piece of that lovely cake.'

'I bought it in the French pâtisserie. I'll make the tea. You get your things off and have a seat.' She did as she was told, feeling comforted.

'How did your holiday go?' she said when Van came back with the teapot. 'Did you do a lot of walking?'

'Every day. We were in an organized group. We stayed in a large house which runs those things, and set off each morning with a packed lunch.'

'And maps with plastic covers round your necks?'

'Right, and we had to check our haversacks every day to make sure we had everything, not to mention a whistle and a large piece of silver foil to wrap yourself in, in case of accidents.' She laughed with Anna.

'So you enjoyed yourself? You tell me about it and then I'll tell you about Mish's apartment. I'm getting quite good at saying "apartment" not "flat". And his girlfriend, Karin.'

'I've finished with William,' she said, pouring the tea. Some slopped into the saucer.

'Finished!' Her surprise was genuine. She hid her

delight. It had never seemed right. 'Oh, I'm sorry!' She meant that, as distinct from any pleasure at the news. 'What happened?'

Van poured milk into Anna's cup and handed it to her. The cup rattled in the saucer, but her voice was level. 'He met another girl. She was pretty and what Mrs Armstrong called "tricksy". Not like me. I'm neither of those things but I thought . . . our interests, and . . . anyhow he preferred her to me. Dorothy. "Call me Dottie," she said. She was the life and soul of the party. She wore neat little shorts. He was captivated by her . . . tricksiness.'

Guilt overwhelmed Anna for her unspoken criticism of William. The little runt, she thought. He had seemed so *reliable*. 'I thought you were the best of friends, both planning to work in the Westminster Bank. Not that they were to blame,' she said, but Van didn't smile. 'What *happened* to him?'

'Dottie happened. Neat little Dottie in shorts. Well, look at me.' She shrugged. 'I couldn't compete. I'm not elegant like you. I'm awkward. I look a sight in shorts.' She held out the plate with the French gâteau on it. 'Have a slice.'

'Thanks. It looks delicious.' It must have cost her a fortune with its filling of orange confectioners' custard and mandarin segments arranged in a pattern on the frosted icing. She cut herself a piece with the silver cake knife Van had provided. She had forgotten nothing. 'Far too expensive, Van.' And then: 'I'm really sorry about William.'

'But having a hard time trying not to show your delight?' Her smile was one-sided. Her eyes were dark with pain.

'That's not fair. I wouldn't have believed this of him. Didn't he say anything, try to explain?'

'Oh, yes. He apologized. He said Dottie was sorry too, but he'd made a mistake about me. We weren't really suited. I think his parents liked her better than me. Especially his mother. We never had much to say to each other. She was obsessed by her neighbours. It was as if she'd brought them with her, all their foibles, on and on. He said I would thank him in time.'

'Perhaps you will.'

'I thought . . . with him . . . I would have an ordinary life, a home, and babies. We'd wait three years to save up before we got married. We talked about it, and I persuaded myself that was what I wanted, to be comfortable, and not to think of all those other people who were . . . crying for help, and that everyone would be pleased . . .'

Anna got up, went round the table and knelt beside Van. She hugged her. 'It's tough. I can understand about William because I'm miserable too. It's hard to take, rejection. Van, there's no hurry about getting married. Look at me.' She tried to smile. 'Tell yourself that if William . . .' She hesitated.

'. . . ditched me.'

'All right, ditched you for someone else, he wouldn't have suited you anyhow. His horizons were too narrow.'

'You don't get it, Mum.' She sat up straight to look at Anna. 'It was my only chance. You talk about other boys. They'll always go for girls like Dottie whether they're clever or not. Gordon showed me how really unattractive I was, always would be, but then when I met William I thought someone really liked me for myself. It wasn't that I was unhappy going to college and working part-time at the home. I love it, all the poor souls there. I *knew* I was different from the other girls . . .' She was suddenly weeping, difficult, heart-rending sobbing which went on and on.

Anna still knelt, miserable in the awkward position, miserable because she was partly to blame. She drew the weeping girl towards her. 'I'm so sorry, Van. I hate to see you hurt like this.' She restrained herself from maligning William, remembering, never-theless, how she had been funny about perks for jerks in banks, and merry hikers, and so on. 'Cry your heart out if it helps.'

How could she say to this daughter of hers whose self-esteem had received such a bitter blow that there *was* a point in being interested in one's appearance and clothes, if only to boost one's morale. How could you explain style? It was an artistic expression, a feel-ing for colour and line. Mish had it, Van hadn't. She wasn't interested. She wanted to succour. Had the Good Samaritan style, or Jesus? And why did this daughter of hers make her feel so unworthy?

Van got three A levels, which were good enough to give her entrance to a university, but she wasn't inter-ested. Anna did her best to refrain from criticism and took her out for a little celebratory dinner in an Italian restaurant which she knew. It didn't work. Possibly Van could feel her mother's disappointment in her reluctance. She didn't drink, and Anna took more than she should and then grew morose and guilty at the thought of driving back home.

'You must take driving lessons,' she said when they were safely back. 'Then you could use my car. I could have loaned it to you if you'd been going to a university.'

'I *said* I didn't want to go.'

The drink made her incautious. 'It's such a waste.

I'm not objecting to you doing charity work, it's just that a degree would have helped you to get a responsible job. The people who run Oxfam will all have degrees.'

'But, don't you see, I could be helping poor people *now*?'

'Yes, for nothing. During which time I have to keep you.' All her resentment against Ritchie was in the remark, which wasn't even true. He had always been generous.

'I'm sorry about that.' Her eyes darkened. 'I hadn't thought –'

'Charity begins at home, you know.'

'I could stay in at Low Wood the way I did when I was at school.'

'But she wouldn't pay you. You'd just be a dogsbody, wiping up their messes.' Oh God, she thought, from bad to worse.

'But I would be off your hands. That's what you want. I annoy you. My presence annoys you. You want a smart daughter like Dottie . . .'

'Oh no, Van, no, I'd *die* with a daughter like Dottie. It's just that you're so stubborn, and you won't let me help you. You could come into the studio with me. I could give you lots to do there, teach you. You might get involved.'

'I wouldn't be any good at it. I'd botch things up.'

'Okay. I'm sorry, sorry. This was meant to be a celebration night. It's a failure. I seem to do and say the wrong thing with you all the time. Did you ever look at it that way? I have a splitting headache. I'm going to bed.'

She didn't weep. She felt too alone to weep. She sat in front of her mirror at the dressing-table, not seeing herself, feeling bereft. Life was a bitch. Ritchie didn't want her, and her daughter despised her.

There was a knock at the door. 'Come in,' she said. She turned a bright face to meet Van who stood disconsolately in the doorway.

'I came to apologize.' She sat down on the edge of the bed. 'I know I'm stubborn.'

'I was the same with my mother. It's all right. We were both tired and I'd drunk too much. I was just as stubborn about your father before we were married. I refused to give him up although my mother didn't think he was good enough.' She laughed. 'And now he's a famous painter!'

'But he's left you.'

'Thanks very much.' Her voice shook.

'I didn't mean it that way. It's just men in general. You've always loved him, believed in him.'

'Living together is difficult, married or unmarried. I'm not nearly as good at making allowances as Jean, or accepting things as they are. Look how difficult *we* find it.' She smiled unsuccessfully, feeling the smile wobble. 'Dad will be very proud of your results, just as I am. I'll phone him first thing tomorrow, and you can speak to him.'

'I'd like that. And don't worry. Dad will come back to you. He couldn't exist without you, Mish said.'

'Did he?'

'It's true. Would you like a cup of tea?'

'That would be nice.'

'Well, you pop into bed and I'll bring you one.' She went quickly out of the room, intent on her errand. She is happy when she is succouring, Anna thought, that's when she is happiest. Maybe Mish had his sister's helping of self-esteem as well as his own. Was it that *she* was responsible for Van's lack of it? And, a new thought struck her, could it be that Van had always been jealous of Ritchie's affection for her? Daughters were supposed to be like that. Well, she thought, as she got into bed, she has no cause for worry now.

Van brought the tea on a silver tray with a box of petits fours she had found. 'I thought you'd like a titbit.'

'Thanks,' she said, and smiling up at this daughter of hers whom she couldn't handle, '*you*'re a titbit.' Van's smile was like Jean's, illuminating her face.

She telephoned Ritchie from her bedroom early the following morning, because she had scarcely slept and the night seemed never-ending. She steadied the trembling in her voice. 'It's Anna.'

He sounded sleepy. 'Anything wrong?' and then he was alert. 'There isn't anything *wrong*?'

'No, it's good news. Van got her three A levels. All good, and an A for English. But she still doesn't want to go to university.' She was thinking, this is unreal. Ritchie, my own husband, lying in bed in far-off Spain, possibly with another woman . . .

'Don't push her then. We've been through all that.' His voice was louder. She got the impression that he was sitting up.

'I'm *not*.' She could have wept. 'It's just that I don't want her hanging about the house, doing nothing. It's bad for her.' She listened to the impatience in her voice. That was why they were estranged, why he had left her for Maria.

'I understand how you feel.' His voice was level. 'Why not send her over here?'

She was surprised, and pleased. 'That's a good

idea. I'll put her on in a minute or two and you can ask her yourself. William's given her up for someone else.'

'The little bugger!'

'I told you it wouldn't work.'

'Well, you have the satisfaction of being proved right again . . .' His voice changed, became tender. 'Forget that. How are you, Anna? I really want to know.'

'Oh.' She was taken aback. 'I'm feeling better. Maybe I don't sound like it. My hormonal imbalance – that was Gerald Masters' fancy name for it – seems to have steadied. He said it would take time. And my holiday with Mish and Karin was a great success, at least for me. I liked her.'

'I'm glad about that. I suggested he should visit me here.'

'Yes, I think he should. With Van? Is this to meet Maria?' It cost her a lot to say that.

'Possibly, but mostly because I miss . . . my family.'

'Well . . .' Do you miss *me*? I can't sleep without you . . . 'How *is* Maria?'

'Very well. I'm working a lot. The ideas are there, all right, but the execution is . . . faulty.' There would be distractions, naturally, she thought. She listened for any noises off, but there were none, no rustling, no stifled laughter. 'I'll arrange that, then. Do you think Van will like the idea?'

'I'll get her and you can ask her yourself.'

'Anna, before you go . . . are you managing all right?'

'Yes.'

'I'm so sorry.'

'It's a bit late for that, isn't it?' There was a pause.

205

She wanted to weep, to say, 'Come home, I need you . . .'

His voice when it came was flat. 'I'm paying money regularly into your bank. Let me know if it's not enough.'

'I've had a note from them. It's more than enough.' She felt wooden, a puppet with someone putting words into her mouth. The unreality hit her again. This wasn't Anna and Ritchie, those great Glasgow lovers talking to each other, she lying alone, he with his mistress lying beside him possibly fondling him in what had been *her* places. It was not to be borne. 'If Van visits you I'll go to Glasgow. I'm due to visit Mother and I'd like to see Jean. I'd go on to Kirkcudbright.'

'Good.'

'I'm sorry you're having difficulty with your work.' She only wanted to keep him talking to her.

'So am I. I seem to have lost my zest or my zing or whatever you call it.'

'You're probably having too gay a life.' She thought of Maria in her white swimsuit with the tendrils of hair lying on her cheek. She would make a lot of demands. And there was the child, the beautiful little Ana. He would have to go about with the two of them, be taken to see her Spanish friends. She, on the other hand, had been careful that their social life never impinged on his working time. That came first. 'I'll get Van.'

'Anna . . .' His voice sounded wistful.

'What is it?'

'Never mind.' She thought she heard him sighing. 'It's nothing.'

'I'll get Van.' When she came in she left her with the telephone and went to have a bath.

* * *

206

Mrs Sanderson took Van on for three days each week, in a voluntary capacity. Unfortunately she had her rota of paid helpers, she said. On the days when Van didn't go to the home, she sometimes went up to town. This surprised Anna, especially as she never came back with any purchases.

'What do you do up there?' she asked once.

'Moon about. Look in at the galleries trying to spot Dad's work. There's quite a lot.'

'Does it look good?'

'I'm no critic, but it jumps off the wall at you when you go in.'

'It's called impact.'

'I told a man he was my father and he seemed very impressed. And, do you know, he had one of Aunt Jean's! It was nearly all sky. A kind of boiling sky.'

'Oh, great. Oh, that's marvellous!' She couldn't have been more delighted. 'The cunning thing. She never said a word.'

'She's very modest about her work.'

'Not like your father. From the time he was eighteen he believed in himself. Although when I was talking to him on the phone – that time you had a word with him . . .'

'Yes. I said I'd like to go to Spain.'

'Good.' At least that was something positive. 'Yes, he said he'd lost his zest. If his stuff is all over London he'll have to keep it going for the sake of his public.' She had been good at chivvying him, discussing techniques, listening to him. And she always criticized his work honestly. 'You're clear-eyed,' he had said . . . How nice it was to talk like this together, as mother and daughter should.

'I looked up Adelaide,' she said. Her eyes were on Anna, waiting to see how she would jump.

207

'Did you?' She was casual. 'How was she?'

'She's still living with her brother. She looks after him.'

'Is he ill?'

'No. He had polio when he was a child and he doesn't get about much outside. He has a wheel-chair.' Her lovely smile came. 'He makes me laugh. He's funny.'

I'm glad someone does – but she was learning not to make remarks like that. 'That's good. Well, I must get on. Would you cook the supper?'

'You know I'm no good at it. I mean, those lovely dishes you turn out.'

'Scrambled eggs or bacon. I don't care. Have a bash.'

Her work was proving her refuge and her conso-lation. She was putting to good use her interpretation of the Indian paintings she had seen in the Metropoli-tan Museum in New York, she had sold two clock faces in Bond Street with a request for more. The hammer as always proved the best way of getting rid of her anxieties, but nights were the worst time.

She lay awake longing for Ritchie, writhing in bed sometimes in an agony of wanting, despising herself for this need which had always been so strong in her. She was fiercely jealous of Maria Roig and the fact that she had taken her place. She would rise in the morning unrested and unrefreshed.

Van was generally at the breakfast table, anxious to please in the small things. 'Toast, Mum?' Did it never occur to her that if she had gone to university she wouldn't have to face this mother who obviously made her feel guilty, or even resentful? And it cut both ways. If she had been able to throw her arms round Van and waltz with her as she and Ritchie had

208

often done round the kitchen table, it would have broken the barrier between them. If I were Van, she thought, and had been rejected twice by men, I'd say to hell with them and make a career for myself. But Van was different.

Anna was relieved when Van said one morning, 'This is a letter from Dad enclosing a cheque to cover the cost of my ticket to Barcelona. Mish will meet me there. He's given me dates.'

'That's splendid. When does he want you to go?'

'From the thirteenth onwards, for a fortnight. It's all the time he can spare.' She looked worried. 'That's over Christmas. He's very apologetic and says we've only to agree if it covers the time you'll be away too.'

'It could be arranged.' She was becoming adept at hiding her misery. *All the time he can spare* . . . From gallivanting about with Maria? 'I think it's a good idea.' It would be better than Van staying at home.

She saw her off from Heathrow with plunging spirits, but kept the smile on her face until it felt stiff. Did it mean that her children would be spending Christmas with her husband's lover? Mish would like Maria, and possibly think how well suited they were. Van was unpredictable. And Maria's daughter wasn't deprived. There would be no one for her to succour unless she went out and gave pesetas to the beggars in the *Ramblas*.

She went home and started to pack.

Nineteen

'Are you excited about your children coming?' Maria asked. They were in her large sitting-room in the Barri Gòtic. Ana was in bed; Josita, the housekeeper, was out for the evening. Josita was a divorcée of forty, almost as smart as Maria, but she had as well the attributes of many Spanish women, she was a good organizer in the home, businesslike and efficient, a good cook, and firm and kind with her small charge. Isobel, the nanny, had gone back to England. Josita had never tried to usurp Maria's influence in any way. She had a daughter of sixteen who was at boarding school.

'Yes, very much.' Ritchie got up and walked across the marble-floored room towards the tall windows and looked down on the narrow street. The bell of the cathedral tolled, sonorous, heavy, eleven chimes. What a time to eat, he thought. They had just finished dinner. A wave of nostalgia swept over him for his childhood home in Glasgow, the shining kitchen with the table set for high tea – bacon and eggs, pie and chips, or cold ham and salad, flanked by bread and homemade scones. Six o'clock. A sensible time.

He never slept well if he stayed here. He preferred the house he had rented – the flat had been too small – or even better, the large warehouse in Barceloneta where he worked and where he kept a studio couch for the nights when he didn't want to drive home. He had said in the letter he wrote to Anna in explanation that he didn't intend to live with Maria, as if that made it any better. He had admitted to being infatuated with her. It would have been kinder to say that he wished to be alone for a time, and he was beginning to think that was partly true.

'You're restless, Ricardo,' Maria said.

'I'm working out that mural for the *Departamento de Justicia*. It's stuck. Manuel says to leave it, but I've never done that in my life. I need someone to give me an objective viewpoint.'

'Don't I give you that?'

'Of course.' He didn't turn. He was watching a girl in a doorway, or he thought it was a girl. He had hardly known what a transvestite was when he lived in Glasgow. The woman was so aggressively feminine that he thought she might be a man. Their legs gave them away. 'But we're involved. I said objective.' That was unfair when what he meant was that he craved for Anna's viewpoint, involved or otherwise. She was as straight as a die. Once he had thrown a pot of paint over a painting she hadn't liked because he knew she was right. 'Mish must have an educated eye now. I'm looking forward to his opinion.'

'But he's involved, so isn't my opinion good enough?'

'Yes, but I need . . . oh, I don't know what I need.' A swift kick up the backside. Maria wouldn't understand a colloquialism like that. She was formal in speech although not in behaviour.

Maria had a tape measure of a mind when it came to criticism. If he said that, she would look at him

211

with narrowed eyes and smile, but she would be cool for a day or two, not like those summer storms of Anna's which were over quickly. Maria had to be wooed out of her coolness, unlike Anna who gave as freely in her loving as she did in her criticism. In her case everything came from the heart, not a costing of the painting's material worth, but a combination of the clear-eyed estimation and logicality of the Scot allied with an unerring eye for design which Mish had inherited.

'Isn't your daughter artistic?'

'No, poor myopic little Van! I think her bad sight made everything a blur until we realized she needed glasses. People interest her, the poorer the better, the more deprived the better.'

'If she'd been a Catholic she could have become a nun since probably she won't marry. She hasn't the elegance of her mother.'

'Oh, she's not religious in an orthodox way.' He ignored the other comment, but it was true Van walked with rounded shoulders and downcast eyes as if she had to protect herself from something. 'There's no "Come to Jesus" stuff with her, just infinite compassion.'

'But that *is* "Jesus stuff", as you put it, my darling.'

'Practical Christianity? I suppose so.'

'We'll leave everything for Josita. Come to bed.' Her voice was seductive. 'I haven't seen you for days.'

'I've been busy.'

'Manuel says you're getting behind with the *Departamento de Justicia*. I must have a look at what you're doing. I have three other murals being done – graduates from the Art School – but you have to bring on the young.'

'Perhaps I'm getting too old,' he said, feeling wistful.

She laughed at him. 'Do not roll your eyes at me like a woman. Come and finish your coffee and then you will show me in bed whether you are getting old or not.' Her hair was a heavy gold swag over one eye, the other side was pushed behind her ear to show a large marquise earring. She looked ravishing, but the thought of lovemaking made him feel more tired than ever. He wanted to lie quietly in bed and visualize each section of the mural, try and see where the fault lay.

'Ricardo! I want you . . .' The childish voice came from Ana's bedroom.

'Go to sleep,' Maria called. 'Haven't you heard the time from the bells? It's getting late.'

'I want Ricardo.'

'I'll go, darling,' he said. 'It won't take a minute.'

He had grown to love the little girl. She enchanted him with her small perfection, but chiefly because she seemed to love him. She always greeted him by throwing her thin little arms round his neck and putting her cheek against his. 'I like to have a papa,' she had once said. 'You will be my papa.'

She greeted him in her usual affectionate way. 'You forgot your story tonight, Ricardo.'

'But you were late going to bed, Mama said.'

'I need my story. The last time Wee Magreega was . . .' Ritchie swallowed a smile at the bizarre pronunciation of a Scottish hero of his childhood. His mother had doted on the pawky little Scots lad, reading Ritchie his exploits from the *Daily Record*. In the course of his stories to Ana, Wee Macgregor had become intertwined with Para Handy and had embarked on a series of madcap adventures 'doon

213

the watter' which went flowing on like the Clyde.

To hear the Spanish voice of the child repeating the names he had learned at his mother's knee gave him infinite pleasure. And the fanciful tales he made up brought back to him his parents, and Glasgow. The warm feeling he had for it was totally unlike the lukewarm regard he felt for Renton and London.

Barcelona had appealed to him because it reminded him of Glasgow. The first time he had been in it when he arrived as a recruit with a few other daft idealists to 'fight for democracy', he had been struck even then by its vitality, its warmth, and the *Ramblas* which reminded him so much of that noisy bustling street which ran parallel to the Clyde, Argyle Street. He had thought at the time that he could live here.

Why was it so many Scots were expatriates? Restless, or lack of appreciation at home? He thought of Charles Rennie Mackintosh who had been considered too 'avant-garde' for his time and had died an early death in comparative obscurity far from home.

'Para Handy was steering the boat into the pier,' he began. 'The sailors got the big rope ready, calling to their friends who were standing waiting to catch it.'

'Wasn't it too heavy for the sailors?'

'No, it was attached to a thinner rope, and it was that they threw and then the big heavy one was pulled after it on to the pier.'

'*Si, si,*' she said impatiently.

'Aw right, Wullie!' they shouted.

'Aw right, Wullie,' the childish voice repeated. 'Mind how ye go.' Her eyes were shining. 'And watch they trippers.' She knew this rubbish by heart.

He thought of that time he had sailed into Kilcreggan Pier and Anna had stepped onto the deck, light, lively, black hair and white cardigan, how her eyes had lit up when she saw him and how she had gone naturally into his arms . . . 'The big seagulls were squawking roon the pier,' he said, 'hoping the weans would throw them the crusts from their jeely pieces . . .'

'Jeely pieces,' the little Spanish voice repeated, 'that is the bread with the sugared fruit spread on it. I should like a jeely . . .' He looked down on her. Her eyes were closing, the beautiful little face with the foreshortened chin, the dark eyelashes sweeping the olive cheeks. The thin little nose was unlike Maria's, which was bolder. Perhaps she resembled her father. Maria never spoke of him. He must have hurt her deeply.

She was in bed, naked, and when he undressed and got in beside her she rolled over on top of him. She always demanded a lot of exhausting foreplay, at least it seemed exhausting to him tonight, and she was sophisticated in her techniques, which perhaps she had learned from her husband.

He obliged and gradually joined in, thinking as he did so that he and Anna had never worked out anything like this. Didn't this elaborate ritual take away some of the spontaneity, he thought, as he felt Maria sliding down his body and the immediate thrill in his loins as he responded. He lifted the sheet to look at her and himself. It was as if his body was working apart from him, a willing slave.

But when it was over he felt stale and unsatisfied in the deepest sense. Maria was asleep, spread-eagled across him. He rolled her off and covertly looked at his watch. It had taken an hour, and he wanted to think carefully about his mural, lie quietly and let it fill his mind. The subject was a part evocation of the

215

time he had spent as a soldier on the Ebro. He didn't flatter himself that it had the impact of Picasso's *Guernica*, nor the weight, but it was to be his angle. Me and Gaudí, he thought. But now came the bad bit, the guilty bit . . .

If he had been with Anna they could have talked it over, she would have burrowed into his motives and exposed them to him, pointed out where she thought he had gone wrong. She externalized his own thoughts. But Maria only wanted the finished product. 'I have the job of finding its place,' she had said. 'The other part is your problem.'

But he was tortured by the feeling of betrayal. He tried the familiar excuses. She was partly to blame with her fault-finding and her whingeing, that pale face. But he should have guessed, since her behaviour was so untypical, that she wasn't well. You never thought of the female side of things with Anna. She was the most fastidious of people.

And there was her harping on about Van all the time, and how she couldn't possibly leave her alone in the house. Surely with her usual competence she could have got round that difficulty? He had become convinced that she didn't want to be with him, and was using Van as an excuse . . .

His hand lay on Maria's bare buttock, and he suddenly thought: what *is* this, Laidlaw? What the hell are you doing in bed with a strange woman, and a Spanish woman at that? The crude remark of a father to his son in a film he had once seen came back to him: 'You think with your pecker, my lad, not your head.'

The bare buttock rolled away from his hand, and now under it there was a small mound . . . 'Tinto Hill' he had called it in his lovemaking with Anna, based on the memory of his walks with his father beyond the Clyde Valley. 'You can see the Lakeland mountains from here,' he had told Ritchie as they had climbed. Ritchie had described his elation to Anna on reaching the top, and she had said, 'Unimaginable delights.' She always understood. And that's what it had been with her, unimaginable delights.

He looked down, leaning on his elbow, at Maria's sleeping face. She liked the table lamp left on. The heavy eyelids with their short eyelashes moved, the pink half-open mouth showed gleaming teeth, her musky odour engulfed him. 'Want you,' she whispered, sounding like her daughter. 'Want you . . . don't waste time . . . thinking.' He blew out his breath in a bemused fashion, and collapsed on the pillow beside her.

Later, lying exhausted but wide awake, he thought how easy it had been to slip into an affair with a woman as sensual as Maria, who flattered by implication and knew how to fan his infatuation until it became an obsession. But the difference was obvious. Anna's lovemaking was always wholehearted and wholesome; Maria's was like a sweet which when sucked left a bad taste in one's mouth.

What a fool you're making of yourself, he thought. You're gullible. Long ago, Christine Bouvier, now Maria Roig. Largely, it's curiosity, a painter's curiosity, which taken beyond its bounds always lands you in trouble. You had the good sense to marry the only woman for you and then you toss her aside for a whim. Soul mates, they had called themselves, and then he had cheated.

He got up, dressed quietly and slipped out of the flat. He needed to breathe some fresh air. Outside the deserted streets, dark shadows, rearing black

217

buildings, splashes of Spanish colour in the shop windows was a new, exciting mural, but he needed Anna, if he started it.

He was overjoyed to see Mish and Van, who arrived separately but on the same day. Mish's American suit made his trim figure even trimmer, and he wore on top of it a bulky anorak like a down quilt which he said Karin had given him for an early Christmas present.

'We're used to cold weather in New York,' he said. 'She wanted me to be prepared for here.'

Van was merely bulky in a smart red coat which seemed to make her feel ill at ease. She moved inside it, undid the buttons, seemed glad to get it off.

'You look very smart, Van,' Ritchie said. 'It isn't often I see you out of trousers.'

'It was Mum's idea,' she said. 'I've to keep up with the Barcelona girls, she says.' Did she mean Maria? 'How is she?'

'She came back from seeing Mish looking very good. She liked your girl, Mish,' she said to him.

'Yes, they got on like a house on fire. Karin relates to most people. She has a lot of Middle European aunts and uncles in Brooklyn Heights whom she insists on trailing me to see. She wants them to like me. Perhaps it's to influence her mother.'

'Doesn't *she* like you?' Ritchie asked.

'I'm a goy. She has bitter memories. I don't blame her.'

'She'll come round if you and Karin stick together. Now, the drill is, we stay at our house in Arenys de Mar along the coast. It's near Manuel Folguera, who told me about it. I think you'll like it. I go into Barcelona every day to work and you can come with me if you like. Otherwise I'll leave you to your own devices.'

'Where does Mrs Roig live?' Van asked.

'Maria? For God's sake don't call her Mrs Roig.' He saw the immediate confusion in Van's eyes. 'In the Barri Gòtic, the old part of the city. You'll be meeting her quite soon.' He felt embarrassed. Mish, urbane as always, waded in.

'I'll take you in charge, Van. I'm never going to see all the places I want to in the time. And I'd like to see where you work, Dad, and what you're working on.'

'I'm rather stuck just now. I'm going to take a few days off over Christmas. Maybe a rest away from it will do me good.'

'Mum was great at telling you what was wrong,' Van said. He looked at her. She wasn't being malicious. 'I did admire how she could stand in front of one of your paintings and . . . dissect it.'

'She has an eye.' Mish nodded. 'I think since she doesn't use colour it's even better. There's no distraction. We're interested just now at the gallery in a painter who's turning out abstracts like Hartung. He says he sees colour in black.'

'Does it work?' Ritchie asked.

'No, because basically he's a colourist. He's got about twenty different shades of black already and he can't keep his brush away. Too much.'

'You and I are going to have a lot to talk about.' He saw Van's face. Was one of the problems with her that she felt disadvantaged, wrongly, in this family where she was the only one who wasn't artistic? She had never complained about their endless discussions, but that didn't mean anything. 'Have you any special thing you'd like to do, Van?' he said.

219

'Just potter.' She gave him her swift shy smile. 'Look at people. Probably go with Mish part of the time – as long as he doesn't go to the Bullfighters' Museum.'

'There's the Christmas Fair round the cathedral, on till the twenty-fourth. Cribs and children.'

'I'd like that.' She nodded.

'We'll meet Maria there. It's all arranged.' He felt awkward bringing her into the conversation. What did those two grown-up children think of him leaving their mother for someone else, however temporarily? Were they surprised, disgusted, ashamed, apathetic? And yet how could he explain this infatuation for Maria which had been all-consuming – but was now wearing very thin? He and Anna had been going through a bad time, but that was no excuse for introducing Maria into the situation. He should have been more understanding.

He had a great desire to say, 'You two, what do you really think of me?' but he couldn't. 'She always takes Ana, her little girl,' he said. 'And you'll see the *sardana* danced.'

'That sounds good,' Van said. Mish thought it would be interesting.

When they were eating, Mish said to Van, 'I was sorry about you splitting up with William. Mum told me.'

Her dark eyes fixed on him. Her mouth rose slightly at one corner. Was there an element of scorn there, or was it disappointment in him? 'We didn't split up,' she said. 'He preferred someone else.' The dark eyes again: you should know all about that . . .

'Oh,' Mish said. 'I'm still sorry. Never mind, you'll meet plenty of men when you go to university.'

'I'm not going.' Mish's eyes met Ritchie's. He signalled to him to keep quiet.

'She's thinking of her options. Have some more of this pork. It's a Catalan dish.'

'I thought they ate nothing but paellas,' Mish said.

'A popular misconception. In Renton the neighbours thought we fed you two exclusively on porridge.' They laughed.

Ritchie thought Van looked pale. Her skin had a muddy tinge and her figure had thickened. She would have to find something to do which she enjoyed and forget about this further unhappy episode in her life. William was no great loss, nor had Gordon been, but it would be a pity if rejections became a pattern.

They drove along the coastal road with the lights following the dark mass of the Mediterranean. Van was enchanted.

'Can you see the sea?' she asked. 'I mean from the house?'

'Yes.'

'Oh, I'll love that.'

When they arrived, he showed her the bedroom she was to occupy. 'Is that all right, Van?' He wanted to please her because he loved her.

'It's fine. And you *can* see the sea. And I like the bed, Dad. All that carving.'

'It's not genuine, but they're good at beds. The room's rather bare, I'm afraid. I have a daily woman, but she hasn't the deft touches Mum had . . . has.'

'I can buy one or two things if you like. I can make this my little home. I don't even have to go out much. I will have your meal ready, let Mish trail round galleries and museums on his own.'

'Yes, but you have to move around too?' Where

221

did this sense of insecurity in her come from, the need for a womb? She'd had the same upbringing as Mish, the same opportunities. As far as he knew there had never been any favouritism. But Anna had never really understood her, had been baffled at her lack of interest in feminine things, and especially her choice of friends. It's that Rose, he thought, not for the first time, and her ridiculous snobbishness. If Anna had gone to school in Glasgow and seen some of the children with bare feet swollen with chilblains in winter, she might have had different ideas. He sat down on the edge of the bed. Van was still standing at the window. 'Van,' he said. She turned around, apprehension on her face.

'Yes?'

'I'm not going to lecture you, don't worry, nor pry. I appreciate that you don't want to go to a university. I respect that. It's your own life. But could you tell me why?' She turned sharply away from him. The downward dejected angle of her head made him wish he hadn't spoken. 'You're clever. That side shouldn't worry you.'

'No, it doesn't.'

He said in the vernacular which used to amuse her, 'Cm'on, be a wee pal. Spill the beans.'

She snorted. 'It's . . . I'm . . . frightened . . .' She was still not looking at him.

'Not of the professors or anything like that? Not of being away from home?'

'No, it's not that.' She raised her head and turned to face him. Her face was white, her eyes wide and stretched-looking. The half-smile was pitiful. 'I'm frightened of . . . I'm frightened at the thought of being amongst a lot of students, of young people.'

'Oh, come on!'

222

'Don't say, "Oh, come on!" You and Mum don't understand. You're so confident, so *right* looking. They don't *like* me. I seem to say the wrong thing. They're *born* knowing all that chit-chat. And they go in packs and I'm never included.'

'Come here.' She came reluctantly. 'Sit down. I'm not going to eat you. This is your old dad.' He put an arm round her and pulled her against him. '*I* don't make you feel like that, do I?' He wouldn't mention Anna. Nor the sadness that Anna was Anna, practical, clever, critical. She couldn't change.

'No.' Her voice trembled.

'Well?'

'You see, Dad,' she said, 'you and Mish and Mum are lucky. You can see beauty in paintings. I envy you. I try to, but I don't see it. It's just . . . paint to me. I stand and stand and pretend to look wise but I *still* don't see it. Now there's a boy in Low Wood, Johnny. He's a spastic and hydrocephalic. He can't even hold up his head and his legs cross like scissors if he tries to stand up. And when I hold him it's like trying to hold an eel, he slips and slides all over the place.'

'Poor soul.'

'No, pity won't do. It's not enough. Not very often he manages to lift his head and look at me. It's as if he was trying to get through, shut up in that damaged envelope which is his body. It's not "Thank you" or anything like that, it's a kind of "Hello, you out there," or even, "Just look at me. This is me. I'm here." Do you know what I mean?'

'I think so.'

'Well, that gives me the same feeling I expect you get from looking at a painting. There's a kind of . . . truth buried there, deep inside, the answer to why he's like that, and why no one strangled him at birth and why he's still living when on the surface it would be far better if he were dead. And how everybody gets weary coping and stringing him up in a net to bath him, and putting nappies on a boy of ten but keep on coping, just for that look they get when sometimes he manages to lift his head. Is it truth, do you think?'

'Beauty. But truth is beauty.' He was profoundly moved. He sat silently, feeling closer to her than he'd ever felt, as close as he had with Anna on their first days together. He cleared his throat, 'Mother's . . .' he cleared it again '. . . pretty busy, is she?' His eyelids pricked, he tightened his arm round her.

'Yes . . . pretty busy.'

'That's good.' His throat ached. 'I miss her.'

'Yes. She was . . . very low when you left. She was straight – you know her – she told us the truth about that, but she came back from New York with determination written all over her face. This Karin of Mish's had done what I couldn't do.' Her voice was bitter. 'She had that look, you know that look of Mum's, chin up, "I'm going to have a bash."'

'I know it. I'll tell you something, Van. I miss all that, I miss her straightness. I miss her like anything. This was only a trial separation. I was being a silly bugger about Maria . . . Do you mind me speaking like that?'

'I've heard worse.' She laughed.

'Men are like that, especially at my age, I suppose. I'm pretty mediocre. But sometimes a separation is good for a couple. They get on each other's nerves, just as no doubt we get on yours.'

'You'll have to go down on your bended knees if you're thinking of coming back to her.'

'No, you're wrong there. You know her as a mother. I know her as a wife. Anna wouldn't have anyone begging for favours. She gives freely or not at all.'

'When she thinks it's time. Oh, she knows what she is about.' Again there was the bitterness in her voice.

'Perhaps.' He sighed. 'I'm going to make a suggestion to you. Would you like to come and housekeep for me?'

She sat up and looked at him. 'But that would be like taking sides.'

'Not necessarily. It might do you and Mum good.'

'What would I *do*?'

'Keep house. I can introduce you to Spanish girls. You could go to a college and learn the language, regard it as widening your education for a few months. What do you say?'

She sighed, then looked at him, shaking her head. 'I can't, Dad. It would be like university and all that I said. A language college and those smart Spanish girls ganging up with their swinging earrings . . . there's no *need* for me to get into a situation like that – not when I could be doing other things.'

'Like what?'

'Mrs Sanderson would take me back. I'll keep looking for a paid job, but meantime I can help there. It's the only thing I'm good at. If you could see some of them! They're so deprived, so deprived . . . It makes any feelings I have about myself, about smartening myself up, seem so puny. I've learned that no boy's going to look at me when there are so many tricksy girls around. That's what Mrs Armstrong said about Dottie, the girl William fell for, "tricksy".'

'Who on earth wants you to be "tricksy", for

God's sake?' He was suddenly furiously angry, and impatient with her. 'You have to get rid of this feeling of inferiority, Van. You put yourself down all the time.'

'No, I don't. Everyone in our family has talent; I'm the odd one out. I'm lucky in a way I've found my métier – that's the word, isn't it? And I'm sorry I give you all this worry.'

'But we love you, Van, don't you see?'

'Yes, I know you love me, deep down.' Her face had such sadness that he drew her to him and hugged her.

'I could murder William,' he said, 'throwing away a jewel like you.' He laughed to hide his emotion.

'Some jewel.' Her voice was muffled against his shoulder. 'You wouldn't have liked him for a son-in-law anyhow.'

'You're right there.' He could have wept. How had he and Anna acquired this strange bird in their nest? The realization that they couldn't do a thing about it was like a screwdriver boring into his heart. '*Wee chookie birdie, toll, loll, loll . . .*' He sang softly the old refrain. 'My mother used to sing that to me when I was a wee lad. Do you know it?'

'No,' she said. He thought of his mother, who hid such deep compassion under her stern kindliness. She could get close to this girl. She had been reared in a far harder school than Anna.

Nevertheless, the three of them soon fell into some kind of pattern. Mish was in his element touring the city and the galleries religiously. Van sometimes joined him, other times she preferred to stay in the house, treating her room as an eyrie. She had meals ready for them when they came home. Often he

would arrange to meet Mish in the Plaça de Cata-
lunya, 'opposite El Corte Inglése,' he instructed him,
so that they could drive back together.

He confided to Mish that he wasn't getting on with
his work as before. 'I had ferocious energy,' he told
him. 'I was like the big waterfall on the Clyde at
Lanark, enough force to take on anything I was given
and more besides. Ideas gushed out of me. Maria
doesn't say much, but I get the feeling she's disappointed in me. There are younger painters coming
along. Their stuff's crude, in my opinion, but the
vitality's there, the way I was, not now.'

'I see nothing wrong with it,' Mish assured him.
'It's technically more sophisticated, perhaps a little
more contrived, but it would go like a bomb in
London.'

'You see I'm working for the *Departamento de
Justicia*, and there's a time limit.'

'Don't get anxious. It's a pity Mum couldn't see it.
She'd put you right.'

'I haven't the nerve to suggest it.' He laughed rue-
fully. 'I hope you don't make the same mistakes as I
have. How do you get on with Karin?'

'It's a more . . . level relationship than yours and
Mum's. We occupy our own space. That's an American saying.'

'So do your mother and me.'

'Mmmh.' He didn't sound too convinced. 'I'm looking forward to going to Señor Folguera's tonight. Will
Maria be there?'

'Yes, I think so. Manuel generally invites us
together. He knows . . . She'll have her little girl with
her, I expect. She's only twelve, but like most Spanish
children she's allowed to stay up till all hours.'

'Van will be pleased. She likes children.'

227

'Only if they're poor and deprived.'

'She should go to Lower East Side. She'd get an eyeful there.' Ritchie marvelled at his son's urbanity.

Van was waiting for them wearing a white dress which was too bunchy round the waist and had puffed sleeves. She couldn't be more unlike Anna, he thought, with her impeccable taste in clothes. 'You look nice, Van,' he said. 'Are you ready?'

'Yes, I'm looking forward to it.' Her smile was strained, her voice determinedly cheerful.

'Showers first for us and then we'll all have a drink. There's no hurry. We aren't expected before nine. I used to get so hungry waiting for that late dinner that I could have eaten a cuddy!' She laughed.

'I'd forgotten that word for horse. "Hop on your cuddy." Mother never uses any of them now.'

'She's been subjected to Renton ladies more than I have.' Her lipstick was too bright, he noticed. It was like a wound in her pale face. Vanessa, he thought, *Vanessa cardui*. This tenderness he felt for Van, was it because of her vulnerability, as if she had one skin less than everyone else? Perhaps they had made a great mistake in shortening her name.

The thought pursued him as he vigorously soaped himself five minutes later. 'Vanessa', a beautiful concept, and it was matched by her eyes, dark, brilliant, expressive. If Maria patronizes her I'll be flaming mad, he thought. She wouldn't, of course. She was too well-bred, but the look of cool disdain which sometimes came over her features would be enough.

Mish got on well with Manuel. Of course he would meet many like him on the New York art scene. They immediately fell into an amiable discussion, exchanging information about their respective backgrounds. He gave Mish the names of curators in various galleries. 'Just mention mine. They'll open their secret coffers to you. Only a tenth is ever on show.'

Ana was dressed in what Ritchie thought was too sophisticated a manner for a girl of her age, a polka-dotted navy dress with navy pumps to match. She made Van look like a Christmas tree. Mish seemed intrigued.

'This is Ricardo's little boy,' Maria said to her. Her pared-down elegance was subtly un-English.

'Do I kiss the boy, Mama?' Ana looked under her eyelashes at him.

'No, precious, not on the first occasion. Your hand only. But why not give Vanessa a little one, on the cheek?' Her daughter did not look entranced at the suggestion.

'Is she my cousin, like Lucia?'

'No,' Maria said.

'What is she?'

'Ricardo's little girl, but not so little.' Maria's small smile could not be said to be unkind, neither was it warm. Van blushed and looked down at her gold slippers. They shone garishly beside Maria's discreet bottle-green kid.

Manuel interrupted. 'Come and see my house, Vanessa, and leave all this chattering. Your father tells me you like the sea. I have a tower where you can get a wonderful view.'

She went gratefully, and when she came back she looked relaxed as she smiled at Ritchie. 'It's better than ours, Daddy! Of course, we haven't a tower. Señor Folguera tells me he climbs the stairs every morning to see the sun rise.'

'It's as good as going to the gymnasium,' Manuel said. 'Your charming daughter counted the stairs for me, all of sixty-nine.'

The food as always was delicious – young rabbits cooked in rum, and a *zarzuela de mariscos*, a mixture of shellfish and squid served on rice. And *crema Catalana*. 'A light meal,' Manuel said. 'We must keep our appetites for Santa Llúcia's Day, the Crib Fair.'

'They're coming to me that day,' Maria said, 'and staying the night. You are welcome too. And Calvo.' Ritchie had never met Manuel's friend. He was not *aristocratico*.

'Thank you, but we have our own arrangements. We visit our families.'

Ana was beguiling and wilful by turns. Not for the first time Ritchie thought she was too much in the company of adults, and over-indulged by Maria, who made up for her absences during the day by taking her most places with her.

She declared her *zarzuela de mariscos* '*demasiado*' and pushed it away from her fretfully. Anna would have made short work of her, he found himself thinking. She had always insisted on good behaviour from the children at the table, a throwback from Clevedon Crescent formality.

'Did you enjoy yourselves?' Ritchie asked on the way home.

'I liked Manuel,' Van said. 'He's very kind.'

'*Simpático*,' Mish said. 'Very enjoyable, Dad. I've invited him to look in and see us when he comes to New York. That child was a bit of a pest, though.'

'She's spoiled,' Van said.

'Still, she's a little beauty.' Ritchie noticed she shut up at that remark.

230

Twenty

❦

Anna stayed first with Rose because it was better than staying with Nancy. Mother gave her breathing space. She had strict times for resting, for her hairdressing appointments, her bridge, which only an earthquake could change. And it gave her a good feeling to be there. Rose must be lonely at times. And it was always good to be back in that room she had shared for so long with Jean and where they had had so many secrets in common.

Rose looked older. Her makeup was more pronounced, the powder filling and emphasizing the lines round her mouth, her hair was thinner and too rigid for her gaunt face.

The kitchen was still meticulous and cosy with the Aga, and a ginger kitten was lying in a basket near it which Bessie proudly showed her.

'I thought you weren't going to have any more when the last Tumshie died?'

'So I wisnae, but guess who brought it to me in its own wee basket? Your mother-in-law, Mrs Laidlaw.'

'Well, I never.' How easy it was to slip into the old way of talking. 'Sachernalia', as Ritchie called it, sloughed off her in two shakes of a lamb's tail. 'I didn't know she came here.'

'Och aye, she comes yince a month or thereabouts.

On your ma's invitation, of course, but Mrs Laidlaw tells me she likes fine to see her and then she can let you know how your ma's keepin'.'

'That's kind. Yes, she always tells me, but I thought it was just that they wrote to each other. I must go and see Ritchie's parents.'

'A widnae bother. She was here the day afore yesterday and she telt me they were aff to your faither-in-law's sister in Mauchline. She's just lost her husband. They're stayin' on for a bit to console her. She's a fine wumman, that. Her and me get on fine. She even gies me a haun wi' the dishes afore she goes away. I'd let her, but I widnae let your ma.'

'She wouldn't offer.'

'No, she's no' been brought up to it. But she comes in here from time to time for a chat. I think she likes the wee cat tae. Remember how she couldny abide Tumshie?'

'Yes.' They laughed together. Anna stroked the tiny kitten. 'What do you call this one?'

'Whit dae ye think? Ginger.'

'Well, who would have thought it?'

'You always had a quick tongue in your head. Away you go and sit wi' your ma till I get the dinner ready. She's been that excited aboot you comin'. You'd think you were the Queen of England.'

She and her mother drank a sherry together from the heavy crystal glasses which had been inherited from her grandparents. The silver tray they stood on was polished to an unbelievable brightness. They must sell better stuff in Glasgow for cleaning silver than she could buy in Renton, or perhaps she didn't use enough 'elbow grease', one of Bessie's indispensable ingredients.

'I'm sorry Ritchie isn't with you,' Rose said. 'What

nonsense is this of him being away over Christmas?'

'It's pressure of work, Mother. He's become famous, you know.' She had prepared her story in advance. 'And since he's seeing too little of the children, we both agreed it would be nice if they could spend Christmas with him. Mish was keen to see the galleries in Barcelona, and it was by way of a little treat for Van after she passed her A levels. With distinction.' She always found herself bragging to offset her mother's consistent playing down of anything in her life – in case she got above herself with living 'down there'.

'A levels? What's this nonsense about A levels?'

'It's the same as the Highers I got at Westbourne.'

'It won't be so good. Scottish education is renowned. What does she intend to do? Is she thinking of getting married? I'm all in favour of couples getting married young. It keeps them out of mischief.'

'I'm afraid that's broken off, Mother. I'm quite glad. I think she's far too young. She was probably taken by the idea of having a boyfriend, like the other girls. That's why I was pleased she was going to Spain. She should see something of the world, not tie herself up with the first person who interests her.'

'Well, I don't know. Chance is a fine thing. She's not what I call a very *taking* girl, from a man's point of view. I remember Gordon saying something like that to Nancy and she passed it on.'

'Trust Nancy.'

'Now, don't miscall your sister. In a way he's right. Girls are so smart nowadays. Look at Wendy. A real beauty. I'm surprised you haven't taken Vanessa more in hand. Tell her to pull back her shoulders. And those glasses. None of my girls wore glasses.'

'That's the luck of the draw, Mother.' I could *scream*

already . . . 'How are the happy couple, by the way?'

'Gordon and Wendy?' She looked peevish. 'I haven't seen them for quite a time. Nancy should pull them up there. And Mrs Armour has quite let me down. I went to a lot of trouble to get her into one of my bridge fours and then she said she was afraid she was too busy. And I was only invited to Gordon and Wendy's new home once, right at the beginning. That's gratitude for you, and when I think what those Edinburgh crystal glasses cost me! I was hoping for an occasional dinner invitation. They aren't too far away at Hyndland and they must realize I'm alone here.'

'Well, it's a busy time in their lives, making new friends, setting up their new home. You know what it's like.'

She softened. 'Yes, you're right, and Nancy says a little bird whispered in her ear . . .' She made elaborate gestures with her hand towards her stomach, then put her finger to her lips. 'Of course, it's early days.'

'Is she . . . ?' Anna said, playing along with this pantomime.

'We have to go to Nancy's tonight. Maybe she'll say something to you. I don't count nowadays.'

'Now, now, Mother.' This woman who once had irritated her so much now only did so momentarily. She would let her thoughts drift to the happy days she had spent here when Ritchie was her whole life, a bright, shining experience, and that closeness with Jean, a completeness, always in the background. She could think of her father who had kept the peace so often with his brood of women, of times when they were all gathered round the table and Bessie would come in with Tumshie at her heels. And Mother's eagle eye. 'I've told you time and time again,

Bessie . . .' And Tumshie's retreating rump. A nod was as good as a wink to the estimable Tumshie.

Happy days, she thought. Nancy with her golden hair and her capacity for reducing her and Jean to helpless giggling with her prejudiced remarks. 'Mother, stop those twins laughing at me! It isn't fair . . .' And dashing every morning to the Art School, the three of them, jumping on the tram in Great Western Road, jumping off at Renfrew Street and climbing the hill, knocking against each other with their heavy satchels of paints and brushes and hammers and chisels.

And Ritchie on the steps waiting for her, stocky, curly-haired, open, charming smile – 'There's your boyfriend, Anna . . .' She heard Rose's voice.

'I said this is a very nice sherry. Amontillado. You can always rely on Coopers.'

Nancy and James had changed. That was the first impression. Nancy had a drawn expression, and like her mother, wore heavier makeup. Her clothes were fussier, her nail polish too red. There was about her an air of defiance, which was strange. What could she be defiant about, Anna wondered.

James seemed drier. His handclasp was dry as if he had chalk on his fingers, and his hair looked as if it had been dusted with it.

The meal was faultless, but like Nancy, too fussy with exotic sauces whose ingredients she explained to Anna at great length. 'You get such original recipes in *Good Housekeeping*. Do you take it "down there", Anna?'

'No. I'm afraid I don't read magazines very much. I'm busy working.'

'You and Jean! I just don't have the time for my

watercolours these days, what with this and that. I'm like Mother. I have a sample of my paintings here and that's the lot.' She nodded to the wall above the fireplace.

'Yes, I noticed it as I came in. It's good, Nancy. Where is it?'

'It's a corner of the Crathie gardens. We did a tour of the Scottish gardens with James's Association years ago, before we started going on cruises, didn't we, James?'

'I enjoyed that.' He looked wistful. 'Scottish history . . .'

'James would be an old stick-in-the-mud if you'd let him. I thought the rose trellis gave it a good focus.'

'Yes, it does.' And spoils it. Nancy and Mother had grown tired of their own competence in watercolours because there had never been any struggle.

'Of course, Ritchie is the star turn these days,' James said. 'I read a piece about him in the *Herald*. "Famous Expatriate", it said. "What we lose the world benefits from." Well, that's as it should be.'

Rose was tired with this discussion. 'Are Wendy and Gordon coming tonight?' she asked. 'Later on?'

'No.' Nancy suddenly looked brittle. 'She's not been feeling so good, Mother.' Anna saw the forced smile, the chest rising. 'I'll let you into the secret. There's a baby on the way.' Her mother's face broke, it seemed, into pieces of delight, her mouth widened, her head inclined.

'Now, that's what I like to hear! Morning sickness.' She nodded sagely. 'It sometimes goes on and on. How I suffered. People said when you were on the way, Nancy, "I don't know how you can face it, Mrs Mackintosh, after all you went through with the twins," but, well, we wanted a boy.'

'I must have been a disappointment to you, then,' Nancy said, lifting her chin, then bending and spooning her raspberry mousse as if it were responsible for her very existence.

'Now, that's no way to talk,' Rose said, all smiles now that Nancy was a prospective grandmother. 'You've always been my little girl, until you became James's.' She smiled beatifically at him. 'The daintiness of her then, James! She was like a little doll. People in trams –'

And now she's like a big doll – Anna often carried on imaginary conversations with Jean. It was a substitute for the real thing and brought her closer.

'Do you have trouble with the servant problem down there?' Nancy veered away from the subject of babies. 'My woman has let me down this week. It's too disheartening, especially as she always comes in to help me when I'm entertaining.'

'What a shame. We'll wash up together. I don't have a servant, I have a woman, two for safety. That way I'm never bereft. And a man for the garden. It's very big and I need help. Ritchie's away so much.'

'Staying in your Spanish property?' 'Property' was a word much in favour with Rose instead of the humbler 'house'.

'Yes. Sometime you must come and see it. It's airy, on the side of a hill, with marble floors. Bougainvillaea grows over the terrace.' She laid it on thick. 'He's on a very big project for the *Departamento de Justicia* and there's a time limit.'

'I don't know why you don't go too. Have some of this raspberry mousse, Anna. Devonshire cream.'

'No, thanks, I'll wait for the cheese. I wanted to see you all, and besides I'm building up a body of work at home. I can't work there.'

'I don't know why you bother when Ritchie could keep you. You must be *rolling* in it.'

'Not so as you'd notice.'

Yes, she's as brittle as thin toffee, Jean. I'll get it out of her later . . .

In the kitchen when they were washing up she said, 'Am I imagining things, Nancy, or are you a bit on edge? I know Mother can be trying –'

'You don't know the half of it! You aren't subjected to it all the time, questions, questions, questions. No, it's not her altogether . . .' The words burst out from her. 'The baby's due any minute, at least any time before Christmas.' Five months. Anna made a rapid calculation. 'I don't know how I'm going to tell her!'

'But . . .' she kept her face solemn '. . . you mean she was pregnant when they got married?'

'Yes. Four months. They didn't tell us. I could have *killed* Gordon, not to mention her. That huge wedding! Everybody'll laugh, you know what they're like.' She became indignant. 'She must have tricked him into it.'

'Oh, Nancy!' She forgot to be sympathetic. 'Don't talk a load of rubbish! They both got carried away. It'll all blow over. What does James say?'

'You know James. He doesn't get . . . excited. He's disappointed, but he says, like you, it'll blow over. But it's the thought of all that sniggering, and them saying fancy her going down the aisle in white and not saying a word . . .'

Did she expect her to shout it on the way down, Jean?

Don't be so supercilious, Anna. Poor lass. I know the dread, the feeling of inevitability. You can *hear* time marching on.

'People aren't unkind, Nancy. "It might have been

238

me," they'll be saying. What about Mrs Armour?'

'She blames Gordon. She says he must have been too impetuous. Well, that's a new name for it.'

Think of Gordon, Jean, po-faced in his morning suit, having made an honest woman out of Wendy.

'I'll tell Mother if you like, Nancy. I'm leaving in a day or two, so I won't have to listen to her for long.'

'Would you, Anna? She's got to be told but I can't face it. It was the size of the wedding . . . a *white* wedding . . . it must have cost the Armours a packet! When you think of the ingratitude of the young you wonder why you ever have them. I feel such a failure. I never thought Gordon would do a thing like that. It's so *common*. You're lucky with your two, so far, anyhow, especially Hamish. I'm not so sure about Vanessa, but maybe she'll improve now that she's got a boyfriend. Mother was telling me.'

'No longer. He's thrown her over. Do you remember long ago, Gordon doing the same thing?' Her sister looked blank. 'When he was going to take her to the tennis hop and he ditched her for Wendy. Went out on their yacht?'

'I remember something like that. But she was only a schoolgirl. It wouldn't mean much to her.' She dismissed that triviality. 'And you and Ritchie. Him so famous! Some people have all the luck.'

'He's so famous that he's gone off with another woman, temporarily, I hope.' Jean, you should have seen her face, the quick look of delight immediately smothered.

'Oh no, Anna. Oh, you poor thing.'

'I don't feel at all poor. Just disappointed in him as you are in Gordon. They're both immature, but there's more excuse for Gordon. He's young. You pull up your socks, Nancy. Don't let it get you down.

If you're worried about talk, go off on another cruise with James.'

'Funny you should say that. We've actually booked one for January. But I'll have to see Gordon's baby first, and make sure it's all right. I wonder what they'll call him? Mr Armour's Robert – that's all right, but shortened to Bob . . .' she screwed up her face '. . . and Bobbie's worse. Oh, you have cheered me up, Anna! It just lets you see everybody has troubles. Fancy Ritchie! And you always so smart and elegant too. When you think how mad he was about you when we were at the Art School . . .'

'It just goes to show,' Anna said.

'Yes, it just goes to show.'

She took quite a delight in breaking the news to Rose before she left for Kirkcudbright but it was momentary, and she was sympathetic as she consoled her with a glass of sherry, and then another. 'Don't let it worry you, Mother. It happens all the time.'

'It will worry me. If it happens in the family, it happens to me.'

Twenty-one

❦

Ritchie was uneasy about their proposed visit to Maria's flat. Van and Mish were bound to make comparisons with their mother. He said to Maria the night before she was entertaining them – he had told them he was staying overnight in Barcelona and left them to think it was at his workshop – 'It's difficult for them.'

'Don't treat them as children.' She smiled as if at a child. 'They are grown-ups. You tell me your son lives with a woman, and the girl must have had some experience at her age.'

'Not very happy ones. She feels inferior with the opposite sex. She's only happy with the handicapped and the deprived.'

'Or superior. You have made a mistake with her, or your wife has. Artistic people often do that, a Bohemian attitude. You should have sent her to a finishing school. Ana is already booked at a prestigious one in Madrid, for the best families. Your daughter is gauche.'

'She would be the first person to agree with you.' He was cold with anger. 'I don't consider her gauche, nor does anyone who can see through her shyness to her true worth. Unfortunately she feels herself

241

lacking with people like you, sophisticated, worldly.'

'Well, naturally.' She was thick-skinned as well as critical. 'Tell me, Ricardo,' she said, turning to him. They were lying on top of the bed having showered together. Her short towelling robe was untied. 'What do you intend to do about me?'

'Do?' He was astonished at the quick change of subject.

'Is this an affair, or do you intend to leave your wife altogether? You said you would tell me. I am a Catholic. I only permit irregular relationships to go on for a certain length of time.'

'You want me to get a divorce?' The idea was preposterous as he said it.

'I want you to make up your mind. You've changed since your children came. I can see it. The young man wouldn't mind what you did, but the girl doesn't like me. It's in her eyes.'

'It isn't you, it's *me* she can't understand.' Nor can I understand myself, he thought. Could there have been a secret gratification in the very idea that he, an ordinary Glasgow boy of poor background should actually be making love to this Spanish lady of high degree?

Get with it, Laidlaw, he thought now. Where do you get this 'boy' stuff? You're halfway through your life, for God's sake. You may be a well-known painter, but you're an immature fool. You need Anna to keep you straight. And with that thought he knew it was over with Maria. He'd go back if Anna would have him.

From desiring Maria a moment or two ago he now felt cold, unstirred, a fine thought, he realized, lying as he was with his hand between her thighs. He wanted to go home, not back to Renton but to

Glasgow, back to his roots to get some sense knocked into him.

'Love me, Ricardo,' she said, turning on her side and bending over him. 'You think too much.'

He gave in because it was easier than resisting. Once you knew the book of rules it was like turning on the ignition key. It followed the same pattern every time. With Anna there was no pattern. One minute they could roll like puppies (including playful bites), the next they were themselves, closely held, mature.

With Maria there were techniques, the shower and the lotions before and after. Cleanliness took the place of passion. All was hygienic. There was no sweating, no peculiar noises – unless they were detailed in the book. The procedure was extensive. It generally took the best part of an hour and yet it lacked depth. When finally she groaned and said, 'Ah, yes, Ricardo, yes, yes . . .' it was like being let out of school. Yes, it was over.

And more importantly, he wasn't working. She inhibited him rather than inspired him. She exhausted him. He only wanted to lie in bed and rest. It didn't work. He smelled the musky smell from her which he noticed after she'd had an orgasm. He had never dared tell her. That smell now in his nostrils was strange and foreign. 'Take a cat of your own kind,' his mother had always said.

True, he and Anna belonged to a different class. The Mackintoshes were well-off townees but Anna's grandfather had been a fisherman, and their roots, the Mackintoshes' and the Laidlaws', were nourished from the same soil. He needed that strong, familiar base if he were to consolidate his success as a painter. He had got it from Anna, whereas Maria, in spite of all her technical knowledge, came from a different culture.

Van and Mish came the following afternoon and they all went out to see the Crib Fair round the cathedral, and afterwards to drink Spanish champagne and eat fishy tapas in a *cava*. Mish was full of enthusiasm, Van looked slightly worried.

'You liked it, Van?' he asked her.

'Oh yes, beautiful, but too grand.'

'You should see the *Merced* in September,' Maria said. 'That would surprise you. I daren't take Ana to that. She would be trampled underfoot.'

'They have big giants in the streets,' Ana said, 'and fireworks and parades and people with torches. Lucia is allowed, Mama? Why not me?'

'When you are Lucia's age perhaps.' She spoke to Van across the table. 'You mustn't mind some glitter, Vanessa, it is part of life. Highlights. It is the same in living. Up and down. You must have known some highlights.'

'A cat had kittens in my bed when I was quite young.'

'What a highlight!'

'I've never forgotten it, the look on the mother cat's face, when I went off to school: "Please leave me till I get this over."' She smiled her rare smile and looked beautiful.

'Ugh!' Ana said. 'A cat in your bed! Did you get the maid to wash the sheets?'

'Mum would.' She looked at the little girl. 'That's interesting, Ana. I never thought of that.' Maria caught Ritchie's eye. 'I told you that you should have sent her to a finishing school,' her expression said.

Josita had prepared a wonderful meal for them when they got back, *suquet de peix*, a mixed seafood dish, and turkey, and wonderful sweets. Van didn't eat much. She had probably seen live turkeys in the street market this morning. Ritchie was inclined to agree that perhaps a finishing school could have persuaded her that you couldn't be one great ache for everything in the world, and if you were, you made people feel damned uncomfortable.

It was a beautiful evening, and about midnight they went out again to be amongst the people and to look at the lighted cathedral in all its glory. He felt he was beginning to see sense in things, and that perhaps Maria had unwittingly helped him. He had his arm round her shoulders because it was his nature. He saw Van looking at him. There was no malice in her look, which was worse than if there had been.

He was mildly drunk. 'I've brought my conscience along with me,' he said to Maria, nodding at Van.

She was acute. 'I have noticed too. If I were you I should be worried about that one. She is lacking an essential skin, that of self-protection.'

They went into a *cava* to have drinks and to give Ana a rest. She was looking tired. It was past midnight.

'You'll soon be tucked up in bed, little one,' Maria said. 'We haven't far to walk.'

'I won't sleep unless Ricardo comes into my room and tells me more about Wee Magreega.' Her Spanish pronunciation sounded comical with the emphasis on the last syllable. Van and Mish laughed.

'Of course he will,' Maria said. 'You will all stay the night. There are two spare bedrooms.' She looked at them.

'Ricardo sleeps with Mama,' Ana said.

Vanessa's eyes were dark.

*   *   *

245

For the first time in his life Ritchie was unable to make love. Maria laughed at him, saying he was getting old. He tried hard, even resorting to conjuring erotic images in his head, but it was no good, and in the middle of his disappointment in himself he went to sleep.

He woke the next morning with a sour taste in his mouth. He drove them back to the house and said he must get on with his work. 'We'll have a quiet dinner tonight,' he said, 'at home.' He thought they both looked strange, as if they found him strange. It had been a mistake having them here. Children of Ana's age would accept anything, but he had made those two grown-ups uncertain of where they stood. He wasn't the father they knew.

Their visit seemed to fizzle out. Mish had seen all the galleries, he said, and Van stayed more and more in the house when they went to Barcelona each day. The weather was cold, rainy and miserable. Ritchie's painting block was almost complete. He sat every day on a stool in front of the mural he was working on and saw it as a confusion of shapes and colours with no meaning.

On one occasion when he was deep in thought he realized Manuel was at his elbow. He had a cat-like tread, light-footed as a girl. 'It doesn't flow,' he said. 'You've lost it.'

'It's only the second block I've ever had. Once, long ago, in London . . .' There had been a woman in his life then too, Christine Bouvier. Was she still in a mental hospital, he wondered. He had never bothered to find out.

He made up his mind. Anna would be due to come back from Kirkcudbright any day now. Van was going back to start work in the children's home, she had told him, and Mish's holiday was up too.

'I'm travelling back with you,' he said to her, 'if you don't mind. I booked my ticket today.' She smiled at him, her face lighting up.

'Mum will be pleased to see you.' And then, her eyes darkening: 'Oh, I hope she will.'

'We'll see.' He felt ashamed, and yet there was the lingering belief that their love for each other had withstood his foolishness. And there was Van and Mish. What did two elderly children think of a father who strayed away from someone like Anna? He daren't think any more. He knew how the Prodigal Son must have felt . . .

Twenty-two

Jean was waiting for her at the station, wearing a cape of loden green and flat brogues. Her hair was wild. She's dressing up in her role as local artist, Anna thought, as they hugged each other enthusiastically.

'Have I missed you!' They seemed to breathe it together.

'I have the car parked at the back. Come on. Do you want me to carry something?'

'Yes, take this holdall. I'll manage the rest.'

'Why didn't you drive?'

'I'm afraid of fog.' She had felt too uncertain of herself to face the long journey in winter by car. She would tell Jean about Ritchie later.

'God, this is heavy!' She shook the holdall.

'Christmas presents. I'm too mean to post them.'

'I've got your stashed away in the spare bedroom. We're a couple of meanies.'

'You look striking, Jean, a combination of *Wuthering Heights* and the Countess of Strathmore or whoever is the grand lady in these parts.'

'I like capes and I do a lot of walking to think about my pictures. The hair is all my own. More like the mad wife in the attic but I've just washed it.'

'I guessed that. How is the painting going?'

'Well. I'm selling. And I've struck a vein in London, not exactly a rich one but a vein. John doesn't mind how much time I spend in the studio. He's hoping for early retirement on the proceeds.'

'Van saw one of yours in London.'

'Yes, I have an agent down there. "Down there"!' She laughed as she opened the door of her car. 'Give me that and I'll put it in the boot.' She came back and got in beside Anna, turned the ignition. 'Here we go on a tour of that well-known centre of artistic effort, that little gem of south-west Scotland. How about *your* work?'

'Bashing on. I have a small but select clientele "down there".' They laughed as they half sang the words together. 'In my case it's "up there". You always go "up to town" with the Renton ladies. Where's Roderick?'

'He has this job in a garage. I told you. He wears green overalls and a cap with "Shell" on the front, and he thinks he's the boss. After the first shock for the inhabitants of Kirkcudbright at seeing the doctor's son working in a garage, they've come to terms with it. You can get used to anything but hanging, as the saying goes.'

They had time for a 'wee chin-wag' before either Roderick, Sarah or John arrived. Jean had a good fire burning in the sitting room, and a small table was drawn up in front of it with a tempting supply of scones and cakes.

'Lovely,' Anna said, and, jokingly, 'You've been busy.'

'Not me. Since Janet married her farmer I have Mrs Roberts who does for me, and accepts although doesn't understand that I'd rather spend my time painting than cooking or baking. John agrees.'

'And Sarah's at home?'

'No. Didn't I tell you? She is the receptionist at the surgery now. She took a training so that she could be near Alastair every waking hour.'

'Is that still going on?'

'That affair was made in heaven. But he's a man of principle, our Alastair. He wants to pay back his partnership loan before he pops the question. John told him there was no hurry, but he said he wouldn't feel right, hooch aye, a true Highlander. Sarah supports him in his decision, so everybody's happy. They're not what I would call a fiery couple. Unlike us.' Anna accepted her cup of tea.

'All fire and no sense. Oh, I'm sorry, Jean. I wasn't casting aspersions.'

'It's water under the bridge now. Water . . . there I go. It's fallen into the category of love's young dream now, and I'm not being banal. It *was* a dream. I see it as a scene which two other people were enacting . . .' Her beautiful eyes rested on Anna, who saw again that like Van's they had a blue intensity, a way of darkening or lighting with a variety of expressions, a reflection of her thoughts. 'How about Ritchie?'

'That dream's shattered too. He's left me.' She felt she was making the bald statement partly for effect.

'I don't believe it! Not Ritchie. You two are joined at the hip.'

'No longer. There's a Spanish siren.' She would be truthful. 'It's a kind of trial separation. Whether I'll take him back or not is another question.'

'You haven't anyone else?'

She shook her head. 'You know me. Faithful unto death. It's physical, mental and spiritual with me. I just couldn't see anyone else in his place. Men are different.'

'I'm disappointed in Ritchie. But it's only a fling. He's inclined to act and then think – except when he's painting.'

'Yes, you're right. Oh, I'm aware of my limitations. I nag at him. I'm intensely critical. He thinks I'm hard on Van, soft on Mish.'

'Are you?'

'On the surface, yes, because Mish never lets me down and she does.'

'But if she's not letting herself down?'

'That's another way of looking at it. You're right. All she wants is to be left alone so that she can pick up all the waifs and strays who cross her path. I know that's laudable, but fifty per cent of the time I think she gets conned. There's the black girl called Adelaide, for instance. She moved to London but I think Van still sees her.'

'Are you racist?'

'Of course not. But even you must feel that they're different.'

'I have no problem. I love their skin tones. I'm dying to find one to paint but they don't frequent Kirkcudbright.'

'The colour wouldn't matter. It's just that I don't *like* her.'

'Okay. So what are you going to do about Ritchie?'

'Damn all. Get on with my work, which is always there, try and make a success of it, travel. I enjoyed New York and Mish's girlfriend, Karin. She's Jewish.'

'Another label. Are you prejudiced about that?'

'You're an annoying devil. I'm *not* prejudiced. And it's just that I don't want to see Van selling herself

251

short. She's so vulnerable, simply not equipped to discriminate . . .'

'If you're talking about being equipped, how do you think I feel about Roderick? He's seventeen now. He's a big strong boy who looks like a young man, but inside he's a child who doesn't understand . . .'

The door opened. Sarah and Roderick came in. She spoke first.

'Here you are!' She bent and kissed Anna. 'Dad said you'd be having a chin-wag.' She was such a wholesome girl. *She* would never give any trouble.

'You look blooming, Sarah. How is Alastair?'

'He's fine too.'

'Anna,' Roderick was gesticulating, 'Roderick's bursting to show you his garage outfit.'

'It's nifty, isn't it, Aunty?' He revolved slowly in front of Anna, finishing with a low bow. They all laughed.

'Very impressive,' Anna said, 'especially the cap. I'm sorry I haven't the car with me so that I could see you working the pumps.'

'I run the garage at lunchtime when Mr Johnson's away. All by myself. Don't I, Mummy?'

'So you tell me.'

'Oh, I haven't given Aunty a kiss yet.' She was enveloped in his enthusiastic embrace.

'Roderick's my very best friend,' she said guiltily. There had been a strong smell of sweat from him, rank, not a boy's smell. 'Talk about a bear's hug!'

'Oh, I'm big and strong!' He flexed his right arm. 'See that! Me Tarzan!' He giggled, then sobered. 'When I'm older I'm going to marry Alice.'

'The pretty Logan girl?' Anna looked at Jean.

'Yes, the younger one. You met her once. Go and get your overalls off, Roderick, and have a bath.' Had she seen her instant recoil from him? 'Go on, please. Alastair will be coming home with Daddy for supper.'

'Alastair is my friend.' The boy stuck out his chest. 'He gives me books to read, and sometimes he takes me runs in his car with Sarah. He's just like one of the family.' He nodded sagely.

'That's nice.'

'Go on, chatterbox.' Jean got up. 'I'll just finish off the supper.'

'I'll come and help you.' Anna rose to her feet also.

'And I'll hurry this lad along.' Sarah pushed Roderick playfully in front of her. 'I'm going to change.'

'It's all done, really,' Jean said in the kitchen. 'Mrs Roberts cooked the roast and prepared the vegetables, and Sarah has made a *tarte aux pommes* — she's going to cookery classes to prepare herself for feeding Alastair when they're married.'

'Are you happy about them?' Anna asked.

'Absolutely. They even look the same. Wait till you see him again. They will be indistinguishable in a few years.'

'They're both sandy-haired, aren't they?'

'Yes. And they'll have children the same and they'll all ride ponies and win the Junior Cup at the Agricultural Show . . . yes, I'm very happy. It makes up for Roderick.'

'You've coped there, Jean.'

'As far as I can. But there might be problems ahead. He has no real friends, and he needs people to love him. The lads in the garage joke with him at work but they'd never ask him to join them at night. He's still the doctor's son. Now tell me about your Glasgow visit. How did you find Mother?'

'Very Rose-like, and Bessie has a ginger kitten who's called Ginger. I felt lonely without you in that great bedroom we shared.'

'Happy days – some of them unhappy. Gosh, you were mad about Ritchie Laidlaw! I can't believe what you're telling me about him.'

'He's always been susceptible to women. You must know that.'

'I know women would have done anything for him. That smiling face, and those curls. He looked like what he was, a painter, slightly raffish, slightly arrogant. I was too much in love with Frederick or I would have joined the queue. But a woman in Spain! It must be a momentary infatuation.'

'More than that. She's quite striking, upper-class Spanish. She looks as if she's used to getting what she wants. It's lowered my self-esteem. That's what I can't forgive him for. My work has been a great help all the same. You can say, "Well, to hell with them." I'd love to see some of your work, Jean. I miss not having Ritchie's to criticize.'

'Yes, you're good at that. Tomorrow we'll spend the morning in the studio.'

Supper with the family was a happy affair. Jean was right about the similarity between Alastair and Sarah. They were so alike that it hardly mattered which one of them you addressed. He was a florid young man with the face of a true Highlander, long chin, high cheekbones, the ready smile of the untroubled and possibly unimaginative.

John had aged, but almost imperceptibly. There was a greater gentleness in his expression than

254

before. He would grow into a gentle old man but would always adore his Jean, and he would be content to let her follow her own pursuits.

'Did you know I have a famous painter now for a wife, Anna?' he asked her.

'Not from her. She's too modest, but fame will out. I know.'

'"Scottish Painter with European Approach," the *Herald* said, and then it was copied in the *Scotsman*.' He spoke proudly.

'Kirkcudbright won't be able to hold her soon.'

'Hey! You'll make me big-headed,' Jean laughed.

'She lets *me* have a go,' Roderick said. 'I can paint better faces than her. Hers have blue cheeks and red hair sometimes. Remember the one I did of you, Daddy? Even the tie had the same stripes as your real one.'

'Yes, that was a masterpiece. You'll be in the papers too. The talk of the town.'

'I *am* the talk of the town. Everybody says "Hello", except Mr Johnson, and he says, "Look slippy, Roderick!" Honestly,' he looked around the table, 'I'm never off the go from morning to night.'

'Poor soul,' Sarah said.

'Would you like me to give you a line to get off for a week?' Alastair teased, exchanging glances with Sarah.

'No, thanks. To tell you the truth, Dr Alastair, he couldn't get on without me.'

'I believe you.'

'Thousands wouldn't,' Sarah said.

That evening, Anna felt relaxed and happy, mostly because she was with Jean. When their glances met they smiled at each other. 'It's good to see you,' they said with their eyes.

255

At ten o'clock the telephone rang and Jean answered it. 'Really,' she said as she got up, 'not at this time of night.' The doctor's wife, Anna thought fondly.

'I'll go, John,' Alastair said, 'if it's a call.'

Jean came back after a few minutes, her face alight with excitement.

'It was Nancy! And you'll never guess. Wendy's had a baby girl!'

'But . . . ?' John said, and stopped himself. 'Well done.' He buried his face in his cup.

'You're pulling our legs, Jean.' Anna looked at her, trying not to laugh.

'Would I ever do such a thing?' She, too, was trying to keep her face straight. 'Wendy's fine, the baby is eight and a half pounds, and then . . .' she was struggling for composure '. . . Nancy said, "I dare you to laugh, Jean Whitbread!"'

'What's funny?' Roderick said. 'What are you all laughing for? Mummy, what is it?' He suddenly shouted. His voice, on the edge of breaking, had an ugly sound.

'Lower your voice, Roderick.' John was stern for once, and then, his mouth working, 'It's your Aunt Nancy. She isn't very good at maths.'

'I am, I am!' He shouted again, then cast an apologetic glance at John. 'I could easily give the customers their change but Mr Johnson says I'm not old enough yet. When are you old enough to give change, Daddy?'

'In about five months.'

They all burst into laughter.

Twenty-three

❦

They went to dinner at the Logans a few days before Christmas. It was to be a proper dressed-up party, black tie and long dresses because Tim Logan liked formality, which was strange in a painter, Anna said, but then he wasn't a real painter, according to Jean. His forte was flattering portraits of the County set, combined with the role of gentleman farmer.

'He's no gentleman,' she said. 'There's talk about him, and I know by what Christine *doesn't* say that he's anything but faithful. I can't stand him myself.'

Anna looked at her set face. 'I get the picture. Is he any good as a farmer?'

'Not even that. He leaves it all to a factor. It belongs to Christine. Her parents were wealthy, and she met him in London when she was coming out. He was at the Slade, though how he ever got in there God alone knows. Still, his chocolate-box efforts please the gentry.'

'Funny how painters push through all barriers.' They looked at each other and laughed.

'At least Ritchie's likeable.'

'Who said anything about Ritchie? Stop reading my mind.'

Bunty, Sarah's friend, was there with Nigel, her boyfriend, a member of the local hunting set, as was

Bunty. She had her mother's love of horses. Alice, her sister, now sixteen, was still hurtingly beautiful, Anna thought, as delicate as a piece of china with her fair fine skin and blonde hair. She should be preserved in a china cabinet, safe from prying eyes.

At dinner, Anna turned to Tim Logan who was on her right at the head of the table. 'Have you still got that marvellous Guthrie?' she asked him. 'The one like his *Midsummer*? Your wife let me see it the last time I was here.'

'It's my prized possession. If you'd like to see it we'll have a look at it after dinner.'

'Jean raves about its dappled tones. I'm hopeless about colour, but it reminded me of summer holidays long ago . . . on Loch Long.'

He raised his eyebrows, smiling. 'You don't like colour and you're married to Ritchie Laidlaw, one of Glasgow's best exports?'

'It certainly looks like that. He's in Barcelona just now.'

'So you're footloose and fancy free? We're honoured to have you in our neck of the woods. You and Jean are quite exotic for poor little Kirkcudbright,' he paused, 'Mrs Laidlaw.'

She looked at him, slightly puzzled by his tone. 'I'm more used to Anna,' she said. She longed suddenly for Ritchie.

'Fair exchange then. Tim.'

She didn't like him, nor his type, like a wily auctioneer. His double role was reflected in his appearance, the florid complexion of a man who spent a lot of time outdoors, but his knife and fork were held by the hands of a painter, or at least someone who had never held a spade. He shot her an amused glance and she felt uneasy under his bold look.

258

'What's happened to Satan?' She said the first thing which came into her head.

'Satan? Oh, he's as busy as ever!' He laughed, a short 'Ha-ha'. 'Oh, you mean Sarah's *horse*! I thought there was a *double entendre* somewhere. We simple country folks . . . I believe he's in comfortable retirement somewhere around the place. You don't want to see him, do you?'

'No, no . . .' She felt foolish.

'You'd be much drier underfoot looking at the Guthrie.' She turned away from him and joined in the general conversation round the table. She felt Tim Logan's eyes on her.

Afterwards they were having coffee in the large comfortable sitting room and she joined Christine Logan who was sitting with Nigel, Bunty's friend. He got up eagerly and offered her his place, glancing towards Bunty.

'I'm sorry your husband isn't here,' Christine said when she sat down. 'It's not often we capture a painting lion.'

'It's difficult to cage Ritchie. He's a devil for work, and his deadline in Barcelona was getting uncomfortably near. I've got used to it.'

'Fame has its drawbacks. Tim isn't in the same class but I don't see much of him either. He's often asked to stay when he's doing a portrait. He's becoming an authority on stately homes, and, to tell you the truth, he loves being fêted.'

'That's what I call combining business with pleasure.'

'Men are experts at that.' Was Christine Logan reading between the lines, or was it that she wasn't happy with her own husband? She looked around the room and saw that Alice and Roderick weren't there. Perhaps they had gone to the games room. She remembered hearing Christine asking him if he played table tennis. 'Daddy taught me,' he had said proudly. She always seemed to show him kindly consideration, unlike her husband who ignored his presence.

'Are Roderick and Alice playing table tennis?' she said, turning back to Christine. Her husband was there.

'If you could call it that.' He gave his short barking laugh. 'I came over to ask Anna if she'd like to have another look at our Guthrie, darling. We were talking about it at dinner.'

'Oh, please don't bother,' she said.

'But he loves showing off, Anna.' Christine's voice was brittle. 'And see if they're in the games room while you're there, Timmy.' Anna, looking at her, thought she had aged since the last time she had seen her, about four years ago. Her cheeks had sunk, but not into smooth hollows. The skin looked loose. Her hair was brittle and dry-looking. Had she been ill? Jean hadn't said, but she was the last person to gossip.

'Come along, Anna,' Tim Logan said. 'I think this little lady has an eye, Christine. She's probably her husband's sternest critic, as *you* are, my darling.' He laughed his short 'Ha-ha', like the bark of a fox. She got up and followed him out of the room, wishing she had never suggested seeing the Guthrie.

'I thought it used to be in the upstairs hall,' she said, as they passed the foot of the stairs.

'No. We changed it to my study, along this corridor. The games room is at the end. I think I hear the fairy-footed Roderick.' She didn't reply. She hoped

Christine didn't think she had engineered this. The atmosphere had been, well, tense.

'Here we are.' He preceded her and switched on a light directly above the painting. The rest of the room was in shadow.

'Oh, yes . . .' She forgot him as she moved towards it, feeling she was walking into it, into all the far-off summer days of her youth, Kilcreggan and the long grass of the fields swishing about her bare legs, the loch sparkling below her at the foot of the hill.

If more painters modelled in colour, she thought, she might change her mind about colour. But then Ritchie had spoiled her for representational work, unless it was a gem like this, and with the thought of Ritchie she remembered he was with Maria.

She was so burning with resentment, suffused with hate that she was hardly aware of Tim Logan's hand slipping slowly between her arm and her side. She looked down and saw it, like an abstraction, saw it coming to rest on her left breast, felt its pressure. Her hate was so consuming that it took her a moment to realize what was happening. She watched, with a detached interest, the fingers of the hand bend, grasp, knead, felt his body press into her from behind. Her voice burst out, rough like a street hawker's in Argyle Street on a Saturday night: 'What the hell do you think you're doing?' She wrenched herself free and wheeled round to face him.

He gave his barking laugh, 'Ha-ha', and the short sharp sound nearly blew her head off with anger. 'What's the joke? Have you gone out of your mind? Or . . .' she glared at him '. . . have I been incredibly naïve?'

'Oh, come on, Anna.' He was not discomfited. 'Looking as you do. Don't come the sweet little innocent with me. I know your type, you and your sister . . .'

'Leave Jean out of it!' She was shaking with rage. It was a joke, really, to be taken as a philanderer when she and Jean were the most faithful of wives. Jean had laughed with her at the mirror, once. 'We're so sexy-looking! What a sell for some men!' Like this fool just now.

Logan suddenly grabbed her by the shoulder, and again, because she wasn't thinking fast enough, she was caught out. He kissed her roughly, forcing her mouth open, pushing his tongue down her throat and making her gag. 'Come on, I know you like it. You and your sister,' he tried to imprison her hands, 'playing hard to get . . .'

'You filthy –' He was strong.

'The exotic twins,' he said, 'pretending to be so high and mighty . . . when all the time . . .' he was forcing her backwards '. . . you're dying for it . . .'

His head jerked back, his grasp loosened, there was a high-pitched scream somewhere near which went on and on. It was a girl's voice, Alice's, high, frightened, wailing, 'Stop, stop, Roderick! You're hurting . . . me!' Anna's heart turned over, sickeningly. 'Stop it, Roderick!' Now a scream: 'Mummy!'

Logan pushed Anna aside, shouting as he ran for the door, 'Coming, darling! Coming!'

'He's . . . hurting . . . !' The cries were hysterical. 'Mummy!'

Anna ran after Logan into the corridor. They were all there. She saw Christine's distraught face, Jean, pale as death, and then she was running with the others into the room at the end of the corridor.

Roderick was spread-eagled on the floor on top of Alice. Anna stood with her hand to her mouth as Tim

262

Logan wrenched him off by the scruff of the neck. 'You little bugger!' His face was scarlet with outrage. 'This is my *daughter*, my daughter! Can you understand, you halfwit!' He shook Roderick violently, and she caught a glimpse of the boy's face, his bewilderment, his stupid grin. 'What do you think you're *doing*?'

'For God's sake, stop that, Logan!' John was there.

'It's all right, Daddy.' Roderick was the most composed of the three. 'Playing, Mr Logan. Just playing weddings. Honest! It's what the minister said, "To have and to hold," but Alice kept on wriggling . . .'

Anna heard Jean moan.

Logan turned and addressed the stricken faces around him. His was boiling scarlet with rage. 'In a civilized house . . . the filth!' He shook Roderick like a rat.

'Stop it!' John shouted. 'You'll kill him! For God's sake, let him go.'

Tim Logan pushed him aside. He was much the stronger of the two. 'I'm entitled to ask, aren't I? Come on, what were you up to?' He didn't release his hold on Roderick's collar, but John, with unexpected strength, had grabbed his son by the shoulders and dragged him out of Logan's grasp. Christine rushed forward and helped the shivering, weeping girl up from the floor, cradling her in her arms, stroking her back.

'Come with me, sweetie. It'll be all right. He didn't harm you, did he? He was only playing . . .'

'He jumped on me and tumbled me! He frightened me! The dribble was running out of his mouth . . .'

Jean was beside them, her face deathly pale, but speaking calmly. 'He's rough, Alice, but he wouldn't harm you. He thinks the world of you. Please don't cry. See, he's crying too.' Roderick was making grunting noises, wiping his eyes with the back of his hand. His little eyes were going from one to the other.

'It was a game, so it was. I'm telling the truth, Mummy. Daddy?' He looked pitifully at John. '"To have and to hold." I remembered it from Gordon's wedding. I said to Alice we'll play at weddings but she didn't understand. She thought I was being rough . . .'

'You little swine! It's sickening . . .' Tim Logan made another grab at Roderick. 'I'm not going to listen to any more of this.'

'For God's sake!' John stood in front of Roderick. 'Don't make the situation worse.' His face was as white as a sheet.

'He bloody well attacked my daughter. Laugh *that* off!'

'Horse play. Remember, it's Roderick. He doesn't understand everything . . .'

'Well, what in God's name are you doing letting an imbecile like that loose in a decent house? I've said it to Christine often . . .'

There was a dead silence.

'Oh, Tim . . .' Christine looked round from comforting Alice who was sobbing on her shoulder.

Jean spoke. She was rigid. The colour which had drained out of her face made her look years older. 'You stay, John, and talk to Tim. Try to explain to him. I'll take Roderick home. Tell him he didn't mean any harm.' She touched Christine's shoulder with her hand, almost timidly. 'You understand, Christine, don't you?' Christine didn't turn her head. Anna saw Jean was shaking. 'He wouldn't ever harm Alice, not

264

in a hundred years. Tell Alice you're sorry, Roderick.'
He hung his head and she pushed him forward. 'Go
on, say it.'

'Sorry, Alice.' His head was still down. He was
giggling. 'It was a wee game. Weddings . . .' Nobody
moved. The only sound was the girl's weeping,
quieter now.

'If you think that's the matter finished you're very
much mistaken.' Tim Logan stood, legs apart, breathing hard as if he had been running.

Alastair and Sarah were there with the coats. Bunty
and Nigel were hovering, Bunty grim-faced, Nigel
looking belligerent. 'Come along, Jean,' Alastair said.
'Leave it to John.'

'Yes, on you go. Is there any place where we could
talk, Logan?'

'My study.'

Nigel nodded approvingly. 'Quite right. It can't
just be brushed under the carpet.'

'Shut up, Nigel,' Bunty said. Her smile wavered at
Sarah.

Alastair bundled them into the car, Roderick between Jean and Anna, Sarah with him at the front.
No one spoke. They raced through the quiet streets.
Everyone must be indoors, the children tucked up,
counting the days until Santa came. Others would be
at parties, the socials, the church soirées – sandwiches and lemonade, paper hats.

Roderick said as they rounded the last corner in
old High Street before they came to their house, 'It
could have been a good game, that.' And, after a
pause, reflectively, 'Girls are no use.'

Anna looked at Jean. She wasn't weeping. She was
staring straight ahead as if into a bleak future.

* * *

265

When they got into the house Anna said, 'I think a cup of tea would be a good idea. What do you say?' Jean shook her head as if she hardly heard her.

'Not for me. I'll go up with Roderick and see him into bed.'

'Will you come down again?'

'I don't know . . .'

Neither Sarah nor Alastair wanted tea. He said he would have to get back in case there were any night calls in, and Anna sat in the sitting room, hearing their soft voices in the hall, and then the long silence. Kissing, she thought. Lucky Sarah. She got up and went upstairs.

Jean was in Roderick's bedroom folding his clothes. She looked up when Anna appeared in the doorway.

Anna said to Roderick, 'So you're in bed, are you?'

'Yes. Mummy's sad, but it was a good party, wasn't it?' He giggled. 'I hope I didn't blot my copybook?'

'I hope you didn't.' She looked at Jean. She wanted to say, 'Don't crucify yourself over this,' but it was too soon. 'Anything I can do?'

'No, thanks. I'll wait for John. I don't want to talk . . . yet.' The tension in her face was pitiable.

Anna nodded. 'Right.' They had husbands now, and husbands came first. 'You go downstairs to the fire and have a stiff drink while you're waiting. I'll get off.' She said to Roderick, 'Good night, you.'

He made a smacking noise with his mouth on his raised hand then blew in her direction. 'Catch, Aunty!' She went through the motions, grabbing in the air. 'Well held, sir.' He bounced down on his pillow, giggling, pulled the bedclothes up to his chin, and pretended to snore.

Anna looked at Jean, then went out of the room. She couldn't share her grief, yet.

There was only John at the breakfast table when Anna went downstairs the following morning. He looked up with a wan smile. 'Good morning, Anna. I told Jean to stay in bed. I had to give her a sleeping pill eventually.'

'I'm not surprised.' She had scarcely slept herself, worrying about Jean, and the outcome of Roderick's behaviour. She knew the affair wouldn't blow over with a simple apology. Christine Logan might be sympathetic but her husband was a different matter. 'You don't think it's over?' she asked John.

He shook his head. 'Far from it. I'm going to suggest that Alastair should examine Alice, but I don't think Logan will agree. No, it's only the beginning.'

'You think there's trouble brewing?'

'I'm sure of it. He told me last night he would take the matter further, as he puts it. That's what kept Jean awake all night. She dislikes him, doesn't trust him.'

That makes two of us, she thought. Sometime she would ask her . . .

'She says he's quite capable of asking for an official order to have Roderick . . . put away.' His face was tragic.

'Oh, but that would break Jean's heart!' She was horrified.

'And mine. You see, Anna, he's seventeen now, he's a strong lad, and he doesn't understand his own feelings. I've tried to tell him about the facts of life but he just laughs. Once when I was floundering he said to me, "Like the two dogs, Daddy?" God knows what he was on about.'

'I do. Didn't Jean tell you? He once saw two dogs . . . at it, down at the harbour.'

'Yes, it comes back to me. It obviously made an impression on him.' He sighed. 'Thank God you're here, Anna, to cheer her up.'

'There's not much I can do. I don't want to interfere.'

'At least you can be with her.' He looked at his watch. 'I've got to get back to work. Alastair can't manage on his own.'

'Van won't be home until after Christmas. I'll stay on as long as I can be of any help.'

'Thanks.'

Jean came into the room. She was tidy. Her hair was damp at the front as if she had used a wet comb to flatten the black frizz.

'How are you feeling, Jean?' she asked her.

'Not bad, but a splitting headache.'

'Would you like a cup of tea and an aspirin?'

'No, I don't want to be more dopey than I am.' She gave a wavering smile in John's direction. He was standing with the morning newspaper in his hand, his eyes running over the back page. 'John's checking up on who's kicked the bucket, aren't you, darling?' He looked guilty.

'Ghoulish, isn't it? I'll have to get to work. Anna tells me she'll be able to stay on for a few days yet.'

'As long as you need me. Even if Van comes home she's old enough to be on her own. Probably prefers it.'

'Thanks, Anna. I think I'm in shock yet. But there's going to be trouble, I know it. Did John tell you Tim Logan is putting it in the hands of his lawyer today?'

'More or less. You and Christine have always been such good friends, Jean. Won't she talk him out of it?'

268

'I don't think so. There isn't much love lost between them, if you want to know the truth.'

John was flicking through the newspaper before he put it down. 'My God!' he said suddenly. 'Well, we needed some light relief. Listen to this! "To Gordon James and Wendy Grace Pettigrew (*née* Armour), of 20 Beechgrove, Hyndland, Glasgow, a daughter, on 19 December 1962."' He looked up, paused, 'It says, "Premature".'

There was a silence, then Jean said, 'Rose is behind that. What do you think?' She turned to Anna.

She nodded. 'Ah well, life is not all sorrow.' Their laughter was as genuine as the tears rolling down Jean's face.

'I'm definitely away now,' John said. He kissed Jean, drawing his hand down her cheek.

I wish I had Ritchie looking at me like that, Anna thought.

They passed part of the day by going for a long walk, Anna acting on the principle that a good blow would help Jean's headache.

'Of course,' Jean said as they trudged along the road past the library, 'I never liked him – Tim Logan.'

Anna looked at her. 'This isn't the right time to ask, but has he ever, you know, tried it on?'

'Me and a hundred others. He thinks he's God's gift to womankind.'

'I'm one of the hundred. He's a shallow buffoon. But dangerous.'

'Oh, yes. It goes without saying. *My* theory is that he doesn't really like women, especially if they rebuff him. It's a matter of conquest.'

'He tried to add me to his list last night.'

Jean turned to her. 'I should have warned you.'

'Alice's screams nipped it in the bud.'

'They'll take him away.' Her mind was on Roderick again. 'There's no kindness in him. He would have barred Roderick from the house if it hadn't been for Christine. I've lived in fear of something like this happening ever since I saw him growing, becoming a man in stature, becoming curious. I know by what he says. He must have feelings like other boys. He's always been amongst older people because his own age group quickly grows tired of him. First it was the fishermen, now the garage. He hears things, gets ideas.'

'Maybe Tim could be made to understand if you went to him and apologized on Roderick's behalf, tried to explain –'

'No, it wouldn't work. He dotes on Alice, really dotes on her. I'm afraid, Anna, for my poor love, I'm so afraid . . .' Her voice trembled. 'I feel there's an inevitability about the whole thing.'

Things moved fast the following day. John came home at lunchtime and said Mr McAlpine, Tim Logan's lawyer, had asked him to call that afternoon to discuss a certain matter.

'How did he sound?' Jean asked.

'Impartial, the way all lawyers sound. But he's their lawyer, and the Logans are more important in town affairs than we are. He's very generous, Tim, new playing fields and the like.'

'With Christine's money.' She looked wistful. 'I thought she would have telephoned me.'

'I rather think she's been warned off,' John said. 'And Mr McAlpine tells me that he's arranging for a doctor to see Alice, but not from my practice.'

Anna hid her alarm. The thought of Roderick being suspected of sexually molesting that little fairy princess was absurd, wasn't it? Not if you faced facts. 'He couldn't have a personal vendetta against you?' she asked John.

'Not that I know of. Doctors in general aren't of much account in the hunting set unless they hunt too, and I suppose I've let it be known that I don't approve of blood sports.'

'He can't stand disability of any kind,' Jean said. 'I've seen him looking at Roderick . . . He gives large donations to the local spastics' home, but Christine told me that when they asked permission to have their annual picnic in one of the Logans' fields, he refused. She had a terrible row with him over that.'

'He doesn't want to be reminded of imperfection. He'd rather dote on Alice.' John stood for a moment, then said, trying to look cheerful, 'Well, I've got to go. Try not to worry, Jean.' He was off. Anna thought that despite the assumed cheerfulness, the glance he had directed at her was full of foreboding.

Twenty-four

The news spread about the town. It could only have come from Tim Logan. Bunty would have a loyalty towards Sarah, and Christine had never gossiped. She was regarded as 'uppish'. Jean and Anna were having a walk the following afternoon down by the harbour when one of the fishermen stepped in front of them, a middle-aged man with the weather-beaten face, keen eyes and straight lipless mouth of many of his kind.

'Could I have a word with you, Mrs Whitbread?'

Anna walked on up the Mote Brae and stopped to wait for Jean out of earshot. When Jean joined her she was agitated. She took Anna's arm and hurried her on.

'Jock Fairbairn was warning me that there's talk already about Roderick. He heard him discussed in the pub.'

Anna was infuriated. 'It could only come from one source! Is it you he's getting at, Jean?'

'No . . . unless it's pique.'

'What do you mean?'

'Well, one day he turned up at my studio, to see my work, he said. It started with the usual wandering hand. I told him to cut it out and that seemed to infuriate him. "I've heard something about your lurid

272

past," he said, "so thought you wouldn't be averse to having some fun." He grabbed me, and I clouted him good and hard with my hand. My fingers, thick with paint, made a new pattern on his fancy cravat, not to mention his Bond Street shirt, and he was furious, called me a bitch.'

'How original! I wonder how he would explain the paint marks to Christine?'

'He'd hide them. They lead separate lives. I think it annoys him that she and I are such good friends, or were.'

'It's strange, isn't it?'

'That we were friends?'

'No, that we seem to give the "come on" sign to men, when in actual fact we're faithful unto death to our husbands. I wonder why it is?'

'Maybe it's our appearance. Makeup isn't all that common amongst Scotswomen of our age.'

Anna's mind veered to Ritchie, and she felt the usual stab in her heart. 'I've been absolutely faithful, always will be, and yet Ritchie leaves me for a Spanish woman!'

'It's chauvinism. Still, he's an angel compared with Tim Logan.'

Christmas Day could scarcely be called enjoyable, although they all made an effort. Only Alastair came to dinner. Roderick had been going around weeping most of the day because his job at the garage was over. Mr Johnson, the owner, had called to see John at the surgery and said there was too much talk going on about Roderick and it wouldn't do his business any good.

John had been polite and said he understood. He had recognized the herd instinct when he saw it, more noticeable in a small town than in a city.

Mothers with young daughters would start saying it was a crying shame that Roderick Whitbread was allowed to roam the streets without proper supervision. One patient asked him when Roderick was going into a home. 'Better to be safe than sorry,' another one said.

They couldn't discuss the matter when Roderick was around, and they felt guilty doing so when he was in bed. As John said, it was as if he was being condemned without a trial.

The day after Boxing Day Jean and John went to a meeting with the Logans in Mr McAlpine's office. The lawyer was impartial but firm. 'My client Mr Timothy Logan has laid down an ultimatum. If you arrange to have the boy consigned to a hostel or permanent place of residence suitable for his condition Mr Logan will drop charges. If you don't, he has no alternative but to proceed.'

They came back shaken and miserable.

'If we don't put him in somewhere he's going to charge us with assault,' Jean told Anna. 'We've worked so hard to give him a normal life, and love. I thought we were being supported in that. Christine was good. She never minded him going to the farm with Sarah. Mr Johnson was kind in giving him a job. It suited Roderick's capabilities. I thought people were helping us. He's a lovable boy. It will kill him to have his freedom curtailed . . .'

'A cup of tea is indicated,' Anna said. She couldn't bear the look of anguish on Jean's face. She stayed in the kitchen for a long time. When she came back Jean was calm, but her eyes were red with weeping.

'Good,' she said, 'just what we needed, Anna.'

'I'll have to go.' John got up. 'It takes two of us for

the evening surgery.' He kissed Jean and went away. He looked worn and ten years older.

'Do you feel better now?' Anna asked her as she handed her the tea.

'I feel like a failure. Everybody I've been involved with has a jinx on them because of me. Frederick, then John . . .'

'That's not everybody, silly.'

'Everybody who matters. John was all right until I came along.'

'Roderick is his as well as yours. What you have to decide between the two of you is what's best for Roderick. He's going to be bored out of his mind hanging about the house at his age. No one will employ him in Kirkcudbright now. And you'll be constantly worried about him. He's growing older, stronger, it's natural for him to be interested in girls, and there isn't much chance of him marrying, is there?'

'No. Except to someone like himself.' They looked at each other. Why not, Anna thought.

'What does John want you to do?' she said.

'He thinks we should have had to face up to the problem quite apart from Tim Logan. We could find a good home, he says, think of it like a boarding school in a way. That the onus is always on me to supervise Roderick – doctors are never much at home for their children – and that it's too demanding.'

'And Sarah will be getting married before long and she'll be too busy to be of much help. He'll miss her, miss his job, he might get into mischief . . . imagine how you'd feel if he attacked another girl.'

'He didn't attack Alice! You keep on saying that! It was friendly, like a playful bear.'

Bears aren't always friendly, Anna thought. 'I

know it must break your heart to feel that you're being pushed into this by Tim Logan, but John's right.' Jean sat in silence, eyes unfocused. Don't say any more, Anna warned herself.

Jean looked up at her, eyes bitter. 'There's a certain dull satisfaction you've never known in having it confirmed once again that things will always be hard for you. But you've had it easy, great children, famous painter for a husband . . .'

'What utter rubbish!' They glared at each other. 'I have a lot of trouble with Van, and a husband who strays –'

'Tosh! You're for Ritchie and he's for you. And Van is at least normal.'

'Oh yes, you can whitewash it all, and of course it isn't tragic like Frederick's death, and then your child's, but Roderick is loving, and he'll have talents and skills which could be discovered at some remedial home or whatever they call it. Had he been normal he would have been leaving home soon in any case to go to a university.'

'You were always logical. It only fails you when it comes to dealing with your own family.' She got up suddenly.

'Where are you going?'

'To the garden. There's something on my easel.'

'And that's another thing. You have a great talent. You'd have more time for it if Roderick hadn't to be looked after. I've seen what you have to do, his bed-wetting, his dirty habits in the lavatory . . .'

Jean went out of the room, banging the door behind her.

Now there was a hiatus when the subject wasn't mentioned. Anna did her best by taking Roderick

276

out on expeditions with her, sometimes to Gate-house of Fleet which she liked, and Dumfries which Roderick liked because of the bustle and the shop windows. He enjoyed having people around him, and he missed being in the garage with its daily contacts.

'I liked it, Aunty,' he said. 'Everybody coming in and saying, "Hello, Roddy." I don't know why Mr Johnson has decided to dispense with my services.' His forehead screwed up. 'What does that mean, "dispense with my services"?'

'Just that he can't employ you any longer. I expect trade's not so good in the winter and he can't afford to pay your wages.'

'No, it doesn't.' His little eyes narrowed as he looked at her. 'You're not telling the truth. It's because I jumped on Alice. I heard him saying to Jimmy, that's the mechanic, "You don't know who'll be next, with him on the loose." Then he laughed when he saw I heard them. I explained to them that I had only been playing at weddings.' He smiled, remembering. 'It was nice when she wriggled, and then struggled. If only she hadn't screamed I could have gone on doing it and she would have liked it . . .'

Anna was silent. A home was essential, but did they recognize in homes that children like Roderick had the same feelings as anyone else? And single sex homes weren't a solution.

She was beginning to feel superfluous, and yet felt she couldn't go until a solution was reached. Jean might need her. At the moment she didn't. She stopped accompanying Anna on walks and during the day shut herself up in her studio. She often took Roderick with her in an attempt to amuse him. He showed Anna the daubs he had made, but any talents he might have didn't lie in that direction.

When John came home he and Jean sometimes closeted themselves upstairs. John apologized, saying it was all boring legal matters they were discussing, but he did show Anna the prospectuses he had got from residential homes.

'Jean can't contemplate it yet,' he said, 'but she's beginning to see that we can't have our son's name dragged through the mud by that man.' Anna agreed, but suggested they might introduce the idea of a home to Roderick to get his reaction. He was convivial. It might appeal to him. John's eyes brightened. 'That could ease her mind . . .' Maybe there was light at the end of the tunnel.

Anna decided she would take a leaf out of Sarah's book and wait. Phlegmatic as always, Sarah was out most evenings, either with Alastair or at her badminton club.

None of the Logans came to the house. Sarah heard from Bunty that Alice and her mother had gone to her sister's home in Sussex. She didn't know if Alice had been medically examined or not. It was an impasse.

For the first time in her life Anna felt cut off from Jean, but when she said she would go home, Jean put her hand on her arm. 'Not yet, Anna, please. You help me to see straight. John is so patient, and loving. He's even said he'll let Tim Logan go ahead if I can't bear to part with Roderick.'

'It's up to you, then,' she said. 'I'm going for a walk.'

She answered the telephone one afternoon when she was alone in the house. To her surprise it was Van. She sounded cheerful. 'How are you, Mum?'

'Fine. I'm thinking of coming home soon, now that I know you're back. Did you enjoy yourself in Barcelona?'

'Very much. I've got a part-time job in London now. In a battered wives' home.' Anna sighed, she hoped inaudibly. 'At least they pay me, even if it's not much.'

'Well, I'm glad you're occupied at least.' She was surprised she didn't mind more. Perhaps she had too much to think about at the moment. She decided not to tell her about Roderick meantime. 'I'm looking forward to hearing about your trip.'

'Just a moment, Mum,' Van said. 'There's someone here who wants to speak to you.'

'Who?' But Van wasn't there.

'Hello.' It was Ritchie's voice. 'I came back with Van. I've been waiting for you to turn up.'

'Really?' She was stiff, but inwardly shaking.

'Could you come home, Anna? I have a lot to say to you. I can't talk on the phone.'

'There's trouble here. With Roderick. It's too involved to tell you about it just now.'

'I could come to *you*.'

'For God's sake, no. Neither Jean nor John is in the mood for entertaining.'

'I'm working hard, trying to finish up odds and ends. I'm stuck on the one I'm on. It's a dead loss. Anna, I've been giving a lot of thought –'

'It's good of you to spare the time.'

'Don't be sarcastic. Keep it for when you see me. Have you *got* to be with Jean?'

'Strangely enough, I think the time's ripe for me to come home. I can't help her any more.'

'Well, come back. You can help me. Tell me to my face what you think of me. You'll enjoy that.'

'You're as cheeky as ever, Laidlaw.' Tenderness was welling up in her.

'It's to hide my nervousness, and my guilt. I need you, darling, I've never needed you more. Please come home.'

'I'd like to tell you what's been happening here. It's about Roderick. Another viewpoint . . .' She was desperate to see him.

'When will you come?'

'Tomorrow.' She had always been able to make quick decisions. 'Of course there's my work, and the house must need a good clean . . .'

'Yes, it's filthy. Anna, I've been daft as a brush.' He was boyish and she loved him. 'I'll meet every train. Van's staying up in London most of the time. At Adelaide's pad, I think.'

'I thought she might.' There was the familiar sinking feeling but she banished it.

Jean said she was glad when she heard Ritchie was at home waiting for her. 'On you go. You won't believe it when I tell you that you're soul mates. Give him a longer leash. He'll always come back to you. It was only a little flutter.'

Twenty-five

❦

When her train came in at Renton Station Ritchie was waiting for her. He stood on the platform in a shapeless old anorak and cords, his black hair longer than she remembered. He came forward and took her bag with a hesitant smile. 'Am I allowed to kiss you?' he said.

She proffered her cheek. 'You look like a golliwog.' She thought he looked beautiful. 'Are you growing your hair?'

'Not deliberately. It keeps you warmer in winter.' They were walking towards the car park in front of the station with the wife-chauffeuses sitting at their wheels waiting for the commuters. She never missed Renton. It was a feeder town for London, not a place in its own right, like Glasgow.

They got into their own car, he started up and drove into the main street. 'The warehouse in Barcelona is damned cold. Maybe that's the cause of my block.'

'You've got a block?'

'I told you on the phone.'

'So you did.' What did he expect her to do, this recalcitrant lover? Kiss it better?

'Van kept the house at Arenys de Mar beautifully cosy. She's a good little housekeeper.'

281

She would have liked to say, 'I haven't seen much of it,' but that would be going in with all guns firing. Besides, Van had been sweet to her when she came back from New York with the tea ready and the French pâtisserie.

When they got into the house she found it quite tidy if undusted, and Ritchie had the central heating humming.

'We'll have a drink,' he said. 'It's tiring, travelling.'

'Fine. You pour it out while I go to the lavatory. I'm dying.'

'You never go on trains. You're daft.'

'Permit me my little idiosyncrasies.' The lack of plumbing disturbed her.

'Anna . . . ?'

'What?' She turned at the door.

'You look so good. So smart and pretty.'

'It's the good bones, as you once said.'

When she came back he handed her a gin and tonic. 'We could go out and eat at that place on the river.'

She didn't want to do that. There was too much to talk about, Roderick for a start, then their own affairs. She wanted privacy to shout, if necessary. 'Is there anything in the house?'

'Lots of stuff. I gave Van money to stock up. There's honey-cooked Virginia ham.'

'That shiny pink stuff? No, thanks.'

'Fricasseed chicken?'

'That would do. Have you wine?'

'Lots of it.'

'Well, we'll stay in. I want to tell you about Roderick.'

'Roderick?' She saw him changing gear. 'Fire away, then.' He liked the boy, had been able to play with him when Roderick was younger far better than she could. She thought of Ritchie's mother saying of her husband, 'There's a sweetness in his character.'

She told him the details, and he was immediately involved. 'The malicious bugger! He can't lay down the law like that, force Jean and John to put him away. Roderick is theirs!'

'I agree, but on the other hand, it could happen again. Jean knows that. He's a big lad, developing fast, aware . . .'

'. . . that he has a prick.'

'I was going to say, "aware of his masculinity".'

'Same thing.'

'It might be better to put him in a home than to make him a virtual prisoner in his own house.'

'I'll give John a ring later, see if there's anything I can do.'

'I felt I couldn't help Jean, the first time in my life I've ever felt that. It's between them. John will let *her* decide, but he wouldn't want her to be influenced by me.'

'Quite right. But you could help *me*, if you like.'

'You?' She took what she thought was the first sip from her gin and tonic and found that the glass was almost empty. She must have been gulping the stuff. But, what a nerve he had!

'With my work. I'm stuck. There's nothing coming out of me. I stare at it hour after hour and I don't know how to advance it . . .'

'So you come home when you're in trouble? I'd like another gin, please.'

'Sorry.' He got up and refilled her glass, handed it to her. 'Does it sound like that? Anna, I need you, and everything that goes with you. I was only away a day – well, a day and a half – when I realized it.

The work's only a part of it, like the flag explorers stick up in the air when they're buried in an avalanche.' The analogy was pure Ritchie, *Boy's Own* stuff.

'Let's start with the work.' The second glass was making her feel benevolent.

'It's the key. I've lost the key. My mind's full of images but I can't unlock them, images to do with Spain. Manuel and Maria are beginning to be impatient. It's results they want.'

'I thought Maria would give you a special dispensation, straight from His Holiness.'

He shook his head. 'I'm too undisciplined. I never work like that, as you know. And the stakes are high. They're paying me the earth.'

'Didn't you ask Mish to look at it when he was there?'

'Now, he surprised me.' He looked surprised, as if Mish hadn't been his son for twenty-three years. 'He's like *them*. He can only judge the finished results, the final impact. He can't think creatively, he can't read a picture the way you can, even when it isn't finished.'

'Flattery will butter no . . . thingamajigs.' Her head was reeling slightly.

'Here!' He looked at her. 'You're drinking that too fast. I'll get you some crisps.'

'No, I want my dinner. My stomach's empty.'

'Right. It's fricasseed chicken, then, and Van has left prepared veg to be cooked.'

'You get it all going, then, I'll sit here and think.'

He was gone a long time because he was no Mrs Beeton. She could hear doors banging, drawers opening and shutting, the distinctive slam of the oven door. He came back at last, red-faced.

284

'Van said I was to be sure to cover the chicken with silver foil, and I forgot, but I got it out again and then I couldn't find the foil, but I've put greaseproof paper over it, so everything's under control now. Well, have you thought yet?'

'I hadn't started.' She was feeling unreal, or surreal, and full of power. He needed her. He needed her needling and her nitpicking, as he'd called it, because at the bottom he knew she was good. She took another sip. 'The Whitbreads go in for sherry as an aperitif. I never got a gin and tonic there.'

'Well, you can make up for it here. Go on, Anna, help me.'

'I'd have to see it.' She thought his astonishment was overdone.

'That's the answer,' he said, nodding, a judicious look on his face, 'that's it.'

'I didn't say I would. Let's have dinner.'

'Yes, you must be starving.' He got up. 'I have a bottle or two of Rioja. We'll light the candles and we'll talk and talk. I've been a fool . . . no, I'll leave that till we're eating.'

He had the table set and he lit candles while she lifted out the fricasseed chicken, heated a tin of peas and sautéed the cooked potatoes. There was ice cream, and cheese in the fridge and some wizened apples if he wanted cheese and fruit. He liked an apple and a piece of Stilton, she preferred a pear. You only found out things like that when you had been living together for a long time.

When he had poured the wine and sat down, she said, eyebrow lifted, 'You said you'd been a fool.' She wished she could work up some of the burning resentment which had been so familiar to her, but seeing him, and the trouble with Roderick, had damped it down. Now it seemed trivial.

'A weak fool I should have said. That last time I went to Barcelona I felt you had lost interest in me. Remember, I begged you to come with me? The thing was,' he looked like a small boy, 'every time I went back,' he looked at his hands, 'Maria was there. That's where the weakness comes in. Her house in the Gothic quarter was handy. I got into the habit of looking in there for a drink before I drove home, and then one night I just . . . stayed.'

The burning resentment had turned into ash. 'Was it good?'

'Technically perfect. There's a Spanish book somewhere which tells you some of the positions only Spaniards know.' She frowned at his bad taste. 'I don't know what makes me so stupid.'

'You like being flattered. And you're curious about women. You've got a painter's curiosity.'

'Although you don't believe it, I never went the whole hog with Christine Bouvier. Maria was my first mistake.'

' "Cynara". "I have been faithful to thee . . . in my fashion." Ernest Dowson, Victorian poet.' She was pleased at his astonishment. 'I've never even dallied. I thought for a long time we were quite exceptional. Jean always said we were soul mates. Can you imagine the blow this is, in spite of the wine? Can you imagine my imagination, and how it's working overtime? I thought of you with Maria, does she do this, that, is it different, better?'

'It's different. That's where the curiosity comes in. But it isn't better. I'm hating myself as I listen to myself, how I threw away the greatest thing in my life, you. There was this kind of ultimatum, you getting nothing out of Barcelona, fed up with me, and Maria said, "Find out if she's no longer interested in you," and it was at that stage I wanted you so badly to come back with me to Barcelona to prove that you did. But instead you went with Mish to New York.'

'You didn't take into account that I wasn't well, off colour, seeing the doctor.'

'No, I didn't. You've always been perfect in my eyes, maybe too perfect, maybe my . . . thing with Maria was a kind of an *equalizer*, no, what rubbish, but your family was so different from mine, and here was an aristocratic Spanish woman thinking I wasn't half bad . . .' He stopped, looked at her pleadingly. 'Does that make any sense? And then, being an only son with no sisters I've never been any good with women's complaints. But I'll try to do better.'

Bathos, she thought, but I utterly love him. He was the young Ritchie she had known, gazing at her over a table in the Regal Café in Glasgow, so adoring, so lovable. Her heart melted.

'Let's eat,' she said.

She thought the fricasseed chicken was quite good. Why had she slaved away with a casserole and all that fiddle-faddle for so long? She was an artist, not a slave in a kitchen. 'In all of this,' she said, 'you never gave a thought to *my* work, which was the real reason for me not staying on in Barcelona. I didn't seem to be able to get any commissions there, although Maria and Manuel said there would be plenty. I was getting them at home. It took time, but I've built up quite a few connections. Mine is a field which isn't over-populated. I can do quite well if I allot more time to it. Didn't it ever occur to you that I was bored out of my mind hanging around in Barcelona while you locked yourself up all day, or had consultations with Manuel? Or Maria? Women never have the same egotism as men. They *defer*. And yet they're keeping about a dozen balls in the air whereas men can be single-minded because the decks are cleared for them. It makes me sick . . .'

'I'll make you an offer,' he said.

'What is it?'

'I'll come out to the barn as soon as we finish this and spend an hour looking at your work, if you'll do the same for me.'

'That would mean Barcelona.'

'Yes, that's what it would mean. And if you think I should give up working there, I'll do it. Anna, you're more important to me than anything else. I knew the moment I saw you stepping out of the train.'

'I'll think about it.'

They went into the dark garden, he carrying a torch to light them through the orchard. She had had electric light installed in the barn, and when they went inside and she switched it on, it was still like a cave because of its size and the high rafters, but a cave with jewels.

The pewter boxes she had been making were like miniature treasure chests, inlaid with polished glass which gleamed like jewels, rubies, emeralds, aquamarines, and she had tall pairs of candlesticks set in the same way. The mirrors were her particular joy, some severe with raised embossing, others Gaudíesque in their jewel-encrusted extravagance.

'It's not surprising,' he said.

'What isn't?'

'All Spain is here. You had to be away from it first.'

'I never thought of that! But do you like them? I

have quite a few designs. The mirrors sell well.'

'Don't make too many. Leave the fatal facility to Nancy or your mother. Yours are on a par with Jean's work.'

'Oh, no,' she said, pleased, 'I'll never be like Jean.'

'You'll never paint like Jean, but you've got something else, a stronger sense of design. If that stuff was in one of the boutiques round the cathedral with a draping of red velvet at the back, the Spaniards would flock. You've caught their character in your work. I never feel the Spaniards quite belong to this century.' He smiled at her, almost shyly, for Ritchie. 'Let's go back and go to bed.'

'That's cheek.'

'It's cosier. We can talk there, or watch television.'

'You can't just *presume*, Ritchie.'

'I'm far from presuming.' He took her hands. 'I'm asking you to forgive me. Please.' He was beguiling, as he would always be for her.

'I wouldn't even think of it, if I hadn't drunk too much.'

'That's when your inhibitions go. Maria is finished. It won't happen again, with anyone.' She couldn't believe that, but her head was spinning slightly, and she had to lie down.

'Why not?' she said. 'After all, we're married.'

She had a bath and he had a shower. The same difference as the apple or the pear with Stilton. They got into bed and she clung to him, trembling. 'You have made me feel inadequate,' she said, 'telling me about the technical perfection of Maria.'

'Anyone can buy the book,' he said, 'but ever since we met at eighteen, you've been my life and my work, hopelessly intertwined. You're straight as a die, and I love you for it. If you say so, I'll give up the whole commission and come back here. But I quite liked the idea of you and I having a house in Spain and flying off into the blue yonder whenever the spirit moved us . . .'

'For God's sake,' she said, 'will you stop talking and love me?'

Twenty-six

Anna felt very happy, except when she thought of Roderick and Jean. She shouldn't feel so happy when Jean was feeling miserable. It was a nervous, difficult-to-contain kind of happiness. She raced through her housework, she hammered in the barn early in the morning, for although she couldn't sleep she still had a lot of energy to get rid of.

When Van telephoned and said she wouldn't be home at the weekend, she said spontaneously, 'I'm coming up to town with some work I've finished. I could look in and see you at Adelaide's flat, if you like.'

'But that will mean you getting a late train home, Mum.' She didn't sound very enthusiastic.

'I don't mind. I'll park my car at the station. I'd like to see you. We might go out for a meal. I have a lot to tell you, about Daddy, and Roderick . . .'

'Is Roderick all right?'

'Well, he's all right, but there's been some trouble. I want to tell you about it. And I think Dad will be coming home for good. He's had enough of Barcelona.'

'That will be nice for you. I know how you miss him.'

'So, if you give me the address I'll be there around six, if that's all right.'

'I don't think Adelaide will be here.'

She stopped herself saying, 'Even better'. She was full of this bubbling kind of happiness which had to be shared. Who better than her own family?

'Have you heard from Mish recently?' she asked.

'Yes, he's fine. I had a letter from Karin too, a nice one.'

'You'd like her, I'm sure. See you on Saturday, then.' She hung up. Life was good.

Adelaide's flat was easy to find. It was quite near where she and Ritchie had lived when they were first married, and it brought back memories as she walked along Farringdon Road. There was an atmosphere in this part of London, Dickensian. Ritchie had captivated it, delved beneath the surface to find the old Fleet River, put it on canvas.

And Mr Wolf had believed in him and taken his work. What had happened to him? And Christine Bouvier? Had she recovered, or was she still incarcerated somewhere, poor soul? She was full of loving kindness. She must ask Van if she had ever noticed Mr Wolf's gallery. Perhaps it had gone.

She found the address, a tall block of flats, well enough built, but not well-maintained. There were children playing in the forecourt, and some of the walls were chalked. The grass in the front garden was patchy and strewn with paper. Some of the railings were missing, and the inevitable dogs of all shapes and sizes nosed around. There should be a law against unattended dogs.

To her surprise and pleasure, because she had been anticipating climbing flights of stairs, the flat was on the ground floor. 'Carradine', the nameplate said. It was brass and brightly polished. At least someone cared. She rang the bell and almost immediately she heard quick footsteps and Van opened the door. Always, at the back of Anna's mind was the scarcely formulated wish that her daughter would have suffered a metamorphosis into a tall, slender, elegant creature. But it was the old Van, pale, hair standing out in its usual triangular shape, the pinafore dress nondescript and waistless, the glasses slightly awry, giving a lopsided appearance to her thin face which contrasted oddly with her plump body.

'Mum!' she said, smiling shyly, and submitting to Anna's embrace. 'So you found it?'

'It wasn't difficult. Daddy and I used to live in Clerkenwell, remember? Before your time, and before he went to Spain to fight.'

'Ages ago.' They were in a dark corridor, and saying, 'This way,' Van led her down it and towards a half-open door. 'I told you Adelaide wasn't in but Eb's here, her brother. I don't think you've met him.'

'No, I don't think . . .' Her voice wavered and stopped. She had the absurd impression for a second that she was looking at Adelaide in men's clothing. Seated in a wheelchair was a young black, thin, his legs seemed excessively thin so that the trousers draped round them, with long black hair and the fleshy-mouthed grin of his sister. She noticed the blue-whiteness of his nails against the dark skin of his hands at the same time as she saw that his hair was plaited into myriad little plaits.

'Hello, Mrs Laidlaw,' he said, holding out his hand and grinning widely. 'Come right in. Excuse me not getting up, but your daughter insisted on me staying right here so that I could get about on my own.'

'Don't apologize,' she said, taking his hand, and

searching wildly for something to say. 'I met your sister when you lived in Renton.'

'Addy? See any resemblance?' He smiled as if for a photograph.

'Yes . . . quite a bit.' She could hardly look at him.

'She's landed a good job in a house up the West End. Lives there most of the time, so Van's looking after me meantime. Mind you, I'm quite self-supporting, but you know what those girls are like, especially Van.'

'Yes, that's Van,' she said.

'Sit down, Mum.' Van pointed to a chair, and she sank down gratefully. She felt as if she could hardly breathe.

'That's better,' Eb said. 'I know what a seat means. Polio in my case. When I was eight. Mind you, I could have been a lot worse, so they tell me. Still, mustn't grumble.'

'It must be difficult . . . not to.' She looked at Van. 'I thought you were living in at that place?'

'The battered wives?' Van helped her. 'Only part time, so I'm able to come here and help Eb out.' She smiled at him, her lovely, enveloping smile.

'You know Van, Mrs Laidlaw,' Eb said, 'always willing to lend a helping hand.' He transferred his answering smile to Anna. His gums were red against the purple of his lips.

'Don't let's go out, Mum.' Van looked anxious. 'I always make a roast at the weekend. Eb gets enough of fry-ups during the week. It's all ready and set in the kitchen.'

'Oh no, there's no need.' *In the kitchen* . . . The Clevedon Crescent dining room with its careful table appointments rose up before her for an instant. But that was trivial. Here was yet another situation with

Van, this daughter of hers, whom she loved dearly, who was so kind and thoughtful to her . . . she remembered her kindness when she came back from America, the tea and the French pâtisserie. Now she was cooking roasts at the weekend for this man and only staying in part time at the battered wives! 'No need, really,' she said, 'it's too much trouble.'

'But we'd *like* you to.' She was aware of the man sitting watching her, smiling, but watching her . . . Van was living here with him, committing herself . . .

She went on protesting. 'It's very kind but please don't include me. I just wanted to see how you were, Van. I think I'll catch an earlier train. Going home in the dark . . . there was a burglary in Mrs Hutton's house last week and I'm nervous when Dad isn't –'

'Now, don't you worry about things like that.' Eb shook an admonishing finger at her. 'You have to try Van's pot roast before you go.' The wide smile slipped into place again. 'You just haven't *lived* until you taste Van's pot roast.' He was very jolly. She said she would stay.

She sat very still in the train while it trundled out of Marylebone Station and through the dirty hem of London to the suburbs which grew leafier as they drew near Renton, ordinary suburbs with ordinary daughters who went to university and met someone of their own class and tastes, and married in due course, or daughters who went up to town to a secretarial college and became smart personal assistants to city stockbrokers or the like whom they married, and went to live in Surrey in a detached house with a garage for two cars.

She was surprised at herself entertaining such ideas when she knew she had nothing in common with the type of person she was imagining. She and Ritchie didn't fit into the general Renton milieu except for a few close friends. The English background which produced women with high-pitched voices who ran things, and men who commuted daily to London and talked incessantly about gardening, was something she had never known, being city-bred. They seemed to take their cue from the Royal family in their behaviour and interests, whereas the average middle-class Scotswoman and many of the working-class had wider interests, just as their conversation was wider. Perhaps it was the Scottish education, or their Celtic roots, a temperamental thing which she had seen in all classes. They didn't have the veneer, the stiff upper lip of the English; they were sentimental, sensitive, creative, curious, volatile and quick to anger, less quick to forgive. Their feelings were nearer the surface.

In view of that, why did she shudder at the thought of Van and Eb Carradine together? Because it was her inability to accept it which was at the root of her misery. Had Rose subtly built up for her a role model of the ideal husband for any daughter, based on her own ideal, which it was impossible to ignore, at the same time as you knew it was impossible to live up to?

Yet, other people's daughters married well – whatever that meant. She and Ritchie had always been critical of marriages such as Gordon and Wendy's, with its pretences and emphasis on the wrong values, so why did she hanker after something which she in her heart despised?

When she walked through the darkness and got into her car, the name 'Rose' came to her mind like a flowering, like a small rose-coloured bomb bursting there. Rose. She had never freed herself from her mother's influence although on the surface it seemed so – her steady determination to marry Ritchie against Rose's wishes, to move away from her influence, to live a different type of life.

She put the key in the door and walked into the dark hallway. In spite of her remarks to Van and Eb Carradine she was totally unconcerned at the thought of Mrs Hutton's burglary. She had never had any fear of living alone. All her fears were inward fears. She liked her own space. She could share it willingly only with Ritchie.

She poured herself a gin and tonic. There had been no offer of liquid refreshment by Van or her friend, which was a good thing surely, remembering the many near-inebriated dinner parties she had attended with Ritchie.

As she sipped, the thought came clearly and stayed in her mind, fully formed. She would only be free of Rose when she was no longer there, and even then it might only be a lessening. Jean, for some genetic reason, had escaped her influence; Nancy's resemblance was surface only, a liking for shopping and afternoon teas in snobbish tearooms. *She* was the one who carried the genes.

Twenty-seven

Ritchie rang her the next day from Barcelona. He was full of enthusiasm and very loving. 'I've had a talk with Manuel. He agrees that I should scrap the mural I've been working on, but says my contract covers a replacement done *in situ*. He says he must see it in its developmental stage. He was interested in my new ideas.'

'I suppose that's fair enough.' She had wanted him home sooner, but the main thing was that they were together again. 'Have you seen Maria?' It had to be said.

'Yes, I took her for lunch and told her I'd seen you, that I'd been foolish and hoped she would forgive me, but that our affair was over.'

Had he held her hand when he was telling her? She had some sympathy for Maria Roig.

'How did she take it?'

'She surprised me. She's a career woman first and foremost. She shrugged and said that as long as I finished my contract to her and Manuel's satisfaction my usefulness in other directions didn't matter.'

'How do you like being called useful?'

'If anything was hurt it was only my ego. I'm disposable.'

'Serves you right.'

'Yes, I despise myself, Anna.'

'But not for long.' She wanted to tell him that she loved him, always would, but thought he should suffer a little longer. 'It suits me you not coming home immediately,' she said. 'I have quite a few commissions to finish. I took some up to London the other day.'

'You're finding yourself. I shouldn't be surprised if you leave me behind.'

Yes, you would.

'I saw Van. She was in Adelaide Carradine's flat. She seems to live there part of the time. Adelaide wasn't there. Her brother was.'

'What's he like?'

'Black, of course, polio victim, early twenties.'

'Poor chap. And you think she's living there?'

'I know she is, when she's not in that battered wives' home. I'm trying very hard to take it, Ritchie. I should know the pattern by this time.'

'We can't do a thing about it.'

'No, but it doesn't stop me feeling distressed. I had such hopes for her.'

'It's her choice.'

'You accept so easily. I know she's a far better person than I'll ever be, but I see nothing but unhappiness for her if this relationship lasts. There's enough misery in this world without going looking for it.' She saw Eb's fleshy-mouthed grin as she spoke, the braided black hair, then the draped trousers round the wasted limbs. Her chest was tight with pain. 'When do you think you'll be home, then?' She tried to steady her voice.

'Two, possibly three weeks at the most. I'll work like a Trojan – then London will be my base. But I'll always love Spain. It's very special to me. We'll keep on the house and you and I will love it together.'

'Okay,' she said, 'hurry home.' She sat down and had what Bessie used to call a 'guid greet'. 'Hae a guid greet an' you'll feel better.'

The following evening Van rang her. Her voice was timid, apprehensive. She was trying to please.

'I'm sorry I didn't go out with you, Mum, when you came. You seemed disappointed, but I had cooked the roast. Eb can't do a great deal for himself.'

'Yes, I saw that.'

'He can walk with a stick, but I think he was shy about you seeing him, you know, his gait . . . it's . . . awkward.'

'He can't help his condition.' In spite of her decision to control herself, the words were out before she could stop them. 'Van, I don't want to presume you're living with . . . Eb, when you might just be helping Adelaide, but I think you should tell me. Is there anything between the two of you?' She waited. The silence hung between them. She could imagine it like a heavy, rain-filled cloud. 'Van,' she said, smoothing her voice so that it was just a mother's voice, naturally interested, 'just tell me . . .'

'I'm very fond of him . . .'

'How long have you been . . . very fond of him?'

'It's always been there, but now that I'm older I realize how much . . . we're happy together.'

'He could never keep you. Most girls think of that.' The rain-filled, cloud-like silence again. 'Van?'

'I don't think like most girls. You should know that by this time.' Her voice rose. 'You visited Mish. You found that girl Karin living with him, but you accepted that! You even said how much you liked her!'

'There's no comparison. They're both independent,

able to take care of themselves. Karin doesn't demand anything of Mish nor he of her.'

'She demands affection.'

'But it's equal, don't you see? One isn't leaning on the other.'

'We could go on and on, Mum. I know I've never pleased you. I was phoning to say that I would come home this weekend since you're going to be on your own. Adelaide will be in the flat then.'

Her heart ached. She couldn't face it. She couldn't think of them being in the same house with this misery between them, mother and daughter. I am actually afraid to be incarcerated with my own daughter, she thought, while her ready tongue, experience against youth, was making excuses. 'That would have been great, but I might not be here. I'm holding myself ready to go to Jean's. If she decides to put Roderick in a home I would want to be with her.'

'Oh, I understand that!' Her voice was unloaded, sincere. 'You're so close and you need each other at difficult times. Don't worry. I'll be glad to see Addy. It was just that she would have taken care of Eb.'

Shame flowed redly inside her, it seemed, as well as flushing her cheeks. 'I tell you what, I'll ring Jean to see what the situation is, then ring you back. I really would have liked to see you. Just give me time to get in touch with her . . .'

'Are you sure?'

'Yes. It would be nice . . . this must be costing you a fortune, Van. Hang up. I'll get back to you.'

She actually buried her head in her hands when she replaced the receiver, suffused with deep, bitter shame.

There seemed to be some non-celestial being

releasing the screw which was boring into her heart, hurting it so much.

When she got through to Jean her sister's voice was full of surprise. 'We really are telepathic. I was standing at the phone just going to ring *you*.'

'Is anything wrong?'

'I don't know if it's wrong or right any more, but we've made up our minds about Roderick.' Her voice faltered, then steadied. 'This weekend he goes into a home we've chosen at Dumfries.'

'I think you're doing the right thing, Jean. He's growing –' She was interrupted.

'John can't come with me. He's booked for a confinement, a difficult one. He daren't leave the district.'

'I'll come up. I'm alone anyhow.'

'I didn't mean –'

'I want to come. We'll try and make it fun for Roderick. A tare.'

'What would I do without you?'

'Lose your head and get somebody to sew on a button.'

She rang Van and was able to be truthful at least. 'Jean needs me.' It lessened the ache a little, but it didn't put it away.

Roderick sat importantly in the front seat with Jean, whose only sign of grief was a perfectly made-up face, even to eyeshadow. She looked like a well-bred lady clown or a tart on her first night at the game. Anna, who had a fair dollop of makeup on herself, didn't dare make any comment.

Roderick was in a new tweed suit, a blue shirt with a tweed tie and a cap of the same material at a jaunty angle. He was especially proud of his well-polished brogues which he had given a last-minute shine to enhance their already glossy surface before they had left home. 'All right in the back there, Aunty?' he said.

'Very comfortable, thank you, Roderick.'

'We don't want any back-seat driving, do we, Mummy?' The snorting giggle.

'Certainly not. You keep her in order.' It was to be a 'tare', as they had both agreed.

'We're off to my castle, you know.' This joke came from the home's title.

'Where you'll be king, I expect?'

'Right first go, Aunty. But I'll have plenty of chums, and I'll learn all sorts of things, Daddy *assured* me.'

'What kind of things?' Anna, who had read the prospectus at Roderick's behest until she knew it off by heart, played her part.

'Woodwork, and gardening, and biology and . . .'

'That sounds interesting. What's biology?'

'Splitting mice open, I think.'

'Dissection,' Jean said. 'Daddy told you. But mostly plants and flowers.'

'I'd rather split mice open. And dancing. I'll give a ball in my castle and ask Alice.'

'You forgot rounders and football.' Jean stopped him in his tracks.

'And swimming. Did you see my new swimming trunks, Aunty? Pretty nifty, eh?'

'Yes, you showed them to me.' Ten times at least.

'I'll dive right to the bottom.'

'You'll have to learn to swim first or you'll never come up . . .' Oh, silly, silly remark . . .

'You *float* up, Aunty! If you didn't you'd lie there

303

drowned at the bottom and the fish would eat you up.'

She saw Jean's face, immobile. Frederick Kleiber . . .

'Whoever heard of fish in a swimming pool!'

'A king can have anything he likes.'

They were driving now through the outskirts of Dumfries. They must be very near the Castle Home. Anna looked at the tremor in her hands. Jean's would be the same on the steering wheel. Her knuckles would be white. 'Did you remember your mouth organ?' she said.

'My harmonica, if you don't mind.' He sang boisterously, ' "I'm a wee melodiman, melodiman, melodiman, I'm a wee melodiman and you all join in . . ." ' again and again until Anna thought she would scream.

'Here's your castle, sir,' Jean said, turning into a gloomy drive lined by dusty laurels. Her voice was rasping, not her own low-toned voice at all.

'I don't want to go, Mummy . . .' He suddenly started to weep, ugly gurgling sounds because of his chronic catarrh. He flung himself about in the seat.

'Use your handkerchief, Roderick.' Anna spoke sharply. 'Kings don't cry. Now here's the door of your castle and look, there's a nice lady and gentleman standing to welcome you. And a boy as well.'

Jean stopped the car. Anna got out and held the door open for Roderick. 'They're waiting for you. Give Aunt Anna your hand.' She didn't look at Jean.

'Hello, Roderick!' the man said. He was middle-aged with a thin grey face lit by bright eyes. There was a kindness in them. Roderick would be all right with him. 'I'm Mr Walker, and this is Mrs Walker. We're going to be taking care of you.'

304

'Shake hands, Roderick,' Anna said, and smiling at the man: 'I'm not his mother.' He understood.

Anna saw Mrs Walker with her arm round Jean, heard her say, 'If you will give me the keys of your boot, Jimmy will take Roderick's case upstairs and show him his dormitory.' Jean was speechless. Her agonized eyes outlined with kohl were grotesque compared with her rouged cheeks.

'Hello, Roderick!' the boy said. He was a Down's child, dark-skinned where Roderick was fair, more Asiatic in appearance because of his slimness. 'We're just going for a game of football. Like to come?'

Anna saw about half a dozen boys of various ages had joined them, crowding round, chattering, curious, giggling. It was like visiting an alien country. Surely it was wrong to segregate them. Jean's way had been best – if it hadn't been for that bugger . . . it did her good to think of Tim Logan like that.

'That would be fun, wouldn't it, Roderick?' Jean had joined them with a fixed, unfamiliar smile firmly in place. 'You go upstairs with Jimmy and get on your new shorts and striped jersey. Remember you packed them?'

'Will you watch, Mummy?'

'D'you think I'd miss it?' The smile had no mirth in it. 'Mr and Mrs Walker will show us where to go.'

'Come and have a cup of tea while you're both waiting,' Mrs Walker said. She was a round, jolly woman shaped like a bun-loaf.

'That's a good idea, Jean,' Anna said, smiling at the bun-loaf. They would call her that afterwards, if she could make Jean laugh. 'I'm Roderick's aunt, by the way.'

'I guessed as much. I'm glad Mrs Whitbread has

you with her. It's hard, I know how hard. I'm lucky.
I have my son beside me, Jimmy.'

'The boy who took Roderick . . . ?'

'Yes. That's why we started this place. You need
have no worries about Roderick,' she spoke to Jean,
'he'll be happy here. He's gregarious. You can have
him home at the weekends, which will help to soften
the parting, but not for the first month until he settles
down. We try to give all the boys some sort of trade
or skill, and the town council pays for it, simple
joinering and such like. He'll be kept occupied.'

They had tea and then they were led down the
long drive and along a side path to the football field.
Roderick was there, dressed in short shorts and a
vivid blue and white striped jersey. He came prancing
up to Jean when they appeared. 'Not a bad get-up,
eh?' He swivelled round on his fat legs.

'Very smart,' she said.

'Do I look like a left outside, Aunty?' This had been
a joke between them.

'Right inside, I should say.'

Roderick bent double with laughter. 'Oh, you kill
me!'

Mr Walker was beside them, skinny in the same
outfit, smiling in his quiet way. 'On you go, Roderick,
with the rest.' He put a whistle to his lips and blew it
loudly. 'Right, boys!' he shouted. Roderick lingered,
unsure.

'That's for you,' Anna said. 'Give Mummy a kiss.'
He flung his arms round Jean, suddenly agitated,
then Anna.

'On you go,' Jean said with that practised smile
which only succeeded in looking fixed and strange.

'Right!' He clenched his fists like a boxer, hesitated
a second, then ran across the field to join the other

boys, lifting his legs like a trotting pony between shafts.

They waited for a few minutes to wave to him should he look their way, but he was racing about in all directions, regardless of any rules. Mr Walker was having a fine time trying to keep him in order with his whistle.

'Come on, Jean,' Anna said, 'he's all right.' They walked back to the car.

Jean drove steadily away from the home with the tears rolling just as steadily down her cheeks. Anna stood it until she could stand it no longer.

'Pull into this lay-by. I have to fix wipers to your eyes or you'll kill us both.' When she drew up Anna took her in her arms. 'I know, I know,' she said, stroking the wiry black hair, like Van's.

She and Jean had never gone in for much hugging. There was the Scottish bit, the dislike of 'softness'.

'You'll get used to it,' she said.

'I'll never forget his face when he suddenly realized . . . he knows I've let him down. He can't fathom it.'

'Think of him scooshing about that football field, not caring. He's gregarious. Mrs Bun-loaf spotted it.' Jean didn't laugh. She wasn't ready for Mrs Bun-loaf yet. 'He's a creature of habit. He'll love the discipline and the company.'

'He'll bear me a grudge for the rest of his life.'

'No, he won't. He'll be boasting to you in no time about the skills he's learning. What do you bet he'll come home to visit you with something he's made, a book-stand, maybe. He'll be tickled pink. He didn't have boys of his own age to play with at home, and doctors are never about for their children. That's why he went down the Mote Brae to the fishermen.'

307

'I'll never forgive Tim Logan, that miserable bastard, wrecking our lives because of his stupid ideas about his precious Alice.'

'He *is* a bastard but you would have felt the same if anyone had molested Sarah.'

'You keep on saying "molested"! You're a fool, Anna Mackintosh. I always knew it. He was only playing! He didn't mean any harm.'

Anna sighed. 'A seventeen-year-old's idea of playing is different from a seven-year-old's. Tim Logan actually did you a good turn.'

'Oh, go to hell! I don't know why I ever listen to you!' She shook herself free of Anna's arms and huddled away from her in the corner against the door.

'Because you know I'm right. Oh God, Jean, I feel what you're feeling, it's torture, worse than I've ever felt about Van, because she isn't incarcerated; she could walk out if she wanted . . .' Don't go on about Van now, she warned herself. Concentrate on Jean, her feeling of failure. She said, 'If you're up to it, I think we should start for home. John and Sarah will be waiting to hear how it went.'

Jean sat up, got behind the wheel and turned on the ignition, put the car into gear and drove off. 'You're right, of course. Self-pity is destructive.' When they were getting close to Kirkcudbright, she said, 'The thing about us, we can say absolutely anything to each other. There's no one else in the whole world I can do that with, not even John.'

'I've told you before, we're joined at the hip . . . worse luck.' They laughed, a barking, painful kind of laughter which changed to a stupid childish giggling although they were forty-nine years of age.

When they got into the house Anna said, 'I'll help

you in the kitchen with the supper. John and Sarah will be home soon.' Sarah usually came with her father in the car.

They chopped vegetables side by side at the kitchen table. Anna lit the oven while Jean went to the larder and produced a sonsy steak and kidney pie which had been covered by the butcher (a complimentary service if the meat had been purchased from him), in a rich, flaky pastry. It was a special favourite of John's.

When Anna heard the key in the door and John and Sarah's voices in the hall, she said, 'I'm going up to my room. Call me when you're ready.' She passed Sarah who was rushing into the sitting room, John behind her, grim-faced. 'She's in the kitchen,' she said. She went on up the stairs.

Nothing like a family, she thought, getting together, consoling each other, sharing their thoughts and anxieties. 'What will he be doing now?' 'How did he look?' 'Were the owners nice, kind?' 'Do you think he'll like it?' 'Playing football already? Trust Roderick.' 'Into everything . . .' 'Oh, what do you think he'll be doing now?'

It was fully an hour before Sarah's voice floated up from the foot of the stairs. 'Aunt Anna? The pie's on the table. Would you like to come down?'

The faces round the dining room table when she went in had red eyes and determined smiles. Jean looked up and gave her a watery smile, a real one. 'I hope the pie isn't ruined.' She became businesslike with a knife.

'They take a lot of punishment, Brechin's pies,' John said. There was a glimmer of humour in his eyes. He was right for Jean. He would see her through this.

'Were you busy at the surgery today, Sarah?' Anna asked.

The girl's nose was red, her smile also watery. 'Not bad. The same old complainers. You'd think they would get fed up coming.'

'The backbone of general practice,' John said. 'How's the pie, Anna?'

'Delicious. You can't beat them. If they moved to London they'd make their fortune.'

'He looked quite happy, running about the football field, didn't he, Anna?' Jean said.

'Not a care in the world.'

'Gravy, Anna?' John was proffering the gravy boat. His eyes were saying, 'Change the subject.'

'I'll take another spoonful of cabbage, please, John,' she said.

The telephone rang when they were having lunch the following day. Anna had been saying she would leave tomorrow, and Jean was talking about going as far as Glasgow with her. She was due a visit to their mother, and also it might be a good opportunity for them both to go and see Wendy's baby. Nancy would never forgive them if they didn't. They joked about teasing her about the *Herald* announcement.

John answered it, muttering that he couldn't even get his lunch in peace. 'It's Bessie,' he said to them, covering the mouthpiece with his hand as he turned towards them. His face was grave. He listened, they heard him say as if repeating what Bessie was saying, 'Yes, the Western,' then went on listening. Anna shivered. If it was Bessie on the telephone it could only be concerning their mother. But she was *never* ill. They sat in silence, not daring to look at each other.

When at last he hung up the receiver and came

310

towards them, she drew in her breath. 'Prepare yourselves,' he said. 'Rose is in the Western Infirmary. She was taken ill in the middle of the night.'

'Oh . . . !' The moan escaped from Jean. 'But Mother's never . . . Did Bessie say . . . ?'

'She doesn't know. She was very sick, vomiting, and in awful pain. It could be anything, appendicitis, even peritonitis . . .

'We'll go up right away,' Jean said. 'That's the only thing to do. Will you be all right, John?'

'Of course I'll be all right. Sarah's here, and Mrs Roberts. Depending on what you find I'll arrange surgeries with Alastair and drive up after you.'

He went off, saying that Alastair and Sarah would fall in with anything.

Anna said, 'I think I'd better phone Van, tell her about Mother . . .'

'I should wait until we find out more. There's no need to alarm her. She has a tender heart, your Van.'

'Yes. All right. And I shan't ring Mish either. We'll wait and see.'

'You can't imagine Rose ill.'

'I don't think she could ever imagine herself ill. That's why . . .'

'Why what?'

'She would hide . . . anything.'

'What are you getting at?'

But she knew. They both knew. It wasn't to be voiced.

They spent the remainder of the day shopping and packing. John had telephoned the doctor in the ward who had said there was no immediate danger. The patient was sedated. They could visit tomorrow.

Mrs Roberts was sympathetic. She would take care

of the house, look after the doctor and Sarah. 'Don't you worry, Mrs Whitbread. Troubles never come singly and I know how your heart must be aching for that lad. I can tell you there are quite a few folks in the town who haven't a very high opinion of Mr Logan.'

'I'll away and telephone the home and tell them I have to go up to Glasgow.' She went out of the room very quickly, her head lowered.

'Poor soul,' Mrs Roberts said to Anna. 'Maybe this trip will be a blessing in disguise, as long as it's no' serious.'

'Maybe,' Anna said. 'Well, I'll away too and get on with my packing.'

She decided she would wait until she got to Glasgow before she telephoned Ritchie. No need to make a song and dance. Rose was a fixture. She was just giving them a wee fright . . .

Twenty-eight

❦

They arrived in Glasgow at midday and drove straight along Argyle Street to the Western Infirmary. There was a flower-seller with her basket sitting at the gates and they bought a bunch of wilted but expensive hot-house roses from her.

'Cut a bit aff the stems and gie them a good ploonge in water,' she said. 'They'll freshen up like magic.' And then with the good-natured curiosity of her kind, 'Is it yin o' your weans you're going to visit?'

'No, our mother,' Anna said.

'Ah, ye canna replace your maw, can ye?' They paid her and walked on quickly.

The infirmary was like a warren, and it took them at least a quarter of an hour to locate Rose's ward. When at last they found it, the nurse who spoke to them looked reproving.

'Visiting's not till two, but I'll see Sister.'

They sat on a bench, not speaking to each other. Anna heard Jean's stomach rumble. They should have stopped long enough to have a cup of coffee. They had passed a café near the Art Galleries.

The Sister, who arrived after a further wait, had a pleasant open face which cheered them. 'Have you come far?' she asked them.

313

'Kirkcudbright,' Anna said in case Jean would say they were staying in Glasgow.

'A friend was in earlier, a Miss Tait. She's not long away. You're the patient's daughters?'

'Yes.'

'Another one phoned. Mrs Pettigrew.'

'Nancy,' Anna said, 'our younger sister. We haven't seen her yet.'

'Your mother's seriously ill. I'm afraid I have to tell you. It's cancer. She hasn't had any treatment. I can't understand it. It's far advanced. Miss Tait, whom the doctor asked to see as she lives with your mother apparently, said she had been losing weight and not eating. She had worried about it but Mrs Mackintosh had dismissed her concern.'

'Where is the cancer?' Jean asked. Her eyes were huge, dark, the skin muddy underneath them.

'In the liver.' The woman's eyes were sympathetic.

'Could we see her, please?' She and Jean hadn't looked at each other.

'Yes. I'll show you the way.' She turned and walked in front of them, her skirt flicking to show a pair of shapely legs. Wasted in a hospital . . . No, she couldn't have *cancer* . . .

Rose had lost some of her hair. That was the first impression. Her scalp showed pink through the thin blondeness. Her eyes were sunken in her head, but she had taken the trouble to smear some colour on her cheeks and on her mouth. The lipstick was badly applied. She looked like a clown.

'Where did you two spring from?' Her voice was faint.

'I was at Kirkcudbright, Mother,' Anna said, taking her hand. 'We came right away when Bessie phoned.'

'That silly woman! I told her to keep quiet until we

314

got the doctor to move me to a nursing home. This won't do me at all. I'm used to a certain standard . . .' her voice faded away.

'Don't talk too much, Mother,' Jean said.

'Did you get Roderick safely away?'

'Yes. He's very happy.'

'I'll never know why you didn't do it years ago.' Neither Jean nor Anna spoke.

'Will you girls see Dr Thompson? That place in Great Western Road with the columns at the front would suit . . . me . . . fine.'

The Sister was suddenly at the bedside. 'That will do for now, Mrs Mackintosh. Your daughters will come back.'

'All right, Sister.' She was meek. Her eyes closed.

'She wants us to fix up –' Anna began.

'Never mind that,' Jean said, suddenly bossy. 'We'll be back at seven o'clock tonight, Sister, if that's all right.'

'Seven-thirty is visiting time. And bring your other sister too, but one at a time, remember.' She looked down at Rose. 'She's very tired.'

They walked through the dreary corridors without speaking. Anna had the impression that they were underground, long lanes running beneath the city. The air was stale with a whiff of carbolic in it. They got into Anna's car and drove silently to Clevedon Crescent. They would telephone Nancy from there. 'Mother has cancer.' That would make it a fact. Then she would feel something . . .

Bessie had the appearance of an old woman when she opened the door to them. 'The two o' ye,' she said as a greeting. 'Come away in. Did you see her?'

'Into your kitchen, Bessie,' Anna said. 'We'll all have something to eat.'

'Your mither wouldny like it, you two in the kitchen . . .'

'Yes, she would. We're starving.'

They went into the warm kitchen. The ginger cat was curled up on a chair near the fire. It opened one eye and closed it again. Long familiarity told them where to find the tea caddy, the square tin where Bessie kept the sugar, the milk in the new-fangled refrigerator, where they also found eggs and cheese and some 'best sliced ham'.

Jean made sandwiches and Anna infused the tea. The hot tea, when they sat down at the table, did more for them than anything else.

'Had you noticed any signs, Bessie?' Jean asked her.

'Signs of what?' She was cagey. 'She got thinner, and wasn't eating much, but that's natural as you get on a bit.'

'She's got cancer.'

Bessie's head nodded, slowly. Her face was grey. She didn't speak for a second or two, then: 'I won't deny the thought crossed my mind. But not your mither, a telt masel.'

'Yes, she's got cancer.' The tears were running down Jean's face. 'Our mother.'

'Jean's sad about Roderick too,' Anna said. 'Dry your eyes, Jean, and take a drink of tea.'

'Aye, your mither telt me. You'll get used to it, Jean, but she's a different thing altogether. I'll tell you now, lassies, I felt terrible aboot her, often. Sometimes her sheets were . . . stained . . . wi' bluid. Yince I caught her trying to wash them in the kitchen sink. My word, did she no' gie me a telling off for being nosey! "I want you to keep this to yourself, Bessie," she said. "It's just a woman's complaint." I

316

should have telt you then, but I . . . respected her wishes. Nobody wants to admit to having cancer . . .' Her voice dropped.

Anna could have wept, like Jean, with sorrow, and at the Scottish attitude to the disease, something to be hidden, to be ashamed about, but Jean was sad enough without her joining in. It was this terrible, deep-seated ache in her heart . . .

'I feel better for that tea,' she said briskly. 'We'll leave you, Bessie, while we phone Nancy. She's to go to the infirmary with us tonight.'

'An' she'll want you to see that bairn o' Gordon's. Margot, it's called.' She shook her head. 'The names they gie them nowadays!'

Nancy always had a soft heart at the right time. 'Terrible, terrible,' she said when Anna told her what was wrong with Rose, then: 'I'll come for you two girls at six and bring Polly with me. She can keep Bessie company while we're at the infirmary. It's a pity to leave her on her own when you've just broken the news.'

She came, city smart in pale blue with a jaboted blouse, high-heeled, fur-coated, contrasting comically with Polly in her costume of navy-blue serge, hat pinned firmly on her bun. 'I'm right sorry to hear Mrs Mackintosh is ill,' the woman said. 'A right joco woman with never a hair out of place. Bessie often said to me she was the best mistress that ever lived.' Bessie was frowning at her kitchen door.

'Come away ben, Polly,' she said. 'The ladies will want to get off to the infirmary.'

Anna led Nancy upstairs to the drawing room, her arm round her. 'There's time to sit down for a few minutes.'

'Mother's favourite room,' Nancy said and burst

317

into tears. 'I promised James I'd be brave.' She mopped at her face with her handkerchief. 'Wendy and Gordon are with him. She's a grand daughter-in-law, and just wait till you see wee Margot.' She spelled out the name slowly. 'It's French.' She plumped the sofa cushions around her. 'She could charm the birds off a tree. Can you believe it about Mother, girls? And not telling us?' She scrubbed her face. 'And here's me crying. I'm ashamed of myself. How's Roderick, Jean?'

'We've put him in a home.'

'Oh dear! Why?'

'He was a bit rough with a friend's daughter and he objected. We had to.'

'The nerve of some people! That's the worst of those wee provincial places, narrow-minded to a degree.' She smoothed her skirt and got up. 'Well, we'd better go. They're strict at the Western. They'd fling you out as soon as look at you. But we'll get her transferred to a nice nursing home.'

'We'll see,' Anna said.

They weren't strict at all. The Sister took them to see a tired-looking young doctor, who advised them to leave Rose where she was meantime.

'What do you mean, Doctor?' Nancy said, raising her voice because she was afraid.

'She's very weak. It would be unwise.'

'Can we see her?' Anna asked.

'Of course, but just for a few minutes.'

'Sister said one at a time,' Jean said.

'If you're quiet I'm sure she would like to see you together.' He looked tired to death. Anna saw his eyelids drop for a second.

Rose's hair was immaculate. The blue veins showed clearly on her white forehead. She must have asked them to leave on her rouge, because the dots of colour showed up clearly on her cheekbones. Trust Mother, Anna thought, her heart beating slowly with fear. They stood in a row, silently, looking at her, the closed eyes, the hand which seemed to flicker a welcome.

'It's us, Mother,' Nancy said softly.

Her eyelids moved. 'The three of you.'

'Yes, Mother. The doctor said –'

'Did you fix up that . . . place?'

'The doctor –' Nancy began.

'It'll be all right, Mother,' Anna said. Rose sighed. Her lips moved. Anna bent down. 'What did you say, Mother?' The lips moved again.

'The one . . . with the columns.'

Anna put her hand on Rose's cheek. 'That's the one,' she said softly, and straightened.

They stood, not looking at each other, not touching. It's unbelievable, this, Anna thought. I'll shut my eyes and when I open them again we'll be sitting round the table at Clevedon Crescent and Mother will be at the top wearing her rose-pink and pearls, Bessie will be thumping at the door with her tray . . .

She swayed, the image went and her mother was there, on the hospital bed, thin blonde hair carefully arranged, the rouged cheeks – the remains of her mother, immobile except for the hands with their rose-pink nail varnish. The hand waved.

'Move closer till I see you.' They did. They waited. Her eyes opened. They looked glazed, and yet there was a buried brightness behind them, as if she was looking through a veil. 'I'm glad . . . you're different.'

'Have you any pain, Mother?' Jean said.

She shook her head. 'The young doctor . . . a good jag.'

'Don't tire yourself,' Anna said, 'talking. We'll give you our news. Ritchie's coming home to work in London, for good.'

'Maybe.' Her mouth stretched. 'Maybe aye, maybe hooch aye.' That wasn't like the polite Rose. Perhaps inhibitions went when . . .

'Sarah's getting married in June,' Jean said.

'You can give . . . your attention . . . to the wedding . . . now. I always liked a good . . . no expense spared. You were . . . lovely brides.'

'Wee Margot's feeding nicely,' Nancy said.

'No wonder . . .' She made a vague, billowing movement with the hand in front of her chest. 'Wendy . . .' Her mouth lifted. She was a caution, Anna thought. 'I was no good . . . Ostermilk . . . builds bonny . . .' her eyes closed, there was a pause, 'babies.' They could scarcely hear her.

The Sister was there, taking her pulse, smoothing her hair back from her forehead. 'She's to get another injection from the doctor before he goes off duty. You should say your goodbyes now.'

They looked at each other, like children, embarrassed, unsure how to behave. Rose didn't like kissing or that sort of thing. They exchanged glances again. Jean's eyes looked as if they would fall out of her head. Nancy's were full of tears.

'Goodbye, Mother.' Their voices came in unison, in a whisper. 'Sleep tight,' Anna said.

Rose's head nodded. There was a slight smile on her face which suddenly changed to a grimace. She moaned, her head rolling on the pillow, moaned again, louder, higher in pitch, a keening. The young doctor had materialized. Anna noticed there was a crumb in the corner of his mouth. The nurses could have been feeding him chocolate digestives.

'Would you leave the room, please,' he said. They no longer existed as people.

They walked once again in the bowels of Glasgow, so it seemed to Anna, dreary, dank corridors. Sometimes they met porters, whistling, nurses laughing, once they stood aside for a draped figure being pushed on a stretcher.

Nancy drove them expertly to Clevedon Crescent. 'Send Polly out,' she said, 'and you two get to bed. You've had a long day. I'll phone in the morning.'

'Thanks, Nancy,' Anna said, as she got out.

'Yes, thanks,' Jean said. 'You always turn up trumps.'

Anna sat with Bessie in the kitchen while Jean rang John, more for comfort than anything else, she said. Anna knew what she meant. She came back to the kitchen. 'John says there's hope yet. There will be tests, examinations. They have a good man in the Western . . . Roderick's had quite a happy day, Mrs Walker says. He loves the company.'

'Good. Well, we'd better get to bed. I'll do my phoning tomorrow,' Anna said. Her heart was aching badly. No aspirin would cure that. 'How about a cup of tea, Bessie, before we go? We'll have to be stirring early in the morning . . .' The telephone rang. 'I'll go this time.' She walked, holding herself together.

The receiver seemed very heavy to lift. 'Yes,' she repeated, the words fell on ears like dull blows, 'Yes . . . Yes . . .' The voice was kind in spite of the starched uniform. 'Passed away peacefully. Thank you.'

She went back to the kitchen. Bessie and Jean were sitting at the table, their hands on it. Their eyes were on her. The ginger kitten raised its head then let it fall again. 'She's died,' she said, 'passed away peacefully.'

'Sit down,' Bessie said, pulling out a chair. 'You're like a ghost.' Her voice rose indignantly, 'I've seen it time and time again! You come home, thinking, I'll have a rest, I'll go back the morra, and then they phone ye . . .' Her face screwed up. She put her hand to her mouth.

'What else did they say?' Jean said. She was dry-eyed.

'It was after the injection. She just . . . died.'

'Heart failure,' Bessie said. 'Too much for the puir soul . . .' Her hand went again to her mouth.

'Pour Anna a cup of tea.' Jean's hand rested on Bessie's arm, fondly. 'And take another yourself. It'll be nice and strong.'

'Aye.' She poured obediently, inured in obedience. She drank, with loud, sobbing sips. Anna didn't touch hers.

'There now,' Jean said, 'you get off to bed. Anna and I have some phoning to do.'

'To your men?' The tears were running slowly down her cheeks.

'It's sad for you.' Anna put an arm round her. 'Sad for all of us. But don't worry, Bessie. There will always be a home for you with us.' She helped her up. 'Come away now. You need to rest.'

'Aye, but I'll no sleep.' She looked at them both. 'Puir lassies. She's the kind you'll miss.'

Ritchie was full of concern and love for Anna. 'I'll leave tomorrow morning,' he said.

'Your work?'

'Never mind that. I want to be with you. Rose!'

322

She heard the wonder in his voice. 'Who would have thought it, that dainty, rose-tinted lady!'

James answered when she rang the Pettigrews immediately after. They should have come first. 'I don't know how you're going to tell Nancy,' she said.

'She's just got into bed, the wee thing. Dead tired. I'll away and tell her.' Husbands had a hard time too when their mothers-in-law died, helping their wives through it.

Jean was at the sink, washing up the cups and saucers. She swayed slightly when she turned to Anna. 'What a day,' she said.

'Come on to bed.'

When they passed the telephone in the hall, Anna said, 'Van and Mish . . .'

'Tomorrow, leave it till tomorrow . . .'

They went upstairs to their bedroom, undressed, and got into the same bed. For comfort.

Twenty-nine

❦

Van was changing Mrs Leeson's baby. His mother was one of the battered wives. Mrs Leeson was engaged in her favourite occupation, comparing notes with the other battered wives. She heard them above the baby's cooing, babies liked to be clean just like anyone else. She had noticed that most of the ladies had a poor idea of hygiene – not to put too fine a point on it, were downright sluts. Perhaps that had been the beginning of their troubles.

'There you are, my precious,' she said, righting the baby and dancing him on her knee. 'That's nice, Malcolm, isn't it, clean and fresh as a daisy. Would you like to go to Mummy now?' She bundled Malcolm and his shawl in her arms and took him to Mrs Leeson. 'Here's your little son and heir,' she said. 'I have to go and see if Matron has anything more for me to do before I go home.' The woman accepted the baby like a parcel.

'We're just saying, Vanessa, the real cause of the trouble is when you let your husband make a doormat of you. "Bring this," "Bring that", "Run and get me a jug o' beer", "Put a sock in that howling kid, for God's sake." And on top of it they keep knocking you up when the fancy takes them and if you say "nothing doing" they batter you!'

'And rape you,' Mrs Bond said with satisfaction. 'But a nice girl like you wouldn't know nothing of that. Your boyfriend will be posh, a City gent.'

'I couldn't sully your ears with the things mine did to me,' Mrs Carstairs said, anxious to have a share in the action. She had a red face with a coarse skin and a bulbous nose set between small eyes. Van had noticed that none of the battered wives was pretty, not because of bad features, but because of a general air of neglect. They didn't like to wash, their fingers were nicotine-stained, if you got too close to them they had a sour smell. Recently that smell had been turning her stomach.

She felt desperately sorry for them. They had no future because they had no money, and how could any woman keep herself looking decent if she hadn't any money?

Mrs Carstairs was still talking. 'And it wasn't only me he abused, it was my Sally. I came in from work one night earlier than usual and found him with her. And when I went for him he took up his belt that was lying on the bed and hit me across the legs with it.'

'What happened to Sally?' Van asked.

'She's in care. She blamed me too, said I should have noticed. She's damaged, the doctor says, inside and out. She's on treatment. She hates me, that's the worst bit of it. How could I have stopped it? He was a beast, but I never . . . and I was out working when it happened.'

Mrs Branksome was the exception who proved the rule, tidy, hair brushed smoothly, but with a bitter mouth. 'You want to watch it, Vanessa, even if your bloke is a City gent. They're all after the one thing, and then when they get it they don't give a piss for you and chuck you out, even if you're in pod. He thought he could kill it by battering me and then the Welfare came. Betty's right. Don't make yourself a doormat. They never appreciate it. All they do is take away your self-respect. I often wonder what my dear mother would say if she could see me today. Sent me to a secretarial college, shorthand and typewriting.'

'You're always boasting about that there college,' Mrs Carstairs said. 'I didn't go to no secretarial college, but it's still no excuse for what he did to my Sally. They're all buggers, the whole lot of them, filthy buggers, think women are put in this world for one thing, to be their bloody servants. You didn't even get a marriage certificate out o' it, Lily Branksome, just one from your secretarial college. But that won't get you benefit, will it, eh, that won't mend your ruptured whatever-it-is, stuck-up bitch . . .'

'Now, now, Elizabeth.' Miss Tomkins, the matron, was in the room. 'You know I don't like swearing here. Let's keep the party clean, shall we?'

'It's me feelings, Miss Tomkins. They sometimes run away with me.'

'We all feel the same at times, don't we? Things get on top of us . . .' she looked severely at Mrs Carstairs who had let out a loud hoot of laughter, but now covered her mouth with her hand '. . . but we try to control them, don't we?'

'Try controlling my Ernie when he's on the rampage!' She snorted. 'Have you got any word of a place for me yet, Miss Tomkins? I've been the longest here.'

'That's what I came in for. I can tell you there's something definite in the offing. Give me a day or two. Now, suppose you help Vanessa to get tea ready. This is one of the nights she goes home.'

Even with Mrs Carstairs' help, or perhaps because

of it, it was an hour later when she was walking down Farringdon Road towards the flat. She tried to hurry, but it seemed she was slower than usual, almost like one of the battered wives.

Their constant complaints about their husbands depressed her. At first she had winced at the stories they told her, sometimes her eyes had flooded with tears, but she had lately begun to think that their troubles were of their own making. Why hadn't they walked out? Why had they remained to submit to the terrible indignities and cruelty which had been inflicted on them?

That, she realized, was a silly question, a typical middle-class reaction. They hadn't the bulwark of parents of ample means, especially a father who was indulgent and non-critical. But she had spurned that support. She had wanted to make her own life in her own chosen way, not theirs, or, to be more specific, not in Mother's. If Mum only knew it, she thought now, working at the home had taught her more about life than any conventional university would ever have done.

She hurried her steps as much as she could, but there was still that inexplicable lethargy, a weakness in the hollows of her elbows and knees. Eb would be tired of waiting. He would be cross. He would be sulky and she would have to tease him out of his bad humour, say, 'I know how wearisome it must be for you, Eb, but put yourself in their place, the battered wives, they have no one to care for them, no future . . .'

When she had said that last week he had asked her what future she thought he had, sitting in this flat all day waiting for her to come home. Addy had always been in on the dot. She shouldn't have taken a job that didn't have regular hours. It was hard work making him laugh nowadays, or perhaps she had stopped trying. There were only two ways, one was to redo his hair in those innumerable plaits which he liked, and which she *had* liked, or to go to bed with him. She would like to go to bed tonight very much, but alone.

She summoned up her energy and went in with a bright smile. 'Eb, darling!' He was sitting in his wheelchair, which was a bad sign. He could move about, albeit slowly, cook a simple meal, lay the table. It was quite possible for him if the will was there.

It wasn't there this evening. She knew by his mouth. It wasn't the full, rich smile which she loved . . . *had* loved? Nor his greeting, 'Hi, chick!' Was he changing too? Hers had been sudden, almost from one day to the next. It coincided with the dull heaviness which seemed to slow her brain as well as her legs. All she was left with was a hardly-to-be-borne disappointment in herself, the conviction that she had made some kind of mistake, gone wrong somewhere.

She went over and kissed him. 'Sorry I'm late.' She kept her hands on his shoulders, searching his face for the thing which had charmed her, but he pulled himself away petulantly.

'What's with you, Vanny? I'm starving. Of course, if I could go to the shops myself it would be easy. I wouldn't have to rely on you, but I'm not one of the lucky ones.'

'Come on,' she said. 'Don't feel so sorry for yourself.'

'It's a matter of plain fact.' He looked sullen. His features sloped downwards, even his plaits looked dejected.

'I remember when you *did* go to the corner shop, when you *did* have the table laid. You told me it was good therapy for you.' Where had her patience gone, her love? Mrs Carstairs' words were echoing in her head: 'Don't let them make a doormat out of you . . .' But she had never thought of it that way before. She had been happy to do anything for him. He changed as she looked at him. He smiled his Uncle Tom smile, his brown cheeks glowed.

'I know what's wrong, why we're going at each other. Yes, I've got it now. You're still angry with me because I said you shouldn't go to your grandmother's funeral. But it was a long way and you know how I miss you, baby.'

'No, Eb,' she said. 'I'm annoyed because I took your advice.' Yes, that was the cause of the resentment, the bitterness, like a kind of indigestion in her chest, preventing her from feeling well, from loving him, the way she still did surely, doing anything he asked her to do, gladly . . . making herself a doormat?

'Be reasonable.' He laughed, good-natured again. 'You couldn't afford the cost of the ticket from London to that God-forsaken place your family lives in, full of razor-slashers.'

She was furious. 'My grandmother lived in a select neighbourhood, the West End, and my father would have sent me the money like a shot if I'd asked him. I'm going to regret it for ever, not going to my grandmother's funeral. I loved her. I understood her, better than my mother did, her pride, her courage . . . she was special.'

'But you always said I was special, honey!' His full lips were pouting like a baby's, there was moisture in the corners of them. 'It would have taken three days. Addy's got this boyfriend now. She hardly ever comes.' She was suddenly weary of this baby.

'Would you like scrambled eggs and bacon? It would be quicker and you always say I can make good scrambled eggs. I've got sausages too.'

'Only if you can be bothered. You get past being hungry.' His eyes were huge, studiedly pathetic. Where had his sense of humour gone? He used to be such fun.

'It never was any bother, Eb. Besides, I'm hungry too.' She thought of saying that she had been on her feet at the home for twelve hours, but dismissed it. She turned her back but she knew he was looking at her as she went towards the stove, got out the frying pan from the cupboard. Looking and considering.

She heard the squeak of the wheels of his chair and knew he was beside her by the smell. She felt his arm go round her waist. She saw his hand spread across her stomach, saw it black for the first time, with the blue-white nails, and the little clumps of hair growing on the upper part of the splayed fingers. 'If the fat jumps out of the pan your hand will get burned.'

'Oh, go on, Vanny. Be nice to your Eb. I'm sorry if I was cross. But put yourself in my place, alone here all day. We'll have a nice little supper and then we'll go to bed. I'm tired. What do you say?'

Tears flowed into her eyes, suddenly blinding her. A TRAP. The word stood out in capital letters in front of her. She had walked into a trap.

'I have to wash my hair. And be up early. It's my early shift. I'll want to sleep. I'm tired . . .'

'Now you're playing hard to get. That's it, isn't it? Little Miss Hard-to-get. That's what it was . . .'

* * *

'Would you like to drive, Ritchie?' Anna said.

'It's your car.'

She laughed. 'It's your ball. Do you remember? At school? I'm not chauvinistic. Just say. Would you?'

It was after the funeral, a funeral which would have pleased Rose herself, attended by all her friends and even Angus's friends. They had said their goodbyes to everyone, they had seen Sarah, John and Jean set off for Kirkcudbright, had comforted Bessie once more and said she was to take things easily until their plans had been made.

'I'll take it first, then,' Ritchie said. 'I like driving through Glasgow, and then perhaps you could drive when we get near Gretna. We'll stop there and have something to eat.'

'Right.'

She stole covert glances at him while he drove. He was so handsome. She always forgot his features until she saw him again, the profile which was so satisfyingly balanced, both chin and nose strong but not over-strong, the way his hair grew from his forehead, still thick and curly. Somehow or other he had gained from both parents, who were in no way extraordinary, a nobility of appearance which was not apparent in their more ordinary features, the best of both.

'Don't feel too sad, darling,' he said. 'Rose had a good life. Better to go quickly as she did. She would have hated the indignity of a long-drawn-out illness.'

'I wish Van had been there. Rose would have liked her to be there. I feel so guilty. With all the arrangements I forgot to send her money for her fare.'

'But you know *she* knows we should have reimbursed her.'

'Yes. Maybe she had to be at the battered wives.'

She would rather think that than put the blame on Adelaide's brother. 'I'm not missing Rose so much just now because I have you back, but I know I shall. There will be a blank space, there will be so many things which will remind me of her, and then there's the feeling of having moved yet another step nearer my own death. The first time was when Father died. Do you remember that school game called statues?'

'We called it stookies at our school.'

'Same thing. Each time the leader wasn't looking you took a step nearer until you were home.'

'We've still got mine, so use them as a bulwark.'

'I'm glad they came to the funeral. Your mother's wonderful, a survivor.'

'Yes, and Dad through her. I want to take good care of them now. That's one thing which . . .' he stopped.

'What were you going to say?'

'Never mind.'

'You were thinking that it would be a benefit to be nearer to them?'

'Goodness, no!' He sounded embarrassed, looked around. 'That's Glasgow behind us. I prefer it to this.' They were on the nondescript road running through Hamilton. Soon it would be Lesmahagow and then Carlisle, England.

'It was such a shock when the lawyer read out her will and she had left *me* Clevedon Crescent!'

'Nothing to the shock it was for Nancy.'

'Maybe she saw Gordon, Wendy and Margot-spelled-the-French-way installed there.'

'Maybe. Was it a shock when she said in her will that it was because you were most like her of the three girls?'

'Strangely enough, no. I had come to the same

332

conclusion myself. It was a shock to know that *she* had known it all the time.'

'So?' His eyes were fixed firmly on the road.

'What would *you* like me to do?'

'Ah, no, don't involve me in your decision. Did you discuss it with Jean?'

'Not really discuss it. She only said it would be grand if I were in Glasgow. We could meet more often. She's going through a bad time missing Roderick.'

'Would you like to go back?' His tone was too casual.

She watched the ribbon of road in front of her with the regiment of conifers on either side, an artificially created landscape with no charm, planted for profit. In any case, she thought, I'm city-bred, Glasgow bred. She liked the shops there with their obliging assistants – so different from Renton – its Victorian buildings, the Clyde bisecting the city, Jamaica Bridge, the accessibility of theatres and concert halls – St Andrew Hall where the Highland ceilidhs were held beloved by her father – she also liked the ability to get out of the town quickly, from Clevedon Crescent, along Great Western Road to Anniesland and on to the road to Loch Lomond in no time, or south to the soft rolling hills of Galloway where Jean lived.

'My roots are in Glasgow,' she said. 'I could leave Renton tomorrow without a backward glance. London belongs to the days of our youth. The only thing which would pull me towards it is Van, but she doesn't want us. She has chosen her own road.'

'Are you coming to terms with that?'

'I have to. I don't want to lose her. I have to realize that I love her but sometimes don't like her, nor her views. But she's ours. We made her.'

333

'We made her with passion. Shall I tell you something?'

'What?'

'I would like to live in Glasgow again. I'm Scottish, through and through. My painting originated there, was shaped there. I would like to be based there, be part of the Glasgow School. Spain could be my occasional retreat. I knew it and loved it when I fought there, I grew to love the harshness of the mountains, the courage of the Catalonians, quick to anger, quick to forgive. I loved it because it reminded me of Scotland. I think it may have added something to my painting. Then, last but not least, I'd like to be near my parents so that I could help them when they "start going downhill". That's how my da talks.' He laughed.

'Would you like to live in Clevedon Crescent?'

He glanced quickly at her. 'I thought you'd never ask! Would I no'? I'd jump at the chance! I'd share the top storey with you – I'm no' selfish – the light's great there. And think of the view over Glasgow!'

She laughed. 'Spoken like a true Scotsman.'

'Did I grab a wee bit?'

'Just a wee bit. And taking into account the Pettigrews and wee Margot-spelled-the-French way?'

'They're part of it, family. And Da and Ma. And we would have room for Mish and Karin when they came to visit, and Van and . . .' he hesitated '. . . her man.'

'The whole jing bang?'

'Aye, the whole jing bang.' Sunday teas, walks in the Botanic Gardens.

They had reached Ecclefechan. 'Have we still got that Blackie's book of Carlyle's *Essays* at home?'

Ritchie asked as he drove along the main street.

'Yes, I think so. Was it yours or mine?'

'Mine. I bought it at the ABC bookshop for a shilling. Have you read the one on Burns?'

'You're like him.'

'Me! Away you go. What do you say if we stop here and spend the night?'

'Is there an hotel?'

'In Carlyle's birthplace? We'll find somewhere.'

'All right. And you could discuss his essays with me in bed.'

They didn't. They were overcome by the joy of being together again. Neither of them mentioned Maria Roig. She was an irrelevance now. It was like the old days, the early days in Clerkenwell when they had feasted on each other nightly, not believing their luck that it was now legalized, 'legalized concubinage', Ritchie called it. They loved each other until they were weary. She wept for love of him and grief for Rose. She felt as if the girl Anna had come together with the woman Anna and made a fairly sensible human being.

Thirty

February, 1963

She didn't write to Van until they were installed in Clevedon Crescent. Van had telephoned once or twice from the battered wives' home, short calls enquiring if they were all right. She didn't think this was strange as she knew there was no telephone in Adelaide Carradine's flat. And the fact that she didn't mention Eb wasn't unusual. She rarely did.

The letter took some time to write. It had to be carefully thought out, and so, allowing for putting their house in Renton in the hands of a house agent, and deciding what pieces of furniture they would keep, it was another month before she felt she could sit down at Rose's desk, her 'escritwaar', as she used to call it.

> Dearest Van,
>
> You haven't been to see us for ages. I would have been worried except that I've been terribly busy.
>
> You will probably get the surprise of your life when you open this letter and see the heading on the notepaper. Yes, we're here in Grandmother's house, which she has left to me! Dad and I talked it over and decided that we would both like to

come back to Glasgow and live, especially at Clevedon Crescent. So this is now our family home.

It's lovely having all this room. Ritchie and I have the whole of the second floor for our studios, and we still have Bessie, who sleeps in the breakfast room, that was, now her bedroom, since she's not so good at going upstairs, 'no' sae gleg' as she puts it. But there are still five bedrooms on the first floor.

We want to tell you that you are welcome to come here at any time, and stay as long as you like – live here, if it suits you. This is your home. You will have the bedroom above the door which you liked because of the little balcony. And Eb is welcome to come with you. I've written to Mish to say the same thing about Karin, who seems a fixture. I want us all to be happy together. Glasgow makes one think that way. Roots and relationships become important.

So, when you get this letter, ring me since I can't ring you, and I hope you think our move was a good idea and that we can look forward to seeing you whenever you can manage to come. I know you're very busy at the home, and possibly travelling presents a problem to Eb, but I hope the feeling that you will both be welcome at any time feels good to you. Don't worry about the expense. I would gladly recoup you. I felt badly that I didn't say that to you when Grandma died. I had a lot on my mind at the time, but don't let the lack of money ever stand in your way.

I've learned a lot in the last year. I had to come to terms with being a rejected wife, temporary, but still a bitter blow. I hope you never know that.

But in a strange way I was helped when I saw how Jean was suffering when Roderick had to be put into a home.

Then there was your grandmother's death. I miss her more than I can say, more than I ever thought I would. I see her in the house, hear her precise voice, see her beautifully painted face, the careful hair, and know now that I loved her for so many reasons. We'll become friends in this house. I can feel her presence, even as I sit writing to you.

I've learned acceptance. She has taught me that. I forget her foibles and only remember her many virtues. She was always good friends with 'her girls', and that's what I want you and I to be. This is your home as well as Ritchie's and mine. Dad wants me to say that, and it's how I feel, a new beginning. Ring or write to me soon . . .

A week later Van rang Clevedon Crescent. She sounded tremulous.

'Hello, Van!' Anna said, tremulous too. 'Was it a great surprise, us installed here?'

'Yes, a great surprise.'

'Did you like the idea?'

'I think it suits you. You're very like Granny Rose. Mum, I'm pregnant.'

The oak-panelled hall had a sudden startling clarity, the linenfold carving, the gold-framed paintings, then it went fuzzy. The flowers in the copper bowl on the settle which Ritchie had brought her last night as if he were courting her, which in a sense he was, ran into the brown background in a mélange of Kandinsky-like colour. The sepia prints were quiet intervals. She remembered that time in Renton when

338

she had gone to the doctor, thinking she was having an early menopause. I'm the type, she thought, when I'm old, who will have a stroke . . . 'Who's the father?' she said, knowing the answer.

'Eb.' Well, at least she wasn't promiscuous.

'The thing is,' her voice was even more tremulous, 'I've left him. He was making a doormat out of me.'

You were making a doormat out of yourself: that she didn't say.

'He's the father of your child.' There was a peculiar flicker in her heart, a fibrillation – her reading told her the appropriate name – making her breathless. Her voice wouldn't come, although she didn't as yet know what she wanted to say. As usual, she had to deal with this herself. Ritchie would be up a ladder, painting, never about when he was needed. Still, he had brought her flowers . . .

'I know it's a terrible shock.' Van was speaking. 'I won't bother you again, but I wanted to be honest and let you know.'

'I see.' Her voice rasped in her throat. 'What . . . what do you intend to do?' Where was her anger, her desperation at this news? Was it shock which made her sound so calm?

She was almost jaunty. 'Oh, I can stay on in the home. Miss Tomkins will let me keep the baby here. She's used to them, with the battered wives.'

'Have you told her?'

'Oh, she knows. She's good at spotting, you see. Some of the ladies tell her lies, but she always knows.'

'Good at spotting', 'used to battered wives telling lies . . .' This was Van's child she'd be good at spotting, their grandchild!

The ice was cracking over her heart. Some of the

jagged pieces were still embedded there, but she knew what she had to do. 'Van, you must come here. I can look after you, better than Miss Tomkins. There's plenty of room, I told you.'

'No.' She was decided. 'You couldn't put up with it. You'll be like Granny Rose now you're in her house. A place for everything . . . Babies are . . . messy. *I* know.'

'I'm not Granny Rose!' The nerve of it. 'I'm a different generation! I *want* you here! Ritchie will want you here.'

'No, you don't. You're not thinking straight. No wonder. I can imagine your face . . .'

'What's wrong with my face for God's sake – when I have my makeup on!' She heard Van snort, thought, this isn't me, so light-hearted when this foolish child is having a baby, a . . . No, don't specify the colour.

'Mum, I've been so stupid. How can you and Dad ever forgive me? But I loved him . . .'

'Do you still?'

'No. It's over. He doesn't want a baby. He says it's my fault and that he has enough to do to look after himself.'

She could have murdered Eb Carradine, the whole of mankind, at that moment.

'Come home. We'll look after you.' There was a deeply embedded sliver of ice which was going to hurt for a long time.

'You can't mean that. After the worry I've been to you.'

'I do. And so will Ritchie when I tell him.'

Van was offhand for a moment. 'Oh, he'll be all right. But what about Bessie?'

'Bessie will do as she's told.' It was Rose speaking.

'Tell me the day you're coming and I'll meet you at the Central. Just pack up and come.' She listened to herself, amazed. Really, for a well-known conventional West End family they'd done their fair share of jumping the gun, Jean, Gordon, and now Van. And her, but for the grace of God.

'You can't just pack up when you're working, Mum.' Such wisdom. 'I should have to give a week's notice at least.'

'Well, do that. Phone me when your arrangements are made.'

'Mum, are you really sure?' She saw her clearly, the great dark eyes like Jean's, the frizzy hair, heard the tremulous voice. Her daughter, with their grandchild inside her. At least Nancy wouldn't be able to criticize, since Wendy had gone sailing down the aisle with little Margot (spelled the French way) under her wedding bouquet.

'I'm sure. This is your home, Van.' She heard a smothered noise, then the soft click of the receiver being replaced.

She swallowed, pulled her back straight and went out of the room, into the hall and then the kitchen. Bessie had the wooden three-sided board which she used for baking on the table. She looked up. 'I thought a pancake and some of that strawberry jam would be nice for the tea. Whit's wrang, Anna? Your eyes are fair jumpin' oot o' your heid.'

'Van is going to live with us here, Bessie.' She sat down quickly on a convenient chair. 'She's pregnant.'

Bessie put down her spoon. 'Did you say pregnant?'

'I did.'

She turned towards the stove and lifted the kettle, filled it at the tap and popped it back again with a

341

small clatter. She lit the gas. 'Whit aboot the man?' she said with her back still turned.

'He isn't coming. It's off.'

She came back to the table, leaned heavily on it, her lips pressed together. 'I've read o' these things.' She was an avid reader of the *Sunday Post*. 'Puir wee Van.' She looked at Anna, woman to woman. 'Well, that's all right wi' me.'

'I thought –'

'Well, you thought wrong. Besides, it gets me oot o' a tight corner.'

'What tight corner?' She stared at her.

'Mrs Pettigrew's housekeeper, that Polly, you know.'

Why did she call Nancy Mrs Pettigrew and yet she was Anna? The thought passed through her dazed mind.

'Yes, I know Polly, of course.'

'She's been on aboot her and me retiring and sharing a wee hoose at Helensburgh, but this gives me a good excuse. I couldny stand her for long . . .'

Van's pregnancy an excuse! 'Are you sure?'

'Aye, it gives me a grand let-oot. Besides, I liked the hoose best when you were all bairns running aboot it. It will give some life to the place. You and your man are either up there painting and hammering, or you're oot awthegether. It's quiet for me.'

'I see.' She stared at Bessie.

'That's the kettle.' Bessie turned to the stove to infuse the tea.

'It's black, the baby. Well, the father's black. It might be.'

There was a pause, then Bessie turned, the teapot in her hand. Her look held more sympathy than shock. You had to remember Bessie hadn't had the

342

sheltered background she had enjoyed. And there was the *Sunday Post*. 'Well, it's still Van's baby, isn't it?' Anna watched her as she got cups from the cupboard, milk from the refrigerator, poured out the tea. 'There now, drink that. You could dae wi' it.'

Ten minutes later she went upstairs to the first landing, rested a minute – there was still that flickering in her heart – then on to the attic floor. Ritchie would be easy after Bessie.